PRAISE FOR BARBARA ROGAN AND
SUSPICION

"Completely absorbing."

—New York Post

"Rogan's best so far . . . a winning, flat-out all-nighter."

—Kirkus Reviews

"The novel is good fun."

—The New York Times Book Review

"Rogan weaves classic mystery and ghost-story elements together with modern computer technologies to create a novel that twists and turns right up to the end. A well-crafted book that is a pleasure to read."

—Library Journal

"*SUSPICION* puts an energetic, suspenseful, and updated spin on the genre."

—The Seattle Times

"A tightly woven thriller . . . Rogan builds suspense well and effectively updates the classic trappings of a ghost story. Guaranteed to keep readers turning pages into the wee hours."

—Booklist

"This absorbing tale is artfully told . . . [with] rising suspense and vividly nuanced characters."

—Publishers Weekly

"The handling of the elements and the writing are masterful!"

—The Poisoned Pen

Also by Barbara Rogan

Rowing in Eden
A Heartbeat Away
Saving Grace
Café Nevo
Changing States

BARBARA ROGAN

Suspicion

POCKET BOOKS
New York London Toronto Sydney Singapore

This book is a work of fiction. Names, characters, places and incidents are products of the author's imagination or are used fictitiously. Any resemblance to actual events or locales or persons, living or dead, is entirely coincidental.

 POCKET BOOKS, a division of Simon & Schuster, Inc., 1230 Avenue of the Americas, New York, NY 10020

Copyright © 1999 by Barbara Rogan

Originally published in hardcover in 1999 by Simon & Schuster, Inc.

ISBN: 0-7434-0057-7

First Pocket Books paperback printing October 2000

10 9 8 7 6 5 4 3 2 1

POCKET BOOKS and colophon are registered trademarks of Simon & Schuster, Inc.

Front cover illustration by Lisa Litwack; photo credits: Index Stock Imagery; Tony Stone Images

Printed in the U.S.A.

QB / ✹

For Ava,
and in memory
of the indomitable
Pauline

Acknowledgments

Many people were kind enough to share their expertise. The author wishes to thank Craig Copius of the Hempstead Police Department, Kevin Newman of the Farmingdale Fire Department, Lesley Rogan, Joseph Magid, Dr. Bruce Rebold, and the wonderful librarians and staff of the Farmingdale Public Library. Thanks to Steve Kavee and Bob Saul for friendship and moral support, to Laurie Bernstein and Joy Harris for devotion above and beyond the call of duty, and to my family for their love and patience.

Suspicion

1

"MAGGIE WAS right about you," Emma Roth says, breaking a silence that has gone on for too long. She gazes through the windshield at the flat gray ribbon of road that unfurls before her. The city is at her back. Ahead lays territory uncharted on her internal map: the sort of wilderness designated by ancient cartographers with dragons and sea serpents. With every passing exit sign, she feels herself shrinking, curving in on herself. This, she thinks, is not agoraphobia but suburbaphobia, the fear of losing oneself in a maze of identical ticky-tacky houses and strip malls.

"What did she say?"

"That you weren't really adapted to the city. That one day you'd revert to your roots." This is the expurgated version, Emma's sister having majored in sociology and minored in mouth.

"And carry you off to the boondocks?" Roger Koenig gives the matter a moment of his formidable attention. "True but trivial. You knew when you married me you were marrying a hick."

"And you knew you were marrying a city rat."

"Rats can live anywhere. They happen to be extremely adaptable animals; not that I accept the comparison."

They lapse into silence. Roger flicks the radio on, and Charlie Parker fills the car. Another exit sign appears, but Roger keeps to the middle lane, maintaining a steady sixty-five. He likes driving and does it well, a good thing for Emma, who hates it.

"And that's another thing," she says.

"What?"

"Out here people drive everywhere."

"It's not like city driving."

"*I'd* have to drive. Every day."

"True."

"But *not* trivial," she says, and in her tone there is reproach.

Roger hears it and hardens his heart. To prevail in this matter he will need to overcome a great many reproaches, he will need to break the rules that govern their marriage. The reason Emma hates to drive belongs to the class of things not talked about, a class that has ballooned in recent years. He says carefully, "That might not be such a bad thing."

"Ha," she mutters, more or less under her breath. Roger stretches his long arm over the seat back and rubs a knuckle into the base of her skull. He feels sorry for her, for in his mind the deed is already done. Emma, mistaking his gesture, leans back into his hand and narrows her eyes. "Roger," she says, her voice cajoling.

"Can it, babe. You promised me two hours of slavish obedience, and I am calling in my marker."

"Extracted under false pretenses. I thought you had something very different in mind."

He flashes the old boyish grin, and Emma's stomach lurches. You'd think, after twelve years of marriage and all they've been through. . . . But wanting him is an involuntary reaction, like a child's helpless laughter at being tickled—a reflex deepened by habit.

"You hussy," he says. "I'll make it up to you."

"You wish. You had your chance and blew it, bud."

Another green exit sign appears in the distance. This time Roger glides into the right lane of the Long Island Expressway. Emma says, "And don't imagine slavish obedience extends to making any kind of offer on this house."

"All I ask is an open mind."

"Don't have one. Never claimed to. *You're* the scientist."

After leaving the expressway they drive north along a winding road bordered by oaks in full spring foliage. Roger leans over the wheel, taut with anticipation. He's seen the house once, for an hour, long enough for him to make up his mind. Emma has never seen it. She sits back, arms crossed; her expression aims at tolerant amusement but falls short on both counts. He glances at her, sighs, but does not speak.

At a fork in the road, he pulls over onto the shoulder of the road and unfolds a map of Nassau County. Roger can chart the course of an atom whirling through a centrifuge, he can map the path of a comet through infinite space, but to Emma's perpetual bemusement, he can't navigate his way out of a paper bag. She unrolls her window and a warm, salty breeze sweeps into the car. The kind of air people leave the city in search of, but Emma thrives on city air, dense and oily, each neighborhood with its own smell, so you can shut your eyes and know just from sniffing where you are. She tries it now. "I smell the sea."

"The Sound, actually; this is the north shore. If my calculations are correct, we should see it in a moment." He sets out again, taking the right fork. The road, which had been climbing steadily, takes a sudden twist and suddenly the Long Island Sound comes into view. A hundred feet or more below them the land curves inward to form a rocky cove. Two stone jetties jut into the water, framing a small harbor. Farther out, there's a smattering of boats, a mix of trawlers and pleasure craft. Then the road takes another turn and merges with another, and they enter the village of Morgan Peak.

An old fishing village, she thinks, tarted up for the tourist trade, straddling the hills above the cove like a harlot on a two-humped camel. The image pleases her and she files it in the section of her brain marked "For future use."

Seeing her smile, Roger allows himself a mild gloat. "It's an artists' colony. You were expecting maybe Levittown?"

"I can see why *you* like it," she says. "Pure chaos." In fact, the village looks like something that has grown at random out of the hills. There is no flat ground, every building occupies a different level, and if the village has a building code, it must stipulate that no structure may resemble its neighbor in size, shape, or color. On the side streets bungalows rub elbows with mansions, frilly Victorians consort with sleek contemporaries. Morgan Peak is a jumble—though not, Emma reluctantly and silently allows, a displeasing jumble.

"Pretty," she says.

"Pretty, nothing. It's the real thing."

"I wouldn't mind spending a day or two. We could come out this summer, with Zack."

"Three bookstores." Roger speaks softly, as if trying to implant the information directly into her subconscious. "Jewish deli, Italian bakery, top-ranked public schools."

"Get thee behind me, Satan," she replies. But absently, her nose pressed to the window.

"Wait till you see the house," he says, and there is something in his voice, a muted intensity that snags her attention. Stealing a glance at her husband's face, Emma raises her hand to her mouth and gnaws a well-chewed thumbnail. Roger doesn't want many things, but he can be ruthless about getting those he does.

GORDON BASS has the key and could have waited inside the house, but he chooses to pass the time on the shady front porch. The realtor is a portly man in a beige linen suit and a red tie loosened at the throat. It's not the sad business of old lady Hysop that keeps him outside; Bass isn't the superstitious type, wouldn't pay to be in his racket. He just doesn't care for the place, grand as it is with all those gables, the octagonal tower, and arched roof. Give him a nice, vinyl-sided split any day, to live in or to sell. In a village where houses rarely last longer than one month on the market, this old Victorian has lingered eight months without attracting a single offer. Doesn't surprise him, considering it started out with two strikes against it. First strike is its reputation, which knocks out your local buyers. Second is shaky curb appeal. Too bad the old lady's heirs refused to paint the exterior—they were quick enough to clean out the furnishings. The fish-scale shingles that cover the house would have looked charming with a fresh coat of some light-colored paint and a contrasting color for the trim. As it stands, though, even people who claim to love old houses are intimidated by this one; daunted, too, by its location, which in real-estate-speak is termed "private," though strictly between himself and the lamppost Bass would call it downright isolated. The house stands sentry on the farthermost end of steep, unpaved Crag Road, where the cliff falls into the sea; there is no other house in sight save the little roadside carriage house that comes with the property.

The house's isolation didn't bother Roger Koenig, but in Bass's experience, nine times out of ten it's the woman who decides on a house. Now the wife is coming to check the place out. Bass, a born optimist, isn't holding his breath on this one.

He hears the car before he sees it, a big old Buick chugging up the hill. They'd do better with a four-wheel drive if they buy this place, Bass thinks. The car pauses at the foot of the drive beside the small clapboard carriage house, then continues up the drive. Bass descends from the porch, smiling. Roger Koenig parks beside Bass's car and gets out. The men exchange greetings while the woman remains seated, staring through the windshield at the house. Her husband opens her door, reaches in and hauls her out.

"Emma," he says, "Gordon Bass. My wife, Emma Roth."

Gordon Bass has a system of rating women. The unit of calibration is time: how much of it he would lop off the end of his life to nail them even once. Michelle Pfeiffer tops the scale at a year. Movie stars aside, though, Koenig's wife is right up there. Midnight-blue eyes under dark, slanting eyebrows, a hybrid mouth— long and thin upper lip, full, sensual lower. Taut olive skin that stretches over high cheekbones like canvas over a frame; luxuriant black hair you can't help but imagine wrapping around your hands. He can't see much of her body; she wears the American woman's version of the chador, jeans and an oversized cable sweater that covers her down to her thighs. She's tall and slender, though, with a coltish figure, like a young Lauren Bacall. She moves as if her limbs are lubricated.

She casts a clarifying light on the husband. Koenig dresses in classic professorial mufti of tweed jacket over jeans, but moves and speaks with an air of unconscious presumption that smells to Bass, who has a nose for the stuff, like very old money. The wife sews it up: not the sort of woman you'd aspire to on a professor's salary.

He holds out his hand. "Pleasure to meet you, Mrs. Koenig."

"Actually," Roger says, "my wife uses her maiden name, Roth."

"Emma's fine," she says. Her handshake is firm but perfunctory; she meets his gaze for just a moment before turning back to the house. Bass, striving to see it through her eyes, is struck anew by its defiant asymmetry, the multiplicity of angles, and the fierce effect of the overhanging eaves topped with wrought-iron castings. Impressive architecturally; though what she thinks he cannot tell. Bass prides himself on his ability to read faces, but he hasn't the key to hers.

Roger puts his arm around her shoulders. "Isn't it amazing?"

It is a setting that could support the most idiosyncratic of houses. The parking area is downhill from the house, which from their perspective appears to float between sky and sea. Gordon Bass looks at the house, then at the woman's profile, and impulsively says the words that come into his head. "You were born to own this house."

Which is not at all the sort of remark he is accus-

tomed to making. "First win their trust," he tells the
young agents who come and go in his office, "and eventually you will sell them a home." It doesn't do to let
buyers feel you are invested in any particular property,
and indeed this is the last property he would think of
foisting on any client. Nevertheless the words seem true
to him: She was born to own this house.

Emma turns her cool gaze on Bass. He sucks in his
gut and smiles hopefully.

"Really," she says. "Who do I look like to you,
Mortitia Addams?"

They climb the five steps leading up to the porch and
pass between spidery trellises to enter the house. Emma
shivers; on this balmy spring day it is cooler indoors
than out. First thing she notices in the wide entrance hall
is the streaming light, which comes as a surprise, for despite the abundance of windows she has somehow expected gloom. The second is the gleaming, wide-board
oak floor. Emma loves wooden floors, though not
enough to sell her urban soul.

The broker leads them into the living room, a large
rectangular room whose length runs along the northern
wall of the house. With no furniture to distract it,
Emma's eye is drawn first to the burnished wood par-
quet floor, then to the windows. Bass is talking about
the age of the house, pointing out the original Victorian
detail, crown moldings, woodwork. She's not listening;
she has drifted away from the men and come to rest
before one of three floor-to-ceiling windows along the
exterior wall. Outside, the land rises for some twenty
yards between the house and a windbreak of old pines
that limns the cliff's edge. The landward portion of the
cove is obscured from this vantage point. Farther out,

where the bay merges with the sound, the waves are capped with white and the water ripples in complex patterns. It is the kind of irregular regularity that entrances her husband, the only adult Emma knows who can spend hours on his back staring up at clouds. The sky above the water looks like an unmade feather bed, piled high with fluffy white cumulus clouds.

She notices then that the middle window is not a window at all but a pair of French doors leading out to a small terra-cotta terrace just big enough for a little table and a couple of wrought-iron chairs. Suddenly Emma has a vision of herself sitting alone on that terrace, watching the bay as she drinks a cup of coffee. The vision, though vivid, almost hallucinatory, lasts but a moment before she whisks it away.

Yet its effect on her does not pass unobserved. Gordon Bass sees it and is heartened. You never know, he tells himself, a phrase that sums up much of what he's learned through his profession.

"Shall we move on?" he says.

She turns, her face restored to indifference. "Might as well; we're here."

He leads them through the parlor and the dining room. Koenig's questions about the house, the village, and the schools are clearly meant for his wife's edification, since he asked them all before. But Emma listens with polite indifference, as silent as he is voluble. She asks no questions, gives nothing away.

There is tension between husband and wife, and Bass swims between them, testing the currents. More and more he comes to focus on the wife. The husband is sold; *she* is the holdout, but Bass is not without hope. He saw the look on her face as she gazed out at the living room terrace: dreamy yet possessive, the look of a woman taken by a house.

Taken, yes, it can happen that way. In the common course of events, of course, people choose houses. Sometimes, though, it doesn't work that way. Sometimes houses choose people. They reach out, they whisper, they entice and enfold. It's strange, spooky, hardly the sort of thing you'd bring up at sales conference—but more than once in the course of his career, Bass has seen it happen.

Something about this house moves Emma; something speaks to her. Bass understands why she resists. It makes sense to him that anyone who likes this house would like it against his will.

They come to the kitchen. Except for the living room, it is the largest room in the house. Built of stone and brick and oak, it features a walk-in pantry and a sitting nook with built-in benches and a fireplace. No woman accustomed to city kitchens would be likely to resist this one, Bass figures, and Emma does smile wistfully upon the stone hearth, but she doesn't do the things women do when they're serious about a house: open cabinets, pull out drawers, eyeball the plumbing. Roger does those things, while she sits on the bench beside the hearth, waiting as women wait for children to finish playing.

Bass leaves the husband to join the wife. "I believe Roger mentioned that you're a writer."

"Yes."

"Good for you! Published anything yet?"

There is a slight, sticky pause. Roger, who's heard her answer this question before, quits poking about the cupboards and looks with trepidation at his wife. The expression on her face—nostrils flared, one eyebrow

arced—he knows well. For a woman without preten-
sions, Emma tolerates condescension remarkably ill.

She gives Bass a frozen smile. "I understand you're a
realtor."

"Yes indeed, going on twenty years now."

"Sold any houses?"

A PRICKLY SORT of woman, then, Bass thinks as he
leads them up the L-shaped staircase, pointing out the
hand-carved banisters as they climb. One of those who
keep their own names after marriage. Call him a chau-
vinist, but Gordon Bass would not have married a girl
who wouldn't be proud to take his name. Although
Emma is admittedly the sort of woman for whom excep-
tions are made.

Times change, and as Bass often says, you've got to
go with the flow. Nowadays most of his buyers are two-
career couples. Have to be, the price of houses these
days—not like when he was a kid, when Mom stayed
home and Daddy brought home the bacon. Nevertheless,
it is a source of pride for Bass that his own wife has
never worked; he's supported her from the day they
married. Better that way, he feels. When both husband
and wife work, the marital balance of power shifts. Bass
still isn't sure where the fulcrum lay between this couple. Perhaps it is in flux.

He shows the four bedrooms, suppressing his own
dislike of the quirky, odd-shaped rooms, each with its
own gable and assorted unexpected nooks and crannies.
If there is one thing twenty years in real estate has taught
him it is the truth of the adage that one man's cramped
and inconvenient is another's charming and cozy.

He saves the master bedroom for last. The wife

responded to the view downstairs; he watches her closely
now as he throws open the door and stands back. The
room faces north and has twin gables. The views are living seascapes, framed in the gable windows. Once again
Emma is drawn to a window. This time Roger stands
behind her, his hands on her shoulders. They don't speak
for several moments. Bass, recognizing a decisive
moment when he sees one, keeps his mouth shut.

Roger brings his mouth close to Emma's ear. "What
you're observing," he says, "is the intersection of three
basic elements: land, water, and air. Total volatility. All
these forces interact to generate a series of inherently
unstable situations. Place is a petri dish for chaotic phenomena."

"You want us to live in a petri dish?"

"Above it, actually. All the action's down below. This
house is perched on the lip of chaos."

"Very poetic."

"Thank you."

"Can we go now?"

He doesn't move. He's not, she sees, even close to
moving. "You realize that from this window, you would
never see the same view twice?"

"I like seeing the same view twice."

"Tell me this isn't an amazing house."

Emma sighs.

"Tell me Zack wouldn't love it," Roger says.

Now he's definitely stepping. She gives him a scalding look, then turns to Gordon Bass with an air of finality. "What an unusual house. Thank you so much for
showing it to us."

"Oh, but wait," Bass says. "You *must* see the library.
And of course the carriage house."

"There's a library?"

"Yes, indeed. It's the most dramatic room of the house. Perfect for a writer, I should think. You'll have noticed from outside the octagonal tower on the north side of the house?"

Emma turns accusing eyes upon her husband, to whom she has entrusted the secrets of her heart. He wears a look of studious innocence. "You didn't mention a library."

"Slipped my mind," he says.

Bass leads them down the hall to a door Emma hadn't seen before. The door opens into a short, drably carpeted corridor that ends in an ascending spiral staircase. Both sides of the corridor are studded with cabinet handles and drawer pulls: hidden storage with easy access. She can't help thinking of the stacks of boxes that line the walls of the converted laundry room she calls her office—not precisely what Virginia Woolf had in mind when she prescribed a room of one's own for every writer. Cartons of galleys and manuscripts and author's copies of her books, material she needs to keep but has nowhere to store. There is more storage space in this short corridor than in the whole of their apartment. For that matter, the pantry is larger than their kitchen, and their entire apartment could fit into the ground floor of this house. Roger must be mad, she thinks. No way they could afford this house, even if she wanted it, which of course she doesn't.

At the foot of the spiral staircase Bass stands back to let Emma proceed. She climbs the winding steps and emerges through the floor of the most astonishing room she has ever seen. The tower's octagonal shape produces a kind of sectioned openness. The arc of the ceiling is repeated in the windows, one to a section. The afternoon light, pouring in from all directions, creates an air of heightened lucidity. The view is panoramic. Pale ash paneling and built-in bookcases on four of the eight walls anchor a room that might otherwise float off into space.

Perfect for a writer, the realtor had said, and he was right. It *is* perfect. It is a room that cries out for a writer. A room any writer would kill for.

Emma sees her books on those shelves. She sees where she would place her desk and where the armchair would go. She pictures the room as hers and feels the bolt of desire snap into place as surely as the lock on a cell door. She wants this tower. She lusts for it. She feels an immediate conviction that she must own this room, followed instantly by the certainty that she never will.

And who has done this to her? Who has brought her in a few short minutes from perfectly reasonable contentment to this wretched state of never-to-be-fulfilled desire? She turns to her husband, who watches her with a smugness he doesn't trouble to disguise. "You devious bastard!"

Roger's face splits with delight. He winks at the broker. "She loves it."

Emma cyclones down the winding stairs, dealing her husband, in passing, an unplayful punch in the gut.

"She *really* loves it," he gasps, clutching his stomach.

"Lucky for us," Bass says.

ALTHOUGH Emma as a child marched to her own syncopated drummer, she has in recent years become a creature of decided habit. Little routines have sprung up like hedges about her days. Spontaneity is reserved for her work; in her personal life she finds safety and comfort in repetition. Of course Emma is not fool enough to believe that any amount of ritual can protect her from misfortune, which by its very nature falls where it will, when it pleases; but what profit is there in tempting fate?

Two days after their expedition to Morgan Peak, Emma rises at six o'clock to see Roger off. She does this because she always does it, it is part of her routine; she does it even though she is tired and her head aches from fatigue and tension. They've been battling for two days, breaking off whenever Zack comes near, resuming at once in his absence. Emma is unused to such vehemence in Roger; ever since the accident he's shied away from confrontations. On this matter, though, he will not give in. The house is perfect for them, he insists. It is time for a change. Why a change should be necessary is another in the class of things not discussed. Thus is Roger trampling on the central conceit of their marriage: that the past is the past, dead and buried. When she punishes him with silence, he responds by upping the ante. "Zack would love it," he says. "Any kid would. The sea, the space, the freedom."

As if that were an inducement, as if she wants Zack to have more freedom. If accidents happen when they're least expected, then constant vigilance is the key. In the city Zack goes nowhere unescorted by a parent; Emma sees to that. But in the suburbs kids have wheels of their own, bicycle wheels. They ride away from you and then anything can happen, anything at all. What goes around comes around is Emma's greatest fear.

Last night she purchased a twenty-four-hour moratorium on discussion of the house, but at a steep price: a promise that she would not rule out the house, that she would consider it seriously. This morning an eye-of-the-hurricane calm prevails. Roger keeps his word and says nothing about the house. They drink coffee together, sitting on opposite ends of the table. Then he kisses her and leaves the apartment.

Her routine continues. At seven o'clock she wakes Zack, at eight-fifteen walks him to the bus stop on Columbus Avenue. She waits at a discreet distance until the school bus comes—not discreet enough for Zack, who hates her hovering. "None of the other moms wait." He is ten years old and bursting with frustrated independence. Emma hates to cramp him, but on points of safety she is inflexible. Doesn't she know how quickly accidents can occur? Not to mention all the other childhood hazards of large cities.

On the way home she stops at the corner bakery for *The New York Times* and her usual croissant. Back in their apartment on the sixth floor of a prewar building, she pours her second cup of coffee, puts it on a tray with the croissant and the paper, and carries the tray into the living room. She scans the *Times* and turns to the crossword puzzle—Monday's puzzle, the easiest of the week, which she fills in quickly. Then, with unusual reluctance, she goes into her office.

A funny little room, she calls it to friends, though for Emma the charms of coziness have long since worn off. Her desk and printer stand occupy the space once filled by a washer and drier. At the end of the windowless room is the deep, chintz-covered armchair where she writes her first drafts in longhand before transferring each day's work to the computer. A shallow bookcase holds essential reference works, whatever books she is currently using for research, and office supplies. A narrow room made narrower by the stacks of boxes that line the walls.

Normally Emma's tunnel vision blocks out the room and focuses on the work. This Monday, though, she sees it with new eyes. What a dreary hole it is. She sits at the computer and conjures up a program of card games. The second cup of coffee, the crossword, the computer game—all part of the morning ritual she thinks of as booting up her brain. A few hands of hearts and then she will settle in to work. From the gallery of talking heads she chooses her favorites: Grandpa, Gambler, and Southern Belle. They have other names, but that's what she calls them. Usually Emma beats the computer, but today the cards are stacked against her. Twice she ends up eating a solo queen of spades; she loses the game in six hands. "Too bad," says the perky Belle. "Maybe you'll win next time." Emma exits the game and boots up Word.

Last week's pages await her in a leather binder beside the computer. She carries them over to the armchair and settles in to read. Feeling her way back into the story, editing as she goes, her protagonist this time a young journalist writing a series about local haunted houses. Faith Mercer is a sensible, down-to-earth sort of person who doesn't believe in ghosts until she actually meets one, which is just about to happen. Meanwhile Emma has left her on the threshold of her first haunted house, a deserted mansion to which she has finagled the keys.

What has to come next is a description of the house. Notebook in hand, Emma pictures the mansion in her mind. Almost at once certain details begin to emerge.

She writes quickly, not pausing to think, just letting the words spill out. Later she will cut and edit ruthlessly, but not now. First drafts are playgrounds where anything goes.

Suddenly she is finished. The description covers three sides of paper. But when she reads it over, she receives a sickening jolt. The house she has described is in all essentials the house in Morgan Peak. She groans. This is awful. Bad enough the house is roiling her marriage and ruining her sleep; now it is invading her work, the last bastion. Emma crumples up the pages, tosses them into the basket.

She tries again, gets nowhere. The room is oppressive, the air stale. She cannot settle down, cannot get inside the story. Her characters read like stick figures, no life at all to them. She turns to a fresh page of loose leaf, folds it lengthwise, writes "Pro" on one side and "Con" on the other. Like most writers, she thinks best when she's writing, so it's not surprising that when she is most stressed, she makes lists. Itemizing pros and cons is no doubt a primitive mode of organization, but surely better than none at all.

Under Pro, Emma writes "library." Her pen falls idle as she pictures the room that would have been and still could be her own. How beautiful it was; what books could be written in such a room! It would affect her writing, no way that it couldn't. One would have to live up to a room like that. Emma likes to claim that she could work anywhere, and perhaps she could; writing is that essential to her well-being. But that is not to say she is impervious. There is a mutual confluence of life and fiction; each exerts a gravitational pull on the other's orbit. Lately Emma has been troubled by a perception of sameness in her work, a feeling that she isn't so much writing as rewriting.

Oh, the words flow easily enough; they always have. But the ideas don't. For her, it seems, there is only one idea, though many permutations. She writes always of women who are haunted, who try and fail to escape their past. Even when she sets out deliberately to write a different sort of book, she finds her story veering back to the same old theme; she is like Alice in the looking-glass world, who discovered that the path away from the house leads directly to it.

It worries her. Last time they had lunch, she put it to her literary agent, Gloria Lucas. "Was the last book too like the one before?"

Caught off guard, Gloria hesitated a moment before responding. "Ghost stories are a classic genre," she said at last. "They're supposed to follow traditional lines. Nobody wants a sonnet with fifteen lines."

Her true answer, Emma knew, lay not in her words but in the pause that preceded them. "It was, then."

"What are you asking, Emma? Okay, sure, I'd like to see you push the envelope, grow as a writer. But if you're asking me as an agent are you hurting yourself, the answer's *au contraire*, babe. Consistency's a real virtue when you're trying to build a solid base of readers."

All very encouraging, except that consistency is not a quality Emma aspires to or even admires. Prison bars are consistent, pudding is consistent. The writers she admires take risks, try things, dare to fail now and then. Emma doesn't read the kind of book she writes, and this fact troubles her greatly.

But that's what happens when you write in a laundry room, says a voice inside her head. She ignores it and goes on with her list. Under Con she writes "L.I."

A bit of a snob is Emma, possessed of the innocent arrogance of born-and-raised New Yorkers who imbibe with their mothers' milk the words of the city's anthem: "If I can make it there, I'll make it anywhere . . ." She knows the city better than most cabbies; she owns the streets; she has never been mugged. When people she knows flee the city for the suburbs, she thinks of them with pity but also disdain, as having either given up or sold out. How will she see herself if she follows suit? For Emma, it must be said, is prone to a feeling of diminishment. In certain subtle but important ways she is not quite the woman she used to be, and she knows it. Surely burying herself in a small village would be another step on the road to disappearing—not only personally, but professionally as well. In her mind there are two sorts of American writers: those who live in New York City, and those who live in the provinces. In that respect Long Island is as far from Manhattan as Idaho.

Under Pro she writes "public school." Emma has been raised to believe in public education; her parents were passionate on the subject, and both she and her sister received very decent public-school educations, thank you very much. But Roger is determined that his son's education will not be sacrificed to a political principle, and in this instance Emma is content, perhaps even relieved, to be overruled. Zack attends a private school on the Upper East Side. Maggie disapproves, of course, but Maggie would. Emma is troubled more by her own misgivings, which resurface with every gathering of the well-heeled PTA. In Morgan Peak Zack would attend public school. According to Roger, who's done his homework, the district is ranked among the top ten in

the nation. Classes are small, they boast an exceptional
program for the gifted, and the high school has produced more Westinghouse finalists than any school on
Long Island.

Under Con she writes "cost." Her first line of
defense, and the first defeated. The night after their
excursion, Roger told her the asking price of the house:
a hundred thousand lower than her lowest estimate.
Amazing that such a large house could cost less than a
three-bedroom co-op in a decent Manhattan neighborhood; even so, it is more than they could possibly
afford. Of course, when she said so, Roger pounced. Not
only could they afford it, he declared with the air of a
magician producing a rabbit, they would actually reduce
their living expenses.

Nonsense, she replied. Their apartment was rent-
controlled; how could a house possibly cost less?
Roger was, as always, appallingly well prepared, as
befits a man who proposed marriage by presenting her
with a mathematical proof of its logical necessity.
(Which she still has somewhere. "If E = Emma, and R
= Roger, and H = the function of happiness . . .") He
produced a small notebook from his jacket pocket and
opened to a page covered with figures. He showed her
what they would save in tuition and income tax, and
what they would realize in rent from the carriage
house, which had proved on inspection to be a very
nice little house; eminently rentable, the realtor
assured them.

It's true that looked at in this way the house *is* surprisingly affordable; but the down payment would con-
sume practically all their savings, so Emma still feels
justified in listing cost as a drawback.

Under Pro she wrote "space; light." The light an unalloyed good, the space a mixed blessing, lack of it having served her well. When Roger says, "We'll have more room," he means more room for children. She knows it, he knows it, but neither says it out loud. These are waters even reckless Roger scruples to disturb.

Under Con she writes "friends." When people emigrate from the city they always swear they'll stay in touch, and at first they do. Gradually, though, they drift away. It would happen to her.

Under Pro: "Roger wants it."

Oh, how he wants it. Roger grew up on Long Island, and feels he is cheating his son by raising him in Manhattan. All the things that Emma loves most about the city—its cultural largesse, ethnic stew, ever changing human landscape, even the unwritten rules of city etiquette, the delicate grammar of social intercourse— he values less than a Sunday game of soccer on his own front lawn.

Under Con she writes "Maggie." Then underlines the name three times. Maggie is the antidote for what ails her; Maggie is the cure. Maggie will shake her back to her senses. Emma closes the notebook and reaches for the phone.

"THAT IS, without a doubt, the stupidest fucking idea I have ever heard."

"So you're against it," says Emma. They are strolling through the Sheep Meadow in Central Park, Maggie's arm taut as a strung bow in Emma's. It's warm for May; the meadow is dotted with groups of office workers eating lunch, children in strollers, shirtless young men playing Frisbee.

Maggie says, "Are you kidding? Mom and Dad would spin in their graves."

"I don't think so," Emma says. "Considering they were cremated."

"In their urns, then. Jesus, Em, why do you have to be so literal?"

"Occupational hazard. Anyway, I didn't say I've agreed."

Maggie stops dead. She is the younger sister but in personality the more forceful, and this is reflected in their choice of careers. Emma is a writer, a solitary profession. Maggie teaches at Columbia and lectures all over the country on class structure in the United States. She has a doctorate in sociology and is half a dissertation away from a second Ph.D. in economics. In her spare time she serves on half a dozen political and academic committees. Emma has built a career out of daydreaming; but Maggie dwells in the world.

"What scares me," Maggie says, "is you're even considering it."

"Roger really wants it."

"Fuck Roger! That bonehead, who does he think he is?"

Emma smiles. "He thinks he's my husband."

"In sickness and in health; I don't remember anything in the vows about in city or in suburb. He can't make you, you know."

"He wouldn't try."

Maggie shoots her a look of utter disbelief. "That bastard. Wait till I get my hands on him."

"No, Mags," Emma says firmly. She reclaims her sister's arm and they walk on. Their progress across the great lawn creates a ripple of male attention, a moving thicket of second looks. Anyone could see they are sisters, with Maggie the smaller, more intense package. Sharp as a tack, their mother used to say; sharp as a chainsaw, Roger later amended. It's a wonder they've grown up to be as close as they are, for they'd little enough in common as children. Emma played house, Maggie war. Emma read, Maggie played stickball on the street. They were so different that there was never any question of competition.

At the far end of the meadow they come upon an unoccupied bench and grab it. Emma rests her arms along the top rail and raises her face to the sun.

Maggie runs a hand through her black curls, tugging at the roots. "Did I call this? Did I say one day he'd pull this number? The man is a solid bourgeois brick. You move to Long Island, I guarantee you within one year he'll be playing golf and bitching about property values. Don't laugh! Can't you see where this is heading, Em? *You* tucked away in some godforsaken little pit stop, cut off from the world, waiting like a good little wifey for hubby to come home; *him* scampering off to the city every day, free as a bird."

"Roger's not like that."

Maggie sniffs disdainfully. "Roger is as Roger does."

"Trust me: That's not what this is about."

"Oh no? What is it about, then?"

Emma stares across the meadow. A gentle breeze carries the distant strains of a calliope. "The house," she says. "It got to me, Mags."

Maggie groans. "Spare me."

"I can't help it. I keep obsessing over that library, the view. You can see in all directions, three hundred and sixty degrees. I have this weird fantasy that a person who lived there and worked in that room would become sort of a real-life omniscient narrator. You must think I'm nuts."

"Of course you're nuts. It's just a house! Who would your friends be? What would you do with yourself?"

"I know. You're right, I know."

In unspoken accord they rise and head back the way they came, more purposefully now, for Maggie has a class to teach and Emma a son to meet. On the pavement outside the park they kiss good-bye, but as Emma turns away, Maggie catches hold of her sleeve. "You asked my advice, take it. Home ownership is a sinkhole, a trap. The minute you sign that mortgage you're invested in the system. You'd be doubly invested, a landlord as well as an owner. You might think it won't change you, but it absolutely will. Socially it would be a disaster. Long Island teems with Republicans. You'd be surrounded, isolated; in short, the whole idea sucks. But I have an even stronger objection."

"What's that?"

"I'd hate it," she says in the small, tight voice that Emma knows of old as the sound of Maggie refusing to cry. "You're all the family I've got, you and Zack and bonehead Roger. I can't afford to lose you."

Emma puts an arm around her sister's shoulder. "You'd never lose us. Even if we did buy that house, Long Island isn't Siberia."

"Yes it is."

"Well, maybe."

"Tell me you're not serious about this house, Em."

"I'm not," Emma says. "It's a ridiculous idea. I'm dead set against it. Except . . ."

"Except what?"

"Except I can't get it out of my mind."

2

ZACK'S NOT hiding, precisely. More like resting, taking a much needed break from the business of unpacking. And if he chooses to rest in an empty carton, what is that to anyone but him? It's a huge carton, tall enough to stand up in, wide enough to sit in, perfectly camouflaged by all the other boxes and crates piled up in the kitchen. Out of sight, out of mind, or so he hopes. His conscience is clear; he's done his share and more.

He is tall for his age, dark-haired, bright-eyed; he has his mother's olive skin stretched over his father's angled, patrician face. His body is slim but solid and muscular. Once he heard a coach say to his mom that he was built like a natural soccer player. Though Zack still isn't sure what that means, he knows it's good, and that comment has become one of the jewels of his collection. Other kids collect trading cards, stamps, or coins; Zack amasses bits of information, fragments of secrets, shards of the puzzle that is grown-up life—anything he can glean from the adults who rule his world.

One thing's for sure: They aren't giving the stuff away. His parents always put forth a seamless front; it was "Your mother and I feel" or "Dad and I think," even when Zack knew for a fact that they were at odds. Like this move to Morgan Peak. His mom was against it. No one tells him this, certainly not his mother, who loves him most of anyone but never tells him anything that matters. He figures it out himself. "Zack," she says the first time they brought him out here, "you wouldn't really want to leave the city to live here, would you?" And by the way she asks it he can tell she wants him to say no, he wouldn't; which shows how much she knows. This house is, like, a mansion! The backyard is so huge he could have his whole team over to play. Just beyond the trees a steep path leads down the cliff to a cove with a small, rocky beach. The whole place is awesome, totally cool. What is his mom thinking? She might as well ask, "You wouldn't really want to meet Michael Jordan and hang out with him and his buddies, would you?"

"Are you kidding?" is all he could say. "Are you kidding?"

Next she brings up his friends. "They can visit," he tells her. "We can have sleepovers. Jeez, imagine playing hide-and-seek in this place."

"And your team?" she asks.

Zack is stricken. He hadn't thought about that. He can't leave his team. Who would he play with? And he can't not play, because soccer is his life; it's what makes him special.

"You'll play on another team," his dad says. "There's soccer out here, too."

Zack looks from one to the other. "You're sure?" he says.

"Would I take a chance with your soccer career?" his dad says. "I'm planning to retire off your earnings. Relax, Zack. I already spoke to the coach."

"You've been busy," his mom says, and they exchange a look he's not supposed to see.

She was hoping Zack would say he hated it and that would be that, but he wouldn't say it. They decided to buy the house. That's how they put it: *"We've decided . . ."* Now they're here, and tomorrow is the try-out for the Morgan Peak Pirates, the under-eleven travel team. Zack's got to practice, but where are his ball and cleats? Must be in his room, in one of the boxes. He packed them himself, marked the box with a big red *S* for soccer. He shoves back the flaps of the carton, but just as he's about to tip it over he hears voices approaching. He ducks back inside, pulling the flaps down over his head. Two people enter the kitchen.

"And just where is His Royal Otherness?" asks Aunt Maggie, out for the day to help his mom unpack. "Don't tell me, let me guess: out in the yard studying the dynamics of dandelion dispersion."

"Upstairs," his mother says, "setting up my computer."

"Nice work if you can get it."

"Well, we don't want him here, do we? He'd come up with some brilliant new system of organizing the kitchen and I'd never be able to find a thing."

"A perfect metaphor for marriage." There's something jarring in his aunt's voice, a metallic ping of resentment.

A short silence follows. Zack hears the swish of cartons being opened, a chink of dishes, then his mother's mild voice. "I agreed to this, you know. He didn't drag me along kicking and screaming."

A loud sniff from Aunt Maggie.

"Anyway, Mags, you have to admit it's a dynamite kitchen."

"It's a womantrap. You'll start baking."

"Mom baked."

"You're not Mom. And Roger will start barbecuing."

"Oh, Maggie. Are barbecues politically incorrect now?"

The sound of their voices—his mother's pacific and amused, Maggie's sharp, quarrelsome, inordinately dear to him—lulls Zack almost to sleep. He is fond of his aunt, who differs from all other adults in that she doesn't act as if there's one truth for grown-ups and another, unrelated one for kids. Ask her a question and you get back an answer and a half, everything you wanted to know and more. One time only did she hold out on him; but that was a day on which much else was revealed.

It happened last year, toward the end of fourth grade. One day he gets off the school bus and his mother isn't there. She's been late before, not often, but occasionally. When it happens he's supposed to wait at the stop till she arrives. But this time Zack has a better idea. It's a gloriously sunny spring day, perfect for a long walk. He decides to visit Aunt Maggie. Picturing her face as she opens the door, he laughs out loud. He knows where she lives, on Central Park West. Knows the way, too; he's gone with his mom a million times.

He sets off at a good clip up Columbus Avenue, past rows of sidewalk cafés, boutiques, delis, florists, pharmacies, and pizzerias. The smell of food is everywhere. Zack's mouth waters; he is missing his after-school snack. Delving into his pants pockets, he excavates six quarters, two dimes, a nickel, and a stick of gum. He sticks the gum in his mouth and walks on for what seems like miles, though according to the street sign he's gone only fourteen blocks so far, not even halfway to his aunt's. Somehow it seemed shorter on the bus.

No one notices a small kid with a backpack; he's invisible, deliciously free. Not because he's tired, but to celebrate and prolong his liberty, Zack stops in a pizzeria. After checking the price list and counting his money again, he orders a lemon Italian ice and eats it slowly, with immense satisfaction. When he's squeezed the last bit of juice from the little pleated cup, he sets out again. Just past 100th Street, he spies a small pod of teenage boys cruising his way. Zack knows he isn't invisible to them; kids always see other kids. One boy says something to another, who looks at him and laughs. When they're half a block away, Zack ducks into a drugstore and hangs out in the candy aisle. Five minutes later, feeling rather slick and proud of himself, he emerges to find the coast clear.

Maggie lives on the sixth floor of a brick building between 105th and 106th. Raul, the doorman, is a friend of Zack's. He looks surprised to see him. "Yo, Zack," he says, holding out a hand for Zack to slap. "How's my man? Where's your mama at?"

"Home, I guess," Zack says, sauntering past as if he did it every day. "Don't tell Aunt Maggie I'm here. I want to surprise her."

"Hey, man, it's my job to tell. What if you was some kinda bad dude come 'round casing the joint?"

"Then I wouldn't exactly come strolling in the front door, would I?" On that triumphant note, Zack steps into the elevator. But when the elevator door opens, Maggie's there waiting.

She pulls him to her and hugs him so tight he can hardly breathe. Zack's a bit taken aback; Maggie is not, generally, a clutchy-squeezy sort of female. Then she pushes him back, holds him at arm's length, and says, "What the hell are you doing here?"

"I came to visit. I was gonna surprise you—darn that Raul!"

"Oh, I'm surprised all right." Maggie takes his arm and propels him with more force than necessary down the hall to her apartment. Zack drops his backpack in the foyer and enters the living room, as chaotic as his mom's is neat. Books everywhere, stacks of papers on the desk, newspapers tossed aside in evident disgust. He sighs with pleasure at the messiness and says, "Got anything to eat? I'm starving."

Maggie points at the cordless phone on her desk. "Call your mother."

"Can I eat first?"

"Call her *now*."

Zack dials his number. The phone is snatched up before the first ring ends. His mother's voice sounds as if she's swallowed sandpaper. Of course, Zack's known all along that he is breaking the rules, but he figured it was no big deal, worth getting grounded for a day or two. Now for the first time it occurs to him that he might be in serious trouble.

"Hi, Mom. It's Zack."

"Zack, where are you?" The words fly out of the phone. He gets the feeling she expects to be cut off.

"I'm at Aunt Maggie's."

Maggie snatches the receiver from his hand. "He's here. Just strolled in, pleased as punch . . . It's okay now, Em. It's over."

Her voice sounds like the voice you hear when you get decked by a soccer ball or kicked in the head, and people bend over you and ask are you all right. Zack sidles out of the room and turns right. Down the hall to the kitchen; Maggie's addicted to Ben and Jerry's Rocky Road. Zack figures he might as well salvage what he can of his excellent adventure before the feds lock him down for life. Sure enough, there's a full pint in the freezer. He takes out a bowl.

Maggie gets off the phone finally and comes and sits opposite him at the kitchen table. He offers her a taste and she turns it down: bad sign. Her nostrils are flared. That and her blinkered attention remind him of the carriage horses on Central Park South. She's steaming like them, too, pissed as hell. Zack eats his ice cream the way a death-row prisoner eats his final meal: very, very slowly.

"How did you get here?" she says at last.

"Walked."

"All the way?"

"It's not so far."

"Alone?"

"Sure." He meets her look and raises her one. "I took a walk. Can't a person take a walk? What's the big deal?"

"The big deal is scaring your poor mother half to death. What the hell were you thinking, Zack? How could you do this to her?"

"I didn't do anything to her. It had nothing to do with her!"

"No? What did it have to do with?"

"Me!"

Maggie's eyes are sharp and unsentimental. She looks like his mother, only more compact and fiercer. Zack wonders how she is as a teacher. Scary, he thinks.

Wouldn't want to forget your homework in her class. If college kids even have homework.

"I see," she says. "Your maiden flight. And you feel you should be welcomed back to the nest with psalms of praise and bouquets of worms."

He doesn't know about the worms, but she's right about the main thing. This *is* his maiden flight, and Zack happens to think it's a pretty damn good one. But does anyone care about that? Of course not; they just worry about his mom. It's Mother this and Mother that, the same old same old as far back as he can remember. His father's favorite words: "Don't upset your mother." Now he's getting it from Maggie. Is his mother a house of cards, that she should be so easily upset? It seems to Zack at that moment as if his entire family is a joint venture formed solely for the preservation of his mother's peace of mind, a conspiracy to protect, the reasons for which no one has seen fit to reveal to him.

And here is the perfect person on whom to test his hypothesis: Maggie, who never lies, who answers every question put to her.

"Why is it always about her?" he asks.

Maggie narrows her eyes. "What do you mean?"

"You're not mad 'cause I took a walk. You're mad 'cause Mom got all bent out of shape. Why is everything always about her?"

She almost tells him. He sees the truth trembling on her lips. Then her eyes drop to her hands, laced so tightly the knuckles shine white, and she speaks in a voice she's never used on him before, the voice of an adult talking down to a child. "Because she worries about you, Zack. That's what moms do: They worry."

A half-truth at best. Clever old Maggie, talking about moms in general to avoid telling about his in particular. But it doesn't work, because if a person who always answers truthfully doesn't, that in itself is a kind of answer. It means that he was right: Protecting his mother *is* the prime directive.

Why this should be, and what she needs protecting from, Zack still has not discovered; although at times it seems he *almost* knows. It's as if the information is present in his brain, but he's lost the access code.

Then the doorbell rings, and Zack's back in his box, stiff all over and aching to get out. "Who could that be?" his mother says, and Maggie answers, "Welcome Wagon, probably. Ladies in hats bearing gifts. *Good Housekeeping*, knitting needles, white bread, and a great big jar of mayonnaise."

"I could use some mayo." Their voices fade as they move away. Quickly Zack tips over his cardboard cell and scrambles out. God, it feels good to move! What a waste of time; he overheard nothing of value. He runs out the kitchen door and around the side of the house, meaning to enter from the front as if he'd been outside all along. But as he turns the corner he skids to a halt. There's a strange car in the driveway, a lady in the passenger seat, and Mr. Fish or whatever his name was, the man who sold them the house, is at the front door talking to his mom.

HE'S SORRY for not calling ahead. He hopes it isn't inconvenient. He was in the neighborhood, showing some properties to a lady who has her heart set on renting a small house. And it occurred to him that they had expressed some interest in renting the carriage house.

"Definitely," Emma says. "But I'm not sure we're ready. We're barely unpacked ourselves."

"She was very taken with the look of the place, said it's just what she had in mind." Bass lowers his voice, though there's no way the woman waiting in the car hears them. "Professional lady, single, middle-aged: A person could look far and wide for a less troublesome sort of tenant."

Emma is acutely conscious of Maggie standing behind her. She hesitates.

"Go ahead," says Maggie. "Go do your little landlord shtick. I'll get back to work."

"I'll have to find the keys," Emma says, turning back into the house. Where could they be? Emma's surface neatness is just a cover for internal chaos; she is an inveterate loser of keys, mislayer of lists, forgetter of dental appointments. Luckily for her she's married to the world's most organized man—which, she once told Maggie, was why she married him. And trust Maggie to pretend to believe her. "In that case," she'd replied, "marriage is excessive. Why not just let him organize your closets?"

Which reminds her: Didn't he say something last night about keys? They were in the dining room. . . . Sure enough, she finds three sets of keys in the middle drawer of the sideboard, each labeled in Roger's small, neat hand. Emma pockets the set marked "Carriage House" and heads outside.

Bass has driven down to the carriage house, though it's barely fifty yards from the main house. The car door is open and he is seated behind the wheel, speaking into a car phone. The woman is out of the car, standing beside one of the two stone pillars that mark the driveway. She

is gazing at the bay, but at the sound of Emma's footsteps she turns and strides briskly toward her.

Emma takes stock with a writer's eye. Fiftyish, tall,
angular, well-dressed in a tailored suit of natural linen
and matching pumps. (Emma is conscious, suddenly, of
her own grubby work clothes: cut-off jeans and an old
gray Cornell T-shirt of Roger's.) No wedding ring.
Expensively tousled salt-and-pepper hair, forthright
green eyes, just a touch of lipstick. Lots of confidence in
that walk, and the suit is Bergdorf quality. Lawyer, loan
officer, corporate exec? Country-club Republican for
sure. All this Emma gleans before the first how-do-you-
do, much of it to be revised later.

The woman's handshake is firm, her gaze direct.
"Caroline Marks," she says.

"Emma Roth. Nice to meet you."

"Very kind of you to show the house. I gather you've
just moved in yourselves."

"Yes. I haven't even set foot in the carriage house
since we took possession. I'm not sure what shape it's
in."

The woman smiles. There is a warmth to her smile
that eases the sternness of her face. "Then we'll find out
together." Her voice is low and pleasant, her accent
refined by education; though Emma, who has a good ear
for accents, discerns faint vestiges of New Yawk.

They walk toward the carriage house. Bass catches
up on the doorstep. Emma unlocks the door but hangs
back, allowing the realtor to take the lead. She could do
with a tour herself. Indeed, the place seems hardly hers
to rent, so little does she know it.

The basic clapboard structure is about a century old.
Originally it housed the family carriage, later the car,

with an apartment on top for the chauffeur. In those days, Bass reminds them with a sigh, everyone had servants.

"Except, of course, the servants," says Emma, who comes from good peasant stock herself. Caroline Marks smiles. Dr. Marks, it seems, for so Bass has addressed her. What kind of doctor is one of many things Emma wonders about. For a woman of her age and stature, Dr. Marks seems unusually unencumbered. Chronic nosiness is a common affliction among writers, though in this case, Emma has some justification. It's a wise landlady, surely, who knows her tenants.

Bass continues with the tour. At some point, he says, probably in the fifties, the entire structure was converted to its present form. On one side of the ground-floor hallway is a large eat-in kitchen, backed by a combination mud/laundry room. On the other side is a living room, quite pleasant, with a stone fireplace at one end and built-in window seats beneath two bay windows. Upstairs are two bedrooms and a bathroom. The smaller bedroom faces east, overlooking Crag Road and the village beyond. The windows of the larger bedroom face north and west, with views encompassing the main house and the bay. Emma looks out the westward window. The sun is setting behind her house, which seems to glow about the edges. The tower is lit from within. As she watches, a figure appears in the facing window. Roger, she assumes, still putzing around with her computer. They are fifty yards apart, too far to see features. Emma waves. The figure does not respond but rather turns away. Something in the movement and the figure's silhouette suggest a woman. Maggie, perhaps?

Caroline Marks joins her at the window. "Perfect," she murmurs.

Emma looks at her.

"Couldn't ask for a lovelier setting," Caroline says.

"Bit isolated."

"I prefer that." Emma raises her eyebrows, and the older woman smiles. "My work can be stressful. It's good to come home to peace and quiet."

"Then I should warn you, we have a ten-year-old son—not exactly conducive to peace and quiet."

"I hope I'm not yet so old and crotchety that the sound of children playing disturbs me."

Bass joins them at the window. "So, ladies . . ."

"I'll take it," Caroline Marks says to Emma, with a look both confident and oddly vulnerable. "If you'll have me."

Emma fights an impulse to say yes on the spot. She's never done this before; or rather, she's done it from the other side, as a prospective tenant. It's embarrassing to find herself now in the position of landlord. Clearly there are questions to be asked, references sought; yet she feels herself unequal to the task of interrogating this older and patently respectable woman. It seems presumptuous, as if she were setting herself above the woman just because she, Emma, happens to own this ridiculously large property. She remembers what Maggie said: *You think it won't change you, but it will.*

Bass, that improbable knight, comes to her rescue. He has the standard agency application form in his car, he tells them, if that is acceptable to Ms. Roth? It is most acceptable to Ms. Roth; so much easier to let a form ask the questions. The ease with which this has come about seems a sign that it is meant to be; but before anything can be decided, Roger has to meet the woman. Emma invites Bass and Dr. Marks up to the house, installs them in the living room with one of Bass's applications, and sets out in search of her husband.

She tries the library first. He isn't there but her trestle desk is set up, and on it her beloved computer, exhumed from its packing. Emma sits in her leather swivel chair and turns on the computer. It blinks to life immediately. The old familiar screen smiles at her; the mouse nestles snugly in her hand. Her new book is in there, just three clicks away. She feels it call to her. Soon, she promises. Tomorrow Roger goes back to work, and so by God will she. She feels heavy with words, like a nursing mother who's gone too long between feedings.

Next she tries their bedroom, then Zack's, and from Zack's window she hears voices outside. She looks out the window to the backyard. Zack and Roger are playing keep-away. Zack has the ball and he's running rings around Roger, showing off his fancy footwork, both of them laughing and panting.

Downstairs then, and through the kitchen. Maggie's perched on a stepladder, washing shelves. Emma slides to a halt. "You're back?"

"From where?"

"I thought I just saw you up in the library."

"Not me." Maggie stares at her. "So?"

"She wants it. She's in the living room now, filling in an application."

"*Mazel tov.*"

"Did you see her?"

"I caught a glimpse."

"And?"

Maggie scrunches up her nose. "Very ladylike. Republican, you realize."

And though this had been Emma's first impression as well, she feels compelled instantly to deny it. "You don't know that."

"Betcha ten million bucks."

"You're always doing this, Mags, judging people purely by their appearance."

Maggie has a trick of looking at people through half-closed lids, a look designed and engineered to quell student inanities. She turns it, now, on Emma and says with utter finality, "She wears Republican shoes."

"Republican shoes?" Emma cries softly. They stare at each other. "Maybe we should add a question about political affiliation to the application."

"Good idea," Maggie says. "Possibly a tad unconstitutional."

"Mmm. Why bother, anyway, when we can just check out their footwear?"

"It so happens that shoes are an excellent marker, much more reliable than clothes. Everyone wears jeans nowadays. Bob Dole wears jeans. Pat fucking Buchanan wears jeans. But how many Republicans wear sandals?"

Emma gives up and heads out the back door. Roger has stolen the ball from Zack and is trying to dribble past him: not easy, because the boy runs backward faster than most kids run forward. Natural athleticism is part of what makes him such a strong young soccer player, but only part; the rest is grunt work, countless hours of dribbling, juggling, and repetitious drills. So many people have told Emma how talented her son is, and she accepts their praise as well-meant; but to her it seems no compliment at all. Lots of kids are talented. What seems to her praiseworthy in Zack is not his gift but the hard labor he invests in developing it.

"Play with us!" they call to her as she emerges blinking into the sunlight.

"Can't. We have company." And taking Roger aside, she tells him about Caroline Marks.

"What'd you think of her?" he asks.

"Intelligent, a bit reserved. I liked her."

"Fine. I trust your judgment." Roger edges toward Zack, who hovers nearby, juggling the soccer ball and pretending not to listen.

"Hang on there." Emma grabs a damp handful of shirt. "You have to meet her. And we haven't even talked about rent. I don't know what to ask for."

"Bass told us what we could get."

"It seems such a lot."

"It's the going rate for this area, and it's what we figured on in our calculations."

"Are you coming?"

"Dad," Zack wails, abandoning his pretense of deafness. "You promised!"

"You go ahead," Roger tells Emma. "I'll join you in a minute."

"What kind of minute?" she asks; Roger's sense of time is notoriously elastic.

"The sixty-second variety."

CAROLINE MARKS is alone in the living room when Emma returns, carrying a tray with four glasses of iced tea. Next spring, she thinks, she will plant mint; she will grow a whole herb garden in that bed outside the kitchen.

"Mr. Bass went out to use his car phone," Caroline says. She sits in the corner of the leather chesterfield, Bass's clipboard on her lap, a pair of tortoiseshell glasses perched on her nose.

Emma lays the tray on the oak coffee table and sits on the other end of the sofa, her body canted toward Caroline's.

"Iced tea? Instant, I'm afraid, but nice and cold."

"Lovely, thank you."

"About the rent," Emma says. As she states the amount she half-expects Caroline to get up and walk out; but Caroline is unfazed.

"That's fine." She hands over the clipboard with a look of trepidation Emma finds surprising, until she glances down the page and takes in all the blanks.

Under profession Caroline has written "Psychologist"; under current employment "Assistant director of 'Fresh Start' (counseling service for victims of rape and spousal abuse)." The salary indicated is more than adequate to accommodate the rent. But the date of employment reveals that she has only just begun working there, and the space for previous employment has been left blank. Her current residence is listed as the Radisson Hotel, Huntington. All questions regarding previous rentals have been answered "n/a," not applicable. Under references she's listed only one: the manager of the Chase Manhattan Bank in Morgan Peak.

Emma's high hopes tumble. Something is obviously wrong. Caroline's current information looks fine, but the woman has no history—or none she is willing to divulge. She looks up to find Caroline's eyes on her.

"I know," she says at once. "It looked strange to me, too, all those blank spaces."

"Perhaps you feel we have no right to ask—"

"No, no, of course you do." Caroline takes off her glasses. Her green eyes are troubled, distant. "It's your house, you have every right. I should have realized these questions would be asked. It's been a long time—"

"Since you rented?"

Another silence. Then Caroline meets her eyes with an air of decision. "I'm so sorry. You must think I'm hiding some deep, dark secret, when in fact it's merely embarrassing. You're right; until a year ago I owned my own house. We, my husband and I, lived in Ardmore, outside Philadelphia."

Emma nods. She knows Ardmore as a well-heeled suburban enclave.

"About a year ago I found out my husband had another woman. It was not a casual affair. It was a two-year relationship, and it was still going on. Everyone knew: his colleagues, our friends, everyone except me. I was that pathetic old stereotype, the clueless wife. You can see why it's not a story I enjoy telling."

"I'm sorry."

"I gave him an ultimatum. He refused to end the affair, and I divorced him. There were no children to consider. I had my doctorate, though I hadn't worked in years. There was nothing to hold me to my old life, so I decided to start a new one. I found a job and moved here. That's it in a nutshell."

"Quite a nutshell," Emma murmurs.

"I'm asking you to take a lot on faith. If it would make your decision any easier, I'd be willing to pay in advance."

Emma blinks. "The whole year?"

Caroline shrugs. The shrug tells Emma that money's no object. "We sold the house. I'm not without means. In a while, if the job works out and I like the town, I may look into buying a house. In the meantime, your carriage house would be perfect. I'm looking," she adds, with a tremulous smile, "for a quiet, private place to lick my wounds and heal."

Before Emma can answer, Roger erupts into the room with Gordon Bass, who performs the introductions. "Dr. Koenig, Dr. Marks."

"Roger," he says, shaking her hand vigorously.

"I'm Caroline."

Roger seizes two iced teas from the tray, hands one to Bass, and drains the other in one long swig. He has wiped the sweat from his face and neck, but his T-shirt still clings to his lanky body and he has a mid-practice edge about him. "Zack's given me a break," he says. "Five minutes on the clock. Delighted to meet you, Caroline. Emma says you like the place."

"I do indeed."

"Any bad habits we should know about? Smoke in bed?"

"Never."

"Wild parties?"

"Hardly!"

"Sunbathe nude?"

"Definitely not."

"Nobody's perfect." He turns to Emma. "She's got my vote. May I be excused?"

"Go," she says, laughing. He leaves, and the energy level in the room drops by half. The others look at her and wait. Laying the clipboard face down on the coffee table, Emma levels her gaze at Caroline.

"The usual two-month deposit will do fine," she says. "When would you like to move in?"

3

MORGAN PEAK PARK is a small, well-equipped community park on the edge of the village, with three soccer fields, two baseball diamonds, a wading pool full of toddlers, a snack bar with shaded picnic tables, and a fenced-in blacktop basketball court where a dozen teenage boys are playing a pickup game of shirts versus skins. Soccer tryouts are called for four P.M. Zack, of course, has been dressed, cleated, and ready to rock and roll since before breakfast. They arrive an hour early and wander around, Zack sticking close to Emma's side, a sure sign of nervousness. Emma—who never sees her son but through a thin, permanent scrim of guilt—believes he does it not so much to anchor himself as to prevent her drifting away. "Jeez," he says, looking around, "can you believe this place?" Emma can't help thinking of their old home field, where parents and coaches waged an incessant battle against the broken glass and other debris that sprouted like weeds on the scraggly field. So perhaps there is something to be said for the suburbs after all.

When boys in soccer gear start to gather on the side of the larger soccer field, Emma and Zack join them. There are green wooden bleachers on the sideline, but someone has spilled a sweet drink on one of the risers and the yellowjackets are swarming. Zack's nerves begin to fray. "Where's the coach?" he asks every thirty seconds. "Gotta find the coach." At ten to four the coach appears, an athletic-looking six-footer accompanied by a tall blond boy. He stops every few yards, shaking hands with the men, hugging the women, high-fiving the boys. Emma thinks of a benevolent king dispensing alms. Zack's last coach was the sort who shmoozed with the dads while keeping his distance from the moms, whom he regarded as mere chauffeurs and uniform washers. This one seems altogether different: an all-American, back-slapping, arm-squeezing, shoulder-hugging sort of guy, a toucher of men and women. His name is Nick Sanders.

She doesn't approach immediately. She hangs back, waits and observes. If Zack makes the team, Sanders automatically becomes his third most significant other. She notices how easily he converses with the women, and how they laugh and flirt with him. She waits till he is alone, crouched on the ground beside his duffel bag, riffling through a sheaf of papers.

"Mr. Sanders?"

He stands and turns toward her. Removes his Yankees cap, revealing thick, brown hair, boyishly tousled. Add to that heavy-lidded green eyes, dimples to die for: The man looks like he stepped out of a Nautica ad.

"I'm not even going to try," he says. "If we'd met, I'd remember."

"Emma Koenig," she says. In family and school mode, Emma finds it easier to use her husband's surname. "This is Zack."

"Glad to meet you, Zack. Heard you're quite a soccer player." Shaking Zack's hand, Sanders takes a good, frank look at him. Then he turns to Emma, and the look he gives her is as openly appraising as the one he gave Zack. As if she, too, were trying out for his team. "Mrs. Koenig," he says. "It's a pleasure." Even before they

shake hands she knows he's going to hold on too long.
He does. His smile has that lethal mix of cockiness and
self-mockery. He's good, but not as good as he thinks he
is; the smile gives too much away. Emma can see him in
high school: athletic and popular, good looks unmarred
by adolescent spots or braces, never a moment's uncertainty about what to do with his hands in movies. A
menace to society.

"Quite a change from the city," he says. "I hope you
like it here."

"So do I," she says. Walking away, she feels his eyes
follow her.

THE TRYOUT starts with dribbling races. Four kids at a
time weave the ball through twelve cones, then turn and
sprint back with the ball held close. Losers are eliminated and winners play each other, till in the end it
comes down to two boys, Zack and the coach's boy.

They line up. An assistant coach blows the whistle
and Zack explodes forward, the ball clinging to his foot
like a dog at heel. As he rounds the last cone, Zack
glances back. The blond kid is two cones behind. Zack
puts on a burst of speed and finishes first by a solid
margin.

A loud silence greets his victory. Zack tries not to
take it personally. All these kids know each other, but
nobody knows him. Nobody talks to him, either, till the
blond kid comes over, looks him up and down, and
sticks out his hand. "Dylan Sanders," he says. "Who the
hell are you?"

"WHO'S THE little rocket?" says a caustic voice some
feet behind Emma. Emma turns and takes in the

speaker's small, harridan eyes, taut cheekbones, down-turned mouth, heavy mascara, and thin, teased hair. *Bitch Alert!* scream her sensors.

Another woman answers the first. "Never seen him before. Must be new in town."

"Hmm," says the Harridan.

Emma understands perfectly. Zack is trying out for an established team. A new kid taken on may mean another kid dropped, which is a shame but doesn't keep her from rooting for her boy. Emma doesn't much care about wins and losses, but she loves to watch Zack play. It seems to her that just as she is most herself while writing, Zack is most himself on the soccer field.

Coaches love him; parents don't always, jealousy a factor. Also, with travel teams there is always politics. Emma pays nearly as much attention to the sideline as she does to the field. The mothers of the Pirates sit back from the field in a cluster of lawn chairs. They pay no attention to the tryout, instead exchanging gossip and demonstrating in every possible way their mutual bond. The Harridan is one of them; so, too, the woman who answered her. Emma feels out of it, ghostlike on the sidelines, smiled at by all but greeted by none. Even her clothes set her apart. She wears a sleeveless denim dress, Birkenstock sandals, and a wide-brimmed straw hat against the summer sun. The locals—for so she thinks of them—favor sneakers, T-shirts and khaki shorts. She will never look like them, Emma thinks. She will never be like them. She will never find a friend.

THE COACH stands behind the net, clipboard in hand. Zack steps up to take his turn. There are five balls in a row, eighteen yards from the goal. The goalie crouches in the net, hands outstretched. Zack runs forward. Eyes fixed on the left corner, he kicks to the right. The goalie buys the fake and dives the wrong way. Zack's second shot soars over the goalie's head, slamming into the far side of the net with a soul-satisfying *thwack*. The goalie manages a mighty leap to catch the next, but the ball's momentum drives him back into the net; "Goal!" rules the coach. Now that he's got the goalie thinking high, Zack bangs in two quick grounders, one to the far post, one to the near. This time, trotting back, he slaps a line of upraised hands.

After the last kids take their shots, the coach calls a water break. Zack runs to the sideline, where his mother waits with the water bottle. He throws his head back and drinks.

"Doing great, Zack," she says.

Well, she would say that, wouldn't she? But he knows it's true. He's the only one who scored on all five shots; some kids didn't score on any. He swigs more water, then squirts some over his head and down the back of his neck. The coach is out on the field, pulling red and yellow pinnies out of his bag. Zack smells a scrimmage. The coach summons them back and sure enough divides them into two teams, assigning positions as he hands out the pinnies. Zack worms his way toward the front.

The coach lays a hand on his shoulder. "What did you play on your last team, Zack?"

"Striker."

"That's my position," Dylan cuts in. He's wearing a red pinny. Zack looks at him and sighs. In his experience, what the coach's son wants, the coach's son gets.

The coach swats Dylan upside the head. "You don'*

own it." He hands Zack a yellow pinny and sends him out to play center half.

Zack doesn't mind. Striker's the glamour position, but center half's a lot more fun to play. It's the key position, first line of the defense and launching pad of the offense. His dad always says that any player worth his salt can switch on a dime from offense to defense and back again. Zack wishes his dad were here. Mom means well, but she always thinks everything he does is perfect; the only advice she ever gives him is to tuck in his shirt. His dad is more realistic and he knows soccer, played it all through school and college. If only *he* could coach; but Zack knows that's impossible. His dad's always worked long hours; since he got promoted, Zack's lucky if he gets home in time to say good night.

At last the teams are in position, four subs per team moldering on the sidelines. Zack thanks God he isn't among them. If there is one thing in the world he hates, it's sitting out. Doesn't happen often; he usually plays the whole game. Sometimes, though, if the team's safely ahead, the coach'll take him out to give the subs extra time. Zack knows this is only fair, but it drives him nuts watching his team play without him.

This coach uses an unusual four-three-three setup: four defenders, three midfielders, two wings and a single striker. The opposing strikers gather for the coin toss, Dylan for the red team and a short, wiry black kid named Marcel for the yellow. Red wins. The strikers return to their positions and the red right wing comes over for the kickoff. Coach Sanders calls out to the goalies, who raise ~eir hands to show they're ready. He blows the whistle.

~ylan tips the ball to the right wing and explodes ~ down the center. Instead of passing forward, the

wing passes back to his center midfielder, who's come up
for the ball. A set piece: Zack recognizes the play; he's
used it himself. Ignoring the man with the ball, he runs
back to mark Dylan instead, plays him close, and when
the pass comes he's ready. A long, high ball: They both
jump for it, but Zack has the inside advantage. He gets a
head on the ball and knocks it down, five yards away.
Sloppy, but Zack gets there first, gathers up the ball, and
keeps it between his feet as he speeds toward the goal.

The red team's stopper lumbers up to challenge him,
big kid, but flat-footed. Zack fakes a pass to the right, at
the last moment lifting his foot over the ball. The stopper buys the fake and leaps to intercept a pass that never
comes. By the time he recovers, Zack and the ball are
long gone.

Zack's won himself fifteen yards of open field. He
considers taking the ball up himself, showing this coach
what he can do. But it's not the right play. The defenders
are converging on the goal, blocking his shot. Pass,
then—but first improve the odds. He puts on a burst of
speed, straight toward the goal. As soon as the red
defender leaves Marcel to come out, Zack chips the ball
over his head. Marcel settles the ball, shoots, and scores.

Cheers from the yellow team. Marcel runs over and
slaps Zack's hand. "Beautiful play, man!" He has the
blackest skin and the warmest eyes Zack has ever seen.

"Nice shot," Zack returns.

"Keep passing like that, man, I'll give you all the
goals you want."

EMMA GLOWS on the sidelines. If it is possible to make
a team on the strength of a single play, Zack has just
made it.

"All I can say, my girl," says a voice close beside her, "is thank God that child can play."

Emma turns. The speaker is a small, sparkling woman, ebony-skinned. She wears a colorful wrap-around skirt and an orange halter top. There are rings on her fingers, silver bangles on her wrist, large hoops of braided gold in her ears. Emma noticed her earlier, sitting with the team mothers, looking like a tropical bird in a nest of sparrows.

"Yolanda Dumont," she says, holding out her hand.

"Emma Koenig. Why thank God? If he couldn't play, he wouldn't make the team, and that would be that."

The other woman laughs. "You obviously don't know Nick."

"No, just met him today."

"My husband used to coach intramural with him. Nick's got his own special way of picking teams. Used to drive Gerard crazy." Yolanda links her arm in Emma's and moves her down the sideline, away from the team enclave. Her voice has a melodious lilt, bubbling with underground laughter. "Every season Gerard would give him a list of players to try for in the draft. Very serious man, my husband. He'd spend hours rating the boys by ability, balancing offense against defense. And every season Nick would go in, stick the list in his pocket, and make all his own picks."

"By what criteria? How did he choose them?"

Yolanda looks down her nose at Emma. "No need to define the word, darlin'. Nick's *criteria* were simple: He picked the kids with the hottest mamas. Didn't matter to him how the boy played or what he was rated, 'cause Nick wasn't picking a team, he was picking a sideline."

All Emma can think is, Thank God Roger isn't here.

What kind of jerk is this coach? If Yolanda's story is true, that is. But why would she make up a story like that?

"What does his wife think of his selection method?" she probes.

"Not much. She divorced him."

Emma stares. "Tell me you're making this up."

Yolanda raises her right hand, and silver bracelets flash in the sun. "If I lie, I die."

"Jesus. If that's how he picks his teams, I can't imagine he wins many games."

"Then you'd be wrong, darlin'. Just because he is a bad man for women don't make him a bad coach. See, he picked those boys for their mothers, but once he picked them he made them into players. Nick's teams win. Last season, this team won the division and the State Cup."

Emma glances over at Sanders, who's demonstrating a move to one of the players. He moves as good as he looks. "I'll bet the moms are grateful," she murmurs. It slips out, the kind of casual cynicism one might whisper to a friend.

"*Very* grateful. Guess how he picks his MVPs?"

"Get out!" cries Emma, but this time Yolanda is teasing; she sees it in her dancing eyes. It dawns on her that perhaps friendship is not impossible even in the outback. She nods at the team mothers. "So you're telling me that this is the cream of Morgan Peak womanhood?"

Yolanda follows her eyes and laughs a full-throated laugh. "Ah, well, when it comes to the travel team, the coach plays it straighter. Wouldn't be fair to cheat a boy who's earned the right to play, would it? Still, Nick being Nick, the minute I saw you I started praying your kid was good. 'Cause otherwise, you know, he drops a player, it could get ugly."

The coach has moved the boys around. Zack's the striker now, and Marcel's on right wing. They work together on an overlap, moving the ball down to the eighteen. Then Marcel centers to Zack, a high, crossing shot, and Zack leaps up and nails it perfectly, straight into the net.

"Goal!" yells the coach. "Beautiful header, son!"

Emma *kvells*, a Yiddish word with no English equivalent, denoting that specific mix of pleasure and pride parents take in their children's accomplishments. Her mother's word. Rosa Roth—Rosie, as everyone called her—was a devout atheist and die-hard socialist who had no time for religion but nevertheless reveled in Yiddishkeit. Her speech, famously earthy, had been peppered with Yiddishisms, which she learned from her mother and passed down to her daughters. In Maggie's case, these expressions serve to enrich an already well-developed scatological vocabulary. In Emma's, they surface unexpectedly in her books, emerging from the lips of the most unlikely characters. And if Emma leaves them in, as she sometimes does because they amuse her, eventually they come back to haunt her in the form of polite little stick-it notes in the margins of her manuscript. "Would Lady Brentwell really call the rector a putz?" or, if the copyeditor was from Iowa or wherever they were importing them from these days, "What's a putz?"

Beside her, Yolanda sighs with pure soccer pleasure. "It's like they've played together all their life."

"Just what I was thinking. That's your son on right wing?"

"How'd you guess? Stepson, actually. You know," Yolanda says, "I think you'd better come meet the girls."

"YOUR SON'S good," the Harridan says grudgingly. Her name is Cheryl. "Where did he play?"

"In the city. We've only just moved out here."

Murmurs of comprehension and welcome. The team mothers gather around, peppering her with questions. "Do you have family here?" "Any other children?" "What school will your son attend?" "Which house did you buy? Crag Road? *Not* the old Hysop place, the house at the end?"

"That's the one," Emma says.

Glances are exchanged; no one speaks. Cheryl laughs, not pleasantly.

Emma looks from face to face. "Something wrong?"

"Better you than me," says Cheryl.

"Meaning what?"

"Meaning nothing at all," says Yolanda. "Girl just loves to run her mouth, don't you, Cheryl?"

The Harridan raises eyebrows plucked to a pencil-thin line. "Let's just say it wouldn't be my first choice in houses."

"Different strokes for different folks. It happens to be a gorgeous house."

"Then you know it, too," Emma says. "You all know it." Again no answer. She picks the most sympathetic face in the crowd, a woman with apple cheeks and a black pageboy, and speaks directly to her. "What's so special about my house?"

"It's very old," the woman replies.

"So are half the houses in the village."

Silence. Emma's skin prickles. Drop it, she tells her-

self, but she can't, it's not in her nature, any more than
it's in Zack's to refrain from driving on goal. Her curiosity, essential to her craft, is as well-honed as the taste
buds of a chef or the nose of a perfumer. Curiosity and
fear: Emma's warp and woof. If her life could be
graphed, those would be its axes. She means to press the
point and would have, but now the children come
spilling off the field, hot, sweaty, and boisterous. Zack
and Marcel walk together, jabbering like old friends.
Yolanda draws Emma aside.

"Don't let Cheryl worry you," she says. "Girl got a
sting on her put a scorpion to shame."

Emma shrugs. She doesn't care about Cheryl. As
bitches go, Cheryl is small potatoes. What she wonders
about is why they all seemed to know her house. She
asks Yolanda. Yolanda shrugs her little shoulders, shakes
her head, and professes total ignorance and mystifica-
tion.

She is a terrible liar.

"WANT TO thank you all for coming," Sanders says.
"Got a talented bunch of kids here. I wish I could take
'em all, but it comes down to a numbers thing. I'm limited to fifteen. Results will be posted by six P.M. Monday
on the soccer bulletin board in the clubhouse. After that,
anyone wants to call, ask why their son didn't make it,
what they maybe need to work on, feel free. The main
thing is, don't let 'em get discouraged. There's tryouts
every year."

As the parents walk in small groups off the field,
Sanders falls into step beside Emma. He nods over at
Zack, drinking on the sidelines. "So, what do you want
for him?"

Despite herself, Emma laughs. But then, the quickest way to a mother's heart is through praise of her child, and Sanders is just the sort of man to know that.

"Not for sale just yet," she says. "We're fattening him up. Where's the clubhouse?"

"Other side of the snack bar. List'll be up Monday, like I said. But I wouldn't lose any sleep over it."

She looks up, reads his eyes, and smiles from the heart. Sanders falters in mid-step.

"I DIDN'T SAY I don't believe you. I just said it all sounded a bit random."

Roger's voice is testy, but Emma's not offended. Roger wrestles with randomness every day at work; when it crops up in his private life, he tends to take it personally.

"That's because you weren't there," she says patiently. "You didn't hear the reaction when I said what house we'd bought. They all knew it. Why would they know it?"

"Small town," he says, rubbing her back with long, downward strokes. It is the hour between the late news and sleep.

"And that woman," says Emma. " 'Better you than me'; what did that mean? It must have meant *something*."

"You're thinking of fiction. In real life, people talk because they love the sound of their own voices."

"If this were fiction I'd do a better job writing it. Such an obvious setup: Who'd be surprised when the house turns out to be haunted?" Emma's joking, of course. How many times has she gotten that question in Q and A's and interviews? "Do you believe in ghosts?"

someone invariably asks, and she replies, "Absolutely not. If I did, I'd never have the nerve to write about them."

Roger yawns. "If I were you, I'd worry more about mice. Never mind the gossips. Tell me about Zack."

"He did great."

"Tell me everything, play-by-play. What position did they put him in?"

"Center half at first, then striker."

"So? Did he knock their socks off?"

"The coach's socks, anyway. He offered to buy him."

Roger snorts. "Yeah? How much?"

"We left it open."

"Did he say anything else?"

Emma turns her head to watch his face as she answers. "He said, 'The list goes up Monday, but I wouldn't lose any sleep over it.' "

Roger beams. "Really?"

"Did you doubt it?"

"I knew he'd make it. Though some of these coaches, you never know. What'd you think of this guy?"

Emma lets her chin sink back onto the pillow. A fork has opened up before her: to tell or not to tell? If she tells Roger and he decides the coach is a flake, he might not let Zack play for Sanders. But if they move Zack to another club in a different town, then every game becomes an away game; every practice, too. Who will drive him? Not Roger, that's for sure. Emma loathes driving and Roger knows that, but he makes her do it anyway. Won't give in to her fear, won't allow her to; for which she is supposed to be grateful, but isn't.

He's waiting, looking at her curiously. Emma doesn't for one moment believe that she has to tell her husband everything. Every marriage has its no-man's-land, and theirs is larger than most. But she doesn't, as a rule, lie to him.

"Bit of a flirt," she says at last. "But the soccer moms say he's an excellent coach. Last year his team won the State Cup."

"A flirt," says Roger. "And we learned this how?"

"Acute observation." Emma turns and presses her body against his: one sure way of subverting the conversation. Roger is appreciative but not totally distracted.

"You're saying the guy came on to you the first time you met?"

"Nah, he just looked."

"Looked how?"

"Like he was hiring for Hooters and I was applying. He asked how I like the village and I was tempted to say"—Emma shifts to a breathy little-girl voice—" 'It's beautiful, but I get so lonely with my husband away at work all day,' just to see his reaction."

Roger groans. "Tell me you didn't."

"I didn't," she says sadly. A good joke sacrificed to prudence.

"This guy sounds like a jerk. Maybe we should look around."

Emma moves in closer. "So what if he's a jerk, as long as he's a competent jerk? I watched him. When he's not flashing his boyish grin he's totally focused on the game. My guess, given a choice between me in the sack and Zack on his team, he'd pick Zack any day."

"More fool him," says Roger, but now his arms are around her and he's lost interest in Nick Sanders.

Later, Emma slides her leg out from under his, slips on a gown, and curls up in the curve of his sleeping body, her body warm, her face pleasantly cool. The windows in this room are old and far from hermetically sealed. It is drizzling outside. The air smells deliciously of rain and brine.

Afterward, when she thinks about it, she will never be able to tell for sure where her thoughts left off and her dream began. One moment she is lying in bed listening to the rain, the next she's asleep, dreaming that she's in bed listening to the rain.

The wind picks up. Rain slams against the windows, and lines of moisture appear below the sills. Upstairs, something bangs, and bangs again: a loud report, like shutters hitting against the house. Emma first tries hoping it will stop; when that fails, she rises reluctantly from her warm bed and goes barefoot out into the hall. The banging is louder from the hall, as erratic as the wind. She climbs the winding stairs to the library, holding tight to the banister. As her head rises above floor level, she sees at once what has caused the noise: not a shutter, but a window that has blown open and is banging back and forth. Hurrying over, she pushes it shut and latches it. It is the northernmost window, overlooking the bay, and as she wipes the rain from her face, Emma looks out. The moon shines bright, which is odd because it's raining hard. A ray of moonlight stretches across the mouth of the bay like a pale finger.

Suddenly there's a loud report, like a shot. Emma whirls around. The window above her desk has blown open, and the wind rushes in, peeling off page after page of manuscript, flinging them about on invisible currents. She staggers across the room, but even as she latches one window another bursts inward, then another. Chaos engulfs the room. Wildly she runs from window to window, but however fast she runs she can't keep up. The room is full of rain and wind and paper, a white blizzard swirling around her. Outside, the wind rages and the waters rise to meet the rain. From far away she hears her name called.

"Emma! Emma!"

It is Roger's voice. She opens her eyes. His face blots out the world. She is amazed to see him here. How did he reach her, how did he get upstairs without her noticing? A moment later she perceives that she is in bed, Roger's arms around her. "You were dreaming," he tells her; but Emma is unsure. It didn't feel like a dream; it felt real.

"Em," says Roger, "are you with me?"

"Oh God," she mutters, "what have we done?"

4

FRIDAY, ROGER takes Zack to work with him; afterward they will go to a Mets game. Emma drives them to the station, then faces a whole long day to herself. She takes a cup of coffee onto the verandah just off the living room, warming herself like a lizard in the hazy morning heat. Below her the bay, crisscrossed by sailboats, dotted with fishing dories. It has not yet sunk in that she lives in this place. The raucous cry of the gulls, the slap of water on the shore, the drone of bees, now and then a barking dog or the distant, desultory sputter of a lawn mower, all set against a backdrop of deep silence: These are sounds she associates with vacations and travel. Somewhere in the back of her mind she is waiting to go home.

She has finished the *Times* crossword puzzle and drained her coffee to the dregs. It is time to work. She's not afraid anymore, she tells herself. There's nothing to be nervous about. She's not a child, to confuse dreams with reality. And it doesn't take a genius to trace that dream to its roots. The stress of moving, the soccer moms' knowing glances, Yolanda's reticence, all tinder to the flame of her own natural anxiety at leaving everyone and every place she'd ever known for a village with customs as strange to her as the Samoans' were to Margaret Mead. Naturally she's anxious; hence the dream. Elementary. Nevertheless, last night's dream of chaotic eruption in the tower inspired an order of fear very different from the sort she lives with every day, and it hasn't dissipated yet. What happened had had the texture of reality, the supercharged air of something crafted to frighten, a scene from a Gothic tale, perhaps, or a Stephen King book, or that old movie, *Gaslight*, in which Ingrid Bergman's husband tries to convince her she's gone mad. And her body had responded as to external menace, heart pounding, muscles tensed. Hours later, long after Roger had fallen back asleep, she lay wide awake, pressed against his solid, sleeping self. Stinking of fear, dying for a shower, yet she dared not stir. Her throat was parched, but her fear was greater than her thirst. Even now the thought of climbing those winding stairs to emerge headfirst into the library arouses an irresistible urge for one final cup of coffee.

Entering the kitchen, Emma hears a faint scuffing sound and suddenly recalls Roger's joke about mice. Not a great joke, she'd thought then—or was it a joke? She freezes in the doorway, scanning the floor with rapid eye movements. Ghosts in the attic, mice in the pantry—give me a fucking break! Suddenly there is a sharp rap on the back door. Emma starts, then clutches herself in relief at the sight of Caroline Marks's face behind the frosted glass.

Caroline has already moved into the carriage house; she took up residence within twenty-four hours of signing the lease. No moving van or U-Haul marked her coming, just three large suitcases she carried herself and, later that day, an Ikea truck loaded with furniture. Emma, spying from her tower window, thought it very strange. Did Caroline sell all her possessions when she sold her house? Fresh start indeed.

That was over a week ago, and since then Emma has been tempted more than once to drop in on her new tenant/neighbor. She has refrained, less for fear of imposing than of being imposed on in return. Writers who work at home are subject to all kinds of interruptions, not so much from friends and family, who know better than to call during working hours (and certainly not from Zack, schooled since infancy—"When can you interrupt Mommy's work?" she'd ask, and he would lisp, "In case of fire or loss of limb"); but there are always people who think of writing as Emma's hobby, a pastime like knitting or whittling, to be put aside whenever something better presents. She hopes her new tenant isn't one of those.

She opens the door. "Hi, Caroline."

"I'm sorry to bother you. I know you're working."

"Ought to be, but I'm not. Come on in."

Caroline enters and looks around. "Great kitchen. Look, I won't keep you. I'm afraid I just did the stupidest thing: I locked my keys in my car."

"Sounds like me; I'm always doing that. Now I keep a spare under the bumper. Do you have one?"

Caroline rolls her eyes. "Sure. Only the spare key is locked in the house, and the house key's locked in the car. Brilliant, huh? I'm hoping you have a key to the carriage house."

"Of course." Emma is in full sympathy. If she had a dollar for every key she's lost she could retire tomorrow. Keys seem to hide from her, or perhaps she is their gateway to an alternate universe. Last time she saw the spare keys they were in the dining room sideboard—no guarantee they remain there, but they do, half a dozen gold and silver keys nestled on their tags like chicks in a nest. One after another she lifts them out, each labeled in Roger's precise hand: "Front Door," "Kitchen Door," "Car," until she comes to the one marked "Carriage House." She grabs it and turns. Caroline has followed her in from the kitchen.

"Got it," says Emma.

"Great. I'll bring it right back."

Emma accompanies her to the front door. "Where's your car?" she asks.

"In the village. I was shopping when I locked myself out of the car."

"How'd you get back?"

"Hoofed it."

Emma eyes her in amazement. Two-inch heels, no less. "All that way?"

Caroline grimaces. "You try getting a cab in this burg."

Emma's car is sitting in the driveway. Her duty is clear. She offers with tolerable grace to drive Caroline back to her car.

"Out of the question," says Caroline, but she lets herself be persuaded. Emma runs upstairs for her purse while Caroline collects her spare set of car keys. Ten minutes later they are in the Buick and Emma is taking deep, anxiety-controlling breaths. Back when she actually enjoyed driving she wouldn't have been caught dead in a car like this. Now she's like an ex-smoker: no discrimination between brands.

"Gordon Bass told me you're a writer," Caroline says. "It took me a while to make the connection, but I actually read one of your novels not long ago. *Call Waiting*."

"Really?" Emma is surprised; she belongs to that great unwashed mass of writers whose books have not yet made the best-seller list, for whom such close encounters with a reader unrelated by blood or acquaintance are few and far between. Besides, Caroline doesn't seem the type to read Emma's books any more than Emma is. "How'd you like it?" she asks.

"Hated it: kept me up reading all night."

Emma flashes a grateful smile before turning back to the road. Thirty yards ahead, a boy is bicycling, hunched over the handlebars, his back to her. She slows, tightening her grip on the wheel. You could never tell what kids would do.

"To tell you the truth," Caroline says, "I picked it up looking for a few hours of mindless entertainment; but it was far from mindless. Some deceptively good writing, and wonderful characterizations."

Emma glows, a slut for praise of her work, and this is praise of the very sort she invents for herself on nights when she can't sleep: imaginary front-page *New York Times* reviews, in which the word "deceptive" figures prominently. Clearly Caroline is a person of unusual discernment. As they approach the boy on the bike, Emma slows to a crawl, swings out wide to pass him. Only when he appears in her rearview mirror does she let out her breath and loosen her grip on the wheel.

She feels Caroline's eyes on her and beats down an impulse to confide. Presently, as if changing the subject, Caroline says, "You must have enormous self-discipline."

"Habits, routines. Tricks to get myself jump-started in the morning. After that there's no problem."

"Really? What kind of routines, if you don't mind my asking?"

A frequent question during the Q and A's that followed readings, though a distant second to the perennial favorite, Where do you get your ideas? "Coffee, cross-word, and computer games, in that order."

"Oh, those computer games are addictive. I play chess on mine, although in times of stress I revert to Pacman, the intellectual equivalent of thumb-sucking."

"Card games," Emma confesses. "Hearts and gin."

They share a guilty laugh. "Still," Caroline says, "writing takes a great deal of discipline. I should know: I tried to write a book once. Hate to tell you how that ended."

"How?"

"Daytime TV. Escape to the soaps. I couldn't believe how difficult it was to create something out of nothing."

"Was it a novel?"

"No, that I wouldn't have dared. A self-help book in my own field. I was going to call it 'Righting the Scales: A Manual for Women Who've Been Wronged.' "

"Good title." Emma wonders if Caroline's book idea

came about before or after she caught her husband cheating. Not, unfortunately, the kind of question one could ask.

"I felt I had something worth saying. But the process was harder than I ever expected. I found I couldn't deal with working in a vacuum, the lack of any external structure and direction."

Emma nods, thinking of her own panic every time she starts a new book peopled with characters who don't even exist yet. Like trying to conduct an orchestra full of empty chairs: It takes blind faith and plenty of it.

They reach the center of the village. Caroline's car, a silver-gray Acura, stands in the rear of the Waldbaums parking lot. Emma pulls up beside it and the women look at each other. This parting has come suddenly and with a sense of interruption. Emma feels the kind of intense curiosity about Caroline that is, for her, a precursor and predictor of friendship. Though she is slender, there is a pleasing solidity to the woman; she reminds Emma of one of those carved Russian dolls with rounded bottoms that spring back up when pushed.

Caroline thanks her. She reaches for the door handle, then turns back. "There's a Starbucks just up the block. Least I can do is buy you a cup of coffee."

"You don't have to work?"

"I start at noon."

Emma feels a warning twinge from the internal foreman who stands perpetual watch over her work time, tapping his foot and scowling, pocket watch in hand. But Zack will be away all day, she argues with him. No need to cook; she can work straight through dinner.

"Love one," she says.

* * *

FOUR CAST-IRON tables, two on each side, flank the
door to the glass-fronted café. Only one is occupied, and
that by a small boy in a baseball uniform holding a large
sort of terrier on a leash, waiting, presumably, for a parent inside. The dog stands and wags its upright stump of
a tail at their approach. Emma holds out her hand and
the dog sniffs it; but Caroline shies away. Inside they
join a line of people waiting to order. The ambiance is
of stainless steel, glass, and snow-white crockery; the
staff are young, attractive, polite but noticeably superior
in attitude. Altar boys of coffee, Emma thinks, inhaling
the warm, earthy incense. The list of offerings is long
and full of flavor combinations that sound much better
than they taste. As they approach the counter, she
notices Caroline staring lustfully at a display of pastries
and croissants. "May I help you?" asks their server, a
tall, thin young man with saintly cheekbones and a long-
suffering look. When Emma orders a cup of the straight
stuff, Starbucks's house brew, he sighs but passes the
order along. Caroline chooses an almond-filled croissant
and a raspberry latte, to which she adds two packets of
sugar. Emma has noticed this in people whose lives contain much bitterness, that they crave sweets.

They take a chair beside the window, overlooking the
street. The little boy has been joined by his mother, who
reads *The New York Times* and pretends not to notice as
the child slips bits of Danish under the table to the dog.
Emma thinks of Zack, who is dying for a dog. For years
he's yearned for one, but there was not enough room in
the apartment. Now that space is not a problem, his
campaign has intensified. Roger, who still keeps pictures of his childhood pets, is sympathetic to the cause
but wary of pushing Emma any farther than he's pushed

her already. She, of course, is the holdout, not because she dislikes dogs but because she hates interruptions. Yet now, watching the little boy outside, Emma feels churlish for resisting. Why not get a puppy? Maggie would say she's gone native, but when *didn't* Maggie have something to say? It's not as if Zack had a brother or sister to play with. A dog would be a friend for him and company for her, once Zack goes back to school. She wouldn't be alone in the house. Not that she minds that, not at all.

But Caroline has been speaking and is waiting for an answer.

Emma turns to her. "Sorry?"

"I was asking if your husband is also a writer."

"No. Well, he writes articles, but that's sort of a by-product. Roger's a physicist."

"Does he teach?"

"He's with Columbia, but he has no teaching duties. Right now he's heading a project on chaos theory as it applies to weather patterns. Don't ask me to explain. Roger's the brains of the family."

Caroline's eyebrows shoot up. "Oh, really! Which makes you what?"

"The protoplasm?"

"Somehow I don't buy that."

"I'm not playing dumb. It's just that I grew up with a brilliant younger sister and married a scientific wunderkind, so I know where I fit into the general scheme of things."

"But your writing—"

"Draws on other faculties," Emma says firmly. Though flattering, the other woman's focused attention is also disconcerting. But that, she supposes, is what happens when you put a writer and a psychologist together: Each tries to out-listen the other. Now it's Emma's turn to pry. "What about you? This place where you work, Fresh Start, what's that about?"

"Just what it sounds like. It's about women doing what they have to do to put the past behind them."

"Through counseling?"

"That's part of it, certainly; my part. I do one-on-one counseling, and I lead the groups. But there's more to the program. We also teach self-defense. Every woman in the program, staff as well as clients, takes some sort of martial arts course. It's part of the healing process, part of taking back one's life. It's what drew me to the organization. We're not real big on victim culture at Fresh Start. We're not passive, and we don't turn the other cheek."

"More Old Testament than New? An eye for an eye?"

"Metaphorically speaking, of course. But yes, absolutely." Caroline sips her latte. "I never bought the old adage that living well is the best revenge. I think it's only half the solution. Living well and sticking it to the other guy: Now *that's* more like it, don't you think?" She dabs her mouth with a napkin, taking care not to smudge her lipstick.

Emma smiles to herself at the contrast between the message and the messenger. What a strange amalgam, a woman with the soul of Conan the Barbarian and the facade of Margaret Thatcher. So much for her sister's theory about the correlation between politics and shoes. Wishing Maggie could hear this gives her an idea.

"We're having some people over next Saturday night. A few friends, colleagues of Roger's, my sister, Maggie. Sort of a housewarming."

"Aren't you brave, so soon after moving in."

"Roger's idea. It's a male thing, like dogs pissing to mark their boundaries. Probably a good idea, though. Anyway, I'd be very pleased if you could come." She pauses, but Caroline does not rush in. Emma supposes she's searching for a tactful way out, and provides one. "Of course, it's very last minute. I'll understand if you have other plans."

"Not at all." Caroline's smile is clearly self-mocking. "My social calendar is not exactly overbooked at the moment. I'd love to stop by."

Stopping by, Emma understands, is not the same as coming; it reserves the option of a quick exit if one is bored or manifestly out of place. The sort of answer she herself might give under similar circumstances. Emma feels a tug of warmth toward Caroline, the baseless gratitude of a stranger in a strange land who suddenly hears her own language spoken. They sip their drinks in amicable silence. Caroline's lipstick leaves a red smudge on her glass. For some reason—perhaps the op-artish decor of the café—Emma sees Caroline as a character in an old movie, one of those pert 1940 career-gal romances starring Rosalind Russell or Kate Hepburn. She is the figure glimpsed in the background, an elegant female in a broad-brimmed hat, examining her face in a gold compact.

An odd image, and Emma is still wondering where it came from when suddenly a large figure looms over the table and she looks up to see Gordon Bass in the distressed flesh. Face red, tie loosened, collar button undone, clearly suffering from the heat, he holds a beaded glass of something pale and frothy. "Hello, hello!" he booms. "Ladies, what a pleasant surprise. May I . . . ?"

"Please," says Emma.

Bass plops down beside her, dwarfing their little table. He settles his iced concoction on the table and dabs his shiny face with a napkin. "Brutal out there. I must tell you, when I see you two together I feel like a real matchmaker."

"Oh, but you are." Caroline smiles. "A match made in heaven."

To Emma, though, it is Bass's appearance that seems providential: the very man she needed without realizing it. "This is good luck," she says. "There's something I wanted to ask you."

"Yes?"

"What exactly is the story with my house?"

Bass runs his tongue over his lips. "I beg your pardon?"

"It's a simple question. Why do strong men pale and women shudder when I mention which house we bought? What's the mystery, Gordon; what gives?"

Gordon chokes on his latte. They pat his back. "Emma," he says when he can speak again, "have you ever lived in a small village before? No? Then allow me to present to you Gordon Bass's lesson numero uno on village life. In a village like Morgan Peak, gossip's the local cottage industry. It's a web that binds people together, like a network of underground telephone wires. If I might offer a word of advice? Don't subscribe. Emma Roth has better uses for her time than worrying over old tattle."

This advice, though well-intentioned, has the usual effect of determining its recipient on the opposite course; cautioning Emma not to listen to gossip is about as effective as warning off a bull with a red flag. She is and has always been a sucker for the stuff. Confided or overheard, old or new—it doesn't matter; the stories people tell about themselves and each other are the chaff from which her flax is spun.

"What is it," she asks, "this tattle I'm supposed to ignore?"

Bass looks at Caroline, but Caroline, without stirring, has withdrawn from the discussion. She sits as still as it is possible to sit and still be present. Only her eyes move, from one face to the other.

"Virginia Hysop," he says, "was a well-respected English teacher for forty-five years. As a matter of fact, she was my twelfth-grade English teacher. Highly intelligent woman, strict but not unfair. Had such a thing about run-ons and sentence fragments that to this day I flinch when I notice one in my own writing. Still expect that ruler to come smashing down. On the page," he adds, interpreting Emma's look. "Not the hand. She was not at all an unkind person; she just had this grand passion for the language. Couldn't bear seeing it abused or mangled, any more than a person who loves animals could stand by and see one tortured. Mrs. Hysop taught well past retirement age, close to seventy, I believe, when they forced her out, and even then she didn't go peaceably. After that she became reclusive. Stopped seeing people, rarely left the house, never had anyone in. Nobody knew what she did with herself, all alone in that big house. So people did what they usually do when they don't understand something: They made up stories."

"What kind of stories?" asks Emma, whose credo, admittedly biased, is that there's more truth to be found in one good story than a whole stack of nonfiction.

"Nonsense," he says shortly. "Trouble is, over time

the rumors become self-perpetuating, and the house became one of those that Girl Scouts avoid when they're selling cookies, and boys challenge each other to touch. They used to go up and ring her bell and run away. Finally she had it disconnected. And then she was really isolated."

"How sad."

"It was. The woman educated half the people in this town. But when she did go out, the children either ran from her or plagued her."

Something's missing in this story; Emma can feel it. "But why?" she asks. "What did they think she'd done?"

"Who knows?" He looks at his watch, drains the last drops from his glass, and stands. Fleeing the interrogation, thinks Emma. Her own damn fault for pushing too hard. Should have flirted a little, drawn him out. Never mind; she'll find out eventually.

"Ladies," says Bass.

5

"I can't tell you," Gloria Lucas says, "how deeply relieved I am. Because frankly, my dear, my first reaction when you told me the news was to phone in the obit."

Emma laughs. "I knew it. I saw it in your eyes."

"Now at least I see. You were seduced. It could happen to anyone, this house is so fucking romantic. Oops." She claps hand over mouth as Zack materializes at her side, holding a laden tray.

Arthur Matthews raises his bearded chin from his chest. "Really, Gloria. Young Zack isn't accustomed to such language, are you, lad?"

"Hell, no," Zack replies. "Thingies, anyone?"

"Zack," says his mother, "watch your language. They're not thingies; they're hors d'oeuvres." She reminds herself, though, to talk to him later. Emma is no more phobic about words than surgeons are about blood; Zack's "Hell, no" was a good joke under the circs, but he'd better understand there's a time and place for everything. She doesn't want any calls home from school.

Friday evening, seven P.M.: cocktails in the living room and a buffet dinner later in the dining room. Gloria, Emma's agent, has stopped by the housewarming en route to her house in the Hamptons. She's a bright-eyed wiry woman of a certain age, all fangs and claws toward recalcitrant editors but fiercely maternal with her clients. Roger calls her the lioness. She calls herself an old hag but acts the imperious beauty she once was and still, in her heart, believes herself to be. Doesn't win every fight but defers to no one. Roger likes her, and Emma feels well-protected in her den.

Beside her on the leather couch, deeply absorbed in his malt whiskey, sits Emma's long-time editor, Arthur Matthews. Arthur arrived without his wife this evening, and from his general air of bereftness Emma infers that she's left him again. The wonder is not that Alison leaves but that she keeps coming back; for Arthur, despite what he calls his underlying faithfulness, is a notorious seducer of female authors and colleagues. He's an unlikely-looking Lothario, round and bearish, with a thick beard and a graying ponytail; more Friar Tuck than Don Juan. British by birth,

Arthur has lived in New York for fifteen years without sacrificing a jot of his Oxbridge accent. In recent years he's published the memoirs of a self-avowed sex addict and a brace of self-help books for the hopelessly libidinous, but according to Gloria they haven't done a thing for him. Gloria herself had a brief fling with him a million years ago, a Frankfurt affair, one of those champagne-fueled book-fair trysts; didn't outlast the plane ride home and had remarkably little effect on their business relationship. She still sends him clients, though not without briefing them first, because despite his idiosyncrasies Arthur is a fine and conscientious editor, who, for his part, regards his seductions as logical, even altruistic extensions of his professional duty, sort of an alternate route to getting inside the writer's head. Stories abound, possibly apocryphal, of Arthur in the throes of lovemaking being struck by bursts of inspiration so orgasmic that the sexual tryst devolves into a frenzied editorial conference.

There's nothing coercive about his advances, no hint of the casting couch; if anything, Arthur's desires add a dollop of power to the author's side of the scale. He bears no grudges when they fail, as they have with Emma, whom he now regards with an erotic wistfulness that she finds rather touching. Roger, it must be said, finds him considerably less charming.

They spear bits of shrimp toast and mini-quiches from Zack's tray. As the boy moves on to another group, Arthur rouses himself with an effort. "I'm not sure romantic is the word I'd use."

"The eternal editor," Emma teases. "What word would you use?"

"Atmospheric, perhaps? Come to think of it,

wouldn't this house make the perfect setting for one of your books?"

"Don't encourage her." Roger joins them, standing over the back of Emma's chair, resting his hands on her shoulders. "She's already half-convinced the house is haunted."

"Liar!" cries Emma. "You know I don't believe in ghosts, except as plot devices."

"Make a great story, though," Arthur says wistfully. " 'Haunted-House Writer Buys Haunted House.' "

"Oh, please. Roger made that up. All I ever said was that there's a mystery about the previous owner."

"Publicity would kill for a hook like that."

"No, Arthur."

The doorbell rings. Emma starts to rise, but Roger presses her back. "Got it," he says.

She listens for voices in the hall, but the sound of the heavy front door opening and closing is followed by a perplexing silence. Minutes, not seconds, elapse before Roger returns with the new arrival: India Robbins, his assistant. They enter talking and drift to a halt in the center of the living room, India's luminous eyes fixed on Roger's face, her hand on his sleeve. And how strange it seems to Emma, how ominous in some unexamined manner, that India does not glance around, neither at the room nor its occupants. She wears high-heeled sandals and a white, off-the-shoulder dress cut low enough to display the swell of her dark breasts. India is twenty-six, a beautiful mutt, the unlikely product of an Argentine mother and a Swedish father. She has witch-hazel eyes, flowing black hair, skin the color of honey, and, according to Roger, a mind like the proverbial steel trap.

"My oh my," breathes Arthur, his desolation clearing

like a summer storm. It is actually possible to see his muscles tense, his movements slow to the pace of a stalking cat. "Emma, darling. Who is that vision?"

"Roger's assistant."

A quick sideways glance. "You let him work with that?"

"Shut up, Arthur."

"Hmm. Married?"

"No, but last I looked *you* were."

"Not for long." He lumbers to his feet. "Emma, I'm in love. I am hopelessly smitten."

Emma almost believes him. Arthur's sincerity is no less real for being serial and short-lived; for him, brevity is the soul of passion. From Gloria's corner, however, there comes a loud snort. "Idiot. You've never even met the woman."

"A minor detail, soon to be remedied. Introduce me, Emma."

Emma leads him over. Is it her imagination, or does India blush at her approach? Certainly she drops Roger's sleeve. "Emma," she cries, "congratulations! The house is wonderful! And so close to the water!"

A wave of distrust sweeps over Emma; but then she is a stickler for punctuation and would tend to suspect anyone who speaks in exclamation points. "India, this is Arthur Matthews, my editor. Arthur, India Robbins."

Arthur envelops her hand. "Delighted to meet you, India. I understand you work with Roger."

"Well, for him. He's my boss." She looks at Roger, and this time her blush is unmistakable.

"Where's Alison tonight?" Roger asks pointedly. "We were hoping to see her."

"Couldn't make it," Arthur mutters. "Sends regrets."

"Pity. Brilliant woman, his wife. Photographer. Exhibits all over the country."

"Gosh," says India.

"Actually, we're separated," Arthur says. A very old, generic sort of look passes between the two men, a lion-in-mating-season look.

"India," Arthur says, "would you do me an enormous favor? I've just inherited a manuscript on chaos theory, a subject of which I am utterly ignorant. My head is swarming with fractals and butterflies flapping their wings in Tokyo and smooth noodle maps; the terminology is delightful, but I am utterly clueless. I need someone who can explain the basics of chaos in words of one syllable."

"You should talk to Roger. He knows much more than I do."

"Roger's useless; he knows too much. Anyway, you're prettier than he is."

"I'm devastated," Roger says. "Anyway, it's not all that complicated. I take it the book is written for laymen?"

"Supposedly."

"Then if it's any good you should be able to follow it. Basically, chaos theory is a mathematical tool for finding order in complex phenomena, not by reducing them to their constituent parts, as classical physics tried to do, but by seeking out underlying patterns in nonlinear dynamical systems. Chaos is the interface between science and natural phenomena that operate within certain parameters yet seem, in their particulars, impenetrably random. Turbulence, for example, or migratory patterns, or next week's weather. In short, chaos explores order without periodicity."

"See what I mean?" Arthur asks India. "Clear as mud. I pity his students."

Roger smiles. "Haven't got any, fortunately."

"Why fortunately?"

"Distracting. Too many extraneous agendas interacting."

"Then it sounds like the classroom is the perfect laboratory for your work," Arthur says. "Or is human behavior too complex even for chaos theory?"

"Generally speaking, no, not nearly as challenging as traffic patterns or the arc of an epidemic. But I don't think we need trot out the heavy guns to analyze yours."

"Oh no?"

"From what I've observed, your behavior is perfectly periodic, linear, and remarkably free of variables."

Arthur turns to Emma, who tries without success to smother a laugh. "Is that what passes in mathematical circles for an insult?"

"No," she lies. "It's what passes for humor."

"Way over my head, I'm afraid. Come, India; let me ply you with liquor and pick your brains." India looks back over her shoulder as Arthur bears her away, her arm tucked firmly under his.

"Her brains my ass," Roger mutters.

"Mmm," says Emma. "He's in love."

"Only you would call it that."

"She's a big girl, darling. And you did warn her."

The doorbell peals again. This time they go together and open the door to Maggie, who kisses Emma and clicks her heels at Roger. "Herr Doktor," she says; "Dr. Fluff," he replies. With her are the Chrises, as they are known in tandem: Christine and Christopher Palmer. Friends from the old West Side neighborhood, they're among the few Emma and Maggie have in common. Tall, blond, and gorgeous. Goys in the hood, Maggie calls them; their mother used to call them the gorgeous Aryans. Christine looks like the girl from Ipanema, Christopher like her twin brother, though in fact they're man and wife. He's a pediatrician, she's a vet. After hugs, kisses, and handshakes, Christine says, "We brought you something."

"But decided against giving it?" asks Emma, seeing that they're empty-handed.

"Nope. It's in the car."

"Her idea completely," says Christopher, raising his right hand like a man in court. "Don't blame me."

"You're a stand-up guy," says his wife. "Emma, if you don't want it, it's absolutely no problem. We'll take him back."

"Him?" says Emma.

They step outside, Emma and Roger shivering a little in the cool night air. Christine opens the back door of their Mercedes and bends over a cardboard box that takes up half the seat. When she turns, she's holding a puppy.

Emma takes it from her arms, surprised by its weight. Soft and warm, and that wonderful puppy smell. The puppy licks her face.

"It looks like a German shepherd," Roger says.

"Very good!" Christine says. "Fourteen weeks old, pick of the litter, and the dam's a lovely bitch. Emma, what do you think?"

"He's darling," says Emma. She draws the puppy toward her, stroking his downy fur. The puppy nestles against her breast like a sleepy baby, setting off a sudden wave of maternal longing.

"Only, Jesus, guys," Roger protests, stroking the puppy's head. "Bunch of flowers would've done just fine. This is too much."

"Not to sound cheap," says Christine, preening, "but the best part is, he didn't cost a cent. Got him in settlement from an owner who couldn't pay his bill."

"Nice precedent," says Roger. "What's Christopher do if his patients can't settle up, take a kid?"

Zack is in the front hall holding an empty tray when Emma carries the puppy inside. "Oh my God," he cries as Roger relieves him of the tray. "Where'd this come from?"

"From the Palmers," Emma says, placing the gangling pup in Zack's arms. "Want to keep him?"

For the first time in his life, Emma's son weeps for joy.

THE LAST TO ARRIVE is Caroline Marks, carrying a crystal vase filled with long-stemmed red roses. Emma introduces her around, ending up, not accidentally, with Gloria. This is a token of friendship Caroline may be unequipped to recognize; where Emma comes from, an introduction to one's agent ranks as high on the scale of significant gestures as bringing a boyfriend home to Mom and Dad.

"Caroline's a psychologist who works with battered women," says Emma. "She has the most wonderful idea for a book. You don't mind my mentioning it, Caroline?"

Caroline looks surprised but answers promptly. "Not at all; but you know, ideas are a dime a dozen. It's the execution that counts."

It cannot be said that Gloria shifts into agent mode,

for she has no other. But her attention sharpens. "What's the idea?"

"It's called 'Righting the Scales: A Manual for Women Who've Been Wronged.' "

"Great title. Half the battle right there."

"What's it about?" asks Maggie, joining their group.

"I have observed," Caroline says, "that women tend to blame themselves whenever something goes wrong in their lives. Their husband's unfaithful? Clearly he's not getting what he needs at home. He beats his wife? She must have provoked him. Kids get in trouble? Mother failed to instill the proper values. A tree falls in the forest? She should have caught it. There is no limit to some people's capacity to absorb blame. My contention would be that before we can deal effectively with our abusers, we have to stop abusing ourselves."

"Hear, hear," says Maggie. "But, if you'll forgive me, very sixties. Don't we know this?"

"We know it here"—Caroline touches her head—"but not here"—then her heart. "The women I work with might say they hate their abusers, but to a woman they come into the system blaming themselves."

"To a woman, you say. So you see this as strictly a gender-based phenomenon?"

"Not strictly, no, though there certainly seems to be a correlation. I heard a story recently that pretty much sums it up. Scientists have finally invented a device to end all wars: It's called the estrogen bomb. Drop it on a battlefield and the fighting stops instantly. Soldiers drop their weapons, turn to the enemy, and say, 'Sorry; all my fault.' And everyone starts cleaning up."

Amid the general laughter, Roger turns thoughtful

eyes on Caroline. He's been so busy glaring at Arthur Matthews, Emma thought he hadn't heard a word anyone had said.

"If I might play devil's advocate for a moment," he says.

"Go right ahead."

"You seem to be implying that your clients bear no responsibility at all for their situation, but is that really true? I'm talking, of course, about situations of ongoing abuse, not a one-time assault."

"You're saying they bring it on themselves."

"Not the initial attack, no. But by tolerating that first assault, staying in the relationship, aren't they permitting it to continue?"

"Devil's advocate indeed," Caroline says. Bright red spots have appeared in her cheeks. "You've captured the batterer's mind-set perfectly. 'She knows she's got it coming; why else would she take it?' "

"That's not what I said."

"Isn't it? You're skating on thin ice, Roger, right out there with men who claim that date rape is impossible, or that marital rape is a contradiction in terms."

Bitterness leaches from her voice. Maggie and Gloria exchange glances. Roger is mute, silenced by old-fashioned notions of what is due a guest in his home. It's left to Emma to break the silence.

"You're talking to the wrong man, Caroline. Roger hasn't got a sexist bone in his body."

Caroline lowers her eyes. "Forgive me if I jumped to conclusions. I never meant this to be about gender politics. In my book, female doesn't equal right, or male wrong; on the contrary, women can be every bit as destructive as men. My subject is really misplaced blame, the tendency to look inside oneself when the real fault lies outside."

"Sounds fascinating," Gloria says tactfully. "I'd love to see it."

"I'd love to write it. So far, Emma's kind words notwithstanding, it's all up here." Caroline, now fully restored to civility, taps her temple.

The conversation drifts away. Among the guests there is an abatement of tension, a sense, almost, of danger averted. But Roger remains silent, hiding behind the impenetrably courteous facade Emma calls his Wasp banker face. It is the look of the man he might have been had his parents had their way with him; the man he'd have been, perhaps, without Emma. The space around him vibrates with the effort required to contain his indignation. When Emma's sandaled foot brushes against his ankle, Roger pulls back from the contact.

Emma sighs. She and Caroline might yet be friends, but not Caroline and Roger. Her husband has many good qualities, but a propensity to forgive and forget is not among them. In this respect he shares the fault of Jane Austen's Mr. Darcy, whose good opinion, once lost, is forfeited forever.

"JUST AS I suspected," says Arthur, "the perfect setting for an Emma Roth novel. A house like this requires a ghost. Wouldn't surprise me if your next book turns out to be nonfiction." They've finished touring the second floor, and are waiting for stragglers at the foot of the winding stairs.

"It would amaze the hell out of me," Emma says. "I wouldn't stay ten minutes in a haunted house, if there were such a thing."

"Me neither," Gloria says with a shudder.

"Nervous?"

"Not a bit."

"Care to spend the night?"

"Not on your life."

"Still," Arthur says, "one might investigate. Do you know, I recently met a psychic, the most unexpected person you could imagine. I should get you two together."

"I don't think so," says Emma. "I'm not into spiritualism."

"Neither is she, that's what's so interesting. Never met a more down-to-earth woman in my life. Name's Ida Green."

Emma laughs. "You're kidding."

"I'm not. She is the widow of the late Murray Green, CPA. Sixty-eight years old, looks like your generic Jewish grandmother. 'What's a nice lady like you doing in a profession like this?' I asked her when we met, intending merely to break the ice, you understand, but milady bristled like a hedgehog." Arthur puts his hands on his hips and raises his voice an octave. 'So what do you think, I should waste my time playing mah-jongg? Excuse me, Mr. Big-Shot Senior Editor, but I am surprised that a person like yourself would make such a remark. Would you advise Carl Lewis to spend his life spit-shining shoes? God gives you a talent, you use it.' "

"Very forthright," Emma says. "What's her talent, fraud or self-deception?"

"My thinking exactly, till I met her. She told me things about myself my own mother doesn't know. We checked her out before we took on her book; don't want to wind up with egg on our faces. She's worked with the

NYPD and the Nassau County police. The cops I talked to swear she's the real thing."

"I'll believe it when I see it, which hopefully will be never. I'm for the coward's creed: What I don't know can't hurt me." Now, her guests having assembled, Emma leads the procession up to the library. Roger brings up the rear with India.

"This is my room," Emma says. "This is where I work." She poses a bit self-consciously before her desk, facing her audience. Her cheeks feel warm. This is like the first public appearance with a new lover, and not just any lover. A Tom Cruise at least; a Liam Neeson. Emma, that is to say, feels more than she wants to show.

The game plan is to play it cool, keep an ironic purchase on the situation. But it's turning out to be harder than expected, because Emma has feelings about this house so strange she hasn't even confided them to Roger. She has a sense of symbiosis with the house, a feeling of mutual acceptance. They are like partners in an arranged marriage who discover to their amazement that they've fallen in love.

All very fey, and Emma not your fey sort of woman, no matter what kind of books she writes. There is nothing animate about a house, therefore no mutual interaction is possible. Emma knows this. Yet as she shows it off, she cannot altogether repress a deep satisfaction that arises not so much from pride of ownership as from her sense of being owned, of belonging to the house. This feeling is amplified in the library, which has in a very short time become the very room she'd imagined when she first laid eyes on it. Her desk beneath the southern window, armchair beside the shelves. Her books, lovingly arranged, nonfiction by topic, fiction by author. One whole case devoted to her own work, displayed face out. Hard- and softcovers, American, British, and foreign editions.

Arthur whistles softly. "You'll have to do some damn fine work to live up to a room like this."

Emma nods approvingly. Arthur has the editor's gift of seeing to the heart of things. He's right, of course. You have to deserve a space like this. You have to earn it.

Caroline turns from examining her displayed oeuvre. "Very impressive. You've made quite a career for yourself."

"With a little help from my friends."

"Emma," declares Gloria, "I forgive you."

"I thought you forgave me downstairs."

"No, my dear. Downstairs I understood you. Up here I forgive."

"I wish you could see it in daytime," Emma says wistfully. "It's like sitting on top of the world, like inhabiting a watchtower." At night the windows reverse their function, enclosing instead of opening. The bay is invisible. Reflections of the room surround them. In one window she glimpses India whispering to Roger, their heads canted together. What is she saying? Whatever it is, he nods without smiling, his features thoughtful, graver than they should be at a party. Then Christopher calls, and Roger goes to him. India is left alone, but only for a moment. Arthur approaches. The editor smiles, he speaks, he oozes charm with every word and gesture; but India pays no heed. Her eyes, dark and full of longing, follow Roger's every move. He is the only one she sees. And thus, as writers often do, Emma learns through a reflection what she failed to perceive in real life. India Robbins loves her husband; this fact is suddenly clear. What is not at all clear is whether Roger knows.

But how could he not? Maggie can joke all she wants about absentminded scientists with their heads in the clouds; Roger doesn't miss a trick. Besides, India doesn't exactly hide it. And if she moons over him in public, God knows what she gets up to when they're alone.

Emma has never been a jealous wife. Too secure in her man and in herself; too arrogant, perhaps, to worry. But a demon voice, a lot like Arthur's, whispers in her ear. *Look at her. She's beautiful, she's available, and she's in love with him.*

This is not just any woman. This is the woman who works at Roger's side, day after day. No bimbo, but a brilliant, sexy, younger woman who knows more about his work than his wife does.

But Roger loves me, Emma reminds herself.

Ah, murmurs the demon voice, *but look at it this way: What man could resist India served up on a platter?*

She stares across the room at Roger, trying to penetrate inside, but for once her view remains stubbornly external. She sees a tall man with an athlete's body, an aquiline face, eyes that reveal an almost painful intelligence. Saturnine complexion, angled cheekbones, small, precise ears, graying brown hair receding at the temples. Try as she might, she sees no deeper than this. Not for the first time, Emma bemoans the stubborn opacity of real people. Why can't people be more like their fictional counterparts, who have depth allied with transparency? Real people have greater density; they're apt to surprise you, and they're inconsistent. You think you know them, then they turn around and do something you'd have thought totally out of character.

Emma loves her husband, but that it not to say she knows him through and through. Their marriage is not a merger but a partnership, and Emma has always considered that its greatest strength: that they are not one, but two together.

But in such a marriage many things must be taken on trust. And it's the undigested bits of him, the areas outside her grasp—his otherness, his analytical mode of thinking, the natural opacity of the adult male—that pose the greatest risk.

Love is no safe harbor, she thinks. We just pretend it is.

" 'S'UP WITH YOU, big sister? You look like you swallowed a fly."

"Mags, that girl's in love with him."

Maggie follows her eyes and snorts. "India in love with Arthur? He wishes."

"Not Arthur. Roger."

"No, duh!"

"Now there's a lovely expression."

"Learned it from my students. Very useful in class."

"So it's that obvious."

"You only have to look at her. I thought writers were supposed to be observant."

"Not this writer, apparently."

Maggie looks at her, then takes her arm and pulls her close. She switches to sister frequency. "Don't look so stricken. Smile at your guests. If it's any comfort, I'd bet the ranch *he's* clueless."

"You don't think she's a pretty tempting package?"

"Compared to what he's got at home?"

"Do men think that way?"

"Do they think at all is the larger question. In Roger's case, I think you can factor in some intelligence."

"I'm being dumb?"

"Mildly paranoid."

"Thanks, Mags."

"Any time."

MAGGIE WATCHES her sister reenter the party, mingling with her guests as she makes her way toward Roger. Graceful as all get-out; Emma's always had it over her in that regard. Killer charm, too, even as a kid. Whenever they got into trouble at home, Maggie would try arguing her way out of it and end up digging herself in deeper, whereas Emma would deny everything, so charmingly and with such fabulous, extravagant lies that their mother would end up laughing.

Emma reaches Roger and whispers something in his ear. He smiles, slips an arm around her waist.

No way, Maggie tells herself. If he were fucking India, he'd keep her far away from us. He's cool but not that cool.

And if I'm wrong, I'll slit his miserable throat.

6

WITH ROGER at work and Zack away, Emma has the house to herself. Zack has gone for a week to visit Roger's parents in the Newport house they call their summer cottage: a rank misnomer, in Emma's mind, for a house with twelve rooms, a swimming pool, a tennis court, and two acres of gardens. Not that she's ever seen it; when the elder Koenigs want Zack, they send their car and driver. Having him to stay for a week or two in the summer is their method of maintaining a relationship with their only grandchild while minimizing contact with his parents.

If it were up to Roger, Zack would not go. Roger has never forgiven his parents their rejection of Emma, nor have they have ever sought forgiveness for a judgment they regarded, and no doubt still regard, as perfectly justified. Their problem with Emma was not merely that she was, in Walter Koenig's quaint term, "a Jewess." Her unsuitability went much deeper than religion: It was an offense against class, a renunciation of the rights and privileges that were Roger's birthright. No matter that Roger had eschewed those rights and privileges; they were still his to claim when he would. What was Emma, on the other hand, but a prole, a peasant, two generations from the ghetto? Anti-Semitism not the issue here, as Walter Koenig explained to Roger and Roger subsequently relayed to Emma; it's just that there are Jews and there are Jews. Had Roger settled on a Rothschild, say, or a Brandeis, perhaps his parents would not have been altogether pleased, but they could have worked with it. Emma's people, on the other hand, were simply the wrong sort of Jews: the common or Brooklyn variety.

So much for Roger's father. For a short while Emma harbored hopes of the mother. Two days after Roger informed them of his engagement, Alicia Koenig had telephoned Emma to propose a meeting. Just the two of them, she'd said; a chance to get to know one another. Of course Emma accepted. Alicia invited her up to their pied-à-terre, as she called it, on Park Avenue. Emma opted for a more neutral venue. Not too neutral, though; she chose the Museum of Modern Art, where she and Roger first met.

Their appointment was for three o'clock the following day in the museum restaurant. Emma arrived ten minutes early to find Alicia already seated. A petite woman, well-tended and toned, with lovely posture and a cameolike profile. If she had lost a minute's sleep over her son's engagement, it did not appear in her ice-blue eyes or porcelain complexion. Her hair, honey-blond and carefully tousled, looked like it cost more to maintain than Emma's apartment.

Emma had chosen her most conservative suit, an Ann Taylor, fine gray wool with a fitted jacket and a short, straight skirt that showed off her height and her figure to advantage. Alicia watched her approach with an assessing eye and a faint smile.

"Well," she said as Emma stood before her, "one sees how. What remains to be discovered is why."

"Why what?" Emma asked; and if Alicia had known her better she might have taken heed of her tone. Instead, Alicia smiled as if the answer were too obvious for words and said, "Have a seat, my dear."

Emma saw herself turning and walking out, and for a moment she was tempted. Maggie would have done it, and thrown in a few choice words to boot. But this was Roger's mother. Alicia must care for him. There must be something here to salvage.

She took the seat opposite Alicia, who summoned the waiter with a crook of her finger. Emma's coffee was served with unprecedented speed, then the waiter retired discreetly. At this hour the restaurant was all but deserted.

"The first thing I need to know," Alicia said briskly, "is why you are doing this. It is entirely to your advantage to be frank with me; I cannot help unless I know the situation."

How dare she? Emma swallowed hard. "I didn't know Roger's family had money when I met him, I didn't know it when I agreed to marry him, and I don't care now."

"I see." Alicia is all politeness with just a dash of skepticism. "Then we should have one thing at least in common: We both want what's best for Roger."

"Of course," said Emma, and was amazed to hear her voice come out steady and composed. "But do we agree on what that is?"

"Surely it is whatever enables him to fulfill his greatest potential."

"I would have said it is whatever allows him to lead the happiest, most fulfilled life. You're his mother; don't you want him to marry where he loves?"

If by this appeal to maternal feeling Emma had hoped to break through Alicia's mannered fortress, she was quickly disillusioned. Alicia's air of polite attention did not waver, and her silky voice issued forth without a ripple of unease.

"The sort of love you speak of is transient. To marry for that is to build on sand. In addition to your more obvious attractions, you are evidently a very clever young woman, clever enough to understand this. You please him now. But if you marry him, sooner or later he will realize what his marriage has cost him. Inevitably he will regret squandered opportunities. And he will blame you, my dear. He will hold it against you. It will end in disaster for you both." This was said in the kindest possible voice.

"If that's what you think," said Emma stoutly, "you don't know Roger at all. And if you are going to insult me, I would be grateful if you did not address me as 'my dear.'"

A faint blush overtook the porcelain cheek. For the first time Alicia's tone betrayed the steely edge beneath the abundant silk. "I know my son; I know him very well indeed. And I know where you fit into the scheme of things, which is clearly more than you do. Let me tell you, my dear, that you are merely the latest in a series of petty rebellions that has gone on long past its time; you are the last gasp of Roger's childish irresponsibility. When the time comes, as inevitably it will if you pursue this foolishness, you will be cast aside like the hundred other expensive toys and hobbies he's dabbled in and forgotten."

Though nothing in her face showed it, Emma flinched inside. Alicia's words had struck their target. Ever since she'd started going out with Roger, Emma had been waiting for the other shoe to drop. It was common knowledge that guys as good as him didn't exist in New York. Handsome, brilliant, established in his field, straight, sober, and unattached? Gotta be a catch. It took months for her wariness to subside. Now Alicia was stirring it up again.

Damned if she'd show weakness before the enemy, though. Instead she carried the attack to Alicia. "Just out of curiosity, would you mind telling me what exactly your objections are, considering the fact that you don't even know me?"

Alicia's look was pained, reproachful, as if Emma had willfully trespassed on forbidden ground.

"It's true I don't know you. But I know where you come from, and that's much the same thing. There is a saying, perhaps you've heard it: A fish can marry a bird, but where will they live?"

Emma thought about that. "This bird and fish," she said presently, "is one of them a Jew?"

"Don't be ridiculous," Alicia snapped. "We are talking about something much more fundamental. You seem to have made the most of the cards you were dealt. I respect that; but it absolutely does not matter. You will never fit into Roger's world, and he is not meant for yours. Marrying you would hold him back."

"You're assuming that the rest of the world shares your archaic class prejudice."

"It's not prejudice. It is simply a knowledge of how the world works."

Emma laughed.

She didn't mean to, didn't plan it. The thought just came to her: If Maggie could hear this! But Alicia's reaction was as marked as if Emma had reached across the table and slapped her.

"You find this amusing?"

"Not at all," Emma said. "It's actually quite sad. I laughed because I suddenly thought how strange it is that you and my sister should be on the same side."

Alicia's pale eyes glistened as she scented an ally. "Your sister is against this match?"

"Dead against, and for the same reason: class."

"Sensible girl."

"She fears," Emma continued, "that Roger is indelibly stamped with his. But I believe no one is irredeemable, however badly raised."

EMMA WOULD have spared Roger this encounter with his mother, but Alicia did not. Her account left him shimmering with rage and humiliation. When his parents realized they could not prevail upon him to break his engagement, they insisted on a prenuptial agreement. Emma had no objection; it was Roger who refused, and the tenor of his refusal marked the end of a relationship whose deterioration had begun years ago.

They were married in a Unitarian church. Once she realized that Emma would not be swayed, Maggie swallowed her disapproval and threw herself into preparations for the wedding. The elder Koenigs did not attend; indeed, they went so far as to ask their friends to decline, which many did. But the younger set, Roger's contemporaries, came in force, as did Emma and Maggie's friends: an odd mixture indeed. As the guests began to arrive, Maggie stood in the vestibule instructing the ushers on seating. "It's simple. Socialists to the right, socialites to the left."

"Shouldn't it be the other way round?" asked Roger in passing.

"Very clever, Herr Doktor. How about paupers up front, princes to the rear?"

"You're thinking of Kingdom Come, my dear sister-to-be. Though come to mention it, I do feel as if I've died and gone to heaven."

FOR TWO YEARS there was no communication between the Koenigs elder and younger, but when Zack was born, Emma took it upon herself to send Roger's parents a birth announcement. Three weeks later, to her amazement, a large parcel arrived containing a complete layette from Saks and a note penned in Alicia's elegant hand. "To Zachary, from his grandparents. God bless."

That night at dinner she showed the gift to Roger. "We should call and thank them."

"Send it back," he said. "I can't imagine how they even heard."

"I sent them an announcement."

Roger looked at her. "Did you," he said.

"Roger, they're your parents. And the only grandparents Zack has."

"He's better off without them."

She fished Alicia's note from her pocket and passed it over the table. " 'To Zachary, God bless.' You don't think they're reaching out?"

"To him, not us. You notice not one word's addressed to us, the proud parents."

"Who did they think would read it, Zack?"

Roger laughed shortly. "My dear, sweet girl, you don't know my mother. Alicia's built her career on letter-writing: the perfect note for every occasion, subtly nuanced and always in code. She is the grand master of the gracious snub."

"Decode this, then."

"Trivial. 'We'll acknowledge the child but not the marriage; take it or leave it.' I say leave it."

"I say take it."

He stared at her. Roger was a man who, in his own quiet and accommodating way, generally managed to get and do precisely what he wanted. He achieved this not through coercion or bullying, but rather by being the kind of person other people don't say no to. Emma rarely opposed him. But she had pulled an end run on this play, and they both knew it.

Roger didn't know and would not be pleased to hear it, but it was when he was offended that he looked most like his father. The resemblance lay less in physical features than in the tilt of his head, the look in his eye: impressions stamped at an early age. Emma held his eyes long enough to establish that she wasn't intimidated, then returned to her dinner. Her gaze fell on the crystal salt shaker beside her plate, one of a pair her mother's mother had brought from Poland. Precious relics, too formal for their little Parson's table, but she uses them anyway.

"I didn't have a big family," she said, "but what there was of it meant a lot to me. I don't want to be the cause of Zack losing that experience."

"You're not the cause, they are. I wish I'd known your parents, Emma, though if Maggie's any indication they probably would have disapproved of me. But mine are different. All families aren't cut from the same cloth."

"I know. But they're getting older, and we're the only family they have. Maybe they regret things but can't bring themselves to say so. Maybe they don't. The thing about families is that you're stuck with each other, for better or worse."

In all of this Emma was sincere but also not unmindful of the fact that Zack was the only grandchild of two very wealthy people. Roger might disdain his parents' wealth, and she herself might disregard it; between his salary and her royalties, they did not need his parents' money to live comfortably. Nevertheless, Emma was not one to overlook her child's interests.

Of course, she knew better than to advance that argument with Roger. That she prevailed at all was only because Roger, primed by the birth of his son, was ready to be persuaded. His resentment at the time of his marriage had run very deep, but not deep enough to eradicate all attachment. They were his parents, after all, as Emma kept reminding him; and though he denied it to her and to himself, their rift had long been a source of subliminal distress.

So the call was made, an invitation issued, and on the appointed day the elder Koenigs came in state to view the baby. The visit began with all the warmth of a reunion in a walk-in freezer. Handshakes but no embraces; the tone was not conciliatory. Walter produced a bottle of champagne and they drank to Zachary's future. Conversation languished until the scion himself awoke and was produced. Emma carried him to Alicia, who instinctively held out her arms. After a moment's hesitation, Emma gave her the baby, wrapped in a pale blue receiving blanket. It was one of those rare moments that feel significant even as they're occurring. As Alicia gazed into her grandson's face, her frozen countenance melted. She smiled with spontaneous warmth. "Oh my dear," she cooed. "Oh, you sweet little boy. Walter, look at this; he's the image of Roger."

Walter came over to inspect the child. Zack's eyes sought his; when they met, the infant smiled and gurgled. You're doing it on purpose, Emma thought, you crafty devil, you. Walter held out a pinkie and laughed as the baby grasped it. "Fine-looking boy, I'll give you that," he harumphed. "Fine-looking boy."

OVER TIME the two couples have achieved a level of civility, though not warmth. They meet without incident at family functions. Alicia does not refer to Emma as her daughter-in-law but rather as Roger's wife; if Emma hears in this an elided hint of "Roger's first wife," she keeps that perception to herself. Tacit rules of engagement prohibit each side from disparaging the other to Zack. He is the link that binds them. Once a year the boy visits his grandparents. So far Zack seems never to have wondered why his extended family does not gather for holidays. Or perhaps he knows enough not to ask.

Now Emma, having fostered the relationship, is left to pay the price in loneliness. She misses Zack and finds it hard to settle down to work without seeing his face in the morning. Casey, the German shepherd pup, misses him, too. They've been inseparable in the weeks since the dog arrived. Casey follows Zack everywhere, cries when he leaves, and sleeps on the floor beside his bed. In Zack's absence, Casey trails Emma from room to room. She's not sorry for the company. When she's alone, the house seems huge, unconscious but not inert, like a slumbering beast. Sometimes she feels like Jonah in the belly of the whale.

She carries a cup of coffee upstairs to the second floor, the dog at her heels. Just inside the hall leading to the winding staircase, Casey stops short and growls deep in his throat. The hair on his nape bristles.

Emma calls him from the foot of the stairs. Stiff-legged, the dog backs away. "What's the matter, Case, scared of a few steps?" She returns and scoops him up, but as they reach the staircase, Casey wriggles free. He jumps to the ground and crouches, releasing a thin trickle of urine onto the carpet.

"Bad dog!" As Emma storms past him to fetch a brush and detergent from the bathroom, Casey escapes downstairs. Damn, Emma thinks as she scrubs the carpet. And Zack swore it was housebroken. If that dog pees on the Navajo rug downstairs, he is meat loaf. The carpet shifts beneath the vigorous strokes of her brush, and Emma feels the hard, smooth surface directly underneath. There seems to be no padding or underlayment, which means that the dog's urine has probably soaked through to the floorboards. She'll have to pull the rug up, clean underneath.

It's always struck her as odd that this hallway is carpeted while the rest of the house has hardwood floors. Not a very nice carpet, either: cheap synthetic fiber the color of mud. Now she notices that it's not even properly installed, just tacked here and there to the floorboards. From the deep pockets of her denim skirt she turns up a pen, two quarters, half a dozen paper clips, and a small notepad. Using the pen, she pries loose two U-shaped tacks at the base of the staircase and turns back a corner of the carpet. The wide oak floorboards appear to be in excellent condition.

Curious. This is the same floor as outside; why cover it up with a cruddy piece of carpet? She pops a few more tacks and rolls the rug back to where the dog peed. And now she sees the reason for the carpet. The wood at the foot of the stairs is marred by a large, irregular stain. Like a giant amoeba, it extends across almost the whole width of the hall. Something big spilled here, something dark and viscous to have left such a stain. Could be paint, but there's a feeling in her stomach that says not. She tears a clean page from the notepad and rubs it along the stain. Where her fingers pressed the paper to the floor there are streaks of reddish brown, transected by the thin blue capillaries of the lined page. She lifts the paper to her nose and sniffs. There's barely any odor, just a few stray molecules stirred up by the rubbing, but it's enough. Some smells you never forget.

A face appears before her, a young girl's face, huge brown eyes gazing upward. Emma shakes her head and the face disappears. She shivers. It's always chilly in this passageway. Cold spots are a classic sign of haunting in the genre Emma knows so well; fortunately she's far too sensible to believe the kind of stuff she writes. She carries the bucket back to the bathroom and rinses it out. So what if it's blood? Doesn't mean a thing. She scrubs her hands with soap and rinses her face in cold water. When she looks in the mirror, Emma doesn't see the prettiness that others see in her. She sees the toughness underneath; she sees the hidden scar tissue. Get a grip, she orders herself, and goes upstairs to work.

Despite an overcast sky, the tower is full of pearly gray light. This morning, getting out of bed, she'd felt a distinct nip in the air. In two weeks school will begin.

Before settling down to work, Emma makes her usual survey. To the north, sailboats in the bay hover close to the harbor. To the east, beyond her backyard, is a windbreak of hemlocks. To the south is the lower part of Crag Road, the rakish peaks of the village in the background. Westward stands the carriage house, smoke rising from the chimney.

She boots up the computer. First a game of hearts. The familiar faces appear on the screen. Who shall she play with today? Every day she chooses by category: smartest, trickiest, oldest, youngest. . . . Today she picks the kindest. The gray-haired one she calls Grandpa because he reminds her of hers; the always gracious Southern belle; and the gambler, boastful but magnanimous. Emma knows exactly what they'll say when she calls them up, what they always say. "I'd just love to play hearts with you, sugar," Belle will gush. Grandpa will say, "I've been waiting for this, *bubbele*. Hearts is my favorite game." The gambler will grin wolfishly and ask who's dealing.

You can turn off the dialogue but Emma never does.

Though the characters' comments grow repetitious after a while, that is hardly their fault, and it would seem rude to silence them. She double-clicks on her selections and hits Enter. First up is Belle. Her words appear in a bubble above her head. Emma reads these words: "Something's happened to the boy."

Once, visiting a friend's country house, Emma opened a cutlery drawer and a panicked mouse leapt out at her. She feels a similar shock now, amplified by eeriness. Something that cannot happen has just happened, something wholly inappropriate and weird.

She blinks. When her eyes reopen, the words are gone and so is Belle. The old man has come up. "I've been waiting for this, *bubbele*," he says. "Hearts is my favorite game."

The gambler follows in turn. "Who's dealing?"

Everything back to normal. Did she really see what she thought she saw? "Something's happened to the boy." She doesn't ask herself, What boy? There's only one boy in her life. Has something happened to Zack? Emma has no reason to believe it, but neither will she be able to work till she finds out.

The cordless phone is on the table beside her armchair. She punches in the Koenig's Newport number. The phone rings four times, then Alicia's cool, calm voice comes down the line. "Hello?"

"Hello, Alicia, it's Emma. How is Zack?"

"He's fine, of course. Are you all right, my dear?"

"Where is he? Is he with you?"

"I'm watching him as we speak, playing soccer on the lawn. Is something wrong?"

"No, not at all." Emma forces a laugh. "A sudden twinge of maternal angst."

The silence on the other end is dense with speculation. They know her history, of course: the accident, the
depression. Roger didn't tell them, but somehow they
found out. While she was hospitalized they'd offered to
take charge of three-year-old Zack for the duration, an
offer Roger instantly and adamantly refused.

"Sorry to have bothered you," Emma says. "No
bother at all," replies Alicia. They hang up. For three
long minutes Emma sits staring at the phone. Then she
snatches the receiver and speed-dials Roger's number.

India answers. "Dr. Koenig's office."

"Hi, India. Is he in?"

"Oh, hello, Emma. He is but he's swamped. Is it
urgent, or could he get back to you?" Her tone cloyingly
sweet and yes, proprietary. He might be yours at home,
it says, but here at work he's all mine.

"Put him on," Emma says shortly.

Roger picks up. Emma tells him what happened and
what she did.

"You called my parents?"

She prays that India isn't listening in. "I had to. I had
to make sure he was okay."

"Which he was."

"Yes."

There's a longish pause. Then Roger asks, "How
long were the words on the screen?" Mildly puzzled, as
if this were nothing more than a common computer
glitch.

"Five, ten seconds."

"Did you try rebooting the game to see what would
happen?"

"No."

"Try it now."

"Hold on." She carries the phone back to the desk. The screen shows the opening Windows setup; odd, she doesn't remember exiting the program. She reboots the game and chooses the same characters in the same order as before, then, steeling herself, hits Enter.

Belle appears on screen. "I'd just love to play hearts with you, sugar," she gushes. The others follow in due course, with their accustomed lines.

"Normal," she reports. "Just the regular dialogue."

"No repeat?"

"No."

He's silent for so long she thinks she's lost him. "Roger?"

"I'm thinking."

"Think about this, too." She tells him about the stain under the carpet. "I'm sure it's blood."

"So what if it is? It's an old house. Things happen. I don't see the relevance, except . . ."

"Except what?"

"Well," he says with a nervous laugh, "as they say on TV, except as it goes to state of mind."

Now the silence comes from Emma's end.

"You think I imagined it?" she says at last.

"Isn't it possible? You saw the bloodstain, Zack was on your mind . . ."

"So I hallucinated."

"I'm just tossing it out there. And it's not hallucinating to misread a few words."

"Trust me, Roger. I know what I saw."

"You're certain?"

Absolutely, she tells him, but is she? The whole thing happened so fast that the words were gone almost before the sense of them struck her. She'd doubted herself at the time. How sure can a person be when the only evidence is memory?

"Do you want me to come home?"

"And tell India what? That your wife's having hysterics and you've got to go calm her down?"

"What's she got to do with it? I don't answer to her. I'm asking what you want."

"No," says Emma. "Don't come." Tears of humiliation run down her face, but she keeps them out of her voice. "Forget it. I'll see you tonight."

She hears relief in his voice. Go out, he tells her. Take the dog for a walk. Clear your head. Good advice, which Emma is happy to take. She goes downstairs, scrubs her face, and whistles up the dog. They set off down the drive. Just as they pass the carriage house, the door opens and Caroline emerges. She's dressed for work, car keys in hand. "Hello!" she says. They exchange a few remarks, nothing of consequence, yet almost at once Emma feels better, restored to the real world, cobwebs blown away. Then Caroline, hesitating, asks, "Is everything okay?"

Emma looks at her without response, or perhaps she draws back a little, for Caroline says, "I don't mean to pry. It's just that you looked a bit upset."

Her eyes, no doubt. Emma's always been unlucky that way. Some women can cry all day without leaving a sign; she sheds three tears and has to endure twelve hours of red-rimmed eyes and puffy lids. Caroline's face radiates such friendly concern that for a moment Emma's tempted to confide. But she's already made a fool of herself twice today. Three times seems excessive.

"Allergies," she says. "This time of year . . ."

"Awful," Caroline agrees politely, and they part.

7

"A virus," Roger says decisively. "A prank. Someone's idea of a joke."

"You ran the virus scan and found nothing."

They are in bed, Roger on his back, left arm around Emma, whose head rests in the hollow of his shoulder. He says, "They're always churning out new ones."

Emma sighs. If only Roger could have seen it, too. Since he came home they must have booted up the game a dozen times, to no avail. Not that he appears to doubt her story, unlikely as it sounds. Instead he postulates a computer virus, an explanation which Emma, who's had all day to think about it, has already considered. But what sort of virus appears just once, then disappears? Emma feels as if she is caught inside one of those non-linear equations Roger's always tackling, trapped in a field of shifting variables in which what happens depends on who's watching.

"It was too specific for a virus," she says. "It was personal; I felt it was meant for me."

Roger shakes his head. "Random hit, designed to seem personal. Think about it. Zack's name didn't appear. It was 'the boy.' What boy? Any boy. Son, grandson, nephew, neighbor: Who doesn't have a boy in their life?"

"What about the bloodstain?"

"Totally unrelated."

"And we know this how?"

"Give me one explanation that links the two."

Emma is silent. It's not that she can't, it's that she doesn't want to.

"I rest my case."

"Maybe it's something connected to the house," she blurts out. "The computer's unchanged. I haven't added any programs or downloaded anything since we moved."

"How could a house be responsible?" His voice is gentle, solicitous; he is humoring her. "Wood and brick and glass—what can they do?"

"A house is more than wood and brick and glass. It's also its history, who lived in it, the things that happened."

"Now you sound like a character from one of your books."

Silly, he means; lacking rigor. Though Emma is wounded on their behalf, a good part of her agrees with Roger. Despite the disparity of their fields, there has always been a remarkable similarity in the way they look at the world. Each has a feel for patterns, Emma for the rhythms of speech and behavior, Roger for the order hidden in chaos. They share an intense curiosity; and though the objects of that curiosity differ, the light they turn upon them is the same pure, concentrated light, free of sentimentality and superstition—or so Emma has flattered herself, until today. Today a single well-aimed sentence pried her open, and she glimpsed within herself a great reservoir of superstition and dread, a poisoned well just beneath the surface.

She snuggles more deeply into Roger's shoulder. He is so solid, so real. If she could, she would crawl inside him. His arm tightens around her. *Poor kid*, it says, *you've had a helluva day.* Which is not a small part of what she loves about Roger, whose body language is pure Bogart.

"I know a guy in the computer department who's up on the latest viruses. If you want, I could get him to take a look. You'd have to live without the computer for a few days."

"Not now," she replies automatically. In the middle of a book, she'd as soon give up her right hand as her computer.

"I don't know what else to suggest."

"Forget it," she says. "Chalk it up to a virus or a neural glitch."

Roger gives her a nod of approval, and Emma is left to wonder why a man who has made a career of puzzling out the sort of anomalies that give most scientists migraines would seem so dismissive of this one. His solution to the suspicious stain at the foot of the spiral stairs is simplicity itself. "Call in a floor man, have it stripped and refinished: end of problem." As to the hearts game, he advises her to avoid it.

The conclusion is unavoidable: He doesn't believe her.

"Do you think I'm nuts?" she asks. "When I called, did you think, Uh-oh, Emma's losing it again?"

"Of course not."

To her hypersensitive ear his denial enters a beat too soon, as if it's been there all along, waiting in the wings. "Good. Because I'm not. It really did happen."

He nods. "By which we infer that something caused it to happen. Probably we'll get to the bottom of this thing, but there's always the possibility that we won't. Uncertainty tends to rear its ugly head when least convenient."

Someone caused it, she thinks, not something. Even if it is a virus, computer viruses are not spontaneously generated; they're created, written into existence. There was a sentence. Someone wrote that sentence, someone programmed it. It did not write itself. Show me a sentence, thinks Emma, who knows a thing or two about the matter, and I'll show you an author.

SHE WAKES in the morning uncommonly late. Roger is gone, Zack still away, and the empty house surrounds her like an aching tooth. A tepid cup of coffee on her bedside table is cold comfort. Needing more, Emma decides to take a bath.

In the city she was all showers, but the tub here—a claw-footed cast-iron relic of the forties, deeper and wider than modern tubs—is as conducive to long, luxurious soaks as it is hostile to showers. Though she's alone in the house, Emma locks the bathroom door, thinking as she does so of Hitchcock, his permanent mark on the collective unconscious. There may be greater artists, but few who can claim as much.

After her bath she dresses and carries a fresh cup of coffee upstairs. Casey emerges from Zack's room, which he's taken to visiting dozens of times a day, in hopes, Emma assumes, of Zack's miraculous reappearance. The dog accompanies her as far as the hall leading to the spiral staircase, refusing despite coaxing to go any farther. Emma climbs the stairs alone and is once again delivered into the library.

She skips her usual game of hearts and sets right to work. With all the distractions of the past months—the mountains of papers and documents required for the mortgage, the tedious job of packing, moving, and unpacking—Emma is far behind schedule on this novel, the second of a three-book deal. When Emma left off, her protagonist, Faith Mercer, was having her first close encounter with the ghost. She does not yet see him, but she senses his presence. Ghost stories are the literary equivalent of striptease; they have an innate rhythm, a stately progression that cannot be hurried without sacrificing pleasure. Faith must endure a period of suspension between belief and perception.

As Emma writes, the library fades from view. She might as well be back in her converted laundry room for all she notices of her surroundings. She sees what her character sees, feels what she feels. Emma is so immersed in her story that she is not so much alarmed as annoyed by the sound of someone coughing just behind her—a prim, tactful little sound, as if the cougher were attempting to engage her attention without actually interrupting. Even more irritating is the visceral sense of someone standing behind her. If there's one thing she can't abide, it's people reading over her shoulder while she's working.

A moment's thought would have told her that the room is empty. But Emma doesn't think; instead she turns, with the full expectation of seeing someone.

There is no one. Empty space, dust motes dancing in the sunlight.

Who coughed, then? Who stood behind her, so close that the hairs on the back of her neck still bristle?

A strong sense of déjà vu descends on her. It's not her own experience she's remembering, though, but her characters': the stock scene, present in every ghost story she's ever written, in which the protagonist senses, usually through hearing or smell, something her eyes cannot see. Emma realizes now that she never conveyed, because she failed to imagine, the deep befuddlement caused by such a basic failure of sensory agreement. When one sense testifies against another, the very mesh of reality is rent: If this is possible, one asks oneself, what is impossible? What else have I got wrong?

In this case, the solution is clear. Immersed in the scene she was writing, she let her imagination run away with her. A good thing, in a way; she must be writing well to spook herself. Nevertheless Emma feels a sudden urge to call Roger at work. She suppresses it and returns to work, picking up where she left off.

A moment later she stops and sniffs the air. There is a distinct smell of lavender, a scent Emma dislikes and never uses. Where could it be coming from?

Not a profitable question, she tells herself. This is getting out of hand. It's one thing to empathize with one's characters, quite another thing to identify to the point of hallucination. Like surgeons, writers need to maintain a certain professional distance in order to operate. Once again she bends her mind to her work, and this time manages to keep it there.

THAT NIGHT Roger lets himself into a house that is dark and silent except for a radio tuned to NPR, the same interview he was listening to in the car. He follows the trail of conversation to the kitchen.

Emma, working at the counter with her back to him, does not hear him enter. He stands in the doorway and watches as she peels a cucumber with a few deft strokes of a paring knife. Then he glides up behind her and kisses the back of her neck.

Shrieking, Emma spins around, knife in one hand,

cuke in the other. Roger steps back, hands raised in mock surrender.

"Oh Jesus." She presses the cucumber to her heart. "Don't do that to me!"

"Sorry, darling. Didn't mean to startle you."

"Then why sneak up like that?" She turns her back to him, leans both arms on the counter.

Roger encircles her waist and molds his body to hers. "I'll make it up to you."

"You'll have to be very good."

"I'm always good."

"You're always full of yourself."

"It's part of my charm." He kisses her neck.

She smiles. "Hey, babe. Is that a kirby in your pocket, or are you just moderately glad to see me?"

Laughing, Roger lets her go, takes a beer from the fridge and sits at the table, stretching out his storklike legs. "How'd it go today?"

Now is the moment; but even as he asks, she realizes she can't tell him. Roger is a scientist. He would add today's incident to yesterday's and draw the only rational conclusion. He wouldn't say anything, but she would see it in his face; and later, whenever he thought she wasn't watching, she would feel his eyes on her, scrutinizing, vigilant, determined never again to be caught napping.

He doesn't deserve that. Emma knows that what's happening in this house has nothing to do with the other time. She has put it behind her, the darkness that over-came her life then; she does not fear its return. But he will, if she's not careful.

ON SATURDAY Zack comes home, tan and gorgeous, sporting brand-new sneakers: the latest Air Jordan

Nikes, $120 a pop, the very shoes Emma refused to buy a month ago. She says nothing. If his grandparents think they can purchase his affection, let them try. Emma knows her son.

With his return, life itself returns to normal. Spectral coughs and fancies are banished by the boisterous sounds of running feet, slamming doors, laughter, and bursts of frantic barking. Soccer season is upon them, school just a few days away.

8

WHEN ZACK scores his first goal for his new team, Nick Sanders turns to Roger and pumps his hand. When he scores his second, the coach kisses Emma on the forehead and then hugs her: two arms, full contact, duration one micron short of actionable. Emma steps back, and Nick turns his wild-man grin on Roger. "Don't mind me; I get carried away."

"It's her you want to watch out for," says Roger, who now knows exactly what he's dealing with. Sanders is hardly the first bastard to come on to his wife, he's just a little less subtle than most. Something about Emma evokes primitive responses in men. She's not flirtatious; she's just there, like Everest. Age is no barrier. In the city, their neighbor's fourteen-year-old haunted the lobby just looking for a chance to carry her groceries. Gus, the elevator man, seventy-something, used to look at her with the hopeless longing of Moses gazing down upon the Promised

Land. And then there's her faithful editor, Arthur Matthews. Emma affects to see Arthur as a harmless puppy dog; Roger knows him for a wolf lurking just outside the glow of the campfire.

It is useless to complain. The catch with Promised Lands is that they're never promised to just one people. Stake a claim and strife comes with the territory. At the end of the day, Roger knows who's taking her home.

The second half starts with some beautiful give-and-go between Zack and Marcel Dumont. Marcel's parents had come over before the game and introduced themselves. Gerard Dumont is a thin, light-skinned black man in pressed khaki trousers and an Izod shirt. Suburban chic, conservative, speaks with a distinctive and, for Roger, instantly identifiable Ivy League drawl—Harvard, Yale, or Princeton. The wife's a study in contrast, a foxy little thing in a form-fitting purple dress and a turban of kente cloth wound about her head. Roger can see why Emma likes her; she's a breath of city air.

Zack scores again, off a crossing pass from Marcel. This time, as Nick Sanders bears down on his wife, Roger steps into his path. "Want to kiss me, sport?"

" 'For a hat trick?' What the hell." Nick plants a smacker on Roger's cheek.

Roger joins in the general laugher. He's made his point. Remains to be seen whether Sanders will take it.

The Morgan Peak Pirates win the game, four to one. After the players line up to shake hands, Zack and Marcel swagger off the field with their arms around each other's shoulders. "Yolanda," Marcel says, "can Zack come over and play?"

"Fine with me," says Yolanda.

"Why don't you all come?" Gerard says. "We'll throw some burgers on the grill."

Their first suburban barbecue. What would Maggie say?

"LIKE A FISH out of water," Emma says.

"You're telling me?" Yolanda lights a cigarette and drops the match into a quartz ashtray. They're on the lower deck of the Dumonts' contemporary, a house as different as any house could be from Emma and Roger's. Burgers sizzling on the hibachi, the kids shooting hoops in the driveway. "First few months after we moved out here, I couldn't sleep for expecting to wake up and find a cross burning on our lawn. And lonely? Girl, I thought I'd die."

"What brought you out here?" Emma says.

"Gerard shanghaied me. He built us this house."

"Built it?"

"Designed it. Gerard's an architect."

"I don't recall much resistance," Gerard says, joining them. He sits at the foot of Yolanda's chaise, wraps an arm around her bent knees.

"I agreed for Marcel's sake. City's a dangerous place."

"Personally, I felt safer in the city," Emma says with more feeling than she intends. There's a silence. Then Yolanda says, "You're not raising a black boy," and Emma meets her eye and nods. Gerard takes another bottle of wine from the mini-fridge on the deck and tops up their glasses.

"We owe him," he says. "Did you know he introduced us, Yolanda and me?"

"Smart kid," Roger says, "How'd he find her?"

"Yellow pages," Gerard says. Yolanda gives him a look. "Okay, okay. She was his art teacher. Open-school night, Marcel insists I go meet this particular teacher. I find that rather odd, since art has never been his subject, but okay, he wants me to go, I go. He mentioned she's a widow; I picture some sweet old thing. The rest, as they say, is history."

"What about you two?" Yolanda asks.

"We met at MOMA," Emma says. "The Museum of—"

"Modern Art. Heard of it, girl."

"I picked her up," Roger whispers.

"He likes to think so."

"They all like to think so." Yolanda stretches her arms up over her head, silver bracelets jangling. "And we let 'em. Baby, what's that I smell burning?"

"Damn!" Gerard scurries over to the grill.

THEY EAT their well-done burgers at the table on the deck. Zack and Marcel down two each and kill a bagful of chips between them. Then Yolanda leads Emma on a tour of the house. Emma forms an impression of open spaces, vaulted ceilings, golden light spilling across bleached oak floors. There's a startling absence of clutter, no sign at all that a young boy lives in the house. The living room is dominated by a large painting over the fireplace. In the center of the picture, water spews from an open hydrant while bare-chested black boys frolic through the spray, mouths agape with laughter. Behind them, velvet-skinned women in brilliant sundresses lounge sensuously on brownstone stoops. Brilliant color and vitality to the painting, with a touch of Rousseau in the ample, rounded forms of the

women, the way they seem to fill out their skins. Emma
is struck instantly by a rare covetousness, not only for
the picture but also for the life it captured, the city
neighborhood.

"Know what it reminds me of?" she says. "You know
that piece by Duke Ellington, 'Harlem Suite'?" Yolanda
looks at her in pure amazement. "What?" says Emma.

"I can't believe you caught that, girl. I listened to
Ellington the whole time I worked on this."

"You? This is your work?" Emma looks from her to
the painting, then down at the floor. "Well, fuck me.
And here I'm telling you what MOMA stands for."

Yolanda laughs, and it's like music pouring out of a
player piano. "Want to see more?"

"Love to."

ROGER AND Gerard are smoking cigars out on the deck.
Roger's not crazy about cigars but it's one of the few
lessons his father taught him that stuck: Never refuse a
man's cigar unless you mean to insult him.

They've talked about the Yankees and sneered at the
Mets; they've established that Gerard plays golf and
Roger doesn't, and that both enjoy the odd pickup game
of basketball. Roger's edging up to what he really wants
to talk about.

"Some game today, huh?" he says.

"Oh yeah. Kids did real well."

"Marcel's a hell of a ball handler."

"So's your boy. Three goals his first game: not too
shabby."

"So," Roger says, studying the tip of his cigar,
"what's the deal with Sanders?"

Gerard looks at him through a veil of blue smoke.

"Helluva coach, if that's what you're asking. Knows his stuff inside out."

Roger waits. He's not impatient. Gerard's known Sanders for years, coached with him, in fact. He's known Roger less than a day.

"Bright guy," Gerard says. "Used to work for Microsoft. Started his own software company. Doing quite well, I hear."

Roger waits some more.

The other man sighs. "Fond of the women, as you may have surmised."

"I noticed that."

"Thought you might. Business and soccer aside, the man thinks with his dick. But hey, nobody's perfect."

"No," Roger says. "Though some are less perfect than others."

Gerard shrugs. "Look on the bright side. At least, with Nick, you don't have to worry about your boy."

ZACK AND Marcel are playing virtual soccer on Marcel's computer. Not as good as the real thing, but close enough. "Watch this," Marcel says as he switches to the viewpoint of the goalie. The other team's striker takes a shot, and the ball hurtles through the air toward the screen, growing larger as it approaches. The effect is so realistic that Zack flinches. At the last moment the goalie's hands appear on screen. He catches the ball and hugs it to his chest with a loud grunt. You can almost feel the air fly out of him.

"Oh, man," Zack says, "this game is cool."

In fact, Marcel's whole room is cool. Place looks like a Nobody Beats the Wiz ad. Apart from the computer, Marcel's got his own TV, Sony Play Station, and

CD stereo. The room has bunk beds, which Zack figures means there's a brother around somewhere; but when he asks, Marcel tells him no, it's just so he can have friends sleep over. About a million soccer trophies, which Zack has, too, but Marcel's are displayed in a glass-fronted case. The whole house is awesome. Apart from the hoop in the driveway, there's an inground pool in the backyard and a whole separate little house, which Marcel says is his mom's painting studio. Except he doesn't call her his mom, he calls her Yolanda. Stepmother, Zack figures. There's a lot of that going around. Last year his class had an epidemic of divorce, five in one year, which if you ask him really sucks, because why do people even bother having kids if they don't want to stay together?

Just thinking about the whole divorce thing makes Zack nervous. His parents seem pretty tight, but how can you tell for sure? None of his classmates saw it coming; and it's not like his parents would tell him if there were problems. They don't tell him squat, which is why Zack makes a point of keeping his ear to the ground. He knows for a fact that sometimes they fight. Not often, and not in front of him, but he can always tell. His mom's face tightens up and lines form like trenches around her mouth, and his dad goes all bluff and hearty, and neither one looks at the other.

He hates it when they fight. He's afraid to fall asleep at night, for fear he'll wake up and find his mom gone. In Zack's fear-borne fantasies, it's always she who deserts, never his father, which is strange, given the fact that in all the cases he knows of, it's the dads who moved out. Zack knows his mom loves him. She's always telling him she does, though he's trained her not to do it publicly; and even when she's not saying it, her gaze feels like hands cupping his face, lips brushing his cheek. It's not that he doesn't believe her. It's just a feeling he can't explain, that somehow his mother carries within her the potential for desertion, a latent gene of disappearance.

High-pitched voices drift through the open windows of Marcel's second-story room. Leaving the computer for a peek outside, Zack sees his mother and Marcel's crossing from the house to the studio on the far side of the pool. He can't make out their words but he hears their laughter. How long has it been since he's heard his mom laugh? Not since they left the city; maybe longer. He watches them from above. Their hands move as they talk, and their shoulders collide.

Marcel joins him at the window in time to see them disappear into the studio. "Yolanda must really like your mom. She doesn't let anyone in there, not even me."

Mom's found a friend, Zack thinks, and feels a great release inside him. This could be the sign he's been waiting for, the sign that says this move has taken in her, that they're here to stay. It hasn't come yet, and he's been watching for it. For a time it seemed she was in love with her office in the tower, but that's worn off big time; she hardly seems to like going up there anymore. Then Casey came along, and for a while Zack hoped that would be the thing she needed, but it wasn't, or it wasn't enough. She misses her city friends, her sister. Zack misses people, too, but it's different for him. He has soccer to pave the way; and anyway, it's easier for kids to make friends. They share more interests; whereas adults, he's noticed, tend to specialize. Marcel's mom seems like a natural, though, the only woman in

Morgan Peak who looks like she comes from his mother's tribe.

Suddenly things are looking up. Zack feels so happy he can't hold it inside, so he punches Marcel lightly on the shoulder, and Marcel punches him back, and they start in wrestling and keep it up till they fall to the floor laughing.

SCHOOL STARTS the day after Labor Day. Pro forma declarations of misery aside, Zack prances all the way to the bus stop. Emma trudges by his side, one hand thrust deep in the pocket of her windbreaker, the other holding Casey's leash. More than a nip of fall in the air today. The tall maples that line Crag Road show glints of crimson amid the green. How strange it seems to be walking Zack to his bus stop on a winding dirt road, a road bordered by giant oaks, manicured lawns, and picket fences, when just a few months ago the route lay along city blocks whose every store, restaurant, grate, and alley Emma knows as intimately as a beat cop. She feels like a character who's wandered into the wrong book.

Half a dozen children are gathered at the corner of Crag Road and Mill Lane. Four are girls and thus outside the scope of Zack's notice. Of the two boys, one is younger, a first- or second-grader, and the other looks about Zack's age. All the kids stare at Zack, who whistles unconcernedly, gives the dog a parting pat, and separates himself from his mother.

"Bye, Zack," she says, knowing that a kiss is out of the question.

He waves without looking at her. Emma leaves, resisting the impulse to linger. Casey strains against the leash and whines in protest. Emma knows how he feels, but like Orpheus she is forbidden to turn around. At ten paces she hears a boy's voice say, "You the new kid?"

"New to you," Zack replies. "Old to me."

"What's your name?"

"The name's Bond, James Bond."

"Yeah, right!"

"It's Zack. What's yours?"

"Mike. What grade you in?"

"Fifth."

"Me, too. You bought the old Hysop place, right? You ever, like, hear stuff at night or something?"

"Sure," says Emma's son, who combines her knack for fiction with Roger's for friendly accommodation. "Lots of stuff."

A girl's voice asks, "Ever see anything?"

"Nothing much," Zack says with a slight swagger in his voice, "unless you count the headless dude."

Laughing, Emma rounds a bend in the road, beyond which the voices are lost to her. Suddenly there is a black car approaching, taking the curve too fast. She yanks Casey close to her and steps off the side of the road into a patch of tall grass. The car whooshes by, kicking up dust, then it's gone. Emma walks on.

Caroline's car stands outside the carriage house, and Emma is ambushed by an impulse to knock on her door. In the city, her friends with kids always celebrated the first day of school with a moms' day out. But she has Casey with her, and Caroline, Emma has noticed, is not a dog lover. Besides, they don't have the dropping-in-unannounced sort of relationship; which, given their proximity, is just as well.

Emma enters the house through the kitchen door,

pours herself a cup of coffee, and heads straight
upstairs. As usual, Casey drops out on the second floor.
"Be that way," says Emma. She climbs up to the library
and takes her customary turn about the room, checking
out the view from each window. To the north the Sound
is churning, water gray and choppy. To the west, a large
crow rises from the apple tree at the far end of their
yard, flaps its black wings and disappears over the ridge.
Southward, a yellow bus wends its way toward the center of town; to the east stands Caroline's little house.

Tour completed, Emma sits at her desk, facing west
so that the morning sun pours in behind her. She turns
on the computer and pulls up the card-game program,
choosing for today's game of hearts the physicist, the
fireman, and the gambler. She holds her breath as their
opening comments appear on screen, but there's nothing
unusual. Emma has gradually come around to accepting
Roger's view of that event. It was a computer virus, a
random hit that happened to strike home. Either that or
she imagined the words. Which wouldn't mean she was
crazy, not at all. Psychologists classify moving as one of
the most stressful life experiences, right up there with
losing a job. Whatever. Doesn't worry her.

Emma wins the game, exits the program, boots up
Word, and moves over to her armchair. Picks up the
manuscript and, pen in hand, starts reading through the
latest pages. When she left off she was in the middle of
a scene with Faith Mercer, who's a journalist, and her
editor.

"I'm telling you," Faith said. "Something happened. I swear to God I wasn't alone in that
room."

Santini, chewing on an unlit cigar, stabbed the copy in front of him. "What something? I don't see anything here."

"I didn't write it because I can't think of any reasonable way to explain it."

"So you're telling me this bogus haunted house actually is haunted."

She ran her fingers through her cropped hair. "I'm not saying that, exactly. Look, I told you from the start I don't believe in that crap."

"Then what the hell are you saying, Mercer?"

There it ends. Emma pencils in a few changes and carries the paper over to the computer. She pulls the chapter up onto the screen, starts entering the changes. But as she reaches the final page, she encounters a discrepancy. What's printed on the paper is not the same as what appears on the computer. Her first thought is that she forgot to print out the latest version. Then she reads the words on the screen.

Her hands fall to her sides. She pushes back from the desk, but slowly, keeping her eyes on the screen. Sweat gathers on her forehead. She reads the words again.

"I'm telling you," Faith said. "Something happened. I swear to God I wasn't alone in that room."

"Kind of hokey, don't you think?" Santini yawned. "Get the feeling we've been there, done that?"

"That's not my fault!" Faith declared indignantly. "I just say the lines, I'm not the one writing this pulp."

"I know, I know," the editor sighed sadly. "That

bitch can't write for beans. Talk about your talentless hacks!"

"Please, boss, I'm begging you!" Faith said pleadingly. "Get us out of this book!"

9

"LOOK WHAT the cat dragged in," Roger says, entering the house with a guest.

"Maggie," says Emma, "what a surprise." They embrace, then Maggie holds Emma at arm's length and gives her an examining look.

Zack comes bounding downstairs and flings himself on his aunt. "Yo, Aunt Maggie, I didn't know you were coming. How's it hangin', my main aunt?"

"S'up wit' you, Gee?" Under the guise of slapping him five, Maggie slips him a Milky Way, a well-worn routine for them.

"So," Emma says, "what brings you out to the provinces?"

"I didn't realize I needed a reason to visit my own family. Not to mention I miss your cooking. Is that Mom's pot roast I smell?"

"So you two just ran into each other at the station?"

Maggie's eyes consult Roger's for a moment. "Something like that," she says. Then she turns to Zack and asks about his new soccer team, unleashing a covering stream of conversational fire that lasts all the way through dinner. After dessert, under protest, Zack goes upstairs to do his homework.

Maggie stands up and starts clearing dishes.

"Leave them," Emma says. "Shut the door."

Maggie shuts the kitchen door, returns to the table. Emma says, "Tell me again how you two bumped into each other."

"I asked her to come," Roger interjects. "Is that a problem?"

"Depends on why."

"Why not? Christ, Em, I figured you'd be glad to see her."

She ought to be, and maybe somewhere deep inside there's rejoicing; but on the surface Emma doesn't feel much of anything. All day long she's been keeping a lid on for Zack; now the lid's on too tight to come off. "Did you tell her about . . . ?"

Roger shifts in his chair. "After you called, I felt we needed another take on the situation. Your sister may be wrongheaded, but she's not stupid."

"How come *you* didn't tell me? How come I have to hear it from him?" Maggie's voice is sharp as broken glass. Emma calibrates her sister's distress by her accent. Normally it's what she thinks of as Dorothy Parker in the 'hood; but when rattled, Maggie reverts to her Brooklyn roots. Right now she sounds like Brando doing the Don.

Emma sighs. "Because I knew what you'd say, so what was the point?"

"The point is, you're going through hell and you don't say a word. The point is, what the fuck am I to you, you got a problem like this and you don't talk to me?"

"I didn't want to worry you."

"Who you gonna worry if you don't worry me? Jesus wept, Emma, show some sense!"

Arms folded, they stare off in different directions. Roger goes over to the counter. He pours coffee into three mugs and brings them to the table. He sets out sugar and milk. He takes Zack's seat opposite Maggie, so Emma's facing both of them at once.

"Tell us what happened today," he says. "Start at the beginning and don't leave anything out."

She tells the story once again, then hands them each two pages. "The first I wrote. The second I found on the computer."

Roger and Maggie read in a silence that stretches past the reading. They keep their eyes to themselves and their faces blank, but Emma knows these faces too well. Their thoughts are transparent to her; also their distress. Why is it that when she wants to read Roger's mind, it is opaque to her; yet now, having absolutely no desire to know his thoughts, she hears them as clearly as her own? The problem is, they share too many memories. One ambushes her now, a prime candidate for worst moment in a life surprisingly rife with them.

She's in a different kitchen, but the same faces peer down at her where she hunkers in the crevice between refrigerator and wall. Their lips move, they are speaking, but from where she is she can't hear them. There's another face, though, level with hers, plump cheeks stained with dirt and snot and tears, and another voice, the only sound that penetrates the barrier. "Mommy's stuck," it cries over and over. "Mommy's stuck." Emma watches him from far away. He has cried on and off all day, and she has listened as one listens to a child in a neighboring apartment, vaguely annoyed, wishing someone would comfort it. There is nothing she can do. Her body has lost power, suffered a catastrophic breakdown, a complete severance of the fuel line between will and action.

It doesn't hurt. The pain comes later. What a failure she feels then, an utter and complete failure. The diagnosis is depression, but what's in a name? To him it can only be experienced as desertion. Two months in the hospital: not a long time in her life, but a lifetime for a three-year-old.

Emma has long since recovered, she has retaken her body. Knowing, though, as not many do, the fragility of that link. Perhaps it is unfair of her to expect Roger and Maggie to forget what she cannot. The trauma ran deep for everyone. As an explanation of current weird events, a recurrence of her illness has the compelling advantage of simplicity; it is by far the most elegant solution.

And yet she does expect forgetfulness of them; she demands it of their loyalty. And it angers her now to see them sitting in judgment behind their eyes, doubting her, wondering. It injures feelings that ought to be numb by now, because being a nutcase is like being a recovering alcoholic: You can stay sober for twenty years, doesn't matter; for the rest of your life, every time you look a little frazzled or show up half an hour late, the ones who remember will be sniffing at your breath.

"Well?" she says at last, as no one else seems inclined to speak. "Any conclusions? Ideas? Questions?"

"One conclusion." Maggie flicks the page in front of her with a nail bitten to the quick. "This is nasty shit. The other thing, too, the business with the card game: nasty, weird, and seriously hostile. Wherever it's coming from, it started when you moved out here. The solution's staring you in the face: Get the hell out."

"I knew it."

"Dump the house. Take a loss if you have to. Come back home."

"Mom and Pop didn't raise us to cut and run."

"They didn't raise us to be stupid!"

"Running away is a knee-jerk reaction," Roger cuts in. "We haven't even figured out what's going on yet."

Maggie favors him with a look of contempt. "Pop quiz: You look up and see a Mack truck bearing down on you. Do you, a., stand there and calculate its velocity, or b., get the fuck out of the way?"

"Show me the truck."

"Get your head out of the clouds, Professor. Hand like this, smart money folds every time."

"And to hell with Zack, right? You realize he loves it here."

"He'll love it there. It's not like it's new to him."

"Spoken like an aunt," Emma puts in, "not a mother."

Maggie flinches but her voice remains level. "Spoken like a sister. It's you I'm concerned for, not Zack. I think we all have to get our priorities straight here." She cocks an eye at Roger, who answers peevishly:

"Of course Emma's the first priority. That goes without saying. The question is whether such a drastic move would even solve the problem."

"Which is what," Emma says, "in your opinion?"

"You tell me."

There's a long silence. Emma shreds her napkin. No one looks at anyone else.

"*Someone* wrote it," she says at last.

"Granted; this was not a random hit. So the question is, who has access to your computer?" Roger raises three fingers, one by one. "You, me, and Zack. I take it we can eliminate Zack?"

"Of course."

"That leaves me and you. I can assure you I never touched your computer."

"Gee," says Emma, "I guess that leaves me." She flings her wadded napkin at his face. "You bastard! I knew that's what you were thinking. That's why you brought Maggie out, to back you up."

"Emma, please. There's no reason to be defensive."

She bangs the table with both hands. "I am not defensive, I'm fucking pissed! We're married twelve years and you can't tell the difference?"

"We're trying to deal with the problem rationally. We have to look at all the possibilities."

"Then why don't you? All I see you looking at is one. I mean, Jesus. How would you feel if you presented a paper to a gathering of your peers, and the first consideration they took up was the possibility that Professor Koenig falsified his data?"

"Who said anything about falsifying? No one's suggesting that you deliberately wrote those lines."

"Not deliberately!" she howls. "So now I'm delusional."

"Just hear me out. Keep an open mind."

"On the possibility that I've lost mine? You ask a great deal."

Roger casts an anguished look at Maggie, who says, "Shut up, Emma, and let the man talk."

Emma subsides. It's not as if Roger is saying anything she hasn't already considered. It's almost a relief to get it out on the table.

"First of all," he says, "I haven't looked at just one explanation. I have run eight different virus checks on that damn computer, and found nothing. I've offered to take it to an expert; you didn't want that. You work in the house all day. There is no way I can see someone getting in here and tampering with the computer. What *else* am I supposed to consider? What other explanations are there?"

"I'm not crazy," Emma says. It sounds terrible even to her, "I'm not crazy" being one of those statements that, like "I'll be right back" in a horror movie, contain within them the seed of their inevitable contradiction. The others turn their eyes away. Emma understands. She lost it once, they're thinking; she could lose it again.

"What happened back then happened because of the accident." She forces the words out. "Even then I was depressed, not delusional. You have to believe me—I didn't write those lines."

They nod, still avoiding her eye, their thoughts drawn back, as hers are now, conjured by the triangulation of memory. The kitchen fades from view; Emma peers through the streaming windshield, squinting against the glare of approaching headlights. Wipers on high, she surfs a green wave past rows of factories and warehouses on Eleventh Avenue, making time despite the rain. A white car appears heading toward her, headlights reflected in the rain-slicked road. Twenty yards ahead, it veers suddenly into her lane. Instinctively, without thought, Emma hits both the horn and the brake. At once she finds herself skidding, spinning out, hydroplaning helplessly across the road.

Time slows. She sees exactly where and how the crash will come, the intersection of the two cars as inevitable as the path of a billiard ball after the cue has struck. She braces for the blow, but what comes instead is a touch on her hand; Emma shudders convulsively and her vision clears. She is back in the kitchen; Roger is leaning toward her, glancing obliquely but knowingly at her face.

"No one," he says gently, "thinks you're crazy. But I know how you work, I've watched you. You're in a world of your own. You've said yourself that sometimes you're surprised by what you've written."

"I was being modest," says Emma. "I meant I was surprised by how good it was."

"I've also heard you talk about wanting to break out of the haunted-house genre, write something different. Read in that light, those lines, 'Been there, done that,' and 'Get me out of this book' sound like you sending a message to you."

This does give her pause; for fiction, as she well knows, is the medium of unconscious truth. A writer friend of hers once wrote a novel about an affair between a married man and his wife's best friend. While she was busy writing the book, her own husband was sleeping with her best friend. The writer claims that the affair was totally unknown to her at the time, a claim that Emma, for one, has no trouble crediting. Writers lie, and through the alchemy of fiction, truth emerges.

She reads the words again, and her certainty returns. "I *couldn't* have written that excerpt, consciously or unconsciously; and I can prove it."

"Couldn't have?" Roger says. "Why not?"

"Because it sucks." She produces this assertion with an air of triumph.

His face registers surprise, then amusement. "Forgive me, Emma, but haven't you ever—"

"Of course I have," she snaps, for no writer likes to be reminded of her early drafts. "But this stuff sucks in

a different way. This is strictly amateur hour. Look at
the adverbs: 'The editor sighed sadly,' 'Faith said pleadingly.' I *hate* adverbs. Never touch the things if I can
avoid 'em. Look at the exclamation points. One, two,
three, four exclamation points in as many paragraphs.
And those fancy speaker tags? No way, José! I am the
poster boy for your basic 'he said, she said.' "

"That's it?" says Maggie. "A textural analysis, that's
your proof?"

"Mags," Emma says with serene confidence, "I could
be brain-dead and write better than this."

She lies on one elbow, studying her husband's face in
the moonlight. Sleeping, he looks peaceful, happy, years
younger than he looks awake. It used to amaze her how
fast he could fall asleep after a quarrel or an upset. He
could just lie down and shut his eyes, and in two minutes he'd be snoring. Took her years to figure out that
sleep was his way of dealing with stress.

Wakefulness is hers. Sleep is far from her tonight, but
Emma doesn't fret. She finds it restful to be awake while
her family sleeps. She feels she is watching over them,
protecting them from harm as her parents protected her.

It's only when the house is quietest that one can hear
the waves slap against the shore. The sound is repetitious yet unpredictable, just the kind of regular irregu-
larity Roger thrives on. If she's bought this house for the
tower library, surely Roger bought it for this inconstant
beat, backdrop to their days and nights.

Emma shuts her eyes, and the sound of rushing water
carries her back to a riverfront boat landing somewhere
upstate. They're going white-water rafting: she and
Roger, Roger's childhood friend Kip, and Kip's wife,

Jane. Kip and Jane are hale-and-hearty outdoor types with the money to indulge their tastes. Emma's not much of a swimmer, and she's never rafted down a river in her life, nor felt the slightest urge to. But she can't let her man down in front of his friends, so there she is, and there are the boats, not the four-person raft she'd anticipated but two separate rafts, one for Kip and Jane, the other for Emma and Roger.

Roger helps her strap on her life jacket. Then he grabs the straps and pulls her close. She feels the heat of his body. Three months married, and Emma still can't believe her luck.

"You can do this," he says sternly. "This is fun."

"Piecea cake," says she, who was raised on the credo of the city child: Never show fear. Roger takes the rear and puts her on point. They paddle around the boat-launch area and he shows her how to steer by shifting her oar from side to side. It seems simple enough; it seems doable. They set off downriver, with Kip and Jane leading.

For a long while the river runs wide and slow, and Emma begins to enjoy herself, raising her head to the sun, watching the woods slip past. Then Kip, in the rear of his raft, turns around, smiles and flashes the thumbs-up sign. Emma looks beyond him. The river narrows ahead. The raft picks up speed. They go around a bend and suddenly the water is choppy with white spume, littered with protruding boulders. "Oh my God," she screams. "Follow them!" Roger yells. The river hurls them toward the boulders, any one of which will certainly break their bones if they hit it. Emma paddles furiously, first obeying Roger's shouted instructions—"Hard left! Now right!"—then anticipating them.

Through some miracle they get through the rapids without bashing into anything. Kip and Jane are waiting in calm water on the far side. They're laughing. Emma's shaking with delayed fear and excitement. Less than a minute from start to finish, but God, what a minute, what a rush.

They pull up alongside the other boat. Kip and Jane reach across the water and pound her back and shoulders. "Nice going!" they cry. "Well done!"

Roger slides over and hugs her. "See what you can do when you have no choice? Remind me never to get in your way."

The house is quiet, drugged with sleep. It's a false quiet, though, like the calm of the river before the rapids.

Emma gets up and walks barefoot out into the hall. She presses her ear to the door of the guest room. Hearing nothing, she enters silently. Maggie sleeps as she always has, curled up on her side with her fist pressed to her mouth. She has the look of one abducted, not seduced, into sleep: Her sheets are twisted, her quilt is awry. Shame on Roger for dragging her into this, Emma thinks. It wasn't kindly done. Maggie can't help, however much she wants to. All she can do is worry.

Emma untangles the quilt and spreads it over Maggie, who stirs but does not wake. She pushes back a twist of hair that has fallen over one eye. Maggie was fifteen when their parents died, Emma nineteen. The difference seemed enormous then. Though it has narrowed over time, Emma still feels very much the older sister.

Not that Maggie reciprocates. Maggie is and has

always been certain she knows best. You bail, she'd said, as if it were self-evident. Leave. Run like a rabbit and don't look back. And maybe she's right, maybe running is the sensible response. Yet the more she says it, the more determined Emma grows in opposition. Because it's easy for Maggie to say, leave it; she cares nothing for this house or any other. Maggie leads a gypsy life, migrating from camp to camp. In the past ten years, she has lived in six apartments. Sublets, most of them, some quite nice. Flat-sitting when she's lucky; colleagues on sabbatical, that sort of thing. Once she lived with a man; that lasted six months. Stability supplied by her office at the university, which houses her papers and books. As for personal belongings, Maggie boasts of owning nothing she can't fit into two trunks.

A dreadful waste of energy, Emma thinks, all that searching and moving, packing and unpacking; but for Maggie it's a matter of principle, a way of staying light and unencumbered. Whereas Emma, even as a child, showed strong nesting instincts. Not the sort of person to whom you give a house, then snatch it away; let alone this house, which fits her like a second skin. Why *should* she leave, after all? It's her house now. True, she was slow to claim it, she resisted at the start; but it's very much her house now. Why should she walk away?

She's not going anywhere, not without a fight at least. But Emma wonders how to fight what she cannot even see.

She leaves the room and turns aside. Zack's door is ajar. Casey hears her come in, wags his tail but doesn't get up. He's lying on Zack's Dallas Cowboys blanket, which Zack has as usual kicked off. Emma tugs at the blanket till Casey reluctantly cedes it. She covers her son. Moonlight falls on his face. Such a beautiful face, she thinks, and bends to kiss his brow.

As soon as she reenters the hall, she knows it has changed. Everything looks the same, but something is different. She'd thought the house silent before, but she didn't know what silence was until this moment. It's as if all sound has been vacuumed out. There's a resonance to this hush, a pointedness, almost a focus. Like the inside of a cresting wave, it is charged with potential.

She creeps along the edges of the hall to her own door, behind which lies her husband and safety. She clasps the doorknob, and then the sound comes. Out of nowhere comes the distinctive *clunk clunk clunk* of something heavy falling downstairs, a dozen or more quick, loud, descending bumps; then silence.

Emma freezes. The sound came, unmistakably, from her right, from the door that leads to the tower stairs. She dares a quick look behind her. No sign of anyone else. But how could they have slept through such a racket?

She can turn the knob in her hand and be safe in her bedroom. She can wake Roger, and he will comfort her. He will look behind the door so she will not have to.

But what if he does, and there is nothing to see? Then he will add aural hallucinations to the list he is compiling, in which case he might as well scrawl QED at the bottom. No, Emma decides. She'll do it herself. But she doesn't move.

Something cold and wet touches her hand. Emma starts, but it's only Casey. The dog leans against her leg, head low, neck outstretched, tail tucked between his legs. He's staring at the door at the end of the hall. Emma kneads the thick ruff of fur around his neck, inordinately pleased to see him. "You heard it, too, didn't you, buddy? Good boy. Come."

With her hand on his neck she can feel the fear coursing through him, but to her surprise the dog cleaves resolutely to her side as she approaches the door to the spiral-stair corridor. With her hand on the knob she hesitates. It has occurred to her that she is in a perfect lose-lose situation. Nothing she can find behind this door is going to make her happy, including nothing, which is probably the best she can hope for.

Casey looks up, whines expectantly.

"Okay, okay," she says. "Keep your hair shirt on."

Emma opens the door. Staircase and corridor are illuminated from above by the moonlit library. She can see at a glance that the hall is empty.

10

MAGGIE ORDERS a double black espresso, earning a nod of approval from the Starbucks altar boy. He recognizes Emma and greets her with a marked diminution of enthusiasm. "Let me guess: house brew?"

Emma orders espresso to spite him. They find a quiet table by the window and sit down.

Maggie nods toward the counter. "Does that kid have something against you?"

"Nah, he's just a coffee snob. House brew doesn't cut it."

"Well," says Maggie, who supports an eight-cup-a-day caffeine habit, "it *is* a bit like ordering Dubonnet with a twist in a trucker's bar." She's dressed for work in a charcoal suit with a pencil skirt and black stockings, severe yet sexy. Emma feels a prime suburban frump in jeans and a pink sweatshirt. The shirt, a gift from Roger and Zack, reads, "If Mama ain't happy, ain't nobody happy."

Roger took an earlier train, and Zack is in school. The sisters have half an hour before Maggie's train takes her back to the city for her twelve o'clock class. "I wish I could stay longer," she says for the third time.

"It's okay," Emma says. "I'm fine."

"You don't look fine. In fact, you look like shit."

"Thank you so much."

"Bad night?"

Emma looks at her, then down at the table. She doesn't want to tell Maggie about last night. What's the point, she asks herself. Who does it help? But the fear is so great inside her, it exerts so much pressure, she doesn't trust herself to speak.

"What?" Maggie says.

"Nothing."

"Don't nothing me, girl."

Emma slides her chair closer to Maggie's. "Promise you won't laugh if I ask you something?"

"Try me."

"Do you believe in ghosts?"

Maggie leans back and looks at her. "I don't believe you're asking me that. We hearing bumps in the night now?"

"So you didn't hear anything?"

"Like what?" says Maggie.

"Like something heavy crashing down the tower stairs."

"Get out! When?"

"Late last night."

"You were dreaming."

"I was wide awake," Emma says firmly.

"What'd you do?"

"Went and looked. Nothing there."

"Jesus," Maggie breathes, her face pale in the fluo-rescent light. "Catch me sleeping under your roof again."

"Thought you don't believe in ghosts."

"I don't, but. You know, Em, this whole thing is start-ing to sound like one of your books."

"That's what Roger says."

"Or that movie, what's it called? The revival we saw at the Paris? With Ingrid Bergman."

"*Gaslight?*"

"That's the one."

"I don't think so. In *Gaslight* it turns out to be the husband who's behind it."

"Whatever," Maggie says. "Any way you look at it, it's all the more reason to bail the fuck out."

"We've had this conversation."

"Obviously it didn't take. You are so damn stubborn!"

"*I'm* stubborn?"

It's an old argument. They look at each other and laugh the kind of laugh that's half sigh.

They walk to the train station. As the train pulls in, Emma leans toward her sister for their usual peck good-bye. Instead, Maggie hugs her tight. "Call any time," she says in her ear.

"I will. Don't worry."

"Don't cut me out."

"Go already," says Emma, and gives her a push.

*   *   *

A FINE, BRISK DAY. Wind from the north; the air smells of brine. Emma's in no hurry to return home. Work is out of the question; today is a day to recoup, to gather her wits and think things through. A day to indulge herself. She walks slowly from the station, up the hilly cobblestone road that is Morgan Peak's Main Street. Checks out the storefronts, stops in a bakery for a loaf of corn rye and a blueberry pie. The clerk is young, cheerful and chatty. "Have a nice day," she tinkles as Emma leaves. Next door is an art gallery featuring an exhibit of book illustrations. She considers going in, decides to return sometime with Zack. Then she comes to the library.

She has not yet set foot in the library. For weeks it's been on her list of things to do: She needs to apply for a card, scope out the reference facilities. In addition, there's a piece of research she's been meaning to get to—an unexceptionable excuse to malinger.

The library is housed in a large stone edifice, vaguely Gothic in aspect, set back from the street and raised above it by six wide marble steps. Just inside the entrance is a circular check-out desk staffed by bustling women, rather like a nurses' station. To the right is a children's room, to the left, the fiction stacks, where Emma is cheered to find two of her older books and a copy of her latest on the "Recent Releases" shelf. At the far end of the stacks she emerges into an open area of tables and chairs, presided over by the research librarian's desk in the corner.

The man behind the desk looks like no librarian she's ever seen. A regular Adonis, her mother would have called him; Emma imagines that the teenage girls of Morgan Peak must make assiduous use of the library.

He's a young guy, mid-twenties perhaps, with wide shoulders and a massive neck, black hair, blue eyes, and a square chin shadowed by a day's stubble. His hands dwarf the book he's holding. He looks up as she approaches. "Hi, can I help you?"

"I'm doing some research on a family that used to live here," Emma says. "I wondered if you could suggest some resources."

"Sure." He marks his spot in the book, closes it, and swivels toward his computer. "What's the family's name?"

"Hysop."

He looks more closely at her. "Welcome to Morgan Peak, Ms. Roth."

Does she know him? No, she'd remember. "How do you know my name?"

"Small town. I heard the Hysop place went to a writer. Figured you'd turn up here sooner or later. We've got a whole bunch of writers living in the village."

Emma checks the nameplate on his desk and ratchets up her smile a notch. A well-disposed research librarian is a writer's best friend, as essential as ink. "Then I'm surprised at your welcoming another. You may come to regret it, Mr. Harris; I am forever needing help."

"It's Jeff," he says.

"Emma." She holds out her hand, which he shakes without rising. "Pleased to meet you," he says, and sounds it. "The Hysop family were longtime local residents, so your best bet's probably the *Morgan Peak Observer*; and after that *Newsday*. They're both available on microfilm, and the *MPO* has an index. *Newsday* does, too, of course, but they make you pay to use it. You could also try the Long Island Studies Institute over at Hofstra. They've got a special genealogy section and a huge collection of Long Island newspapers going back well over a hundred years."

Emma asks to start with the *Morgan Peak Observer*. Jeff rings a bell on his desk and in a moment a teenage page is dispatched to fetch the *MPO* reels. "Do you know how to use the microfilm machine?" Jeff asks.

"I've used them before. I'll figure it out."

"Ours is a little tricky. I'll show you when the kid brings the films."

Moments later the boy is back with a stack of six reel boxes. It's only then, as the librarian emerges from behind his desk, that Emma realizes he is in a wheelchair.

He shows her how to work the machine, then withdraws. In the index, Emma finds three references to Hysop, one for Arthur, two for Virginia.

Arthur's is an obituary. Arthur Hysop, distinguished educator, beloved husband of Virginia, died October 21, 1991, at the age of seventy-one. Cause of death "a long illness"; cancer, no doubt. The more recent of the two articles on Virginia Hysop is dated November 3, 1997, half a year before Emma and Roger bought her house, and it, too, is an obituary. Mrs. Hysop is described rather tersely as a former teacher at Morgan Peak High School, seventy-five years old at the time of her death. Cause of death an accident, unspecified.

Emma wonders what kind of accident. Auto, perhaps; people that age make dangerous drivers. Or some sort of household mishap, the kind common to elderly people living alone. She thinks about the stain at the foot of the library stairs, the crashing sounds last night, and a chill runs through her veins.

The earlier article, dated June 29, 1989, announces

Mrs. Hysop's retirement from Morgan Peak High School after forty-five years as an English teacher. "Mrs. Hysop was the guest of honor at a farewell banquet given by the English department. The dinner, at Morgan Peak Hall, was attended by many notable former students, including Dr. George DeSica, principal of the high school, and Mr. Henry Larkin, chairman of the Morgan Peak School Board. Asked to sum up her career, Mrs. Hysop replied succinctly, 'Short but sweet.' "

That's it: three articles. Not much for two lifetimes of work. Strange that the paper didn't report Mrs. Hysop's fatal accident. A teacher for forty-five years: She must have known and been known by the entire town.

"How're you making out?" says a voice behind her.

Emma swivels and finds herself knee to knee with the librarian. "Not great. I don't suppose you happened to know Virginia Hysop?"

"Hell, yeah," he says feelingly. "Had her my senior year in high school. Last year she taught; just my luck."

"Tough teacher?" Emma asks.

He snorts. "I've known football coaches who were softer. She had a real bug about grammar and punctuation. Woman would crucify you for a missing comma. Scared the dangling participles out of me, I'll tell you that."

"You didn't like her."

"Not at the time. In retrospect, though? At least she cared. So many just phone it in. That one came to teach, and God help you if you weren't there to learn."

Emma smiles. "Not a bad epitaph for a teacher. I was surprised by how little coverage there was in the local paper, considering how well-known she was. The obituary mentioned that she died of an accident, but there was no report of the accident."

"Not surprising. The *Observer*'s motto is 'All the news that's nice to print.' "

"What happened to her?"

He hesitates.

"Please. I want to know."

"There was an accident," he says, looking away. "She fell down some stairs."

She nods as if she's known it all along, which in a way she has. "Who found her?"

"The police. Eventually."

Eventually. What a lot of pain and suffering can fit into a word. Did the old lady die instantly, or did she lie there, helpless and alone, until the end came? Emma can't bring herself to ask.

THE PHONE is ringing as she walks through the kitchen door. Emma submits to Casey's boisterous greeting, drops her bags on the table, and plucks the cordless phone from its mount. "Hello?"

"Emma, my love! Playing hooky, are we?"

"Hey, Arthur," she says. Cradling the phone between her ear and shoulder, she pours herself a cup of coffee and settles down by the fireplace for a talk. Her editor doesn't call frequently—she hasn't heard from him since the housewarming—but when he does, the conversations tend to be long and gossipy.

"You've been on my mind," he says. "How are things going?"

Emma's guilty conscience translates this civil inquiry into *How's the book going?* "A little behind schedule," she says defensively, "but moving ahead."

"No doubt the move set you back."

"You could say that," she says; then, conscious of a certain wryness to her tone, asks, "So tell me, are you and Alison back on line?"

"Sadly, no." He sighs. "This time she seems determined to destroy our happy home."

"Happier for you than for her, apparently."

"*Et tu*, Emma?"

"I really am sorry," she says, swallowing a laugh.

"So am I, for all the good it does me. The woman is relentless. And to make matters worse, I have gotten absolutely nowhere with that wench of Roger's. I begin to fear I am losing my touch."

"India is Roger's assistant, not his 'wench.' "

"Whatever. Couldn't you put in a good word for me, Emma?"

"I could put in a true word."

"Now that is unkind. And I rather think we share a common interest there."

Coolly, she asks, "What would that be?"

"Well," says Arthur, "once she has sampled my charms, she's hardly likely to go on making sheep's eyes at your husband, is she? Not to cast any aspersions on Roger, of course."

"Of course."

There's a brief pause. She hears him sipping something. "Ah well," he says, "if you won't, you won't. Never mind my troubles; tell me about yours. How are you adjusting to life in the provinces?"

"Early days yet. It has its points."

"And that wonderfully eerie old house of yours? Any skeletons turn up in the attic?"

"The house," she says, "is just a house." But she lowers her voice, as if it might hear.

"You sound nervous. Why do I get the feeling you're holding out on me?"

"I'm not," she says.

Silence. Arthur is good at silences.

"It's an old house," Emma says defensively. "All old houses have noises. It just takes getting used to."

"I knew it," Arthur purrs. "Come on, Emma. Tell Uncle Arthur all about it."

She's tempted. Arthur's a great listener, a gift that serves both his craft and his arrested-adolescent libido. But if she tells all, he will think her mad. All those strange little incidents, each a minor puzzle in its own right, taken together form an ominous cloud. And none of them witnessed by anyone other than Emma! How can she help but feel singled out? But the delusion of persecution is the sine qua non of paranoia, the very emblem of insanity. If she tells him everything that's happened, Arthur will exclaim in wonder, he will exude sympathy; but the moment he hangs up, he will buzz his secretary and say, "Lilith, we need to fill a hole in the spring schedule. Emma Roth has lost her marbles." And who can blame him?

"Emma," he says, "I'm waiting."

"There was a noise last night," she says. "Huge crash, like something falling down the stairs from my office. This morning I did some research. Guess what I found out?"

"Do tell."

"The previous owner died falling down a flight of stairs."

Another silence, then Arthur says, "Emma, love, I'm going to make a *shidduch*. Remember the psychic I told you about, Ida Green? I'm putting you two together. You'll enjoy her, Emma, and I assure you she's the real thing. If anyone can suss out this ghost of yours, she can."

Emma's reply is automatic. "You know I don't believe in ghosts, except as plot devices."

"I know you've always said so," says Arthur in the tone of one making a distinction. "Though you certainly write them convincingly. Anyway, love, what have you got to lose?"

It is a telling sign of Emma's distress that she allows herself to be persuaded. If nothing else, she tells Arthur, the experience will be useful. She's never seen a psychic in action. Emma does quail a bit at the prospect of telling Roger; but didn't he himself say they must consider all the possibilities?

LATER, STILL MALINGERING, Emma decides to go down to the beach. It's not much of a beach, really, more a rocky alcove between the bay and the bluff leading up to her house. She sits Indian style, her back against a rock, a fresh notebook on her knee, while Casey frolics beside the water, barking indignantly as the waves lap his paws. The afternoon is brisk, but Emma is dressed for the chill in a tan anorak she's purloined from Roger.

Before he hung up, Arthur had offered some parting advice. "Write it all down, Emma," he said. "Keep a journal. Document *everything*. If I know writers, which I do, you'll thank me someday."

It's not as if he'd suggested a naked stroll through the village; writing things down is second nature for Emma.

She begins with a question—"What the hell is going on?"—and a list of three possible answers. "Poss. #1: There's something in the house." By something she means a ghost, though she can't bring herself to call it that. Because even if ghosts exist, which they don't, how likely is it that she of all people should acquire one? If this were fiction it would be pulp fiction, resting as it does on the sort of coincidence that sets critics howling. But it sounds more like something dreamed up by an overzealous flack.

Nevertheless, Emma is committed to leaving no stone unturned, no explanation unexplored. And she has the advantage of knowing the genre. The conventions of ghost stories are the parameters within which she works; the traditions, the folklore, the literature of "true encounters" are the palette from which she concocts her fiction. In short, she knows the form; and the more she thinks about it, the more her experience seems to fit the mold. She runs through the indications: the fact that nothing of a similar nature occurred before they moved here; the inexplicable sounds corresponding to the house's history of sudden traumatic death; the recurrent sensation of an unseen presence in the library; the cold spot at the foot of the steps; even the dog's aversion to the spot, all classic signs of haunting.

And then there's the house itself, big and old and isolated, a house that, as Arthur said, cries out for a ghost, a house that would surely top the wish list of every discerning spirit: the ghostly equivalent of a three-bedroom rent-controlled apartment on the Upper West Side. If this were fiction, there would be no doubt but that this house was haunted. But Emma is not convinced. Real life is so much messier than fiction that haunting seems too tidy an explanation to be true.

Casey runs up, crouches at her feet and barks an invitation to play. Emma takes his ball from her pocket, lets him sniff it, and chucks it down the beach. The dog leaps off in pursuit and she returns to her list.

"Poss. #2: Someone is targeting me." The most favored hypothesis, though how it could be carried out Emma cannot begin to imagine. The advantage of this explanation is that it accounts for the personal nature of the incidents, as the first cannot. Ghosts, by all accounts, do not target individual people; they offend simply by existing.

It would explain something else, too. Not all, but some of the incidents have reeked of malice. The message, "Something's happened to the boy," was meant to frighten. Worse yet was yesterday's invasion of her manuscript. It strikes her as a kind of rape, a way of attacking from the inside. There was a creepy sort of intimacy to it; she'd felt as if unseen hands were touching her beneath her clothes. These are not acts of haunting, but of hatred.

But if there is a real person behind all these manifestations, it would have to be someone with access to her computer, probably with access to the house: by implication, someone close to her. This is something her imagination refuses to encompass. No one close to her would do this, thinks Emma, which leads her to her third and final hypothesis:

"Poss. #3: I'm losing my mind."

Painful even to contemplate, but she has to consider a possibility that, looked at from the outside, is by far the most likely of the lot. After all, there is a history; Emma has been there. That door is closed, but it doesn't lock. She'd have to be crazy *not* to consider the possibility that she's crazy.

Everything that has happened has seemed as real to

her as the beach she's sitting on, as solid as the rock behind her back; but isn't that the nature of hallucination, to seem real? When she was sick before, she didn't realize how sick she was. She kept denying and denying, going through the motions of her life like a wind-up toy, until suddenly she couldn't anymore and she just stopped. If Emma is delusional now, she wouldn't know she was delusional; she would think everything was real. She would conclude that either her house was haunted or someone was targeting her.

Emma rereads the first two entries on her list and snaps the notebook shut. She hugs her knees and rests her chin on them. What if it's true? she wonders. What if I hallucinated the noise last night and the message in the hearts game? What if I put those words into my characters' mouths, called myself a talentless hack and cried for a way out, then forgot I did it? What if I imagined the cough in the library and the feeling of someone reading over my shoulder?

Why then, she thinks, I'd be mad, totally, hopelessly psychotic.

She's not. Deep inside she knows she's not. But then what *is* going on? Tears well up in her eyes, tears of self-pity and frustration. After a moment's woeful indulgence, she dries her face on her sleeve, gets up, and picks her way to the water's edge. Today the bay is emerald green, the surface lightly shirred by an off-shore breeze. Casey comes bounding up. He nuzzles her hand with his velvet nose and she bends down to embrace him, burying her face in his thick ruff. Sitting on a boulder, Emma removes her sneakers and socks and rolls up the legs of her jeans. Then she gets up and wades into the water.

It's freezing. She has to stop herself from jumping

back. The cold is eminently real. The tingling shock it produces in her feet and calves is real. The pebbles underfoot, the dog pacing anxiously behind her, the bright September sky, the tang of saltwater in her nostrils: all real. Emma, too, is real; she is herself, the same self all the time. No stranger dwells within. The cold water clarifies all; her thoughts are washed clean of self-doubt, her will strengthened.

CAROLINE MARKS, sensibly dressed in Timberland boots, Levi's, and an L.L. Bean lumber jacket, clambers onto the rock jetty that divides Emma's beach from its neighbor in time to see Emma step into the water. Emma has removed her shoes and rolled up her pants legs, but to Caroline's mind she's picked a cold day to go wading. Emma takes another step, and water swirls around her calves. Caroline considers calling out, but thinks better of it. Emma's eyes are open, but she has a sleepwalker's look about her. Then the dog begins to bark and Emma turns around.

Caroline waves.

They meet halfway. "Great day for a walk," she says.

"Beautiful." Emma is smiling, but Caroline can see from her eyes that she's been crying. It's not the first time she's come across Emma looking distraught. Perhaps it's time to reach out.

"Right now," Caroline says, "I crave a really hot cup of coffee. Can I interest you in some?"

"I'd like that," Emma says. "Why don't we go to my house? I have a pot on."

The path up the bluff is narrow, so they climb single file, first Caroline, then Emma, with Casey at her heels. Emma carries her notebook in one hand and her socks in the other. Her feet are wet and squish unpleasantly inside her sneakers, but she hardly notices, for she's deep in thought. Caroline's fortuitous appearance has given her an idea. Emma desperately needs to talk things through with someone. Roger and Maggie are disqualified by love; they are too close, too vulnerable. Arthur is her friend but also her editor; she has a business relationship to protect there. But Caroline Marks is a stranger, impartial and unprejudiced; she is, moreover, a trained psychologist. If the worst is true and Emma is crazy, Caroline would know.

They reach the house and enter through the kitchen door. Emma gives Casey a fresh bowl of water. She pours two cups of coffee and carries them over to the kitchen table.

Caroline hangs her jacket on the back of a chair and sits down. "Your feet must be frozen," she says. "Why don't you put on something dry? The coffee will wait."

Emma leaves her and goes upstairs. She dries her feet and slips on the shearling moccasins Roger gave her last winter. When she returns to the kitchen she notices Caroline hasn't touched her cup. "You shouldn't have waited for me," she says.

"Do you have any sugar?"

"Oh, sorry!" Emma takes the sugar bowl from the cupboard and a quart of milk from the fridge and brings both to the table. As Caroline lifts the lid of the bowl, movement from within it catches both their eyes. It's a squirming, primordial sort of motion, so incongruous in the context of a sugar bowl that comprehension falters. Moments later, two shrill screams rent the air.

The sugar bowl is alive with worms, fat, ugly, blood-red worms, coursing through the sugar.

Caroline's hand arches away from the bowl, and the

lid flies across the room and shatters against the fireplace. She presses her hand to her chest, backs away. The worms are beginning to crawl out of the bowl and drop onto the table. She looks at Emma. The younger woman is pale as death, swaying on her feet. Seeing that she is about to faint, Caroline hurries to her side, puts a strong arm around her shoulders, and leads her to a seat by the fireplace. She pushes her head down to her knees, then goes back and deals with the worms. She sweeps them, bowl and all, into a trash can, then ties up the bag and dumps it outside. She gathers up the pieces of lid. When these, too, are disposed of, she joins Emma, who sits hunched over with her hands between her knees.

"Those were bait worms," Caroline says. "The kind you buy for fishing."

Emma does not reply.

Caroline takes her left hand and presses it between her palms. The hand is icy. "Emma," she says, in a firm, calm voice, "tell me what's going on. Who did this?"

"I don't know." Emma raises her face. Her skin is pallid, with the waxy sheen of fake fruit, and her eyes are black holes. "You saw those worms?"

"Of course I saw them."

"Thank God," she says.

11

EMMA FEELS she's reached a turning point. She's a burst pipe, a spewing volcano of words. Like a woman in the final throes of labor, she is without inhibition.

Until now she's revealed only bits and pieces of her story to three different people, holding back more than she told. When you can't hold back any longer, it's such a blessed relief to let go.

The story pours out, unorganized, chaotic, heedless of chronology. Still talking, she leads Caroline through the house. She shows her the stain under the carpet. Together they mount the winding stairs to the library. There Emma tells about the cough, the feeling of someone standing close behind, reading her work.

Caroline's astonishment is unfeigned. Whatever she expected, it is not this. She listens to the account of Mrs. Hysop's death with a frown of concentration. Emma is grateful for her focused intelligence and for the chance encounter that produced not only a witness but a confidante as well. At last, she thinks, an ally. Then she is ashamed, for what are Roger and Maggie if not her allies?

At last the spate of words trickles to a halt. Depleted, Emma sprawls in her armchair and waits for a response that is long in coming.

"I'm at a disadvantage here," Caroline says at last. "I don't believe in ghosts."

"Me neither," Emma says quickly, though she can't keep from tensing as she says it.

"I wish I could believe in an afterlife; no doubt it would be comforting. But it's not in me to believe."

"So what do you think is going on?" Emma searches her face.

"I'd *like* to think you're trying out the plot of your latest book on me."

"I'm not."

"I know." Caroline sighs. "It's very strange."

Emma gathers her courage and says with a little laugh, "If you think I'm crazy, just say so."

Caroline raises her eyebrows. "Do *you* think you're crazy?"

"No. A little freaked, maybe."

"Sounds appropriate to me."

"So you don't think I'm imagining it all? Projecting or whatever?"

"You didn't project those worms." Caroline's face is grim. "What does your husband say?"

"He's perplexed." Emma lowers her eyes, but feels the other woman's clear-eyed gaze eating into her.

"Was that his idea? Did *he* suggest you imagined these things?"

"Roger's a scientist. He says we have to consider all possibilities."

"I see," says Caroline.

"Yo, Mom! Guess what we're doing in gym!"

"What?"

"Soccer!"

"Oh, so you get to strut your stuff, huh?"

"You bet!" With Casey capering at his side, Zack does his sideways Egyptian strut down the hall toward the kitchen. He halts in mid-step as Caroline appears on the staircase.

"Hello, Zack," she says.

"Oh. Hi, Caroline." She said to call her that and dutifully, he does; but he thinks of her as Dr. Marks, or the tenant. Zack's surprised to see her here, not altogether pleased. He's used to having his mother to himself when he comes home from school; he prefers it that way. And Dr. Marks is no Aunt Maggie. She's not mean or anything, she just doesn't engage. He guesses she's a grown-up's grown-up, the way coffee is a grown-up's drink: what his mom calls an acquired taste.

"I'd better be going," she says.

His mother grasps her hand. "Thank you," she says. "For *everything*."

"For nothing. I hate to . . ." Caroline's eyes flicker at Zack, then cut back to his mother. "Why don't we talk tomorrow?"

"Yes, please," says his mother, in such a heartfelt tone that Zack's ears perk up and he looks from one to the other. What gives?

But Zack doesn't have time to think about that now. He's got soccer practice, and Coach Sanders as good as promised them a scrimmage today.

YOLANDA'S ON the field taking pictures when they enter the park; Emma hardly recognizes her in sweatpants. Yolanda waves but stays where she is, shooting the goalie as he fields practice shots. Nick Sanders is on the sideline holding court among the soccer moms. Pea coats and jeans are the uniform of the day, Emma notes; she's got it wrong again, swathed in Roger's bulky anorak. How do they manage the unanimity? Is there some kind of dress code she's not clued in to? Then Sanders's roving eye falls on Zack and Emma. Forsaking the others, he lopes over to greet them.

"Hey, buddy," he says, holding out his hand to Zack. "Gimme two laps."

"Just two?" scoffs Zack.

"Wise guy. Just for that, give me three."

Zack takes off around the field, and Nick turns to Emma. "Great kid," he says.

"Thanks."

"I bless the day you moved here, you and Zack. Your husband now, him I could live without."

Emma looks at him in amazement.

Sanders winks. "Just kidding."

She smiles vapidly and walks away, her usual line of defense with Nick. But he turns and walks with her. "Staying for practice?" he asks.

"I might. Do you mind?"

"On the contrary, I'm all for it. Though my concentration suffers."

"Then maybe I should stay away."

"Now *that* would be distracting."

His smile is innocent but his eyes are bold. Emma gestures toward the field, where the boys are warming up with the assistant coach. "Shouldn't you be out there?"

"Perks of high office. Stu gets to do the stretches. So how are you settling in? No plans to move again any time soon, I hope?"

She snorts. "Not for a decade or two. I hate moving."

"Good," he says. "How does Zack like playing center half?"

"He likes it fine. It's a trade-off: He doesn't score as much, but he gets to handle the ball more."

"He doesn't score as much? He's averaging better than one a game."

"Playing striker on his last team, he averaged two."

"Huh," Nick says thoughtfully, looking toward the field. Emma takes the opportunity to escape. She heads for the bleachers. Excessively good-looking, she's thinking, and doesn't he know it. Hard to dislike him, though. Nick reminds her of Zack dancing around his room to the strains of "I'm too sexy for my shirt, too sexy!" There's a transparency to his attentions that renders them harmless in her eyes. He is not, she thinks, a serious man, just a player hoping to get lucky.

The assistant coach hands out pinnies and assigns positions. He puts Zack at center half, Dylan Sanders at striker, and Marcel on right wing. Then Nick Sanders runs out and has a word with Zack and Dylan. The two boys switch positions, Zack with alacrity, Dylan with a dirty look. The scrimmage begins. Yolanda hangs in at first, running parallel to the ball handler, snapping pictures as she goes. Ten minutes of that and she staggers off the field to Emma's side.

"Shit," she says, panting. She bends over with hands on knees, camera dangling from her neck. "I have got to quit smoking."

Emma, pleased that they're past the hi-how-are-you stage, asks what she is doing.

"What's it look like I'm doing, girl, baking cookies?"

"Not exactly."

Yolanda tugs a pack of Camels out of her pants pocket, lights one, and draws as if pulling on an oxygen mask. "That's better. What I'm doing is, I'm thinking of doing some soccer paintings. Maybe a series of 'em." She glances sideways at Emma. "What's that sound like to you—suburban brain rot?"

"Well, it's different," says Emma, surprised. She'd taken Yolanda for a serious painter. Would this happen to her, too, given time?

They pause to watch the scrimmage. Zack's running with the ball. He fakes out the sweeper and shoots for the far post. The goalie dives onto the ball. Zack slaps his thigh in frustration, then flashes the goalie a thumbs-up.

"Prom king's up to his old tricks, I notice," Yolanda says, nodding toward Nick.

"Well, he's an old dog, isn't he?"

"Better watch yourself, girl."

"Yeah, I'm shaking." Their eyes meet, and a smile pulls at the corners of Yolanda's mouth. Emma, treading carefully, says, "Can I ask, why soccer?"

Yolanda shrugs, looks away. "It's the faces. All that intense concentration on such young faces."

Which Emma instantly understands, having seen this look herself and wished she could capture it in words. There are times when a player's body and mind are so aligned that they function as one. At such moments, a kicked ball seems willed into the goal, ordained for the net, its arc predestined and beautiful.

She'd once asked Zack what he felt as he watched a shot of his sail into the net. "Nothing," he'd replied. "I just stand there and watch it fly."

An answer made interesting by the fact that it's untrue. Zack has been too well schooled in following his shots to stand still and watch anything; the moment he kicks the shot he's off, charging the goalie. Yet it seems that even as his body automatically positions itself for a rebound, his awareness remains fixed on the ball's trajectory through space.

The illusion that one is a bystander watching things unfold inevitably is familiar to Emma from her work, those blessed moments when her story's momentum allows it to roll forward seemingly of its own accord. Inspiration, she has found, is largely a function of momentum; which seems also to be the case for Zack, who, if allowed free rein with the ball for ten or fifteen yards, builds up such a head of steam he's nearly impossible to stop.

It's all about choices, his work and hers. Every time the ball comes near Zack, he's faced with a series of decisions. Writing's the same. What seems like a continuous story line is actually a myriad of discrete points, each a potential turning point. A story is the sum of its author's choices, its parameters defined by the paths not taken. Completed, a story appears to follow its own inexorable trajectory, but that seeming inevitability is not real; it is art's illusion.

ROGER COMES home late that night. "Departmental meeting," he says. "Did I forget to mention it? Sorry, darling." Emma reheats his dinner and waits till he finishes eating before she tells him about the worms.

He listens grimly. When she is done he says, "I took sugar this morning. There were no worms."

"Caroline dumped them outside in the trash. Go see for yourself."

"Caroline Marks?"

"We met on the beach and came back here for coffee. She saw them, too."

"Was she alone in the kitchen?" he asks.

Emma stares. "For a second, while I ran upstairs to change my shoes. Are you suggesting she did it?"

"How did she react?"

"Screamed; we both did. She threw the lid against the wall. Then she got rid of the worms, cleaned up the mess. Gave me coffee and made me drink it. Talked to me." Her voice quavers.

"And you to her," Roger says with open disapproval.

Emma doesn't like his tone. There's a fight on the horizon. She gets up and checks the hall. Zack's supposed to be upstairs doing homework, but the boy moves through the house like an Iroquois through ancestral woods. "Yes, I did," she says, returning to the table. "And you know what? It felt damn good."

Roger chooses his words carefully. "If you need to talk to someone, that's fine; I'm all for it. But let's find a professional, someone who can really help."

"I don't need a shrink," Emma says stiffly. "I need a friend."

"But why her?"

"Why not her?"

"I don't care for the woman. She has cold eyes."

"You don't care for her because she jumped down your throat the night of the housewarming."

"That, too," he concedes with an air of impartiality.

"You stepped on her toes, Roger. She spends her professional life trying to get victims to stop blaming themselves, and you come along and blame them."

"I wasn't—"

"I know. But that's how she heard it. You stepped on her toes, and she shoved back. Get over it."

"Still leaves the cold eyes." He stares down at his white-knuckled hands. His voice comes out a bitter staccato. "It makes no sense. I can't find the handle. Who would do this to us?" He glances at his watch and jumps up, reaching for the leather jacket slung over the back of his chair. "I'll be right back."

He doesn't say where he's going and she's too proud to ask. She begins clearing the table. By the time she finishes loading the dishwasher he's back, carrying a small brown paper bag with "Home Depot" printed on it. "New lock for the French doors," he says. "I changed all the others when we moved in."

Emma follows him into the living room and flops down on the couch. She watches him work. He has long, deft, patient hands, good for changing locks, good for making love. Which they haven't done for some time now. Lately, either she's too nervous or he's too tired.

Or maybe he's getting it somewhere else. No sooner does the thought occur than she repudiates it as nonsense, a passing notion born of air and low spirits, signifying nothing. Roger would never do that to her.

There is anger in the set of his neck, the overly precise movements of his hands. She understands how hard this is for him, how humiliating. One night, early in their marriage, they were walking up Columbus Avenue when suddenly they heard gunshots. Thirty yards ahead, two young men burst out of a grocery shop. One turned and ran to the right, the other to the left, directly at them. On their heels came the store owner, an old man in a white apron waving a large black gun. That's all Emma saw, because at that moment Roger grabbed her and swung her around, imposing his body between her and the store owner. He shoved her down onto the pavement and hurled himself on top of her. She heard two shots, and footsteps pounding past; she caught a fleeting glimpse of high-top sneakers, and then it was over. Roger helped her up. "Are you all right?" he asked. She nodded. He put his arms around her. They went home and made love. Zack was conceived that night.

Roger can't protect her this time, and it eats at him. So he looks for something he can do, like change a lock. He attacks a stubborn screw as if it were the enemy; he wrests the old lock out of its casing and slaps the new one in with a grunt of satisfaction. She is glad if it eases his mind at all; but to her it's just busywork. Whatever the source of their problem, Emma can't see one lock more or less making the difference.

12

"SUGAR?" ASKS Caroline.

" 'Do I dare to eat a peach?' " Emma says with a smile. "Yes, please." This is the first time she has been inside the carriage house since Caroline took possession. The kitchen is furnished in basic Ikea: a white laminate table, pine chairs with tapered legs, white cups and dishes, Swedish-looking stainless steel cutlery. No pictures on the wall, no clutter on the counters, no frills and no fabric, not even on the windows, which are covered with louvered shades of narrow pine slats. There is nothing old or used here, nothing that looks like it came from her past life. The effect is neat to the point of starkness; efficient, impersonal, remarkable only in how little it reveals.

The only book in sight is a paperback collection of plays by Euripides, lying on the chair beside Emma's. She picks it up, and it opens to the first page of *Medea*. Emma shudders. She hasn't read the play since college, but a woman who carves up her two sons and feeds them to her faithless husband is not a character she is likely to forget.

"This your idea of breakfast reading?" she asks.

"Why not? I take my whiskey neat, too. Actually, I'm reading it for the center. The women have started a drama group, and I'm looking for a suitable play."

"Not *Medea?*"

Caroline smiles. "Hardly. God forbid I put ideas in anyone's head. But one of the others should do nicely. The Greeks wrote the strongest women characters ever to appear on stage. None of that 'Vengeance is mine, saith the Lord' stuff for them. Cross those women and you end up wishing you'd never been born."

"I don't know, what about Shakespeare's women? Lady Macbeth?"

"Went mad, didn't she? Blew it. Ophelia, too, *and* killed herself to boot. Bunch of victims and losers, Shakespeare's women; today they'd be on *Oprah*. Oh no, they don't hold a candle to the likes of Clytemnestra, Electra, and Cassandra."

This is a discussion that, any other time, Emma would gladly have taken up, but coming now, it fails to engage. She makes no answer; she sips her coffee and Caroline hers. Caroline is dressed for work in a pale gray-silk pants suit; her hair is pulled back and she looks professional to the point of severity

"I've been thinking about what you told me," Caroline says.

"And what have you concluded?"

"Not much, I'm afraid."

Emma lets her disappointment show.

"I want to help," Caroline says. "But I don't know enough; and one hesitates to pry."

Emma can see why: Caroline fears reciprocity. There is nothing about the woman that encourages prying. She is, like her kitchen, the soul of reticence. Emma doesn't hold it against her. She has a secret or two herself. Not everything has to be shared.

"Pry away," she says. "I won't retaliate."

Caroline gives her a quick, appraising look. "I guess the first question that occurred to me is who would want to hurt you?"

"If I knew that . . ."

"Yes, I understand. Still, even with the people we're close to, tensions sometimes arise. And most people don't go through life without making an enemy or two along the way."

Standing at a crossroads, Emma discovers that there are, after all, places she doesn't want to go. The other woman holds her in a steady gaze, looking as if she could wait all day. Emma remembers Roger's remark about cold eyes. Caroline's don't look cold to her; they look attentive, thoughtful, often kind. And yet they are the eyes of a listener who absorbs much more than she emits, one who keeps her own counsel. They remind her of Dr. Sloane, her doctor in the hospital. Emma feels the old spirit of evasion rise up within her. She says, "Roger's parents, I guess. They've never approved of me. But it couldn't be them. No access; they've never even been to the house."

"Anyone else?" Caroline asks.

"There are the nut jobs. Writers attract 'em. I've got a file full of letters from readers who accuse me of stealing their life story or conspiring with the devil, real Stephen King stuff."

"Any who wrote repeatedly? Any who phoned, or tried to meet you in person?"

"No."

Caroline gives a slight shake of her head. "We're talking major obsession here. It would almost certainly be someone you know, someone you've met at least. Is there anyone who harbors a grudge? An old boyfriend, a rival, anyone who feels wronged by you?"

So they've arrived after all. The room has taken on a striking clarity. There's a Hopperesque quality of heightened reality to the clear white lines, the swirling currents in Emma's cup, the beads of condensed steam on the rim. She has asked for Caroline's help; what's the point of doing that and then ducking her question? A dark spasm grips Emma, a warning pang, like early labor.

"There is someone," she says. "I've never even met her. But I know she hates me."

Caroline's voice is gentle. "Why does she hate you?"

"There was an accident," Emma says, looking aside. "Rainy night, wet road. Could have happened to anyone; so they say. But of course she wouldn't see it that way. Can't blame her. Look what she lost."

"What did she lose?"

"Her husband," Emma says, "and her little girl."

LATER THAT MORNING, Emma climbs the winding staircase to the library. Talking to Caroline has raised her spirits. She will not let this thing, whatever it is, beat her. Still, she is edgy enough to try with her usual lack of success to lure Casey upstairs.

She sits at her computer and looks at the blank screen, which stares back reproachfully. Behind the screen, her book awaits. Faith, half born and already asserting her independence, waits as well. Emma's not sure she can ever feel the same about the character after what she said about Emma's writing. Of course, Emma realizes it wasn't Faith herself speaking; she retains some grip on reality. But the fact that the words were put in Faith's mouth taints her voice. Emma is by birth and nature more Old Testament than New; she is a jealous creator, and wrathful. *Dis me, will you? Opt out of my book? We'll see about that. What's made can be unmade.*

She turns on the computer and immediately boots up the card program. Stupid, of course. Roger says to stay out of the program, which is like saying be someone else. Even as a kid Emma had trouble with limits. Maggie was the hellion and she was the dreamer, yet it was Emma who could never turn down a dare.

This time, though, she has come armed. Her journal and pen lay on the desk beside the computer. She chooses hearts and selects three players, Computer Nerd, Red Riding Hood, and Grandpa. One by one they appear on screen.

"Good luck," says the Nerd. "You'll need it. My name's Eli, and I'm a whiz at computer games."

"Mama told me to go straight to Granny's house," says Little Red Riding Hood, "but I guess a game or two wouldn't do any harm."

Then Grandpa, with his warm smile. "Did you ever stop to think," he says, "that every day brings us closer to death? And some of us are closer than they think."

Gasping, Emma grabs her journal and copies the words without removing her eyes from the screen. The words remain on screen for four or five seconds, long enough for her to capture them in her book. She writes the date on top of the page, checks her watch and adds the time.

Such documentation would prove nothing to anyone else, but Emma feels a muted glow of accomplishment. There is something about getting words down on paper that gives her a sense of mastery. She has captured something; now it belongs to her.

She plays out the game. Grandpa wins. Is it her imagination, or is there a glint of malice in that twinkly gaze?

Each day's work session begins with editing. Pen in hand, Emma curls up in her writing chair to reread her last chapter. She has expunged the intruder's lines from her manuscript; what she reads is what she wrote.

Her eyes scan the pages. The words fail to coalesce; they remain stubbornly disparate entities. She doesn't hear her characters, doesn't see them. No wonder, with all the other visions and voices jostling for airtime in her head. But this book is leaking vitality. Only recently it achieved quickening, those first faint stirrings of independent life that come about midway through gestation. Still provisional, its viability is already compromised. She could lose this one; it could slip away as easily as a nestling tumbling from a nest.

It's a dismal feeling. Once, when she was three months' pregnant with Zack, Emma woke to find spots of blood on the sheets. She saw her doctor, who examined her and said, "It's iffy; could go either way." He sent her home to wait and see. The spotting continued for five days, then stopped. The bleakness of those five days is the bleakness she feels now.

If only she could pray. *Lord*, she would say, *clean these cobwebs from my brain. Breathe life into my characters. Protect me and mine from those who would harm us. Lead us to safety, Lord. Amen.* That's what she would say. But Emma wasn't raised to pray; she was raised to do.

She pushes the manuscript aside, rises, and prowls

restlessly around the library. Somewhere a car door slams, and Casey, downstairs, begins to bark. Emma looks out the east window. Caroline's Acura is winding down the driveway. Going to work, carrying Emma's secret with her, which Emma can't believe she blurted out. Caroline has a manner of listening as if nothing else in the world mattered. After Emma told about the accident, there was silence. She looked up to find Caroline regarding her with undiluted sympathy. "How terrible for you," she said.

"How much worse for them," Emma answered.

"What makes you think anyone blames you?"

"The child had a mother; the man had a wife. How do you think she feels about me?"

"You probably blame yourself more than she blames you," Caroline had said—a tempting thought, but Emma knows better. She has the cards to prove it. Every year on the anniversary of the accident, a card has appeared in her mailbox, each one bearing the same printed message: "Thinking of you."

They aren't signed. They don't need to be.

The first one, seven years ago, had contained a photo. Emma has it still. She's kept the cards, too, hidden inside an old college text, Kant's *Critique of Pure Reason*. Not much chance Roger would find them there. None that she herself would stumble over them accidentally; Kant was never her idea of bedtime reading.

She is drawn to the shelf where her college books molder. Her hand reaches for the book, hesitates, falls back. But it's too late, she's gone too far. She snatches the Kant, carries it back to her armchair, curls up, and opens the book. Cards spill out onto her lap. Images of somber beauty: autumn woods, a moonlit pond. "Thinking of You" is the message on each.

She finds the photograph. It's a snapshot, unposed and natural-seeming, taken with some skill. A little girl of five or six perches on a Shetland pony. Behind her a tall, handsome man smiles down with fatherly affection. His right hand holds the gathered reins, his left cups the child's shoulder. A cap on his head casts the upper half of his face in impenetrable shadow; Emma can see only that he is dark-skinned and clean-shaven. The girl is fawn-colored, with a wide forehead and huge brown eyes. Even in a snapshot you can see how beautiful she is. She's one you'd stop on the street to look at.

Emma brings the photo closer and examines the child's eyes. No premonition there, no shadow; she is in the moment, and the moment is one of joyful excitement. Emma blinks hard; when she looks again, the expression on the girl's face has changed to fear and confusion. There's a stench of burnt rubber and gasoline in the air, and the wet street, lit by streetlamps and the one remaining headlight on her car, glistens darkly. The child is lying in a puddle, but Emma dares not move her. She gazes up at Emma. "Daddy," she says. "Mommy." Emma shifts to block her view of the wrecked and smoking car wrapped around a telephone pole, the black man's body slumped over the wheel. Awkward in her sixth month, she kneels amid shards of broken glass, holding her belly. The air bag in her car had activated on impact, slamming so hard against her belly that she greatly fears for her baby.

The little girl whimpers. She lies motionless on the road, arms and legs splayed at impossible angles, with the sort of stillness that rules out movement as an option. Emma hardly dares touch her. She strokes her cheek, as soft as rose petals, and murmurs, "Lie still, little one. Help is coming; lie still." Only her eyes seem alive; the rest is flaccid.

Even in the pouring rain, which soaks them both, Emma discerns a different sort of wetness trickling down her thighs. She looks down. There is blood on her sneakers, blood on the ground between her feet. She tells herself it's the girl's, but there's an ache inside, an emptiness that says different. She casts her own pain aside to focus on the child. From far away, sirens approach.

"What's your name?" she asks.

"Rachel." The name emerges swathed in pink froth. The girl's eyes drift away.

"Rachel!" Emma says sharply. No response. "Rachel, look at me. Stay with me, Rachel!" The sirens wail and wail, yet seem to come no closer. Time is running out. She should do something, but what? The child parts her lips as if to speak, but instead of words, blood flows from the corners of her mouth. She sighs, and does not inhale. Her eyes stop.

Emma cries out in protest and swoops down over the child. The sudden movement triggers a quick, sharp spasm in her groin; her thighs are bathed in liquid darkness. She opens the girl's mouth and blows gently, and she goes on breathing for the girl and pressing her chest until the sirens are upon them, flashing red lights and shouting men who pull her away from the child and force her onto a stretcher. A big man with rain coursing down his face hunkers down beside her and asks, "Is she yours?," and Emma says, "No, she's his," pointing to the other car, and then she says, "I'm pregnant," although she knows, even as she says it, that it's no longer true.

DURING THE NEXT few days, Emma adds two entries into her journal.

> Sept. 23, 12:15 P.M. E-mail from Gloria: "Dear Emma, Have been going through my list of clients trying to separate the wheat from the chaff. Must make room for deserving young writers. Fond of you but your stuff definitely chaff. Good luck in future endeavors. Love, Gloria."
>
> Called G. No such letter written or sent.

> Sept 24, 9:40 A.M. Playing hearts. Delay sets off this on-screen conversation:
>
> Grandfather: Bitch is definitely losing it.
>
> Belle: I feel just awful for her poor husband. Such a sweet man.
>
> Red Riding Hood: Shut up, guys; she's back.
>
> Screen goes blank.

She doesn't tell Roger. He'd just fret, and they'd quarrel again about her going into the card program at all. But how can she not? The poison's there whether she looks or not. Is she a child, to hide her head under the covers?

No, he'd said, the last time she'd made that argument: not a child, a sitting duck. Emma doesn't want to hear it again. Doesn't want Maggie's solicitude, either; it saps dearly needed strength. She starts monitoring her calls and ducks two from her sister. Meanwhile, her distress and distraction mount. Her book is stalled and no wonder, when it pales in comparison to her life. Unable to sleep, she carries around a constant throbbing headache. Friday she blows off work altogether and spends the day shopping, cleaning, and cooking. The Dumonts are coming to dinner tonight.

At six o'clock Roger walks in with Maggie.

"Who the hell invited you?" Emma cries, embracing her sister warmly; for however unwelcome Maggie might in theory be, in the flesh she is a solid comfort.

"What, are you kidding? This is better than *Melrose Place*."

"Not scared of our ghost?"

"What, me scared?"

"But you said—"

"No fear," says Maggie. "Yo, Emma."

"What?"

"Can I sleep with you and Roger tonight?"

THE DUMONTS arrive at seven o'clock, Gerard the very image of haute yuppie casual, Yolanda elegant in a dashiki. Emma, with relish, watches her sister. Maggie's response to the news that some new acquaintances were dining that night had been pure condescension. "Great, a chance to observe the native rites. Dare I hope for a soccer mom?" Emma, having refrained from describing her guests, is rewarded for her forbearance by the rare sight of Maggie discomfited. Gerard looks distinguished, Yolanda regal; the Dumonts are not what she expected.

Dinner is roast leg of lamb with potatoes and broccoli. Zack races through the meal, eager to get Marcel off by himself; for they've reached that stage of friendship that necessitates the sharing of secrets. Marcel, however, barely touches his food; and Emma notices he's been uncommonly quiet all evening.

"Marcel, can I get you something else?" she asks. "A hamburger, maybe, or a hot dog?"

The boy shakes his head without looking at her. Gerard barks his name. "No, thank you," Marcel mumbles with a truculent look at his father.

There's a silence after the boys leave the room. Gerard passes a hand over his eyes. "Sorry, folks. Should have left him home."

"Everybody has a bad day now and then," Yolanda says.

"That's no excuse for rudeness."

"Give him a break, baby. It'd be a tough situation for anyone, let alone a ten-year-old kid."

Drinks before and two bottles of wine with dinner have loosened everyone's tongue. Gerard explains that his ex-wife, who lives in the city, has visitation rights every other weekend. But Marcel plays soccer every weekend in the spring and fall, and he bitterly resents being forced to miss games. This weekend he flat out refused to visit his mother. If she tries to force him, he told Gerard, he'll run away and hitchhike home. He begged Gerard to intervene. "What the boy doesn't understand," Gerard says, "is that if I did, it would only make things worse. She already assumes I'm putting him up to it."

"Doesn't his mother realize how much the games mean to him?" Emma asks.

"Oh, she understands perfectly. That's what pisses her off. Yesterday, they're fighting on the phone and she says to him, 'What's more important, your mother or a soccer game?' You can guess what he said. Fool set herself up for that one."

"At least you've got custody," Roger says. "Quite an accomplishment, given the courts' bias in favor of mothers."

"She didn't want it. Cramps her style, having a kid. She'd have kept him for the child support, though, if I hadn't agreed to cough up big time."

"I tell him just be grateful she's such a mercenary bitch," Yolanda puts in, " 'cause otherwise, you know, stay-at-home Mom, workaholic Dad, he wouldn't have had a prayer."

Roger smiles down the length of the table at his wife. "That's why Emma puts up with me. We're joined at the hip. Neither of us would ever give up Zack."

"There's such a thing as joint custody, you know," Maggie says.

Gerard snorts. "So then the kid *really* has no life. You see what it's like for Marcel, and that's just weekends."

Roger nods agreement. "I heard a shrink once talking about joint custody. He said that every time you jerk the kid from one home to the other, you should put aside a sawbuck for his future psychiatric care. It's like the Solomonic solution to the problem of two women claiming the same baby. Joint custody is like cutting the kid in half; any parent who agrees to it is unfit for the job."

Yolanda smiles, looking from Roger to Emma. "Then you two really are mated for life."

"Till death do us part," he says.

"POOR MARCEL," Emma says. "How stupid is his mother, putting him on the spot like that?"

Yolanda lights a cigarette and drops the match in the ashtray. They're in the kitchen, Emma to make coffee, Yolanda to smoke. The others have lingered in the dining room, where Maggie, having discovered Gerard's profession, is picking his brains about a low-income housing project she's involved with.

"Not stupid enough to neglect her own interests," she says. "She took Gerard to the cleaners for that boy."

"Nice mother."

"Yeah, well, divorce rarely brings out the best in people."

Emma joins her at the table with coffee. The men will be waiting for theirs, but this is an opportunity she needs to take. "You sound like you've been there yourself."

"Not me." Yolanda blows a smoke ring and gazes through it. "My first husband died."

"I'm sorry."

Yolanda's shrug might be called Gallic, except that it would be understood anywhere in the world. Things happen, it said. Things happen and you have to move on.

Holding firm to her purpose against a wave of fellow feeling, Emma presses on. "Was he ill?"

"You could say he had a terminal case of being in the wrong place at the wrong time."

"Been there," she says, nodding.

"No shit."

Is it that obvious? she wonders. They think their own thoughts for a while. Then, just as Emma's realizing they should get back to the others, Yolanda says, "Hey, I've got something for you." She takes a thick envelope out of her purse and slides it across the kitchen table. Emma opens it to find a packet of four-by-six soccer snapshots. She goes through them slowly, lingering over a spectacular shot of Zack shooting on goal.

"These are really good," she says. "I'd like to get copies of some of these."

"Keep 'em, I got an extra set."

"Thanks." Emma spreads the photos out on the table. Yolanda's eye for composition clearly carries over to photography, but what strikes Emma is the story contained within the pictures. Each shot captures one moment: an action, an exchange, a moment of celebration or introspection. Taken together, they form a sort of fractured narrative. She begins without conscious thought to rearrange them, pushing them around like pieces of a jigsaw puzzle.

"What are you doing?" Yolanda asks.

"Just playing around. It's almost like there's a story in there somewhere, if you could just get the order right."

"My thoughts exactly. A kid's story."

"Maybe," Emma says. "Why? Are you thinking of doing one?"

"Remember I told you I'd got this bug in my head about painting some soccer pictures?"

"Sure."

"Thing is, I couldn't figure out what I'd do with them if I went ahead. I'm not sure this is something I'd want to exhibit; people already think I've gone soft, living out here. Then it came to me, I could use them to illustrate a kids' book."

"Great idea. And soccer's so popular now, you should have no trouble finding a publisher."

"Just one problem," Yolanda says slyly. "I'm no writer."

Emma looks up and finds her smiling. "Not me," she says. "I don't write kids' books. Whole other ball of wax."

"Is it?"

"Never collaborated with anybody, either."

"Be a first for me, too. But I've got a feeling we could do good work together: your words, my pictures. Will you think about it?" she asks as the men invade the kitchen, demanding coffee.

"I will," Emma says.

ZACK IS SHOWING Marcel around the house. When they come to the corridor leading to the winding stairs, Casey barks disapprovingly and backs away.

"What's the matter with him?" Marcel asks.

"He's afraid of this hallway. Just ignore him." Zack switches on the light.

Marcel, gasping, jumps back. "Those must be the stairs!"

"What stairs?"

"The ones she fell down, old lady Hysop." Then, as Zack stares wordlessly, Marcel says, "Broke her neck falling down these stairs. Police found her days later, dead. Didn't you know?"

"Sure I knew!" says Zack. "You think I don't know my own house?"

Marcel looks like he's wondering. "So, you ever, like, see her or anything?"

Zack frowns in concentration. "Little old lady with gray hair and thick glasses?"

"Yeah, man, that's her!"

"Nah, never seen her."

Marcel punches him in the arm. "So how come you know what she looks like if you never seen her?"

"All old ladies look the same. Man, you been reading too many *Goosebumps*."

"At least I can read!" Marcel retorts, and they tussle for a moment, then fall back laughing. "So how's it feel living in a haunted house?"

"My mom says haunted houses are just figments of writers' imaginations, and she oughtta know. Besides, when people die they go to heaven, they don't hang around earth."

"They do if they're murderers! Everybody knows that."

"So? Mrs. Whatzit wasn't a murderer."

"Oh really!" Marcel crows. "And I suppose killing your husband isn't murder?"

IT'S ONE IN the morning. The house is dark and quiet. Everyone's asleep except Zack, who's thinking about Mrs. Hysop. He's wondering if she really did kill her husband, and if Marcel is right about murderers being condemned to walk the earth. It would make sense in the economy of the afterlife as Zack conceives of it. On the other hand, his mother has always been definite on the subject. Ghosts, in her view, belong with fairies, leprechauns, and ogres, in the realm of imagination.

He's feeling kind of guilty about lying to Marcel, because you're not supposed to lie to your best friend, and Zack's pretty sure Marcel's his new best friend. But if he'd told the truth, then Marcel might be scared and never want to sleep over, which would totally suck. Anyway, Zack tells himself, it's not like he *really* saw anything. It was just a dumb dream; in fact, he'd forgotten all about it till Marcel started in, but then it returned in vivid detail.

In the dream, Zack is searching for his mother, who

is nowhere to be found. After trying the kitchen and her bedroom, he heads up the winding stairs to her office. At first glance he thinks that room, too, is empty; then he notices the small person seated in his mother's armchair. Not his mother but a stranger, a very old lady with a helmet of iron-gray curls and glasses with tortoiseshell frames and a chain attached, so they can dangle from her neck when not in use. Her head is bent; she's poring over a sheet of manuscript paper. There's something tucked behind one ear that Zack can't see clearly until she removes it and uses it to circle something on the page. It's a purple pencil.

Waves of alarm and anger roll over Zack. Mom hates people reading her stuff before she's ready to show it. But this intruder is not only sitting in her chair, she's reading her manuscript; and not only reading, but scribbling on it.

He clears his throat loudly.

The old lady ignores him.

"Yo!" he cries. "Yo, lady!"

She hears that all right. Raises her head and gives him a crusty old glare. "What is it, boy?" she says. Her voice is scratchy, like the old records his parents sometimes play. Blue eyes, magnified behind thick glasses, are as vast and watery as the bay.

"Who are you," demands Zack, "and what are you doing with my mother's manuscript?"

She pushes her glasses down her nose and peers at him over the top. "What a rude little creature it is."

"I'm telling my mom," says Zack, turning on his heel. At the top of the steps he looks back. The woman is gone.

*   *   *

13

SATURDAY MORNING Emma sleeps in. By the time she comes downstairs, showered and dressed, it's past nine-thirty. There's half a pot of fresh coffee on the counter and a single empty cereal bowl in the sink, signs that she reads effortlessly. Zack, who always wakes up ravenous, has had his breakfast; Roger and Maggie had coffee but waited to eat with her. The steady *thwack* of a ball hitting the outside of the house tells her where Zack is. She carries her cup to the window above the sink. Zack sees her and waves. Emma throws him a kiss and goes off in search of Roger and Maggie.

She finds them at last on the living room verandah. They stand at the cast-iron balustrade, their backs to the house, and something about their posture strikes Emma as odd. Without knowing why, she pauses to watch. They face the bay but look at each other. Roger talks intently, gesturing; Maggie nods and at one point lays her hand on his. What's strange about this amicable scene is its lack of precedent. From the start, Maggie and Roger have communicated through sniping, an affectation at first, which gradually calcified into habit.

Emma crosses the room and opens the French doors. Moving as one, Maggie and Roger separate and turn. Emma raises an eyebrow. "Am I interrupting something?"

Roger comes and kisses her on the forehead. "Yes, as a matter of fact. Maggie and I were planning our elopement."

"That's nice. Time for breakfast first?"

"I'm starving," Maggie says. "All this damn country air."

They go inside. Roger nukes the bacon while Emma makes French toast and Maggie sets the table. "Better put out four plates," Emma tells her.

"Zack ate already."

"Trust me."

The smell of bacon acts like a magnet. Zack bursts into the house, followed by Casey. "Wash your hands," says Emma, catching him by the back of his pants.

Zack washes at the kitchen sink, then slides into his seat. "Oh, man, I needed this."

Maggie passes him the French toast. "Didn't you just eat a huge bowl of cereal?"

"That little thing? That's nothing. I got a man's appetite!" He pounds his chest.

Maggie looks at Emma and shakes her head. "Testosterone poisoning."

"Bound to kick in sooner or later."

"Tell me, Maggie," Roger says. "Is it sexism only when men denigrate women, or would your remark also qualify?"

Maggie shoots him a haughty look. "I'm not denigrating; I'm commiserating."

Emma sinks into her chair. Back to normal, or as normal as life gets these days. Zack asks for more bacon, and she forks over the last piece. Then, in the same tone of voice, he asks if it's true that Mrs. Hysop murdered her husband.

Roger chokes on a piece of toast, and Maggie pounds his back.

Emma says, "Why would you even ask such a thing?"

"Marcel told me. He said everybody knows she did it."

"Nonsense. If she'd killed her husband and everyone knew, she'd have been in jail, wouldn't she?"

The speciousness of this logic escapes Zack, who nods as if he'd known it all along and was just testing her.

AFTER BREAKFAST, Roger drives Zack to soccer practice. Emma and Maggie decide to take Casey for a long walk on the shore. It's a bright fall day, a brisk breeze blowing off the bay. Casey regards the water much as he does the mailman: a persistent invader of his territory who can be driven back by some in-your-face barking. Affronted by every wave that slaps the shore, he attacks and retreats, taking care to keep his paws dry.

"That is the dumbest damn dog I've ever seen," Maggie says. "What does he think he's accomplishing?"

"He thinks the water's taunting him. He's showing it who's boss."

"Uh-huh. And we know this how, Dr. Doolittle?"

Emma laughs. She clambers onto the rock jetty separating her beach from the public access strand beside it. In fact, none of the beaches are privately owned; the shoreline belongs to the village. But the shore is too rocky and the tides too tricky to attract bathers; so, apart from occasional hikers and boaters who come ashore to picnic and crab, residents have it mostly to themselves. Too windy today for small sailboats; Emma and Maggie are alone on the shore. They walk without talking, enjoying the rough beauty, the hiss and slap of water meeting rock, the splendid isolation. This is not Maggie's image of Long Island. Morgan Peak itself is more village than suburb, and apparently not entirely provincial. It's not hard to understand the draw; Emma's always been a sentimental sucker for country living. As a girl her ambition was to be a writer in a country house, with five children, one husband, two Dalmatians, and a calico cat. The way she was primed? No wonder the poor sap fell.

She studies her sister, who stands on a rock jetty tossing a stick for the dog. Tall and slender, dressed in jeans and an oversized sweatshirt, Emma looks from this distance like a girl of nineteen. Casey fetches the stick but refuses to let go. They tussle; Emma wins and tosses it again. Her cheeks are bright with fresh air and exercise, and beneath her red cap, her black hair streams in the wind. "You look," says Maggie, as Emma descends from the rocks, "like a fucking Gap ad."

"If it's any consolation, I feel like the poster girl for Bellevue."

"Roger's worried about you, you know. Thinks you're holding out on him."

"If I am, it's for his own good. No point in both of us going nuts over this thing."

"He's your husband, fool. He's on your side."

Emma laughs in amazement. "Listen to you! What next, a chorus of 'Stand by Your Man'?"

"Hey. Whatever his faults, the idiot loves you."

"I should get this on tape. Aren't you the one who predicted that ten minutes after dumping me in the suburbs he'd be screwing around?"

Maggie kicks a pebble down the shore and follows it

with her eyes. "I say a lot of things. Since when did you start listening?" She takes her sister's arm; in unspoken accord, they turn and head back. "You know, for a bonehead, Roger's a pretty smart guy. But he can't help if he doesn't know what's going on."

"He can't help, period. He just looks at me like I'm out of my fucking mind." Emma whistles for the dog.

"That's *not* what he thinks."

"You've been talking about me."

"No, *duh*."

"Behind my back."

"It's the usual way. What haven't you told him?"

Emma shrugs. "Just some more computer crap."

"What manner of crap?"

"If I tell you, you can't tell Roger."

"Bad call, Emma."

"I don't want him worried. He's had enough grief from me."

Maggie's face scrunches in disbelief. "Would you listen to yourself? Roger is not the one who needs protecting here."

But Emma is adamant, and eventually Maggie gives in and promises. Then Emma takes a small red notebook from her pocket and hands it over. Since starting the journal she has backtracked, filling in the earlier computer incidents.

They find a place to sit, a log someone has placed in a sheltered nook in the bluff, and Maggie reads the journal. The latest incidents, new to her, are accorded a second reading. Emma watches Casey tiptoe up to a stranded horseshoe crab: neck extended, nose aquiver, poised to jump back at the slightest movement. She doesn't have to look at Maggie to sense her distress.

Maggie shuts the notebook. She says, "You realize this is harassment. Stalking. You've got to go to the cops."

"Yeah, right! Like they wouldn't laugh me out of the station."

"What are you, nuts? No one is going to read this and laugh."

"Then they'll read it and send for a padded wagon. Or they figure it for a publicity stunt. There's no way I can prove any of this happened. No one else has seen anything."

"What's-her-name saw the worms."

"Right, worms in a sugar bowl. That'll knock their socks off."

"It means someone's been in your house. And it's not an isolated incident. It's part of a pattern. Someone's fucking with your head, Em. That bit about death coming closer every day—that's a threat. Something very sick is going on."

Something evil, Emma thinks. She gets up, gives Maggie a hand, and whistles for Casey, who reluctantly leaves the beleaguered horseshoe crab behind. The temperature has dipped, and the wind blows in their faces as they head back. The sisters save their breath for walking. The sun is behind them now; they are preceded by their shadows.

On Emma's beach, they pause to catch their breath before climbing the path up the bluff. Maggie says, "Have you any idea at all who's doing these things?"

Emma forces a laugh. "Maybe it's the ghost of old Mrs. Hysop."

"Yeah, or maybe it's the tooth fairy. What's up with that, anyway? *Did* she kill her husband?"

"First I ever heard of it if she did. There is some

mystery about her, though. I can't quite figure how she goes from being everyone's favorite English teacher to town pariah. Something happened."

Maggie shrugs off Mrs. Hysop. "Roger says you've been talking to your tenant. What does she think?"

"Probably thinks I'm nuts. She didn't say much. Mostly she asked questions."

"Such as?"

Emma stares down at her clasped hands, her face a study in misery. "Such as does anyone hate me."

Maggie tenses. "What did you say?"

"Well, Mags, there is someone, you know."

"Who?" Their eyes meet. "Oh no, Em. Don't go there."

"She's bound to," Emma says gently. "It's only natural."

"It was an accident. That's what they ruled it and that's what it was."

"Still, if it happened to Roger and Zack, I'd never forgive the other driver, accident or not."

"But why now? And how could she get so close without you knowing?"

Emma shrugs. "I don't know her. Never laid eyes on the woman. Could be anyone, couldn't it?" Abruptly she falls silent. Her brow creases, her gaze turns inward. After a moment she looks at her sister. This time, neither speaks.

AFTER AN EARLY DINNER, all four of them drive into town for the seven o'clock show at the Morgan Peak Showhouse, which is running a *Star Wars* marathon. Zack has never seen *Star Wars* on the big screen. For the adults, the updated sound effects and new footage of the revised movie, together with their own fading memories, make the second time around every bit as good as the first. They come out of the theater awed into silence.

In the car, Zack stares out the window, replaying the movie in his head. Maggie sighs and says, "Could you believe how young Harrison Ford was? God, what a hunk."

" 'What a hunk'?" Roger smiles in familiar irritation. "Is that the feminist equivalent of 'What a babe'?"

"No, actually, it's closer to 'What a piece of ass.' "

As they have reverted to their usual roles, so does Emma, inserting herself into the line of fire. "Interesting," she says, "the attraction between Luke and Leia. Considering what they are to each other, I mean. Little touch of incest there."

"Doesn't amount to much," Maggie says. "Besides, they don't know it yet."

"No, but the writers did."

"I wonder if the actors knew."

"I doubt it."

"What difference would it make?" Roger puts in. "They're actors."

LATER THAT NIGHT, Emma sits at her dressing table, brushing her hair, still thinking about the movie. Maggie was right about the young Ford. Heart-wrenching charm, a total knockout. And what a good shtick for him, the reluctant hero. He's been playing it ever since.

Roger comes up behind her and takes the brush from her hand. "Let me." He brushes her hair with long, deep strokes. Emma closes her eyes when his lips touch her neck. She stands and turns into his arms. Roger picks her up and carries her to bed.

They lie atop the covers. The room is chilly but they don't feel it. His hands are all over her. Groaning at the thought of her diaphragm miles away in the bathroom, Emma starts dutifully to rise, but Roger pulls her back. "Wait," he murmurs, and she stays with him.

Afterward they lie naked under the quilt, Emma's head on Roger's chest; his right hand traces her contours. He says, "Did you and your sister have a chance to catch up?"

"We talked."

"You filled her in?"

Emma turns to watch his face. "I found her surprisingly up-to-date."

Roger grins ruefully. "Didn't buy the elopement story, huh?"

"Not quite."

"Ah well. Best I could do at the moment. Still—she's not stupid, your sister. No point keeping her in the dark. She doesn't much like it, either," he adds, with the wariness of the once burnt.

"No, she doesn't," she says. "But you're so used to thwarting her."

Something has been nagging at her, a comment Maggie made that stuck in Emma's mind like a piece of food lodged between her teeth. "Part of a pattern," she'd said. Emma was struck by the words. They rang true: yet how could they be? Patterns repeat and are therefore predictable; but Emma wakes up every morning clueless, fearful of what the new day will bring.

A different kind of pattern, then, she thinks. Roger's kind, the chaotic variety. She takes her head off his chest, moves far enough away to see his face, and asks if he thinks so. His face tells her he's put some thought into the question.

"Hints of one," he says. "Little DNA strands of pattern, but nothing like a linear progression. My intuition is that if you could find the field, if you could somehow quantify and graph these phenomena in phase space, you'd wind up with something like a strange attractor."

After twelve years with Roger, Emma has absorbed the fundamentals of his work, less by attending his occasional lectures, which tend to be heavily mathematical, than through a kind of marital osmosis. She knows that a strange attractor is the central point or area toward which the motion of dynamic systems is drawn; as such, strange attractors infuse stability and order into systems whose physical manifestations seem, but are not, random. Many scientists, Roger certainly among them, consider them to be a fundamental organizing force in nature whose very existence emerged only recently, as mathematicians began using computers to explore phase space.

Strange attractors live in phase space, which is a graphic way of picturing the changes in dynamic systems. Phase space is located outside real space; it exists only between the ears of those who can conceive of it. What it lacks in reality, however, it makes up for in efficacy: Phase space is a revolutionary tool, a mathematical power drill in a world of stone chisels.

All of this Emma understands, though the mathematics of chaos theory is beyond her grasp. Roger has tried to walk her through a few core equations, but for her it's like trying to play twelve games of mental chess at once: All she gets is a splitting headache. Yet she is enchanted by the concepts, the images and metaphors that chaos scientists use to translate their discoveries. Mysterious and evocative phrases, with a novelistic flair. Strange attractors, the butterfly effect, fractals and bifurcations. The concepts of chaos she understands instinctively, for they describe quite accurately the dynamic of a novel, with its multiple characters interacting with others to produce complex behavior. Even the concept of strange attractors has its fictional counterpart in the climax: the point of resolution, the Mecca toward which all plots and subplots aspire.

There is something else Emma knows about strange attractors. They are the product, always, of multiple forces. Force acts upon force in an endless loop, producing complexity. Mathematically such systems are represented by multidimensional equations, a dimension for each force; she understands this by considering how, in fiction, each fully realized character adds a dimension to the story. "But what are the forces here," she wonders aloud, "and what's the strange attractor?"

"Good question."

She looks at her husband. Darkness cloaks his eyes from her. "But you think there's more than one force in play?"

"I suspect it, that's all. The incidents seem random but smell purposeful: prime chaos territory. To me it feels like more than one force, which doesn't necessarily mean more than one person. Could be a single disordered mind."

Whose? she wonders. Mine? Am I one of the forces, or am I the attractor?

"It's coming closer, isn't it?" she says presently, but Roger doesn't answer. It's possible he's asleep.

14

WRITERS ARE OFTEN praised for self-discipline. Emma hears it all the time at readings, signings, luncheons: "How do you manage," "I'd never have the discipline," and so on. As if she had a choice. Praising a writer for writing is like praising a crack addict for assiduous smoking. Writing is an addiction, and like all addictive substances, it stokes the pleasure centers of the brain. Emma was hooked young. Long before writing became her profession, it was her pacifier. Somewhere in a trunk, a dozen diaries molder that, in their time, anchored her sanity. Now her years of passage, meticulously detailed, await her fantasy biographer. She gave up journal writing after a dull patch in her twenty-third year, when it finally dawned on her that in fiction you get to skip the slow parts.

Whenever Emma first finishes a book, she revels in her freedom. She gets her hair and nails done, tackles mounds of neglected correspondence, catches up on movies she's missed, cooks elaborate dinners. This phase lasts a week at most before the malaise sets in. The writer begins to feel listless, empty, stupid. She prowls restlessly about, searching for something to do, settling on nothing. When she has not finished a book, but for one reason or another is compelled to lay it aside, the effect is even worse, because then she's coming off a jag. Words and phrases, denied outlet, dam up her brain. Left too long they will turn rancid. Much as

Emma loves her family, her favorite day of the week is
Monday.

For too long now Emma has allowed herself to be
distracted, drawn away from her story. She has danced
to someone else's tune instead of composing her own.
Looking back, she sees how passive she has been, how
reactive, like one of those feeble horror-flick heroines
who do nothing but scream their heads off whenever
danger threatens. No more, she vows. She will pull herself together, she will resume control of her life. So what
if the book has been going badly? These things happen.
The cure, she learned long ago, is to keep going, if not
forward then backward. Her method of writing is akin
to spelunking: If one path peters out, retrace your steps
and find another.

This Monday morning she settles in her writing chair,
adjusts the lamp beside her, opens to the first page of the
manuscript, and begins to read. Months since she's gone
back this far. The words are fresh and draw her in. The
pages fly by. Some are marked with amendments in blue
or black ink, which she allows to accumulate on the page
till they get distracting; then she enters the changes and
reprints. One unusual marking does catch her eye, a line
on page thirty-eight circled in what appears to be purple
pencil. In the margin beside it, an unfamiliar, quavering
hand has scrawled "Fragment!" The oversized exclamation point quivers with indignation.

That the circled words are indeed a sentence fragment does not bother Emma in the least; rules, to her
mind, are made to be first understood, then flaunted at
will. The purple pencil and handwriting are more puzzling, along with the annotation itself. When she finds a
problem in her work—a mistake, an inconsistency, an

awkward turn of phrase—she fixes it directly, she doesn't scribble margin notes. But who else could have written it? So far no one has seen this manuscript. Roger and Zack are unlikely suspects; they know how touchy she is about first drafts. She must have written it herself, she decides, though when and under what circumstances she has no idea.

She returns to the manuscript but is almost immediately assailed by the feeling of being watched, a sensation so strong that against her will she casts her eyes about the room. Fool, she chides herself. Settle down; get back to work. And she does, barely stumbling over the purple-penciled markings on pages forty-three, fifty-five, and seventy-nine (two fragments and a run-on). Lunchtime comes and goes; she works on. At half-past three the doorbell peals, and Casey starts howling, "Welcome home, Zack!" in his own tongue. Emma looks at her watch and hurries downstairs.

THEY SIT AT THE kitchen table. Milk and graham crackers with cream cheese for him, coffee for his mother. "How was your day?" she asks, but then forgets to listen. Normally Zack would object, but today he figures it's just as well. From his point of view today's little adventure couldn't have worked out better. He's not just the new kid anymore; he's won himself a rep. But you can't count on parents to see things in the proper light, even though, as he takes pains to explain, the fight wasn't his fault at all. All he did was challenge a kid to a little soccer one-on-one, and he wouldn't have even done that much if it wasn't for what the kid did to him. In front of the whole cafeteria, this big sixth-grade football jock gets in Zack's face and says that soccer is a game for girls and wusses.

Here Zack pauses for his mother's indignation. But she, saying nothing, stares beyond him at some distant point.

"So what I am supposed to do, Mom, you tell me. I can't back down; the whole cafeteria's watching. So I say, 'If soccer's so easy, think you can score on me?' and he says, 'With my eyes shut,' and so we go outside and set up the goals and do it. And I whip his butt. In no time at all I'm up five zip, and the kid's so out of breath he can't even curse. I take pity on him; I go up and ask if he's had enough, but instead of answering the big jerk swings on me. The rest," he concludes modestly, "is history."

His mother finds his face. It takes her a while. She watches him as if he's a computer picture slowly taking form. "You got into a fight?"

Zack rolls his eyes. "Earth to Mom, come in, please." Stupid thing to say; now he's got her full attention.

"Who with?"

"A sixth-grader. Bigger than me. Did we just lose a minute here?"

She looks him over. "Are you hurt?"

"Nah."

"Who won?"

Good old cut-to-the-chase Mom. "Me by a mile," he brags, and almost gets her to smile.

"You get in trouble?"

"Had to see the principal. No biggie." Still, it was a first. He glances sideways at her face. Lucky for him the kid was bigger. She'd kill him if he ever fought a smaller kid; no tolerance for that at all, as he found out once after swatting a friend's pesky little brother. The friend hadn't minded, but Zack's mom had gone ballistic. The problem with mothers, even ones like his, is that basically they're women. Pacifists by nature, they don't understand that sometimes a kid's gotta stand up and fight. (Although, he recalls with a ripple of pleasure, the girls at school didn't seem to mind. Plenty of smiles and eyes turned his way afterward.)

Now his mother assumes her stern look and delivers the standard lecture about fighting—to which, however, no punishment is attached. He's not grounded; he doesn't lose TV or, God forbid, soccer. There's no anger in her voice; her sternness derives from policy, not passion.

Relieved, Zack whistles for Casey. As usual, the dog has been lurking in hope of manna from the table. At Zack's call he leaps up, tail wagging, and they head for the back door.

Halfway there, his mother's voice arrests him. "Zack, you didn't by any chance write on my manuscript?"

He pivots and returns to the table. "Someone messed with your manuscript?"

"Wasn't you, huh? Didn't think so. Never mind."

"What'd they write?"

She cocks an eyebrow. "Just a few corrections. No harm done."

In his mind's eye, Zack sees the old lady from upstairs, pencil clutched in bony hand.

"Pencil or pen?" he asks.

"Pencil."

"What color?"

His mother stares at him. The silence in the room sucks in sounds from outside, shrieking gulls and the deep, glottal thrum of an outboard motor. There's a brightness in Zack's gut. It's a simple question, he thinks; why doesn't she answer?

"Was it purple?" he asks.

She bends down to pet Casey. When she sits up, her cheeks are flushed.

"Black," she says at last. "The usual color. Why purple?"

Zack slumps in his chair and lets out a long whistle. "Just this crazy dream I had."

"Tell it to me."

So he tells her about the dream intruder, the lady with the purple pencil who pored over Emma's pages like a schoolteacher correcting tests. As he tells the story, Zack sees her again, and when she vanishes he tastes the utter stillness of her wake, that explicit sense of absence. He seeks his mother's eyes. "Isn't it strange, though? Isn't it like something out of *Goosebumps*? I dream about someone writing in your manuscript and it turns out someone really did."

His mother smiles her Mona Lisa smile. "More embarrassing than strange. You know how I am when I'm working. I probably just scribbled those notes myself and forgot all about it."

Makes sense to Zack. You hear about absentminded professors and observant writers, but in Zack's experience it's the other way round. His dad is sharp as a scalpel, his mom famously forgetful. Once a week she'll stick a chicken in the oven and neglect to turn it on, or put water to boil on the stove and forget about it. The number of kettles she's burned was a family joke until his dad finally bought her one whose shriek, he said, would wake the dead.

Maybe it had, Zack thinks. Joke. "At least they weren't written in purple. Now that *would* be weird."

Her smile never wavers. "Wouldn't it," she replies.

*   *   *

UP TO HER WRISTS in raw meat, phone cradled to her ear, Emma kneads in spices with more vigor than the task demands. She's making lasagna, Roger's favorite; but will he be home for dinner? He will not.

"Something's come up," he says. The connection is faulty, his voice distant and hollow. "India's going through some sort of crisis."

Emma jabs her thumbs into the chopped meat. "Why? Are the peasants rising?"

"Ha. No, she's been offered a job in L.A., and she doesn't know whether to accept it or stay here and finish her Ph.D."

L.A. sounds good to Emma. Outer Mongolia sounds even better, but California's not bad. There's always the chance it will fall into the ocean. Roger, predictably, sees the matter differently. Best assistant he ever had, he tells Emma, who's heard it before. He doesn't want to lose her.

He's not sleeping with her, she thinks. If he were, he'd never tell me they're going out. He'd make up some excuse for being late. But to say that Roger has not strayed is not to say he won't. Emma has a vision of the two of them sitting at a corner table, heads close together, Roger at his most persuasive, slathering on the charm, India, troubled and trusting, looking to her mentor for guidance. Her hand on his arm. *What do you think I should do, Roger?*

What a fucking setup. Emma wonders if there even is a job offer. A woman in love is capable of any deception. And how could Roger not be tempted? His home life a shambles, his wife a bundle of stripped nerves, and along comes little Miss Adoring Eyes, with her twenty-something body and her brilliant mathematical mind—may she choke on a microchip and die.

A tear drips into the bowl of meat, and Emma kneads it in. Let him dine on her tears; the food will turn bitter in his mouth. But then she feels unjust, for he has done nothing wrong; it's not Roger but her own imagination, freed from its moorings, that torments her. One thing at least she's certain of: India is not to be trusted. But what can Emma do about it without sounding even more paranoid than Roger already believes her to be?

"Emma," he says, "are you with me?"

"Can't you discuss her crisis during work hours?"

"You know what this place is like. I figured I'd take her off campus for a drink and a talk."

She sniffs.

"Care to expand on that?" he says.

"Do you really think it's appropriate? Technically, she's still a student, and you're a professor."

"Since when are you so P.C.?" Abruptly, annoyance caves in to concern. He asks, "Everything okay there? Did something happen?"

And once again the temptation, present from the start, to throw it all on Roger, to burrow beneath his wing. She knows she can bring him home with a word. If she needs him, he will come: part of the basic contract between them, and it still holds, and it works both ways. But Emma is too proud, and perhaps too wise. Age has its advantages, too. Let India play the damsel in distress. Real love requires respect, she reminds herself, and Roger has none for cowards.

"Nothing I can't handle," she tells him.

HALF A MINUTE after she hangs up, the phone rings again. Certain that it's Roger relenting, she grabs the receiver. But the voice on the other end is elderly and female, a nasal honk that sucks Emma straight back to her childhood in Flatbush. Her native tongue, recognized instantly.

"This is Ida Green," the voice says. "Arthur Matthews said I should give you a call. You know who I am?"

"Yes. Yes, I do." Emma wipes her hands on a paper towel and checks the hallway for lurking boys. None in sight. She shuts the kitchen door.

"I understand you got a little problem with your house."

"Strange things have been happening. Things we find difficult to explain." Emma picks her words carefully, cloaking her anxiety. She doesn't want to come across as a nut: an odd concern, considering her interlocutor, but this woman sounds like nothing Emma had expected. No ditzy dame with cotton-candy brains, the owner of this voice, no New Age guru; this woman sounds like nothing more or less than a housewife from the old neighborhood. Emma has an immediate image of the speaker: seventy-something, active in Sisterhood, widowed or pre-widowed; a person with whom Emma's mother might have played bridge, a solid citizen of her class and time. There's a whiff of chlorine about the edges of this voice. Emma adjusts the picture: Mrs. Green is now a snowbird, sitting by the pool, playing canasta with the girls and *kvelling* over the grandkids.

"Arthur told me you heard some banging noises." Mrs. Green is chewing on something. Emma, employing her own psychic powers, envisions a hollowed-out bagel with a *shmear* of low-fat cream cheese. "Let me ask you something. What kind of heat you got in this house? Because nine times out of ten, that kind of banging, it's your steam pipes acting up."

"We have hot air, not steam. And the noises are the least of it. I didn't tell Arthur everything."

"Oy," Mrs. Green says sympathetically. "Don't tell me. Better I don't know too much beforehand."

"You'll come, then?" Emma hears the eagerness in her voice and no doubt the other woman hears it, too. Doesn't matter. When she agreed to meet this so-called psychic, it was out of curiosity more than anything; yet the instant she heard Ida Green's voice, Emma felt comforted, as if it was this she'd been waiting for all along. For one brief moment she feels like a little girl again, tucked into bed in the summer dusk, hovering on the edge of sleep, drifting on the swells of female voices that waft through her open window from the porch next door. The women laugh, their voices ebb and flow; cards slap against a linoleum tabletop like waves against a midnight shore.

"Why not?" Mrs. Green says. "I got a niece lives out by you. How about the day after tomorrow, Wednesday?"

"Would morning be okay? Because my son gets home around three-thirty . . ."

"Ten o'clock I'll be by you."

"Thank you," Emma murmurs. "Should I do anything to prepare? Is there anything you need?"

"You could put up a pot of water."

"Boiling water?" Emma casts her mind back to *The Exorcist*. "Is that for some kind of rite?"

Mrs. Green cackles. "Yes, dear; we psychics call it tea."

EMMA CUTS TWO squares of lasagna and stores them in the microwave for Roger. Clears the table, starts loading the dishwasher; avoids looking at the clock, which is barely moving anyway. Over the rush of water she strains for the distant whistle of the train pulling into the station. If all they did was have drinks he ought to be home any minute.

Her face aches, the muscles around her mouth. All through dinner Zack chattered about this and that, but never returned to the writing in her manuscript. Emma takes this to mean he's bought her act. Good; it cost her enough. Her mother used to warn Emma that if she kept on scowling, her face would freeze that way. Now Emma wonders if the reverse applies: If she keeps smiling when she's sick at heart, will her true face atrophy?

Good thing it wasn't purple, Zack had said, with an innocent twist of the knife. The only good thing is that he doesn't know; nor will he ever, if Emma has anything to do with it. She reminds herself to erase the markings as soon as she's shown them to Roger. She looks at the clock again. How long does a drink take? She reaches out with her mind, trying to sense him, but all she gets is static.

There's a tap at the back door. Emma jumps. She shuts off the water and, wiping her hands on her jeans, hurries to the door.

It's Caroline, holding out an envelope with the rent. Emma takes the envelope and stuffs it in her pocket without opening it. This monthly transaction is an embarrassment to her, a necessary relic of their former relationship. "Can you come in?" she says.

Caroline glances past her. "I don't want to disturb you."

"Roger's working late, Zack's watching TV, and I would welcome the company."

"In that case . . ."

Emma lights a fire and opens the chilled bottle of Riesling she had intended for their dinner. They sit catty-corner on the sofas by the fire, glasses in hand. Caroline asks how she is.

"How's that Paul Simon song go? 'Slip-sliding away. . . .' " Emma smiles to make a joke of it.

Caroline sips her wine. In the flickering light of the fire, her eyes are steady green beacons shining with intelligence. Like the cat in the Saki tale, Emma recalls, who learned to speak and then went from house to house retailing gossip. Only Caroline, she's fairly certain, doesn't gossip. And Caroline, unlike Zack, sees through her smile. "What's happened?" she asks.

"Same old same old. It's all murkiness and one thing after another, and no clear explanations for any of it."

"In my experience there are always reasons, though they may be hidden."

"Explain this, then." Emma relates the coincidence of the purple markings on her manuscript and Zack's dream.

Caroline listens intently, staring at the fire. She doesn't speak for some time after Emma finishes. When she does, it is with characteristic authority.

"Since I don't believe in ghosts, or any form of life after death for that matter, I'm forced to look elsewhere for an explanation. There is one fairly obvious solution that doesn't involve the supernatural; though you may not like it any better."

"What is it?"

"Zack made those markings."

Emma stares. "And the dream?"

"Invented it."

"Why?"

"Don't know. To cover up what he did? Play a joke, get some attention?"

"He wouldn't," Emma says flatly. "I know my son."

"Of course."

"For one thing, Zack wouldn't know a sentence fragment if it bit him on the nose. And for another, he was terrified. And he's not the kind of kid who scares easy."

"I said you wouldn't like it," Caroline says.

"I'm not saying I don't like it. I'm saying it didn't happen."

The older woman raises her glass in a gesture that says she will only suggest; she will never insist.

Emma feels at once she's been unfair. "Sorry," she says. "Shouldn't have jumped on you for doing what I asked you to do."

Caroline shrugs. "It's an awkward situation. If you had come to me in my professional capacity, I wouldn't have hesitated to ask some hard questions. But they're not the kind of questions friends ask each other."

Once again she is asking permission to intrude, and once again, though with a certain wariness this time, Emma grants it. "What kind of questions?"

"Questions like, where does your husband stand in all this? He's a scientist; what's his take on the situation?"

"Roger is baffled, frustrated, and angry."

"Angry at who?"

"He doesn't know; hence the frustration."

With astonishing bluntness Caroline asks, "Does he often work this late?"

Emma's eyes jerk toward the clock. Where is he? As she imagines him still with India, bile fills her mouth.

She swallows hard. "He's with his assistant. They're discussing some job offer she got."

"That pretty young woman who came to your housewarming?"

Emma nods.

"I see," says Caroline with no intonation at all.

"I know what you're thinking and you're wrong. Roger would never—"

"Never what, fall for a beautiful girl who flatters his vanity and worships the ground he walks on?"

"You don't know him."

"You're right," says Caroline. "I don't."

"Roger is a stand-up guy. He's been totally supportive." *And where are you now, my supportive husband?*

"Has he?"

"Why say it like that?"

"Because that day we found the worms, I had the distinct impression you were relieved to have a witness. You seemed to doubt your husband would believe you."

"*I* wouldn't believe me either, given the slightest choice. Can't blame them for doubting."

Caroline looks up with sharpened interest. "Them?"

"Roger and my sister, Maggie," Emma says reluctantly. "Caught 'em with their heads together this weekend. I know they've been talking behind my back."

"Is that surprising, under the circumstances?"

"Surprised the hell out of me. Those two don't chat, they snipe."

"Yes." Caroline sips her wine thoughtfully. "I noticed the Tracy-Hepburn routine."

And at once Emma is obscurely offended. Has Caroline overstepped the line, or are Emma's emotions simply so raw that the slightest touch hurts? She's not sure. Either way, Caroline's observation is not one that pleases. The reason eludes her until she recalls that, although they start out as adversaries, in film after film Tracy and Hepburn end up lovers. Surely Caroline can't be implying a similar relationship between Roger and Maggie. Some things are too ridiculous even to contemplate.

AFTER CAROLINE has left and Zack has been tucked into bed, Emma takes a long, hot bath and slips on a nightshirt and panties. The cotton nightshirt is short, black, and clingy. First time she wore it, Roger said she looked like a high school girl at a slumber party; and to judge by his subsequent behavior he had some undischarged fantasies in that area. Does she choose it deliberately? If asked, Emma would undoubtedly say no. Nevertheless, when she hears him enter the house, just past ten o'clock, she does not go downstairs. Instead she shuts the book she's been trying to read, rises from bed, and arranges herself at her dressing table.

He moves about downstairs; then she hears his tread on the steps. The bedroom door is open. He peers inside, spots her, starts forward, then pauses for a second look. He steps inside and shuts the door behind him.

"Have you eaten?" she asks. In the back of her mind, Maggie snorts derisively. *What a good little wifey it is.*

"I ate at the station. Just missed a train, had an hour to kill." He takes off his shirt, tosses it onto a chair.

Emma brushes her long black hair. "Were you successful?"

"Bagged her," he reports, with such boyish self-satisfaction that half of Emma's fears go the way of nightmares in daylight. He sits on the bed to remove his sneakers. "Told her she'd be a fool to walk away from her doctorate now. She's halfway through her dissertation, for Chrissake. And it's not like she's spinning her wheels with us. Chaos is the cutting edge of half a dozen fields. Wherever she goes after this she'll be welcome."

"Sound career advice."

"Then, to clinch it, I told her that she was by far the least dim-witted of all my assistants, and that I'd gotten used to having her around."

"No points for originality," says Emma. "Wasn't that Henry Higgins's line to Eliza? I trust she was grateful."

"She ought to be." His eyes seek out hers in the mirror. "You don't like her, do you?"

"I don't like the way she looks at you."

A slow smile lights his weary face. "Do I detect a wee note of jealousy?"

"Irritation, more like. Did it take you three hours to persuade her?"

The smile grows beatific. "Of course not," he says. "One to persuade her and two to fuck her brains out."

Gaping, she wheels about. He's waiting for her. Raises his eyebrows, points a finger. *Gotcha!*

"You bastard!" She chucks her brush at his head. Roger ducks, then falls back laughing. She storms over to the bed, straddles him, pummels his chest with her fists. "You pig! It's not funny!" But, broadsided by relief, Emma hears bubbles of suppressed laughter percolate through her rage.

Roger hears them, too. He captures her wrists and pulls them to his chest. Emma, braced above him, is wild-eyed and panting, like a trapped feral cat. Nightshirt hiked up to the top of her thighs, breasts

heaving, nipples erect beneath thin black cloth, and atop
it all the hair of a turbulent angel. No one is laughing
now. He's so hard it hurts. He lets go of her wrists and
reaches up.

There is nothing marital, nothing familiar or soothing
in the scene that follows. No tenderness to speak of, and
less refinement. The urgency is too great. Roger is a
teenager frantic to score before his parents get home,
he's a prisoner on furlough, a sailor on leave. It's not
their usual style of lovemaking, with its time-worn paths
and conventions. This is desperate, defiant sex, back-to-
the-wall rutting, wartime love on the run. This is what
they've come to; this is where they are.

LATE THAT NIGHT a hard wind whips across the bay
and slams into the cliff, shattering into shards of wraithlike moans. Stray gusts surmount the hill and encircle
the house, rattling the windows and trying the doors.
Restive, Roger watches and listens from the shelter of
his bed; but Emma, warm and safe in the arms of her
husband, sleeps through it all.

15

EMMA DRIVES Zack to practice Tuesday afternoon. Midway down a residential street lined by
candy-colored bungalows and basketball hoops, a
small boy on a red bike swings out of a blind driveway
directly into her path. At the first blur of motion Emma
slams on the brakes. Squealing, the car shudders to a

halt ten yards from the child, who stands frozen, one foot on the ground, eyes round with shock, mouth a perfect *O*. "Jeez, what an idiot!" says Zack, seated in the back. Emma pulls over to the curb and shoves the gearshift into park. She leans her arms against the wheel and her head on her arms. She sees another street, another child's face, streaked with rain, peering upward.

Zack's voice is close to her ear. "You okay, Mom?"

"Fine." When she raises her head, the boy is gone.

Somehow she finds the courage to drive on. At the park, Zack grabs his soccer bag and runs. Emma follows slowly. She ought to go home and make dinner, but no way is she driving those two extra trips. Her stomach hollow, she buys a chocolate ice cream cone at the clubhouse kiosk and sits at a picnic table to eat it. The rest of the team trickles past. The mothers smile and call out, "Hello, Emma"; none stops to talk. Emma thinks of Roger, snug in his office. This is his doing, exiling them to this suburban hinterland, putting her in this position. Insisting that she drive, when she would happily have gone the rest of her life without ever again touching a steering wheel; informing her with infuriating equanimity that it's for her own good, and preening as it seemed to work. Emma has grown calmer behind the wheel, she no longer hyperventilates or clamps the wheel so hard her knuckles ache. But all she's really learned is how to fake it. Inside, nothing has changed. She knows she's overcautious; but that plus a token will get her on the subway.

The bench shakes. Nick Sanders has appeared and planted himself beside her. His son groans. "Dad," he says, making it two syllables.

"Go ahead and warm up; I'll be there in a minute." Nick turns to Emma. "Staying for practice?"

"Might as well. It's a beautiful day."

"Very beautiful," he says, staring at her.

Her ice cream is melting, dripping down the outside of the cone. Emma licks around the edges.

"You look like a kid," Nick says. "Ice cream all over your face." With one hand he steadies her chin, with the other he traces the outline of her mouth. It's a gesture of startling intimacy, and the look in his eyes is unambiguous. Emma bats his hand away and wipes her mouth with a napkin.

He produces a hangdog look. It doesn't fool Emma, who sees him laughing behind his eyes.

"Sorry," he says. "Sometimes I get carried away."

"We own a rather large German shepherd puppy," she says. "I've always considered it our responsibility to control him."

"Point taken, Mrs. Koenig. From now on, I promise to curb my inner dog." He holds up two fingers like a Boy Scout taking the oath. If they gave out badges for flirtation, Emma thinks, this one would have made Eagle Scout long ago.

Suddenly it occurs to her that Nick has other talents as well. According to Yolanda, he's a computer whiz who made a bundle at Microsoft before leaving to start his own business. Emma's been thinking for some time of having someone over to check out her computer; but she needs someone savvy. Nick's in the field; he must know someone.

She asks him.

"What's the problem?" he says.

"Someone's been hacking in."

"Doing what?"

"Planting phony E-mail, tampering with programs, changing my text."

Nick stares.

"Also," she adds wickedly, without the flicker of a smile, "I've been getting personal messages over the radio." Nick tries to hide his consternation, but his eyes give him away. She laughs, and he catches on.

"Cute, Mrs. Koenig. Straight up about the hacking, though?"

"Oh yeah."

"I know a guy used to do a bit of hacking in his misspent youth. When do you want him?"

"Is it up to me? Don't we have to ask him?"

"The guy works for me."

"As soon as possible, then. Not tomorrow, though." Tomorrow, Wednesday, Ida Green is coming. They set it up for Thursday at one o'clock and part amicably, Sanders to the soccer field, Emma to the ladies' room in the clubhouse.

She feels queasy, no doubt a reaction to her near accident. The clubhouse rest room is not ornate, but large and sparkling clean, tiled in white, a great step up from its city cousins. There's a fold-out changing table in an alcove, five stalls, a row of white porcelain sinks and mirrors. Emma enters the last booth and slides the lock shut. She doesn't sit, but leans against the divider with her hands on her knees. Gradually the nausea ebbs. She is dabbing sweat off her brow with a sheet of toilet paper when two women enter the room in animated conversation.

"Oh, please," says a familiar voice, strident and shrewish. "Open your eyes. It's all they can do to keep their hands off each other in public."

"All *he* can do, you mean. But that's him; we know that. I haven't seen a thing on her end." This voice, too, is familiar. Emma peeks through the crack between the door and the jamb. Cheryl—the Harridan, as Emma first dubbed and continues to think of her—is examining her makeup in the mirror. Beside her is another of the team mothers, Patty Something, of the sweet face and black pageboy.

Cheryl bends closer to the mirror, penciling in her thin, arced eyebrows. "You are such a Pollyanna. All those cozy little chats: What do you think they're talking about, Wonderboy? If they're not doing it, I'll eat a soccer ball."

Not for one moment does Emma doubt who they're talking about. How weird is this, she thinks. Like being back in high school. Maybe that's the key to suburban living: permanent infantilization. She has to come out now, either that or hide cravenly till they leave. She flushes needlessly and emerges from the stall.

"Ladies," she says, watching the parade of emotions march across their faces: shock followed by shame followed by the question, *What, exactly, did I say?*

"Hi, Emma," says Patty, having concluded that she, at least, has said nothing reprehensible. Pink-cheeked as a novitiate, she is; butter wouldn't melt in her mouth.

The Harridan says nothing. Ice wouldn't melt in hers.

Emma washes her hands, dries them under the blower, and glides unhurriedly to the door. Turning back, she catches them with lips parted, ready to explode into speech the moment the door closes behind her. Her eyes latch on to Cheryl's.

"About that soccer ball?" she says. "*Bon appétit.*"

*   *   *

"*Numero uno*." Yolanda unfolds a stubby, paint-daubed index finger. "She's a bitch. Always was, always will be."

"True, that," says Emma.

"*Numero dos:* She's jealous. Got a thing for him herself; everyone knows it. Seems there's some stuff even Nick won't touch."

"Man knows what's good for him."

"No shit; I swear that thing of hers is lined with razor blades. Just look at her husband. *Numero tres:* She's pissed at Zack. Have you noticed how much time her boy spends on the bench?" Yolanda tips the ash off her cigarette into a ceramic ashtray. They are lounging on her deck, drinking iced tea while waiting for practice to end. Emma had been perched on the hood of her parked car outside the clubhouse—indignation had taken her that far before fear-of-driving kicked in—when Yolanda swooped down and carried her off for tea and gossip.

"That's not Zack's fault!"

"You know it and I know it, but that Cheryl is blessed with the IQ of a bowling ball." Yolanda unfurls her throaty laugh. "Shit, I'd've given five years of my life to see the look on their faces when you stepped out of the stall."

"Wish I'd had a camera. It was classic."

"You go, girl!"

Emma, thoroughly cheered, drinks the last of her tea and wipes her mouth with the back of her hand.

"Come with me," Yolanda says. "I've got something to show you."

Emma follows her through the house, out the back, around the tarp-covered pool to the studio, which looks small from the outside but proves spacious inside. It's a single large room, sparsely furnished, illuminated by windows on all sides and two skylights in the sloped ceiling. An oak refectory table stands flush against one wall, one side strewn with papers, files, sketch pads, glass jars full of pens and brushes, as pleasantly untidy as her house is neat. A computer and printer occupy the far side of the table. There are a couple of chairs, a small settee, and in the middle of the room, a draped easel. Stacks of canvases line the walls, and the room smells of turpentine and paint.

Emma has been in this room before, but this time she looks about with sharpened interest. If Yolanda keeps any photos, mementos of her former marriage, this is where they'd most likely be. Emma is ashamed of her suspicions. Almost from the moment they met, her heart has recognized a kindred soul in Yolanda; but her mind, in audit mode, queries the heart's deductions. Yolanda is one of the few new people who have entered their life. She's a black woman who lost a husband. Kindred soul or not, she fits.

The picture is right on the desk, camouflaged by a small outcropping of framed shots. A man in his mid-thirties, smiling into the camera. Handsome, clean-shaven, skin the color of bitter chocolate, wide shoulders in a beige crew-neck sweater. Yolanda said he died of being in the wrong place at the wrong time. Could mean by accident. Could mean a lot of things. Emma summons up an image of the man in the car, the other driver. The picture comes readily, but it's blurred. She never saw his face in life, never saw the man but once, and then he was dead, slumped over the steering wheel, covered in his blood. At home she has that photograph, but in it a cap overshadows his face. Is it the same man? Maybe, maybe not.

"Be with you in a sec," Yolanda calls. She is sorting through a stack of sketch pads.

"Take your time." Emma glances at the other photos. There's one of Marcel in soccer uniform, holding aloft a trophy half his height. Another of Marcel, Gerard, and Yolanda leaning against a ship's railing; a third of an elderly black couple—Yolanda's parents, she assumes. There are no other children. No little girl. But if there were one, it might be too painful to keep out. Emma picks up the picture of the unknown man and studies it closely.

Something makes her turn around. Yolanda stands like a statue behind her, eyes fixed on the photo.

Emma returns it to its place among the others. "Your first husband?"

Yolanda nods.

"Good-looking man."

"He was that."

Emma is sorry for what she's about to say, but not sorry enough to refrain. "The two of you would have had beautiful kids."

Yolanda looks away.

"Some things," she says presently, "it just don't pay to dwell on."

So Emma has been told, more than once. But can a person choose the things she dwells on? Aren't they rather like mental screensavers of the mind, images that pop up by default in the absence of conscious thought? Yolanda has not answered the implicit question; moreover, she has not answered in a way that precludes further questions. Emma has no choice but to apologize, which she does sincerely.

Forget it, Yolanda says. She hands over a vellum sketch pad.

Emma sits at the desk and pages through a series of pencil sketches, scenes from a soccer game. Drawn with poetic economy, a few lines suffice to capture a moment. Of course they've got to be the right lines. Yolanda's are.

"Wonderful," Emma says when she is done.

"They're just sketches. The actual paintings I'll do in tempera. Have you thought at all about my idea?"

With these sketches in her hand, Emma is tempted to agree. Yolanda is very good, a better painter than she, Emma, is a writer; it would be a pleasure to have her words associated with these pictures. One nagging thought stops her from agreeing outright. What if Yolanda were the one? She's not, of course; but what if she were? Then working with her would be like dropping the drawbridge for the enemy.

"Hey," Yolanda nudges her gently. "You're allowed to say no. We'll still be friends."

At that moment Emma decides: Down with niggling doubts, up with the heart's intuition. "Yes," she says. "Yes, let's do it."

16

EMMA SHAKES out the comforter and with an expert flick of the wrist lays it flat on the bed. She says, "Are you sure you're not needed in the office? Don't you have work to do?"

"Nothing nearly as amusing as the entertainment you've laid on." Roger folds the sheet over the edge of the quilt and pulls it taut. "Which I wouldn't miss for the world. How much does she charge, by the way?"

"Nothing. Arthur says she never takes money. And before you ask, the last thing she wants is publicity."

"Didn't she just write a book?"

"Under a pseudonym. Arthur thinks she's wonderful."

"Now that," says Roger, "is deeply reassuring."

"How condescending. Do they teach that tone in prep school?"

"It's an elective; I took it for the Cary Grant flicks. Will we have a seance, do you think? And what happens if we strike ectoplasm? Do we bring in a priest, or does this woman also do exorcisms?"

"I doubt a priest would oblige, since neither of us is Catholic."

"Maybe the ghost was. Does it go by the ghost's religion, or the homeowners'?"

In answer Emma chucks a pillow at his head. He catches, plumps, and lays it on the bed. "Anyway," he says, "it's not only Catholic priests who do exorcisms. Pentecostals are constantly casting out demons; I believe they're required to cast out half a dozen before breakfast. Maybe we should have one on standby, in case Madame Green doesn't pan out."

"Mrs., not Madame," Emma snaps—but it's her own damn fault. Never thought he'd want to stay, figured he'd laugh it off. He *is* laughing, but he's staying, too. Should have waited, told him after the fact. "Did you or did you not say that we have to explore every possibility, no matter how unlikely?"

"Well, you certainly took me at my word." They eye each other across the vast expanse of the tidied bed. A moment passes. Roger smiles hopefully. "Care to mess it up again?"

"In your dreams. And look, if you're gonna stay, at least keep an open mind."

"I have an open mind. I just can't wrap it around a ghost."

"Is the world only what we conceive it to be?"

"Is Emma turning into one of her own characters? Tune in tomorrow—"

"You're avoiding the question."

"Of course it's not. We all know who had the definitive word on that subject."

"Einstein?" she guesses. "Feynman?"

"No, one of yours: old Will. 'There are more things in heaven and earth than dreamed of in your philosophy, Horatio.' Hangs over my desk, as you well know. But a ghost I'd have to see to believe, and even then I wouldn't."

"I'm not saying I believe it, either. I'm just playing devil's advocate. A ghost would explain a lot."

"A ghost with computer skills."

"Maybe that part's separate," she says, staring at him. "Maybe there's more than one thing going on."

He starts to answer and stops. The doorbell rings. Casey, chained out in the backyard, begins to bark.

"Behave yourself," warns Emma.

"When do I not?" says he.

You'd never pick her out of a crowd unless you happened to notice the little spark of awareness in her eyes, the sort of pilot light by which, for instance, writers are wont to recognize their fellows. Apart from that glint, Ida Green is indistinguishable from several thousand women Emma has met over the years at book-and-author functions: elderly ladies who lunch, avid library patrons, good, conscientious souls who enjoy a dash of cultcha with their chicken Kiev and pasta primavera. Closer to seventy-five than sixty-five, Mrs. Green is short but straight, with leathery sunbird skin and hair layered around her face like silvery aspen leaves. She wears a tailored navy pants suit that Emma figures was $129 at Loehmann's. (Loehmann's had been the site of their mother's biannual clothing hajj. To stave off boredom, the sisters devised a game, competing to predict the price range of each customer, based on her appearance and clothing. Emma usually lost; she had an eye for idiosyncrasy, Maggie for class. The game survives as a useful shorthand for economic standing.)

Ushering her guest into the front hall, Emma introduces her to Roger.

"Ah," Mrs. Green says, shaking hands, "the scientist."

"Very good," Roger says, with a wide-eyed ingenuousness that doesn't fool Emma for a moment.

Doesn't fool Ida, either. "Arthur Matthews told me. He says you're a genius."

"Arthur's the genius; he has a prodigious talent for hyperbole. I see you found your way all right; though I suppose, if you did get lost, you could just follow the emanations." He hums a few bars of the *Twilight Zone* theme.

Ida gives him a thoughtful look over the top of her glasses. "Your wife's directions were excellent."

Emma says, "It was very good of you to come, Mrs. Green."

"About you at least he didn't exaggerate. You're as pretty as he said you are. Call me Ida, dear. We share an editor, makes us *mishpucha*, right?"

"In-laws, at least. Tea?" Emma, nervous of Roger's sardonic eye and unsure of the form in this situation, would camouflage the purpose of this visit beneath a veil of sociability. But, "Tour first, tea later," Ida declares; and though Emma leads, the elderly woman sets the pace. Like a realtor she moves briskly through the downstairs, passing from room to room without a word. Her hands graze walls, windows, and sills but linger nowhere.

Upstairs, Emma opens the door to Zack's bedroom, and Ida walks in. Zack is the fortunate inheritor of his father's gene for neatness. His bed is made, his shelves and desk uncluttered, with no more than a day's worth of used clothing tossed on a chair to prove that he's no Stepford son.

From the desk, Ida takes up a small globe of the world that doubles as a paperweight and cradles it in her hands. She replaces the globe, walks to his bed, touches his blanket and his pillow. "Quite the athlete," she remarks.

"Astonishing," says Roger, seething over this invasion of his son's privacy. "And you got that from touching his paperweight?"

Ida, unperturbed, says, "No, actually, I got that from the trophies on his shelf. Shall we move on?"

She is in and out of the master bedroom in under a minute, pausing only to praise the view of the bay from the turret windows. Emma, suffering under Roger's gaze, feels she's made a first-class fool of herself. There's nothing here, even to one predisposed to find something.

All that remains are the tower room, site of so much assorted strangeness, and the corridor that Casey refuses to enter. Emma opens that door now and leads the way to the spiral staircase. At its foot, Ida stops abruptly. She stares at the floor. She peers up the stairwell, squinting against the dazzle of sunlight. Using the banister for support, she kneels down and presses her palms to the carpet directly above the hidden bloodstain.

Roger looks at Emma, his supercilious smile hanging by a thread. The silence is resounding. Emma, waiting on the third step up, suddenly senses someone standing just above her. She doesn't look. She knows what she'll see, or rather won't: not a person, but the space a person would take up if there were someone there; a compact, ponderous void; an absence as pronounced as any presence could be. She has felt this before, but never with other people present.

Does Roger feel it, too? If so, he gives no sign. He offers his hand to Ida and she takes it, rising with a groan. "Pesky knees," she mutters, and waves Emma upward.

Emma doesn't move. "What is it?"

"Later," says Ida, patting her arm. They mount the spiral staircase, and Ida fails to exclaim over the view from Emma's room or comment on its suitability for a writer. She takes off her glasses and looks around. So thoroughly does she ignore her hosts that Emma and Roger drift together for comfort like ghosts in their own home.

Ida sits in the armchair, with her hands on her lap and her head tilted to one side. There's a listening qual-

ity to her stillness; Emma feels as if to speak would be
to interrupt. She shifts closer to Roger, who drapes an
arm around her shoulders but keeps a vigilant eye on
their guest. After some minutes, Ida rises to walk about
the room, aimlessly at first, then concentrating on the
area around Emma's desk. She spends several minutes
staring out the window behind the desk that overlooks
the carriage house and the road beyond. She handles
objects on the desk—a letter opener, a monthly calendar, the computer mouse. She sits at the desk, lays her
fingers on the keyboard, removes them at once and then
puts them back. Minutes pass. Then Ida turns to Emma
with a speculative look, which morphs at last into a perfunctory smile. It's a doctor's smile, a gesture of meaningless reassurance, and it turns Emma's blood to ice.

EMMA CAN'T TAKE her eyes off the bright red smear of
lipstick on the rim of Ida's mug. They are back in the
kitchen. Ida has removed a ball of sky-blue yarn, two
knitting needles, and a tiny, half-finished sweater from a
bag that seems too small to hold them. She hands the
ball of yarn to Emma and begins to knit. Roger, present
but remote, leans against the counter, sipping his coffee
and smiling behind his eyes. Emma thinks of Bogart
watching Bacall try to con him in *To Have and Have
Not*. There actually is a faint, castelike resemblance.

   "So what's the verdict?" she asks, after several minutes of watching Ida knit.

   "Well, dear," Ida says, "you do have a problem, but
it's not a ghost problem."

   "Thank you, Mrs. Green!" says Roger.

   "For what?"

   "Your unexpected honesty."

She looks at him over her glasses. "Let me guess: You don't believe in ghosts."

"We are rational people. My wife writes haunted-house stories: wonderful yarns, I love reading 'em. But I don't for one moment mistake them for reality, and neither does she."

Ida clucks. "Such logic. Emma writes about ghosts; her books are fiction; therefore ghosts do not exist. In my school days, a thousand years ago, we called that a faulty syllogism."

Roger finds himself regarding Ida with more interest than before, a look she returns with one equally probing. Ida Green has every appearance of a woman who does not suffer fools, hardly a trait he would associate with one of her profession. An astronaut encountering life on the moon could not have been more surprised than Roger at discovering intelligence in such a place. Bowing in recognition, he adopts an altered tone. "We are not the sort of people, my wife and I, to have that kind of problem."

"What kind of problem are you the sort of people to have?" she asks. Her curiosity is of the open, guileless sort, so winning in children and so rare in adults.

"The usual kind, I suppose, not spooks in the attic. The point is, I'm delighted to have you confirm what I've been telling Emma all along: that there is no ghost in this house."

"If you think so, Dr. Koenig, I have not made myself clear. I didn't say there's no ghost in this house. I said the ghost is not the problem."

In the silence that follows, Roger looks at Emma, who looks at the table.

"Let me get this straight," he says presently. "You're

claiming that our house is inhabited by a 'ghost.' " He cannot even say the word without miming quotation marks.

"A *pitzkele*." Ida spreads thumb and forefinger an inch apart. "A little nothing, a poor lost soul wouldn't harm a fly."

"I see. And you know this how?"

"Same way I know we're sitting at this table now."

Emma, arms wrapped around herself, makes a small, inarticulate sound.

"Don't take it to heart, dear," says Ida, who has laid aside her knitting like the prop it was. "It's not so terrible, believe me; there's people would kill for an honest-to-goodness ghost in their house."

"That would do it, presumably," Roger says. "Any chance of putting ours up for adoption?"

She gives him the sort of stare unrelated adults give thoroughly obnoxious children.

Roger laughs. "You're good," he says. "You're very good."

"Tell me something, Dr. Genius. Did you notice how cold that hallway is?"

He doesn't ask which hall, a concession in itself, but he disputes the cause. He points out the lack of windows, the complex patterns of heat convection due to the structure of the hall, the spiral stairwell, and the exposure of the glassed-in tower above; he follows this with a sermonette on the physics of convection, and concludes with an avowal of faith: "There is nothing in that hall that cannot be explained by a few basic equations."

Ida listens patiently but with an air of suppressed amusement. "I don't know from equations," she says. "I got enough trouble just balancing my checkbook. But I can tell you what happened in that hallway. A woman fell and died at the foot of the stairs."

"You told her," Roger says to Emma.

"Did not!"

Ida sighs. "You're missing the point, children. What I'm saying is that poor little spirit is the least of your problems."

Emma licks her lips, which have gone dry. "If that's the least of our problems, what's the greatest?"

"Malice. Strong, focused, and directed at you, Emma. I'm sorry. I came out here hoping to put your mind at ease; but I'm afraid, dear, you have reason to fear."

"Fear who? Who's doing these things?"

"I don't know."

"Of course she doesn't." Roger, pale with anger, approaches the table. "She doesn't know because you don't know. All she's doing is feeding you bits and pieces she gleaned from you."

Ida ignores him, looks only at Emma. "I don't know who. I know this person has been here, all through the house. It's almost certainly someone you know."

"Shame on you!" says Roger.

"Man or woman?" Emma asks.

Ida shakes her head.

EMMA, WALKING her guest to her car, apologizes for Roger's rudeness.

Not a problem, Ida says. Some people aren't ready for the truth.

"Can you tell me more about the ghost? Was it Mrs. Hysop?"

"I don't know, dear. She didn't wear a name tag."

"What did she look like?"

"Old, frail, white-haired. Wore bifocals on a silver chain. Something tucked behind her ear."

"What? What behind her ear?"

"A pencil."

Emma stops and puts her hand out before her as a sudden darkness comes over the world. Then the ground turns to jelly beneath her feet. She falls, and some indeterminate time later opens her eyes to a blur of features that gradually sort themselves into faces. Roger and Ida are bending over her. Above them not sky but living room ceiling. Time and space have been disrupted; she's passed through a L'Engelian wrinkle in time.

"She's back," Ida says.

"I'm back?" says Emma. "From where?"

"You fainted, *maydeleh*."

No way; Emma bristles at the thought. Real women don't faint. Neither, for that matter, do self-respecting fictional women, excluding the swooning heroines of antebellum romances. Emma's never fainted in her life, except that one time playing handball at the gym with Maggie, and then she was two months' . . .

Oh my God.

17

THE MOMENT Zack's bus pulls away, Emma is in her car. Twenty-one agonizing hours have inched by since the light dawned in her turgid brain. Roger would not leave her yesterday, though she urged him to. This morning it was all she could do to wedge him out the door.

She pulls up in front of the drugstore just as the pharmacist is unlocking the door and spends a quarter of an hour choosing from a dizzying array of home pregnancy tests. The cashier, a young woman, says "Good luck" as she hands Emma her change. Two minutes later Emma is headed home, punching the speed limit. For once she drives without thinking about what she's doing, thoughts fully occupied elsewhere.

She parks the car carelessly, runs into the house. Casey, overjoyed, accompanies her to the downstairs bathroom and whines piteously when the door is shut in his face. Emma's hands shake as she tears the cellophane off the pink box. Why pink? she wonders. To differentiate it from male pregnancy tests? And why is she so nervous? It's not as if she doesn't know. The moment she understood about the fainting, all the other clues fell into place. The fact that her period is late: not a lot, a few days, but unusual for her. The bouts of nausea she'd attributed to other causes. It all adds up. The wonder is that she didn't see it sooner. And yet she can't be sure, not absolutely. There could be other explanations. Anxiety alone could account for all of her symptoms; God knows she's had plenty of that.

She pees into a beaker, sets the beaker on the sink countertop, and unwraps the magic wand. One minute is all it takes. Pink, you're pregnant; blue, you're not. In a minute she'll know. Till then there's hope.

She dips the wand into the beaker.

One minute, they said, but the business end of the stick is already blushing as she removes it. Within seconds the color deepens to a fierce, unambiguous rose.

She waits a whole minute. Maybe it will turn blue. It doesn't. She stumbles out to the living room, collapses into the first chair she reaches. The shock is no less for all her suspicion. "Oh my God," she moans, "oh my God." Casey watches from a few feet away with a tilted head and furrowed brow, then approaches and lays a paw in her lap. Emma hugs him, burying her face in his thick ruff.

Like smelling salts, the odor of unwashed dog revives her at once. As her mind clears, Emma begins to take stock. She is pregnant: That's a fact. The timing sucks, another fact. How can she go through a pregnancy when she herself feels so endangered? Babies need a safe, warm nest to come home to; but if a man's house is his castle, theirs has proved both haunted and permeable. How can she bring a baby home to this?

Of course, she doesn't have to. It's her choice; even Roger would agree. Enforced childbirth, he always says, is a form of slavery. But if she chooses abortion, it will break his heart; and it would always be between them.

If he knew, that is. Unbidden, the thought occurs: What if he didn't? Could she do it alone, keep it from him? But even as she asks the question, Emma knows the answer. If choosing an abortion would harm her marriage, having one secretly would drive a stake through its heart.

All of which begs the question of whether she even wants an abortion. Emma consults her feelings; that is, they phone in from all over the map. Dread, of course, lest something go wrong. Fear of tempting fate. Rage at their carelessness, which she sees as deliberate on his part, accidental on hers. But also, on a deeper frequency, faint intimations of joy: a deep somatic jubilation of the cells, a pulse of gladness.

Forcing aside all thought of Roger, she asks herself, Do I want another child? Yes. Can I manage a pregnancy now, let alone an infant? Questionable. But could I bear to end it? To test herself, Emma imagines the abortion. Sees herself lying on a table, feet in stirrups, sheeted knees splayed. At the foot of the table a suction pump whirs. The doctor approaches, dilator in hand. A nurse squeezes her hand. "This won't take long," she whispers.

Emma jerks upright, clamping her knees together. Her heart races as real adrenaline rushes to combat a fantasy. Her choice is made. For better or worse, that is her baby growing in there, hers and Roger's. Unplanned, unexpected, but not, it appears, unwanted. No one is going to take it away. No one is going to harm it; God help anyone who tries.

She lays her hand on her abdomen, dowsing for life. She imagines Roger's face when she tells him, his joy. And Zack's, when he finds out. He has never given up wishing and begging for a brother or sister. But they mustn't tell him too soon, not till they're sure it's all right. As sure as anyone can be, given all that can go wrong.

It is at this point that Emma's thoughts invariably spiral downward as she begins to enumerate all the possible mishaps of pregnancy. This exercise, the very opposite of counting sheep, delivers her not to soothing slumber but to heightened anxiety, and yet she cannot seem to avoid it. It is as if the psychic wound of her traumatic loss had healed askew, derailing all future thoughts of pregnancy by shunting them into a maze of what-ifs, a dire, black-magical realm in which Murphy's Law rules supreme. Whatever can go wrong, will go wrong.

If the mere thought of pregnancy so rattles her, the reality of it must terrify, or so Emma has imagined all these years. But now that the event is upon her, she finds herself floating on calm seas. *All will be well*, the currents whisper, and she is graced with that great wash of calm, the mad, fearless serenity that is the anesthetic of pregnancy.

For the first time since moving to this house, Emma believes she will prevail. The stakes have changed; she's playing for two now. *I can do this*, she thinks. *I can have another child*. She aims her thoughts at the tiny fetus in her womb. *Make you a deal, kid. You grow. I worry about the rest.*

WHEN THE PHONE rings, Emma, certain it's Roger, sits on the bed she's been making and takes a moment to compose herself. This is too good to waste on the telephone. She wants to see his face when she tells him.

It's a man's voice, all right, but not the right man. "Emma, my love!"

"Hey, Arthur." Emma leans back against the headboard, kicking off her shoes. "How are you?"

"Frustrated, horny, and soon to be broke, thank you so much for asking."

"I gather Alison's sticking to her guns."

"Her cannons. She's hired a fucking lawyer. Don't get me started."

"Sorry. No luck with India?"

"Oh, nothing there at all. I'm convinced she's seeing someone. She denies it, but how else could she resist my charms?" He sighs disconsolately. "But enough about me. How did it go with Ida Green?"

"Didn't she tell you?"

"Not a word. Apparently there is a psychic's code of ethics."

"She said we have a ghost in the house."

Arthur whistles softly. "Do you believe it? Do you believe your house is haunted?"

Good question; strange she hasn't asked it herself. Two days ago Emma was aching to know, obsessing over the ghost question. Yesterday she was vouchsafed an answer, and since then she hasn't given the matter a moment's thought. But this is what her life has become, this blind lurching from one crisis to the next. On the scale of crises, an unplanned pregnancy trumps a ghost any day of the week.

"I guess I have to," she says. "It makes sense."

Arthur shudders down the line. "Better you than me, love. If this doesn't bring you back to the city, nothing will."

"I don't know; it beats cockroaches."

"You sound much too calm. Don't you mind sharing your house with a ghost?"

"I don't enjoy it. On the other hand, think what a ton of research this will save me."

"Ha! You realize, don't you," he says portentously, "this is your next book."

Emma laughs. "Oh yeah? How's it end?"

"No joke, love. I mean, it's a publicist's pipe dream, isn't it? Skeptical author of ghost stories buys haunted house?"

"I'll think about it."

"There's nothing to think about, except what a cosmic waste it would be if you didn't write about it. Things happen for a reason. Trust me, love, this was meant to be."

Emma won't commit to a book while her house is caving in around her, but she knows her editor is right: Sooner or later, if she survives this madness, she will need to write about it. By the time she gets off the phone, it's eleven o'clock: half the morning wasted. Emma heads straight for her office. In situations like this, work's a narcotic. After her car accident, Emma had gone directly from the hospital to her desk. Her nonwriter friends marveled at her self-discipline, but the writers just looked at each other and rolled their eyes. They knew that if total obliteration of the self is what's sought, writing beats both drink and drugs.

Casey follows her down the hall but balks in his usual spot. Emma calls him from the foot of the winding stairs, patting her thigh. The dog takes one step over the threshold, then retreats, hanging his head in shame. "Forget you," she says, and goes up alone.

Her office is as she left it, quiet and still, only the dust motes moving in the streams of light that converge in the tower like a reverse beacon. A whiff of reproach in the stale, expectant air, an echo of the unfinished book's lament to its author: "Why hath thou forsaken me?" She sits in her chair, opens the manuscript to a point near the end, and starts reading.

All it takes, usually, is a page or two and she's back inside the story, but today the magic fails her. Her mind keeps slipping back to her own ghost story. Arthur's call primed the pot, now Emma's brain percolates with questions. Was the figure Ida described really Mrs. Hysop? If not, who was it? If it was, what does she want with

Emma, other than to correct her grammar? And wouldn't that be just Emma's luck, getting an English teacher for a ghost? First and foremost, though, is the question of whether there's a ghost at all. Ida's assertion that there is does not stand alone; whatever credibility it possesses derives from previous events. Zack's dream, the purple markings in her manuscript, the frequent sensation of someone standing behind her, the cough, the sound of a body falling downstairs: Though each incident alone admits of other explanations, together they make a compelling case.

But can she really accept it? As Roger said, they are rational people; their hand-picked portfolio of beliefs contains no stock in an afterlife. Flying horses, they'd reckoned such fantasies, sired by Human Egotism on Fear of the Dark. Human life, as Emma comprehends it, is bound by birth on one end, death on the other. She has no understanding of a world in which ghosts are possible, no notion of such a world's boundaries or laws.

Her only points of reference are the ghosts she's known, some half a dozen in all. (That all of these arose from her own fictive imagination in no way eliminates them as objects of study, for the bulk of whatever small portion of understanding Emma lays claim to has come to her through writing. Imagination, as Einstein famously said, is greater than knowledge.) What have they taught her about the breed? Surprisingly little, it seems. Something long hidden from her view is suddenly clear: Her ghosts have never been characters in their own right; rather, they have been plot devices to shake up the lives of her living characters. They lacked *raison d'être*, they lacked substance—a paradoxical charge to bring against spirits, whose very essence might be described as lack of substance, but a grave indictment indeed against fictional characters.

Has she, then, been guilty of a lack of seriousness in her work? Some people would argue that the genre in which she writes precludes any possibility of seriousness, but that is a specious argument; only look at Henry James, Joyce Carol Oates, Kingsley Amis, Paul Theroux. It is not the subject but the depth to which that subject is plumbed that determines quality in fiction; and it costs Emma something in pride to admit that she has fallen short, she has skimped on her work.

To write a ghost one could learn from, one would have to believe in the ghost. But in a writer's lexicon, belief is not a gift but a product, not a prerequisite but a result. Unlike people, characters are made, not born; they're written into life, layer by layer. Starting as bare skeletons, they gradually accrue muscle, flesh, and sometimes, mysteriously, animation. Those are the characters who live on in the writer's mind long after the book is completed, abiding in that section of memory allotted to significant friends and seminal relationships. Some of the most influential people in Emma's life have been characters of her own devising; but none of those has been a ghost. Compared to her living characters, her ghosts are poor, pallid creatures, lacking the essential attributes of motivation, voice, and inner life.

Suddenly an idea comes to her. What if she were to rewrite parts of her novel from the ghost's point of view? The possibilities are intriguing. Seen through the ghost's eyes, every situation would be inverted. Her own situation is a case in point. From Emma's point of view, Mrs. Hysop is a troublesome, unwanted intruder; from Mrs. Hysop's, Emma would be the trespasser.

In her current book, the ghost is both murderer and victim. Why does he remain? What motivates him, and how does he perceive the people who now occupy his house?

She can hardly believe she's never asked these questions before. Asking them now is the writerly equivalent of panning for gold in a virgin-lode stream. Emma's hand flies across the pages of her notebook, filling in sheet after sheet. When the doorbell rings, she starts violently, like a sleepwalker shaken awake. *Who the hell*, she thinks, then suddenly remembers: Someone was coming to look at her computer. She glances at her watch. One o'clock already.

She flies downstairs. Casey's in the front hall, barking ferociously at the door. Through the side vents Emma spies a tall man in a business suit. She can't see his face, he is looking back toward the road. Grasping Casey's collar firmly, she opens the door. The man turns. It's Nick Sanders.

He looks different dressed for work. Older, more authoritative. But the dimpled grin is the same, the hooded eyes and the forelock dipping over his brow.

"Ma'am," he says, "could I interest you in some Tupperware?"

Emma keeps the screen door between them. "What are you doing here?"

"I promised you my best man. That's me."

"I feel scammed. You planned this all along."

He scuffs a shoe on the porch floor, gives her his aw-shucks expression. Maybe he can't help the face, she thinks, but he sure knows how to use it. "If I'd told you, you'd have turned me down."

"Damn straight," she says. Roger will be furious. She

wonders if Nick realizes how close he's come to losing Zack for the team.

"I'm just looking to help," he says. "Might as well let me in, seeing I'm here."

She opens the screen door and Nick comes in. He holds out his hand to Casey, who licks it. Emma is annoyed; dogs are meant to have more discernment. Still, she thinks, what harm can he do her, armored as she is in pregnancy and woe? Oh, he is a wicked charmer, a libidinous Tom Sawyer, but his charm is worthless coin in this realm; Nick is no threat to her.

THEY TALK UPSTAIRS, she curled in her writing chair, he in the desk chair, swiveled round to face her. He has not touched the computer. Unlike Ida Green, who wanted nothing in advance, he demands details: dates and times, durations, texts.

To refresh her memory, Emma consults her journal. She doesn't show it to Sanders, but reads out excerpts, omitting all mention of incidents unconnected to the computer. Those are not his concern, and she is not about to lay out her whole life for any stranger, let alone a man she already distrusts. Even with the omissions, the recital takes nearly an hour, starting with the incursion into the card program, then spreading to her work texts and E-mail. When she comes to the contents of the messages, though, Emma fudges. The prospect of reading them aloud to this man fills her with shame, as if she were a sexual-assault victim forced to detail the attack to an overly attentive male detective. But Nick insists on hearing the exact texts, and at last she complies.

"Read them again," he says when she is through. He

takes a small leather notebook and a gold pen from his briefcase. "This time give me just the texts."

She reads:

"Something's happened to the boy."

"That bitch can't write for beans. Talk about your talentless hacks."

"Did you ever stop to think that each day brings us closer to death? And some of us are closer than they think."

"Useless cunt ought to do the world a favor and pull the plug."

"Her family'd be better off."

"That's for sure."

There's a silence after that. Emma toys with her journal. There's no way, hearing those messages consecutively, to miss the arc of escalation. *You have reason to fear*, Ida had said, and she wasn't the first. Nick's averted eyes suggest a similar conclusion. Or do they? To be so hated implies that one deserves it. Is he wondering what she did to bring this on her head? Or does he suspect, as Roger did, that she is doing this to herself?

"Pretty nasty stuff," he says at last. "What's Roger done about it?"

"He searched for viruses. Didn't find any."

"Ah." Nick's face is expressionless, but Emma detects a note of criticism.

"He offered to take the computer to be checked out thoroughly. I wouldn't let it go."

"Too bad; you might have saved yourself a world of trouble. Had any work done on it lately? Any upgrades, repairs?"

"No. Nobody's touched it except me and Roger."

"Who has physical access to the computer?"

"My family."

"No one else? Workmen, housekeeper, neighbor with a key?"

She shakes her head.

"What's your Internet access?"

"Internet Explorer."

"Who knows you play hearts?"

She thinks for a moment. "Zack and Roger, of course. My sister; she teases me about it. I don't know who else. It's no secret, but it's not the sort of thing that normally crops up."

"Okay, let's have a look." He boots up the computer, then stands and motions her toward the desk. "Would you start up a game of hearts? Do whatever you usually do."

She enters the card program and selects three players for hearts. All appear with their customary introductions. Nick hovers behind her shoulder, out of sight, which normally would have set off alarms; not this time, though. His eyes are fixed on the monitor; for once he's out of flirt mode.

She plays a few hands, then turns to him. "It's not going to happen. It never does when anyone else is here."

"Really? Any disturbances on the screen shortly before you get these messages?"

"None that I've noticed."

He nods, doctorlike, reserving judgment. Emma surrenders the chair and withdraws to watch. Nick studies the icons on the Windows screen, selects File Manager and begins poking around, opening directories and examining their contents. His shucked jacket, loosened tie, and fingers flying over the keyboard remind Emma of newspaper reporters in old black-and-white flicks: Spencer Tracy hunched over his clunky Underwood, forefingers jabbing out the story. All that's missing is the cigarette dangling from his lip.

When watching palls, she retreats to the comfort of her armchair. After a while, feeling herself begin to nod, Emma slides her journal under the seat cushion and goes downstairs to make coffee. When it's ready, she puts two mugs on a tray with milk and sugar. As she enters the front hall, the door opens and Roger enters.

"Good God," she says, "what are you doing home?"

"Nice." Roger kisses her brow. "Whatever happened to, 'Hi, darling, how was your day?' "

"Went out with Donna Reed. Really, what's up? How come you're home?"

"Nothing urgent on today. I cleared my desk and felt like playing hooky. Thought maybe we'd do something, take a walk." He eyes the tray. "But it looks like you've got company."

For no reason at all Emma feels guilty. She says, "I decided to take your advice and have the computer checked out."

"Who by?"

She braces herself. "I asked Nick Sanders to recommend someone. He showed up himself."

He stares. His face registers shock, then anger, then nothing. His mouth tightens and a curtain descends over his eyes; he can see out, but she can't see in. He steps around her and starts upstairs.

"Roger, wait. He hasn't done anything."

He stops and studies her with those blank eyes.

"Why not? Did I come home too early?"

He could shave on the look she gives him then. "I don't deserve that."

"You invited him."

"I asked for a recommendation, that's all. He works in the field; I thought he'd know someone."

"And you really thought he'd pass up an opening like that? What were you, born yesterday?"

Emma is silenced. How could he believe her when she can hardly believe herself? She knows she didn't plan this, but how surprised was she when she opened that door and saw Nick standing there? She'd blamed him for coming, but the moment Roger said his behavior was utterly predictable, she knew he was right. How could she have failed to anticipate it?

Taking her silence as confirmation, Roger wheels around and heads upstairs, taking the steps two at a time. Emma follows at her own pace. When she reaches the foot of the spiral stairs, she hears her husband shouting: ". . . another notch on your belt, you're out of your fucking mind."

Then Nick: "Take a chill pill, Koenig. Ask your wife if I laid a finger on her."

"I know you didn't. You've got none broken."

Then Emma's head clears the floor and she sees them standing nose to nose in the center of the floor. What a tableau of male aggression, what a fug of testosterone pollutes her lucid room! What on earth has come over Roger? Nick is hardly the first man to come on to her. Roger knows she can handle herself; so why the sudden caveman routine?

"Look at you guys," she says. "This is so junior high."

They move apart. Nick takes a step toward her and stops. "I was just about to call you when George of the Jungle here swung in. I found it, Emma. I know how the bastard's getting in."

18

"HERE'S YOUR culprit," Nick says. "The program's called CopyCat. What it does is link two computers via modem. It's typically used by cybercommuters to merge their home and work computers." He sits at the desk, Roger and Emma hovering behind him.

"I went over that hard drive with a fine-toothed comb," Roger says flatly. "This program wasn't on it."

"Crafty bastard hid it good. What he did, he created a sub-directory inside a crowded directory, in this case C:\Windows\system. He stuck the CopyCat files in there and marked both the files and the sub-directory 'hidden.' Files and directories marked as hidden don't appear in File Manager unless you specifically set the search parameters to include hidden files, which most people wouldn't think to do."

Roger says nothing but looks obdurate.

"Then with this program," Emma says, "someone can control my computer by remote control?"

"Yes, provided your computer is turned on. With this program installed in your computer and his, your cyberstalking friend can do everything you can do on your computer. He can get into programs, mess with your E-mail, add, alter, or delete files."

"Computer rape," Roger says.

"Precisely," says Nick. Their eyes meet in a look that excludes Emma; and if there is anger and distrust in that look, there is also a dollop of shared apprehension. "When he's ready to disengage, he simply exits the program, and both monitors revert to the Windows opening screen. That fits with what Emma said happens."

"Any way to trace this computer you claim is linked to ours?" The word "claim" is lightly but unmistakably stressed.

Nick looks at Roger for a beat. "Not that I know of. You can try tracing the incoming calls through your phone company, but I doubt you'll have much luck."

"Why not?"

"Because the bastard who's doing this doesn't want to get caught. Look." Nick clicks his way into Emma's E-mail filing cabinet, while she, cringing inwardly, imagines a cop rifling though her drawers. He opens the fake E-mail from her agent, Gloria Lucas, and freezes the screen on the sender's information. "You can tell just by looking that this didn't come from her agent. Emma naturally would have scrolled past to get to the message itself. The sender is an E-mail forwarding service, one of those blessed services that are responsible for all the spam you get. I tried replying, but the return address is unreachable by E-mail. My opinion, anyone savvy and knowledgeable enough to hide his E-mail address is likely to have rerouted the phone calls as well."

Roger says, "This program's designed to work both ways, isn't it?"

"Been there, tried that, couldn't get in. When you install the program, you get the option of having infor-

mation flow one way or both. Your guy blocked access
to his own computer."

"We know one thing at least," Emma says. "Whoever
is doing this must really know computers."

"Not necessarily. CopyCat's easy to install and use."

"But he'd have to get into the programming of the
hearts game and alter it. We keep saying he," she adds,
almost to herself. "Of course, it could be a she."

Nick looks surprised. "I'd assumed it was a man."

"Why?"

"Uh . . . the language."

Emma has read through those messages a hundred
times without gleaning a clue to their author's gender.
"What about it?"

" 'Cunt.' You hear that word, ninety-nine times out of a
hundred it's a man talking. Anyway, as far as reprogram-
ming the hearts game, that's a piece of cake. I looked at the
program. The dialogue appears as snippets of regular text;
as long as you stay within parameters, it's completely inter-
changeable. I could teach you to do it in two minutes."

Emma looks at her computer and sees a huge black
spider draped over it, poison fangs gleaming. She shudders, and the vision vanishes.

"I don't buy it," Roger says. "Too convoluted. You're
making a major conspiracy out of a computer glitch."

"Computer glitch! Jesus, man, haven't you read the
crap they're sending her? Someone's playing head
games with your wife, and if you don't know that—"

"I'm not convinced. Could be some kind of virus she
downloaded."

Nick sneers. "Smartest damn virus I've ever seen.
And how would you account for this CopyCat program?"

"Could have been there all along, pre-loaded."

"Hidden files in a hidden sub-directory? Why pre-load a program and then go to so much trouble to bury it?"

"For all I know," Roger says, "you installed it yourself." The insult is as deliberate as a slap in the face. Nick stands, and Roger's smile urges him forward. But Nick takes a deep breath and lets it out slowly.

"Fuck you, Koenig, I don't give a shit what you think. I'm here to help Emma."

"She doesn't need your help."

"You're just pissed 'cause you didn't pick up on the program, which I'm saying is not your fault."

"Assuming it was there to find."

"Stop it!" cries Emma, eyes blazing. "We do need his help. We need all the help we can get."

"It's okay," Nick says. "Look, Koenig. I know where you're coming from, and maybe you've got a right to be pissed, coming home and finding me here. But what you've got to understand is, I am not your problem. Somebody out there hates your wife, and it sure as hell ain't me."

They lock eyes for a long moment. Then Roger nods once, curtly, and Nick returns to the computer.

"What do we do now?" Emma asks.

"I can delete the program," Nick says, "which is probably the best option in terms of protecting your work."

She looks at Roger. "What do you think?"

"Does it matter?"

"Of course it matters."

"Then I say get rid of it."

"If we do, there's no chance of tracing this back."

"Worth the price," he says. "Consider your exposure."

Emma stares blindly at the floor, trying to get inside the mind of her tormentor. Cast out of her computer, where would he strike next? She pictures Zack on his bike at the end of the drive, waving his insouciant goodbye, and her decision is made.

"This person is venting rage through the computer," she says. "Who knows what he'd do without it?"

"Come out of the bushes, maybe." Roger's hands twitch in anticipation.

But Emma turns to Nick. "What's the other option?"

"Leave it alone," he says. "Hunker down. Turn your computer off when you leave the room, back up your files every time you use them, and be prepared for a crash."

"You're being unfair." Emma keeps her voice down lest the other diners hear, though there's not much chance of that. When they walked into the restaurant, the maître d' took one practiced look at the mid-quarrel markers—her bright cheeks, his set mouth—and led them to the most private table in the room, a booth in the corner. Zack is having dinner at a friend's; they'll pick him up on the way home.

"I'm being very fair," Roger says. "I said he could finish out the season. After that he'll have his pick of teams."

"But he's proud of playing for his hometown. He loves that team. Plus, you said yourself, Nick's a good coach."

"That was before I knew him. Now I don't want him anywhere near my son, not to mention my wife." He spears a forkful of unresisting greens with unwonted force.

The restaurant is a small, elegant sort of place, staffed by waiters who anticipate every wish and fade into invisibility when unwanted. Glasses of sparkling wine and water appear out of nowhere and are invisibly replenished. Emma eyes her wine regretfully but sticks to water.

It's a relief to get out of the house. There are things that must be talked about, things uncomfortable to say with the house listening in. Besides, there are protocols for eating out. No unpleasant scenes, no raised voices. Roger and Emma are being very civilized. He is nursing his drink, she her secret.

"You know you overreacted," she says. "What has Nick done besides help us?"

"It's what he'd like to do and doesn't trouble to hide. The way he looks at you in front of me."

"How does he look at me?"

"Like a cat stalking a bird. Never takes his eyes off you. I might as well not exist. Don't tell me you haven't noticed."

"Sort of the way India looks at you?" she asks innocently.

Roger's fork pauses en route to his mouth. "India has nothing to do with this. We are talking about Sanders."

"We are talking about jealousy." She slips her foot out of her shoe and caresses his calf with her toes.

Roger stares down at his plate. "Are you trying to distract me?"

"No, I'm trying to seduce you. How am I doing?"

"No challenge." He moves closer, feels the warmth of her thigh against his. "You know I'm easy."

"I hate to admit it, but I sort of liked you in Tarzan mode. Don't make a habit of it, though. And darling, let's leave Zack out of it."

He pulls away, shutters his face against her. Emma knows she's crossed a line; she's trespassing on sacred father-son turf. When it comes to soccer, Roger is not just Zack's father, he's his trainer and manager as well. A month ago Emma would not have interfered, but a lot has happened in a month. The rules that governed their marriage are giving way one after another. Like plaster pillars in an earthquake or umbrellas in a hurricane, they are rigid but brittle, no shelter in a storm. If she and Roger are to pass safely through what lies ahead to emerge with marriage intact, something new will be needed, some quality to which she cannot give a name, but which contains elements of elasticity, flexibility, even play.

"Listen to me," she says. "So far we've managed to protect Zack from all the craziness. This thing with Nick and the computer, that's just more of the same. We can't let him suffer for it."

Roger looks at his wife, which is not hard to do. Her eyes are shining, and her black hair crackles with electricity. The jade jersey dress fits her like a skin; in the city it would pass almost unnoticed, but here in conservative little Morgan Peak it's big news. Every man in sight is stealing glances.

She is different tonight. Something has changed in her, a kind of recklessness has emerged. Tonight Emma reminds him of a woman he used to know but hasn't seen in years: the woman he married.

Is he acting out of jealousy, as she insists? Roger hates to think it, jealousy is such a lowering emotion.

But there's no denying that when he found Sanders in his house, alone with Emma, he was angry enough to make him grateful now that he's never kept a weapon on hand. In retrospect it seems a kind of madness. Not that Sanders isn't a snake; he is. But he's not the first snake or the biggest snake or the best snake; and Emma is perfectly capable of handling a dozen of his kind.

"All right," he says reluctantly. "Zack stays on the team. But that is the beginning and the end of our relationship with Sanders. I won't tolerate that bastard worming his way into our lives, and you better believe he's going to try. Deal?"

"Deal," she says, and holds out her hand. Roger carries it to his lips and kisses her palm. Then he leans over and kisses her mouth.

They separate and look at each other and smile. The waiter appears with their entrees, and they fall to eating hungrily.

OUTSIDE, IN THE parking lot behind the restaurant, Roger backs her up against a wall and kisses her again. He runs his hands along her body, and she presses against him. No lie, what she told him inside; seeing him and Nick squared off over her had set off an erotic avalanche. Very un-P.C., but there it is. Roger, for his part, having routed the invader is eager for the spoils. His hand is halfway up her skirt when a passing headlight strafes them. Laughing, Emma pushes him away and runs toward the car.

Ten feet away she stops short. There is something lying on the ground directly in front of their car. The light is dim in this corner of the lot. Emma glimpses a hank of hair, a tiny, outstretched arm, a twisted leg.

She staggers away from the sight. She covers her face and the parking lot disappears, in its place a storm-swept street. Nearby, a child cries plaintively, *Daddy*, *Mommy*, then falls silent. Rain falls on open eyes.

Something touches her and she lashes out. A familiar voice calls her name. She opens her eyes. Roger's hands are on her shoulders. His mouth moves urgently but she can't hear him.

"What?" she says. "What are you saying?"

His voice comes clear. "It's a doll, that's all. A fucking doll, Emma."

"What?"

"Look at it, for Chrissake." He turns her, guides her forward with an arm around her waist. "Look at it."

It's a Raggedy Ann doll. A large one, the size of a two-year-old child.

"Oh God. I thought—"

"I know."

She looks at him. His face is all angles and shadows; she cannot see his eyes. "I'm sorry."

"Not your fault," he says grimly. "Naturally it threw you. We're both on edge."

Humoring her. Emma's heart sinks. She overreacted, lost it, made a fool of herself over something anyone else would have passed without a glance.

But how did the doll get there? And the way it was positioned, all twisted and bent, and dropped in front of their car: How could that be coincidence?

The conclusion seems obvious, but it's only with great trepidation that she says it aloud. "Someone put it there. Someone set this up."

"Oh, Emma." Roger's voice sounds infinitely sad.

"Don't 'Oh, Emma' me. What other explanation is there?"

"The obvious one: Someone dropped it. A kid lost her doll; happens every day."

"What kid? There were no children in the restaurant. And that thing wasn't here when we parked."

"No," he admits, "it wasn't."

"Someone put it there. Someone who knows about my accident."

A long pause. Then, "It's possible."

"I know it's fucking possible. I'm asking what you *think*."

He stares past her. The skin on his face is so tight it looks as if it will rip at the slightest movement. A pulse beats in his temple. Presently he turns to her and says, "Emma, I don't know what to think anymore."

ROGER SITS ON the window seat, knees drawn up and encircled by his arms, gazing down at the collision of wind, water, and land. Out of primeval, undifferentiated chaos God is said to have formed the world, here to prove it is the ragged seam of creation. Behind him Emma sighs in her sleep. He turns his head to look at her. Raven hair fanned across the pillow, lips parted, she lies on her side. Beneath the sheet her nude body looks ripe, rounded, and succulent.

They'd made love earlier. Two minutes after tucking Zack into bed, they'd picked up where they'd left off in the parking lot. How is it possible that a man in as much trouble as he's in can still feel lust? The same way, perhaps, a man can be grief-stricken and hungry at the same time. The body has its own agenda.

She'd forgotten to put in her diaphragm and he

couldn't be bothered at the time to say anything. It worried him, though, and afterward, he mentioned it.

"I didn't forget," she'd said, smiling. "There's just no point."

"No point?" he'd echoed.

"Ever hear the expression, 'locking the barn door after the horse is gone'?"

Shock his first reaction, shock and dismay. The words "Now of all times" scrolled across his internal monitor. "How did it happen?" he asks.

"In the usual way. I thought you'd be thrilled."

"I am." He forced a smile. "Of course I am. If you are." For Emma, he knew, was perfectly capable of putting up a front; and for once she had reason to fear.

"I was shocked," she said. "But now that I've gotten used to the idea, I really want it." And her eyes glowed with such steadfast serenity, even complacency, that Roger was amazed.

He watches her now, sleeping with a smile on her lips. His wife has many sterling qualities, but he would not have numbered resilience among them. His mistake, he thinks now. She is stronger than she seems.

For him, the news has driven away sleep. Roger gazes out the window and for some reason his thoughts turn to prayer. He is not a religious man. His concept of God, to the extent that he has one, was formed almost in its entirety from the Book of Job, the one book of the Bible he finds both interesting and true to his own experience of life. He equates Job's "comforters" with classical (i.e., non-chaos) physicists. Both view the cosmos as a linear system in which what goes in determines what comes out. In religion as in science, orthodoxy can ill afford to acknowledge its inadequacies; thus Job's comforters assumed some hidden sin in him, just as classical physicists, confounded by anomalous results, blamed experimental error.

The book attributes Job's trials to a wager between God and the devil. Afflict this righteous man, Satan says, and he will curse you; No way! thunders God, and the bet is on.

With as much effect might a lab rat pray to his experimenter as a man to such a God. Roger gave it up after his first year at boarding school, during which he prayed nightly to go home. Tonight, though, the longing comes hard upon him.

The sky is lightening in the east. His wife turns in her sleep, reaching for him. There's a sound coming from upstairs that a fanciful mind might hear as footsteps. Roger considers investigating, but before he can bestir himself, the sound stops.

19

SEVERAL NIGHTS later, Emma wakes to the sound of footsteps above her head. Light, slow, uneven steps, as if someone with a limp were pacing the room above. She doesn't rise from her bed, doesn't stir, barely breathes. There is nothing connected to those sounds she wishes to see.

Oh, she was brave enough on the phone with Arthur. Laughed it off as a nuisance, compared it to an infestation of roaches. But it's not the same, it's not; and tonight she knows it. This unnatural intrusion, eerie and off-putting, stands between Emma and the house she owns on paper only.

After the noises end, she sleeps and dreams of Mrs. Hysop. Nothing wraithlike about her; she's a small woman but as solid and substantial as the table they sit at. They're in the kitchen drinking tea. Emma is embarrassed because the kitchen is a mess, breakfast dishes cluttering the counter, last night's pots soaking in the sink.

Mrs. Hysop stirs her tea with a purple pen. "It's hard to find good help these days," she says. "You can't trust anyone."

"It's all in how you look at it," Emma says.

"Precisely," the old woman replies, laying her finger alongside her nose.

Nothing to it, Emma tells herself later, in the lucid light of morning. This was no visitation, but a simple psychological construct, the effort of her subconscious to grapple with her fear. She avoids asking herself why, in that case, Zack, too, saw Mrs. Hysop in a dream. Like a good surgeon, Emma favors the least invasive procedure/explanation.

In any case, this much is clear: She cannot continue a day longer in ignorance of this person who may or may not still reside in her house. Surely there is more to discover about Mrs. Hysop. No one could live and work so long in a town without leaving more trace of herself than Emma has heretofore found.

She decides to go back to the library; in fact, she'll make a morning of it. There are plenty of errands piled up: post office, dry cleaner, perhaps one of the bookstores for a treat. As soon as Zack is off to school, Emma gathers the dry cleaning, finds her bag, sticks her keys in her jacket pocket and heads out. Her car stands alone; Caroline must have gone out early. A mass of heavy gray clouds lies over the bay like the lid of a cooler sealing in the cold and damp; a foretaste of winter frosts the air. She tosses the clothes onto the passenger's seat and takes her place behind the wheel before realizing she left the library books on the front hall table. "Damn!" She stomps back to the house. But the delay turns out to be lucky; as she turns from locking the front door for the second time, her tenant emerges from the carriage house. Dressed for work, but coatless and in stockinged feet, Caroline hurries up the drive. They meet halfway.

"You're home!" says Emma. "Where's your car?"

"In the shop, waiting to be collected." Caroline hops from foot to foot, hugging herself against the chill. "I was just about to phone for a taxi when I saw you loading your car. Are you by any chance driving into town?"

"Yes, and you're welcome to come if you don't mind a few quick stops along the way."

Caroline doesn't mind a bit, she says, and runs back for her coat and shoes. Meanwhile Emma shifts the laundry to the rear seat and tosses the library books back with them.

It's been nearly a week since she last saw Caroline, and their meeting now is not without awkwardness—on both sides, she suspects, for theirs is a pressure-cooker friendship between two people whose preferences run to the slow-baked variety. Emma has always been one far more apt to receive than to offer confidences, yet to Caroline she has opened windows into her marriage, her secret past, and private anxieties; she has exposed, not only herself, but also her husband and son to this woman's keen scrutiny. She has done this of her own free will, yet in violation of her nature has she done it. Little surprise, then, that every burst of confidence is followed by an equal and opposite drawing back.

As for Caroline, Emma attributes *her* reticence to tact. Caroline never asked to become the depository of Emma's fears (though it may be said that Caroline—intelligent, dispassionate, and *there*—presented an irresistible temptation). From the start she has seemed torn between sympathetic interest and a perfectly understandable reluctance to interfere in her landlords' complicated affairs.

Nevertheless, once Caroline is sitting beside her, Emma finds herself inordinately cheered by their chance meeting. She says so as they drive down Crag Road.

"Me, too," Caroline replies with a smile. "Cab fare aside."

Emma brakes to allow a woman with a stroller to cross the road. The woman smiles and waves, and Emma waves back. They met on open-school night; the woman has a daughter in Zack's class.

Seeing this, Caroline says, "You seem to have settled in nicely."

Like many of Caroline's observations, this one leaves Emma slightly off balance. Is it true? she wonders. Is she losing her city edge, blending in? She consigns it to her waiting list of worries.

"You meet people, and then you run into them everywhere. It's all through Zack, of course. School, soccer."

"Mom and apple pie," says Caroline, smiling faintly, and Emma realizes she's been tactless. How many people has her tenant met? Emma has never seen any visitors to the carriage house, nor has she noticed any personal letters in the mailbox they share. Things are different for a single woman, harder here than in the city. What does Caroline do every morning and night, alone in her little house? Emma finds to her shame she has no idea. They should have done more for her; *she* should have, at least. But her relationship with Caroline is like a river: All questions and concern flow one way.

Now, tentatively, she swims against the stream. "Do you find it very boring," she asks, "living in Morgan Peak?"

"Boring?" Caroline arches her eyebrows. "Oh no, my dear. These months have been the most peaceful I've had in years. And if you'll forgive me, your adventures alone would have precluded boredom."

The post office is a small brick building dwarfed by an American flag on an eighteen-foot pole. Emma pulls into the lot, parks, and goes about her errand. She approaches the brick building with a sense of dread; in the city, a trip to the PO was a chore on the order of doing her taxes. Inside, however, she finds three bored-looking clerks and no line; she's in and out in two minutes.

"That was quick," says Caroline, glancing up from one of Emma's library books.

"Wasn't it? If it weren't for the driving, I could learn to love the 'burbs." Emma pulls out of the lot.

"That's good. Last time we met you weren't so sure. Dare I ask how things are going?"

I'm pregnant, thinks Emma. My house is haunted. Someone has sabotaged my computer. But the first is a secret, the second will not be believed, and the third she is forbidden to reveal; to do so, Roger has warned, would defeat the purpose of leaving the program in. "Fine," she says, a beat late.

Caroline looks at her. "All's well on the home front?"

"Absolutely."

Caroline waits. If silence were a scalpel, she'd be a brain surgeon. "Really," Emma insists. "We're fine."

"So that wasn't Roger I heard yesterday afternoon?"

"Oh," says Emma. "You heard that."

"I wasn't trying to. Voices carry in the country."

"He wasn't yelling at me. He was yelling at Zack's soccer coach. Roger came home early, found him in the house, and jumped to all the wrong conclusions."

"Good Lord," Caroline says. "Never a dull moment."

"Give my eye teeth for one."

"Has he always been jealous?"

"No, never. That's why I was amazed. I mean, Nick's a major flirt, but even so, Roger's reaction was off the scale."

"Hmm," says Caroline. Emma's still gnawing on that "hmm" when they reach the dry cleaner, which shares a parking lot with the village's only 7-Eleven. Caroline waits in the car while Emma goes in. Lee, the proprietor, is busy with another customer but flashes a smile. Emma lays her clothes on the counter and checks the pockets. Roger's jacket yields a crumpled five-dollar bill and change. His pants pockets seem empty at first; then her fingers encounter a small packet. She pulls it out.

It's a condom. In a red foil wrapper. She stares at it as if she's never seen one before.

The door opens and shuts. Emma's fist shuts tight over the packet. The other customer has gone, and Lee is speaking to her. Someone answers with surprising composure; it must be Emma, there's no one else there. When Lee turns away to write up the laundry slip, Emma shoves the condom deep into her pocket.

Years ago, in the spring of her freshman year at college, Emma discovered a lump in her left breast, just above her heart. Her mother having died just six months earlier, she felt both exposed and targeted by a malevolent fate. The possibility of a benign diagnosis, which she eventually received, never even occurred to her. As she fingered the mass, a coldness had spread through her, emanating outward, and her breath had emerged as puffs of gelid particles.

Emma has the same sensation now: She is a block of ice encased by skin. Her emotions are frozen along with the rest of her. When she thaws there will be pain; now there is none.

She finds herself back in the car. A cold rain has begun to fall, blurring the world outside. The key is in the ignition. Emma makes no move to turn it, but sits motionlessly, hands on the wheel, staring into the middle distance. Caroline's voice reaches her from far away. "What is it, Emma? What's wrong?"

She forces her head around. "Roger never empties his pockets."

"None of them do. They see it as one of the perks of marriage."

"This was in his pants pocket." She extracts the condom from her pocket and holds it between them, pinched between thumb and forefinger like a dead bug.

Deep, sorrowful lines emerge on Caroline's face, as if they'd been there all along, undetected. "I gather you don't . . ."

"I use a diaphragm."

Caroline sighs.

The rain gathers force, borne on the wings of a gusty wind. This is not city weather, but the raw, unbuffered stuff. Where am I, Emma wonders, and how did I get here?

"Wait," says Caroline, and then she is gone, dissolved in the grayness outside. A minute later she returns with a cup in each hand. Emma reaches across the seat to open the passenger-side door.

Caroline passes her a 7-Eleven cup. "Ought to be whiskey, but caffeine'll have to do. Drink."

Emma pops the lid and takes a sip. Sweet, milky liquid fills her mouth, and she remembers how to swallow. The coffee melts a trail through her icy innards.

"Forgive me," Caroline says presently, "but does this come as a total shock?"

"Does what come as a shock?" Emma says.

"Ah." Caroline's tone is diagnostic. *Stuck in that stage, are we?*

"There could be other explanations."

"Love to hear one."

"Remember the worms?"

"Vividly."

"Someone did that. Someone could have done this."

"You're suggesting that someone broke into your house and planted that thing in your husband's pocket."

"Yes."

"Knowing, somehow, that you'd be the one to find it."

Emma swallows hard. "It's possible."

"Now I know," Caroline says, "what makes you a writer."

EMMA STANDS ON the steps of the library, balancing her books on one hip. Part of her yearns to go home, climb into bed, and pull the covers over her head. But she's been there, done that; and besides, home is not the sanctuary it once was. It's the battlefront now.

Caroline is gone, deposited, protesting gently, at the auto shop. Kind as she is, her absence is a balm. Alone at last, bathed in silence, Emma feels for the center, the inner fulcrum, and finds it has shifted to her womb. *Poor little one, I had forgotten you. Never mind. Sleep and grow. You're safe with me, whatever happens.*

She enters the library and returns her books at the front desk. She passes through the stacks of new arrivals, ignoring their siren calls, and goes directly to the reference desk. Jeff Harris recognizes her at once and gives her such a welcoming smile that another small part of her defrosts on the spot. "Hello, Emma. What can I do for you?"

"You can tell me about Virginia Hysop." Emma puts both hands on his desk and leans forward. "You went to school here. She was your teacher. You must know what happened to her."

Jeff casts a quick, proprietary look about his domain, then leads her into a small computer room for staff only. She takes a seat, and he wheels his chair around to face her. "What do you want to know about her?"

"The woman's a teacher for forty-five years. When she retires, they give a banquet for her. Ten years later she's the town pariah. What happened?"

"You don't know? No one told you?"

"If I knew I wouldn't be asking."

"Well," he says, seeming at a loss to begin, "her husband died."

"Husbands often do."

"And she tried to bury him."

Emma stares blankly. "Isn't that customary here?"

"Not in the backyard, no, ma'am."

"I see," says Emma, though she does not. Impossible to picture the old lady wielding a spade on the hard, rocky ground, or lugging a man from the house to the garden. "How?"

"There was a guy who used to deliver her groceries, high school teammate of mine named C. J. Freemont. His dad was the football coach. Apparently she asked him for help. I'm not real clear on the details; I was . . . out of commission when it all went down. If you really want to know, you ought to talk to the coach, C. J.'s dad. He's the one went out there and called the cops."

"Would he talk to me?"

"He will if I ask him. I'll call him right now if you like."

Emma glances at her watch. "Wouldn't he be working now?"

"He's retired," Jeff says shortly. He reaches for the phone.

COACH FREEMONT is home, free, and willing. Half an hour later, Emma is ringing the doorbell of a small brick Tudor. The door opens at once.

"Cal Freemont," he says, crushing her hand. He's a large, barrel-shaped black man with a square face and bristly gray hair. Young for a retiree, mid-fifties perhaps. He ushers her into a living room so tidy it looks unused, indicates a chair for her, and takes the one opposite. The focal point of the room is a large combination TV/VCR on the opposite wall, topped by two framed photographs. One is of a young man—C. J., she presumes—in a Notre Dame football uniform. The other is a graduation-day photo of the same young man in cap and gown, mugging for the camera with his arm around his father's shoulders.

There's a settled stillness to the house; Freemont, she feels certain, lives alone.

"Jeff mentioned you're a writer," he says.

"Yes."

"You writing about Mrs. Hysop?"

"No, I'm not. My interest's purely personal; we bought her house."

He nods brusquely. If this is a test, Emma's got the first answer right. "Suppose you've heard a lot of nonsense about her."

"I've heard some things."

"Figures. People love to talk."

"They do, but rarely to the point. I still don't understand what she's supposed to have done. I was hoping you could tell me."

"It's not what she did," he growls. "It's what she didn't do, and what they thought she did—if you call it thinking, which I don't."

As he tells the story, Emma sees it in her mind's eye. February, trees stripped bare, frost on the ground. Honeysuckle vines, planted in happier times but now grown wild, cling with skeletal fingers to the exterior walls. C. J. climbs the steps to the front door, balancing three bags. No sign of anyone at home, but he knows they're in there; they always are. The old guy's an invalid of some sort; and since her retirement Mrs. Hysop herself has gone shy and strange. He lays the bags on the floor of the porch and looks for the envelope she always leaves tacked to the front door. In it, he knows, will be next week's list, a check for the food, and, unfailingly, a two-dollar tip for him. Last Christmas she'd left him a crisp twenty-dollar bill. He'd rung the bell to thank her, but she hadn't appeared.

There's no envelope today, though, only a hand-written note taped to the peeling paint of the front door. "C. J.," it says, "knock." He knocks. Several minutes pass before the door creaks open. Mrs. Hysop blinks hard at the light of day. A whiff of bad air escapes the house as she steps outside and shuts the door behind her.

"I want you to do a job for me," she says, her voice flat, uninflected. Her eyes avoid his face. "I'll pay you twenty dollars."

"What do you want done?"

There's a pause before she answers. "I want you to dig a hole in the backyard."

He looks outside. The ground is frozen solid, glazed with frost. C. J. is a strapping lad, a six-two varsity wide receiver who can bench press three hundred pounds without breaking a sweat. But he breaks one now, standing on that porch with this wisp of a woman who will not meet his eyes. He feels he's stepped into some kind of movie; he can practically hear the organ music in the background. "Why?" he asks.

Again the barely perceptible hesitation, as if she's responding, not to his words, but rather to a not quite simultaneous translation.

"Planting bushes. Spirea. Azaleas. Roses."

He backs away. "I have to finish my deliveries."

"Come back after," she says.

C. J. returns to the store and thinks about what just happened. He's no expert on gardening but even he knows you don't plant bushes in February. The more he thinks, the uneasier he feels. After a while he goes back to the manager's office and calls his dad.

Cal Freemont knows Virginia Hysop, of course, having worked in the same school for ten years. They weren't friends. It wasn't just the age difference; Mrs. Hysop had flunked some of Freemont's best players, knocked 'em right off his roster, which the coach didn't exactly appreciate. They'd gone a few rounds over the years, and even though he could have crushed her with one fist, more often than not she came out the winner.

Still, he knows her, and he knows her husband, Arthur, too. C. J.'s account is troubling, but Cal is more than a little reluctant to get involved. He's got problems of his own and doesn't need anyone else's, let alone Virginia Hysop's. C. J. is counting on him to do the right thing, though, and Cal can't let his boy down.

So he goes out; he drives to their house. By this time it's past seven, full dark, but there's not a single light showing in the house on Crag Road. Cal rings the bell. Nothing. He knocks. Still nothing. He goes on ringing and knocking for fifteen minutes before she quits ignoring him and opens the door.

He's shocked by her appearance. She's lost perhaps a dozen pounds off a frame that was never robust. Her hair is matted, and there are dark bags under her eyes. Cal doesn't wait for an invitation. He steps into the house, and right away he knows. Decades ago he did a stint in 'Nam. There are some smells a man never forgets.

He finds Arthur upstairs. She's rolled him up in a blanket and hauled the blanket to the top of the L-shaped stairs. God knows how she managed; the old man would have made two of her. How she planned to get him downstairs and outside Cal cannot imagine. Looking at her, he doubts she's thought that far ahead.

At this point in the story Cal falls silent. He walks to the window and stands with his back to Emma, looking out at the truculent rain.

"What did you do?" she prompts softly.

"I called the cops." His back stiffens, but Emma does not speak. "I didn't know what was going to happen," he says. "And even if I did, what was I supposed to do: let her plant him in the backyard like a tub of petunias?"

"What happened?"

"Nothing much," he says. He seems tired of the subject, tired of her. "There was some talk of charging her with failure to report a death. He'd been gone three days, the coroner said. But any fool could see how confused she was, how lost. The teachers' union handled the funeral. And I guess some of them tried to help her. PTA ladies called on her, sent cards. But Mrs. Hysop wouldn't see anyone. Had her phone unlisted. Disconnected the doorbell, even, and went on living in that big old house alone."

"And that's it?" Emma asks slowly. "End of story?"

"For him," he says. "For her it was just the beginning. Hell hath no fury, Ms. Roth, like a pack of do-gooders scorned. When Mrs. Hysop shut herself up and the world out, people started talking. Why would she try to bury her husband if she didn't have something to hide? She must have killed him. Rumors started flying around, didn't matter how mean or unlikely or contradictory. The cops were investigating; the cops were covering up. The old man died of poison, he starved to death, he was covered head to toe with bruises. The cops were digging up the grounds, looking for additional bodies. No rumor too outrageous to be believed and repeated. If you've ever seen those nature films of barracuda in a feeding frenzy, you'll have some idea."

"You'd think people in a small village would be more sympathetic."

He turns and stares. "City girl, are you?"

She admits to it.

"Dynamic's different in a village. Consensus rules. When you're in you're in, but when you're out you couldn't be more out. Village's like a body reacting to a foreign presence: It closes ranks and attacks."

Emma thinks about Mrs. Hysop, and her own misery recedes. She sees the old woman clearly, feels close to her, moreover, for reasons not entirely clear.

In the silence that has fallen between them, the thrum of rain fills the room. It's a steady, efficient downfall, like the regulated breathing of a long-distance runner. It has no built-in limit, no parabolic curve; not a cloudburst but a skybreak, an atmospheric sea change. It's the kind of rain you could imagine going on for forty days and forty nights.

"Roads'll be flooding," Cal says.

"I've taken enough of your time."

"Plenty of that." He lumbers back to his chair, pinning his hands beneath his armpits, and suddenly Emma is aware of the size of him, the unused strength: He's like a bear in a zoo, all untapped potential. There's a story here, too; she smells it. A question that earlier lodged itself in the back of her mind now breaks free and floats to the surface.

"Jeff called your son his teammate," she says; and by the sudden guarding of Freemont's eyes, the way he recedes without moving, she knows she's touched a nerve.

"They were teammates, yeah. Harris was my quarterback, best I ever coached. Kid had a hell of a future. Why, did you think he was born in that chair?"

"What happened?"

"Broke his back."

Emma winces. "Playing football?" It's not really a question.

"Now I *know* you're from out of town," Cal says, with a poor attempt at a smile. "There's nobody from around here doesn't know the story. Happened during a game, his senior year."

"The damage is permanent?"

He lifts a heavy shoulder, lets it fall. "Doctors say it is. He thinks different."

Her next question is not the sort she would normally ask—too close to the bone, even for her. Maybe it's the rain, the closed-in, curtained atmosphere that creates a false sense of intimacy, or the impact of the day's revelation jarring something loose.

"When did you retire?" she asks.

Freemont glares and works his jaw. For a moment Emma expects to be turned away, sent out into the rain. Then she sees he's not looking at her at all. "It was a quarterback sneak. Harris made it through the line, but the safeties got him. One hit him high from the front, the other hit low from behind. You could hear it happen. I heard the crack. I knew right away."

He falls silent. The sound of the rain fills the room. Then Freemont shrugs. "You tell yourself risk comes with the territory. Everybody knows it coming in. I used to stand on that practice field yelling at my boys: 'Play harder! Hit harder!' A thing like this happens, you deal with it; you *think* you deal with it. Only next time you go out on the field, you open your mouth and choke. Nothing, not a friggin' word.

"Takes a certain willful blindness to be a coach," he says. "I loved the game, loved the job, used to pray I'd coach till I dropped. Then my eyes got opened. Once that happens, there's no going back."

"No," says Emma, "there's not."

20

"SOMETHING happened today," Emma says. Her face and neck ache with the effort of acting herself all through dinner. It has not come naturally; she's felt like a clever reproduction, a discontinuous composite of sound bites and reconstructed smiles. Everything had to seem normal, for her only hope of finding out the truth was to take Roger by surprise. Now Zack has gone upstairs to do his homework, and they are finally alone. Roger clears the dishes while she loads the dishwasher.

"What happened?" he asks.

"I went to the cleaners." She watches him closely. One flicker of trepidation and she has her answer.

Roger looks up with mild interest; this is not the sort of domestic detail she normally shares. "And?"

"You forgot to empty your pockets."

He smiles unconcernedly. "Careless of me. How much did you make this time?"

She pulls the condom from her pocket and tosses it onto the counter beside the sink. The red foil packet glows and seems to expand.

Roger looks from it to her, his face a blank. "What's this?"

"It's a condom."

"I see that. Where'd it come from?"

"Your pants."

"If this is a joke, it's not funny."

"Do I look amused?"

"It's not mine." He glares at her, daring her to doubt his word.

He's angry, she thinks. How dare he be angry? He's trying to preempt her. "Whose is it, then?"

"You are quick to accuse!"

"It's a reasonable question. Anyway, who are you to talk after that scene with Nick?"

"I never doubted you," he says quickly. "Just him. Emma, look me in the eye and tell me you believe I'd cheat on you."

She looks at him. Sees the pores in his skin, the beard pushing up beneath the surface, the fine lines about his eyes that weren't there six months ago. Images flicker across her mind, scenes from a marriage. The raw tenderness of his face, gazing down on the newborn son in his arms. After the accident: the blessed sound of his voice approaching the cubicle where she lay in her blood, shivering and covered by a sheet. *No, I won't wait! Where is she, where is my wife?* The terror on his face that abated only when she spoke to him, the strength of his arms as he held her. She clung to him as to an anchor and he held firm. All they have been through, all they have survived together comes back to her. It's beyond love now. Life has welded them together.

But even loving husbands stray. Who is immune to

seduction? Caroline's voice sticks in her mind, that curdled blend of mockery and pity. *Now I know what makes you a writer.*

"I won't play the fool," she says. "I won't be lied to. If something's going on, tell me and we will find a way to work it out. But if you lie to me now, I couldn't bear it. I wouldn't."

"There's nothing to tell. How can you not know that?"

She rears back, stung by his tone. "You had doubts about me. When I told you about the hearts game, you thought I was imagining those messages."

He looks away. "I had fears. You know why. But I never questioned your loyalty."

His face is pale; his voice sounds squeezed in the middle. Emma is torn. One moment she feels she's done him an injustice, the next she suspects him of trying to manipulate her. This rapid and extreme vacillation of faith and doubt, feeling and thought, is so exquisitely painful it leaves her gasping inside. A person could go mad, she thinks . . . especially a person so inclined.

With this thought comes an intuition of danger. We all have our weaknesses, genetic dispositions to one disease or another. Emma's is depression. Stress is a known factor. Is her enemy aware of her history? Few people are. Two months in the bin for depression: not the kind of item featured in publicity bios, though it could easily enough be ferreted out. What an intimate enemy this is turning out to be. An enemy of the heart.

Roger stands and begins to pace. His steps are measured but there is rage in the bunched muscles in his neck, the balled fists by his side. Casey raises his head, watches for a moment, then slinks, whimpering, under the kitchen table.

Emma follows with her eyes. She has never seen Roger this angry, not even the time he broke with his parents. If she didn't know him she would have crossed the street to avoid him. This man looks dangerous.

"Tell me how it happened," he says. "Everything, every detail. Where were the pants kept?"

"In that bin in our closet where I always keep the dry cleaning."

"When did you find the rubber?"

"At the cleaners, when I checked your pockets."

"Any stops along the way?"

"The post office, but that was only a minute."

"Wouldn't take but a minute," Roger says. "Did you lock the car?"

"No," she says, "but Caroline was there."

He stops short, turns. "Caroline!"

Emma raises a finger. "Don't start."

"What was she doing there?"

"Her car was in the garage. I offered her a lift."

"Johnny-on-the-spot as usual," Roger says, with such icy contempt that Emma flares up instantly.

"And I suppose she just happened to have a condom concealed about her person. Get real!"

"She had the opportunity is all I'm saying."

"Oh really! And her motive would be . . . ?"

A moment passes. "I don't know," he admits. Emma throws up her hands. "Tell you one thing, Em: I'm not calling it a motive, but that woman detests me."

"You're the one who dislikes her, ever since that silly argument about battered women." Emma hears her voice rising. Let it, she thinks. In his own quiet way, Roger is not above bullying. It's a vestige of class, a potent strain of magic realism endemic to old money: He assumes his wishes will prevail, consequently they do. Emma has learned to pick her battles, but this is one worth fighting. Caroline may be a noxious presence to him, but to Emma she is sanity and common sense itself, even when she's wrong, as she is about Roger.

"It's true," Roger says. "I don't like her. I don't care for her conversation, her demeanor, her cute way of putting thoughts in your head."

"Putting thoughts in my head!" cries Emma. "Why, do you think I have none of my own?"

"That's not what I meant, and you know it."

"I don't know what I know anymore," says Emma, and it comes to her that she has never spoken truer words.

THEY MUST THINK he's dumb, deaf, and blind. He *knows* they think he's some kind of Disney kid, for Chrissake. They imagine it all passes over his head: the looks, the silences when he comes in and goes out, the signs of tears on his mother's face, the anxiety on his father's, the raised voices that penetrate the walls and turn his blood to sludge.

But Zack knows plenty. He sees things. Not enough yet to put it all together—too many pieces missing. But he keeps his eyes and ears open, and he's adding pieces all the time.

Like tonight. They thought he was upstairs doing his homework. And he does go upstairs, but then he sneaks down again. The dishwasher's on, they never hear him. He gets as close as he can to the kitchen—the hallway's dangerous, so he hangs in the dining room, no reason for them to go in there.

It's spying and he knows it, but the way Zack sees it, it's self-defense. It's like his dad says about soccer. To be a really good player, you have to know what your opponent is going to do with the ball before he knows it himself; you have to anticipate. That's what Zack's doing tonight, with the lights out and his ear pressed to the wall: He's anticipating.

His mom can't fool him. All through dinner she was in pert sitcom-mom mode; but in the deep trenches between questions about work and school, distraction welled up, threatening to swallow her whole. If only she would tell him what the matter was, Zack would do anything to fix it.

But she doesn't confide in him. To her he's not a person, he's just a kid.

His knees ache from kneeling on the hardwood floor. He can't hear much, but the tone of their voices tells him they're quarreling. Anger shrills his mother's voice, deepens his father's. Twice he hears a name: Caroline.

He knows who that is: Dr. Marks, their tenant. A middle-aged lady, childless, pleasant enough, harmless, irrelevant, or so he thought. Now he has to wonder: What is she to his parents that they should fight about her?

No answer. Insufficient data.

There is movement in the kitchen. Zack rises, knees cracking, and tiptoes out. Wouldn't do to be trapped downstairs; they always look in on him. He makes his way upstairs, skipping the third and seventh steps, which creak. Knowledge is power, Aunt Maggie always says, a principle Zack not only believes in but applies.

In the absence of openness, vigilance is essential. Let them think they are protecting him; Zack will do what he has to do.

SPARKS FLY AS Emma brushes her long black hair. She watches Roger in the vanity mirror. Standing with his back to her, he empties his pockets onto the dresser top, spilling out keys, wallet, loose change. Could have happened just like that, she suddenly thinks. He could have tossed that thing out onto the dresser with all his other stuff. What would he have done? Palm it instantly, look to see if she'd noticed?

The brush falters in mid-stroke. Like a train switching tracks, Emma's thoughts have taken a whole new turn. She takes her time examining the landscape before turning to Roger.

"What if I wasn't meant to find it?" she says. "What if you were?"

He shrugs. "To what end?"

"You're assuming that, if the condom was planted, it was done here in the house. But why assume that? The pants were never more accessible than when you wore them."

"I think I might have noticed someone sticking their hand in my hip pocket. Besides, I'd be bound to find it."

"Suppose you did. Suppose you're at work, you stick your hand in your pocket and there it is. What would you do?"

"Look around," he says reluctantly; he can see where this is going.

"Right. And suppose someone's adoring eyes are on you, waiting. A little smile of confirmation, a hitch of the eyebrow, and voilà!"

"A joke?"

"A suggestion," she says firmly. "An offer. Don't tell me you've never had one."

He doesn't tell her that. His eyes falter for no more than a second, but that's long enough. *So she has tried, that bitch!* Emma's instinct was right. She resists an impulse to leave the room and call her sister.

Roger feigns weariness. "Are we back to India?"

"Back to the subcontinent herself; yes, I'm afraid so."

"Pretty reckless, wouldn't you say? There's always the chance I don't find it and you do."

"No doubt it would break her heart to cause trouble between us," she says dryly.

"I see you've got this whole *Fatal Attraction* scenario worked out. Take my word for it, Em, it's not gonna fly. It's just not India's style."

Her eyebrows scale her forehead. "Oh, no? What is her style?"

"I wouldn't know, but I doubt it's as sleazy as this."

Emma goes to him then. She wraps her arms around his waist, and though he's surprised he readily returns her embrace. For several moments they cling together. He strokes her flank, kisses her neck.

"She could have done it," she whispers in his ear. "It's possible."

"No way. I'd have noticed."

"Are you sure?" Emma backs away, out of arm's reach. "Check your pockets now."

Roger sighs reproachfully. They're both aware of the erection tenting his khakis. Slowly his right hand slides into the pocket and emerges clutching a gold band studded with diamonds: Emma's wedding ring.

"There you go," she says.

"It wasn't a fair test. You distracted me."

"All's fair in love and war. Arthur's convinced India's in love with you."

He snorts. "Sure; how else could she resist his advances? For Chrissake, Emma, you know the man thinks with his prick."

"True," she says, "but it's a pretty good barometer."

21

WHEN THE doorbell rings, the United States has just scored a goal in a World Cup qualifying match and Roger and Zack are dancing a celebration tango across the living room floor.

"I'll get it," Emma says.

She goes out to the front hall—Casey's already there—and opens the door. Nick Sanders stands under the porch light, dressed in jeans, a Shetland sweater, and a Burberry jacket. All that's missing is the pipe. Poor man, she thinks then; is it his fault he looks like a Ralph Lauren ad?

The October air is a sailor's chantey, flavored with brine and the distant scent of wood fires. Nick looks at her like a man just home from the sea. "Hey, Emma," he says.

"Hey yourself."

"Brought you something." He lifts a large carton from the floor and, without waiting for an invitation, steps past her into the house. "Roger home?"

"Yes."

"Good. Don't want him getting the wrong idea." He lays the unmarked box on a table by the door and bends down to return Casey's greeting. "Your husband's a jealous man. Not that I blame him."

"What's this?"

"Peace of mind, I hope. Open it."

Emma opens the box and peers inside. "Looks strangely like a laptop."

"Didn't see how you could be comfortable working on your own machine, knowing someone's in there with you. This one's straight from the factory, intact. It's a safe place to work."

A safe place to work. How long since she's felt safe working in a room haunted from both within and without? With a laptop she could work wherever she pleased. No one's eyes but her own would read her work. It would be just her and her book, the way it's supposed to be. Emma is amazed at the coach's thoughtfulness. It's the kind of thing she would have expected from a woman friend, or a fellow writer. But of course she can't accept it. She tells him so.

Why the hell not, he wants to know.

She glances down the hall toward the living room, and Nick follows her eyes. He moves closer, lowers his voice. "Who's doing this to you, Emma?"

"Beats me."

"Can't be that many possibilities. Somehow I don't see you having lots of enemies."

"Now you've hurt my feelings. You think I'm a marshmallow."

He laughs. Is she flirting? Emma prefers to think of it as marshaling her forces.

"Please take it," he says. "And if there's ever anything else I can do for you, all you've got to do is whistle. You know how to whistle, don't you?"

"Just pucker up and blow." Emma laughs in his face. "*Casablanca.*"

Unabashed, he flashes his dimples and says, "*To Have and Have Not*, actually. Waited my whole life for a chance to say that line. Meant it, too," he adds softly, looking past her. Emma turns around. Roger is striding down the hall toward them.

"Hey, Roger," Nick says.

"Sanders," says Roger. His hands are in his pockets. "Just passing by?"

"Brought your wife a laptop. Thing was lying around the office gathering dust. She can work on that and not worry about tampering."

Silence, a little beat of chagrin.

"Not a bad idea," Roger concedes grudgingly. "Tomorrow we'll go out and get one."

"What's wrong with this one? Straight from the factory, never touched."

"We'll get our own, thanks."

"Jesus, man," Nick says, "could you be more of a hard-ass? Consider it a loan if you like, but take the damn thing."

Roger looks at Emma, and a quick, silent exchange ensues.

He's trying to help.
Don't want his help.
You're behaving badly.
He's got an agenda.
So what!

"Your call," he says aloud.

Emma weighs her husband's displeasure against the injustice to Sanders and says, "We'll take it, as a loan of course. Thanks, Nick."

"*De nada*. Want you to have this, too." Nick takes a card from his pocket, glances at Roger, and holds it out to Emma. "It's got all my numbers: home, office, and beeper."

Roger intercepts it. He drops the card into his jacket pocket and offers up a rictus of a smile. "Thanks," he says, thinking it'll be a cold day in hell when he calls on Nick.

A long look arches between the two men. "I'm never far," Nick says quietly. "You work in the city. Think about that."

"I'll bear it in mind," says Roger.

LATE THAT NIGHT, getting out of the shower, Emma overhears Roger on the bedroom phone, his voice low and confiding. Who could he be talking to? India, maybe? A knot forms in her stomach. As she enters the bedroom he is saying, "You realize this weekend's Halloween." He turns and sees Emma, and at once his voice takes on a familiar edge. "Are you coming by train or broomstick?"

Maggie, she thinks. Thank God.

"Here she is. I'll put her on." He holds out the receiver. "Your sister."

"Hey, Mags," Emma says.

"Remind me, would you, why you married that lughead?"

"Slips my mind. What's up?"

"Thought I'd come out for the weekend, if Herr Doktor can bear it."

"We'll sedate him. Who was it who said she would never sleep another night under my roof?"

"Who said anything about sleeping?"

Emma laughs with pleasure at the prospect of seeing her sister, tart tongue and all. "When?" she asks.

"Friday evening. Cook something good."

"I have a lot to tell you." She touches her belly, which now feels swollen, though nothing shows.

Maggie's voice is suddenly tense. "Good or bad?"

"A bissel o' this, a bissel o' that," says Emma in their mother's voice. "More good than bad is all we can ask for."

"God, you just sent shivers up my spine, you sound so much like her."

"See you Friday," Emma says. She hangs up and gets into bed beside Roger.

"The whole weekend?" he asks.

"Be nice."

"I'm always nice to your sister. It's like petting a tarantula."

Emma laughs. "Her bark is worse than her bite."

"Tarantulas don't bark," Roger says. "They attack silently when you least expect it." He illustrates beneath the covers. "They crawl up your leg. They creep under your clothes."

"They do not," she protests, laughing, but does not push his hand away.

"They find their way into your most intimate folds and crevices. They explore, moving softly, softly . . . and then they strike!"

NEXT MORNING, making her bed, Emma finds herself wondering about the phone call from her sister. It must have been close to midnight when she called, unusual for Maggie, who keeps late hours but knows they don't. Strange, too, that Emma didn't hear the phone ring. True, she was in the shower; but the phone often rings while she's showering, and she almost always hears it.

Is it possible Roger made the call, not Maggie? But why would he call her? And why wait until Emma was out of the room?

She sits abruptly, suffering a rush of nausea unrelated to her pregnancy. Hates where her thoughts are going but can't seem to stop them. That throwaway remark of Caroline's sticks to the roof of her mind. *I noticed the Tracy-Hepburn routine.* Which is what if not the classic love-hate relationship? Poisonous words; damn Caroline and her knowing eyes. The sort of relationship she implied (if indeed she did imply it, if it's not just Emma's own paranoid fantasy) is doubly impossible: Roger and Maggie love her; and they are honorable people.

She lies down with her cheek on Roger's pillow. The sheets smell of him and her and what passed between them. Unlike her chaotic night table, his is uncluttered; alarm clock, TV remote, and white cordless telephone neatly aligned. Emma stares at the phone and the phone stares back. She sits up, reaches for the handset, hesitates, then snatches it up. She presses the Redial button. Ten quick tones are followed by two rings and a mechanical click.

"You've reached Maggie Roth," declares her sister's no-nonsense voice. "Leave a message."

Emma hangs up.

OVER FRIDAY NIGHT dinner Maggie peppers Zack with questions about his school and social life, an interrogation Zack seems to accept in a spirit of scientific inquiry, for he answers with surprising forthrightness. When she asks how he has been received by his classmates, he says, "They like me 'cause I'm good at sports. And I'm from the city, so they think I'm tough."

"Got a best friend yet?"

"Marcel."

"Because you play soccer together?"

"That, and we just like the same stuff. Plus, we're both different from the others."

"How so?"

"I'm new and from the city," Zack explains. "He's black."

His parents exchange identical looks of amazement. Zack is their greatest joy, in their eyes a delightful child, as bright as he is graceful; but one thing he is not is open. Their son does not confide; he watches. Emma doesn't know if this is simply his nature, as it is hers, or if it stems from her unwilled desertion all those years ago. In either case, Maggie has the purgative effect on Zack of a dose of cod-liver oil. Roger and Emma eat silently, listening with a sense of eavesdropping as the interrogation continues.

"Does his being black matter to the other kids?"

Zack shrugs. "They're friendly."

"But that's as far as it goes?"

"Yeah."

"Why's that, do you think?"

Zack knows what a sociologist is because over the years Maggie has taken care to explain. So he gives his answer some thought, and presents it with the air of an ambassador explaining his native land to a foreigner.

"Marcel's a real good athlete. Not just in soccer; he's

awesome at basketball, too, even though he's short. Sometimes when a kid's that much better than other kids, other kids think he's a snob even if he's not. Plus, to them being black means he's automatically cool. It's, like, they're wannabees and he's the real thing."

Maggie looks at him with quiet approval, then reaches out and musses his hair, which needs no mussing. "And you're the real thing, too."

"We like to think so," Zack says modestly, buffing his fingernails on his shirt, and flushing with pleasure when the grown-ups laugh.

"I don't know," says Maggie, "if it's a tribute to the way you raised him or a sign of the times that Zack regards being black as conveying a distinct social advantage."

Emma leans back in her chair and rests her legs on Maggie's bed. It's a pajama party, the menfolk tucked away in slumberland while the sisters gossip in the guest room. Maggie sits upright on the bed, painting her toenails red. Emma wonders if there's a new man in her life but dismisses the thought as unlikely; Maggie would have said.

"That's his interpretation," she says. "You notice the bottom line is still Marcel doesn't get asked over much. I think his parents are as glad of the friendship as we are."

"And the parents?" Maggie glances up from her task. "Have you gotten close?"

"Heading that way," Emma says warily. She knows her sister's thinking on this subject, which has come up before. And it's not as if the idea never occurred to Emma. There are certain commonalties: the husband who died, a whiff of buried tragedy. But it can't be, Yolanda cannot be that woman, because she didn't follow them to Morgan Peak; she preceded them by several years. What are the odds that of all the villages in the world, Emma and Roger would blindly choose to settle in the backyard of the one person on earth with cause to hate them?

But when she says this to Maggie, Maggie rolls her eyes heavenward and says, "This isn't fiction, Em. Real life is shot through with coincidence. Look at it this way: You moved here and all hell broke loose."

"I know her," Emma says. "You don't. There's no malice there."

" 'One may smile, and smile, and be a villain.' "

"Judge for yourself. We'll see them tomorrow at the game. Yolanda's painting the kids' faces for Halloween."

"Before or after?"

"Before, of course. Psych out the opponents, who happen to be our divisional rivals; we're tied for first place."

Maggie heaves a sigh. "Alas, poor Emma, I knew her well."

And Emma, glimpsing herself through her sister's categorizing eyes, flushes scarlet. So Maggie thinks she's turned into Suburban Soccer Mom. Well, maybe she has; but the real question is, would she go back if she could?

There are nights, it's true, when Emma can't sleep for missing the lullaby of the city: the eternal rush of traffic, the subterranean thrum of the subway, the random strains of melody that waft through the air, the constant beat of the city, which was to her like the heartbeat of its mother to a sentient fetus. She misses her neighborhood (her cocoon) and its nourishing mix of faces: black, white, brown, Asian, Middle Eastern, European, South American, Mediterranean, and all combinations thereof. She misses the ambrosia of accents and argots, music to a writer's ear.

Not a small thing to give up, one's native land; yet for writers there is much to be said for living in exile, as many have found to their profit. And Emma is coming to see that there are phases in life, and that what would be absolutely wrong in one phase may be right and necessary in another. Would she go back? No, not for all the lox in Zabar's. This is her home now. Despite all that has happened, despite the impediments that remain, this is still the house that was meant for her. Let Maggie imagine she took this step for Zack and Roger's sake; to herself, Emma acknowledges the truth. Though their happiness matters deeply, it was her own she consulted in making this move. She wanted this house and the house wanted her; it's as plain and simple as that.

Maggie finishes her right foot and stretches it out to admire. Size six and narrow; Mags' secret vanity. "Who's going to see them?" Emma teases.

"One never knows," says Maggie, starting on her left. "So, what's this news you couldn't tell me over the phone?"

Nothing like novel writing for teaching deferred gratification, though Emma always was the kind who'd eat the outside of the Oreo first. She smiles to herself, resisting an impulse to touch her belly.

"Two things," she says. "The first is, my house is haunted. I'm convinced of it now. Almost convinced. Ninety-nine percent convinced."

"Oh, really?" Maggie examines a cuticle critically. "Ghosts, goblins, or fairies?"

"I'm serious, Mags."

"And I'm the Virgin Mary." But as Emma relates the story of Ida Green's visit, Maggie abandons the nail polish and hugs her knees to her chest. And by the time they reach Coach Freemont's account of Mrs. Hysop's decline and fall, she is gnawing on a corner of the bedsheet, a childhood habit denoting high anxiety.

In the end there's a silence.

"What does Roger say?" Maggie asks in a voice pitched half an octave higher than usual.

Emma looks at her. "He doesn't believe it."

"Score one for him."

"Meaning you don't either?"

"Hell, no," Maggie says stoutly, abandoning the sheet.

"Fine," says Emma. "Then you won't mind coming upstairs with me."

The silence is palpable. Maggie blinks. "Now?"

"Why not?"

She doesn't stir. "I don't think so."

"Scared?"

"And you're not?"

The odd thing is, Emma isn't. Not that she's free of fear; on the contrary, her life of late feels like a minefield. But she no longer fears the presence she's come to identify as Virginia Hysop. The change came on gradually, but Emma knows precisely when it began: on that dismal afternoon in Coach Freemont's living room, when he stood at the window and told a story to her reflection. Since then, pity has driven out fear.

She'd gotten it all wrong in her books, this business

of haunting. It isn't terrifying. It's barely even dramatic. Mostly it's just sad, in the peculiarly dreary manner of an unremitting toothache or implacably rainy afternoon. Painful, like seeing a lost child and being unable to help.

Emma had once conceived of an idea for a ghost story in which an autistic child is the only one in his family who can see the ghost. The child could have normal or even superior intelligence coupled with a complete inability to express himself, which would make for endless complications. She read up on the disease and was encouraged. The deficits of autism were a window into the preprogrammed nature of human socialization, fertile territory for novelists as well as neurologists.

It was good while it lasted, but it didn't last long. Two hours into what was meant to be an all-day visit with a four-year-old autistic boy and his mother, Emma abandoned the idea forever. The child was big and strong, highly energetic, and totally unsocialized. His language comprehension was inferior to that of the average house dog or cat; he seemed to lack the very concept of communication. His mother's wishes meant nothing to him. When frustrated, he tried to bite the hands that restrained him—his mother's, Emma observed, were covered with scars—or banged his head against a wall.

Unutterably dismal; not fodder for entertainment. Which is how she feels about Mrs. Hysop. To be trapped in such a marginal existence, hopelessly befogged, is a fate that Emma (who's been lost herself) cannot contemplate without horror and pity.

That said, she is not about to go up there alone tonight; for while Mrs. Hysop in the abstract may be pitiable indeed, Mrs. Hysop in the flesh, or lack thereof, would be quite another matter. Emma tunes in to Maggie, who is speaking earnestly.

"The thing is, once you start believing in ghosts, it doesn't stop there. You're forced to infer some sort of afterlife, survival after death, and God knows what else."

Emma shrugs. "Don't look at me. Not my doing."

"Thank you, Emma. With all due respect, I hadn't actually mistaken you for God. Tell me—if the old lady was senile, does that mean her ghost is senile, too?"

"I don't believe she was senile."

Maggie stares. "What would you call it, waiting three days, then trying to bury him herself?"

"Didn't start there. She'd already cut herself off from the world, locked herself up. Could have been agoraphobia, but I'd bet on depression."

There's a sudden charged silence. Maggie stares at her toes with fierce concentration. "Depression," she says.

"Takes one to know one," Emma says lightly.

Maggie's eyes dart toward her. "You aren't—"

"No, not at all. Couldn't be better. Actually, that leads me to my other bit of news." She pauses teasingly.

"What?" says Maggie.

"As a matter of fact . . ."

"Nu, what already?"

"I'm pregnant."

Had she not known her sister as well as she knows herself, Emma might have missed the tremor in her gaze, the barest flicker of something that is not surprise. Then it's gone, and Maggie screams and launches herself from the bed, catching Emma about the neck, pulling her into an all-out hug. "Oh my God, that's super, that's great, congratulations!"

And Emma returns her embrace, struck with wonder and doubt; because Maggie is not a squealer or grabber or oh-my-Godder; she's as far from those things as she can be without leaving the planet. Not because she doesn't feel deeply, but because, for Maggie, coolness is a matter of honor and a way of life. Always has been, since they were kids. When Emma announced her pregnancy with Zack, her sister's first reaction was to slap on sunglasses, hide those treacherous weepers behind mirrored glass.

She already knew, thinks Emma.

She couldn't have. No one knows but me and Roger.

But she did, Maggie knew. Which means Roger must have told her, which means . . . what?

22

THE SISTERS are just sitting down to coffee when Roger returns home bearing fresh bagels. He kisses Emma. "Maggie," he says cordially, though with a wary eye, "how did you sleep?"

"Remarkably well, considering your wife's choice of bedtime stories."

"She share her theory on Mrs. H.?"

Maggie nods.

"Tells it well, doesn't she?" he says lightly. "Hazards of marrying a writer. One is constantly tempted to believe."

Last night Maggie refused to hear of a ghost, but if Roger says black, she must say white. "It's not impossible."

"It's not impossible aliens will land in our backyard—but I doubt it."

Emma pauses in the middle of slicing a bagel. "You go on blindly believing what you want to believe," she tells Roger. "I'm just following the evidence."

"What evidence? Strange sounds in an old house, a child's dream, and, oh yes, a psychic advisory."

"Don't forget the markings on my manuscript, and Mrs. Hysop's history: her inability to leave this house, her confusion."

"It's strange story, but that's all it is: a story." He spreads a thin layer of cream cheese onto his bagel, which despite years of tutelage by Emma he still eats open, like an English muffin.

Maggie snorts. "Yeah, that'll work. Might as well tell a mathematician, 'It's only a number.' "

Despite himself, Roger laughs.

Emma watches, not only with her eyes but with her whole self. She listens to what is said and what is unsaid, and for the first time she discerns the ease and deep familiarity that underlie their jibes. When exactly did they become friends, and where was she looking when it happened? It's a discovery that ought to fill her with delight. Isn't it what she's always wanted, what she's urged on them both?

Now Maggie turns to Roger with an air of remembering. "Emma was full of surprises last night, and they weren't all bad. I understand congratulations are in order."

"It was nothing," he says modestly. "Anyone would have done the same in my place."

"True, but minimal as your contribution was, it has to be acknowledged."

"Too kind." He suppresses a smile. "We plan to name it after you, you know, if it's a harpy."

"Good morning," Emma says warningly as Zack, dressed and cleated for the game, follows his soccer ball into the kitchen. They haven't told him yet; Emma wants to wait till she's safely past the first trimester.

"Morning." Zack submits to her kiss.

"Hey, champ," says Roger, holding out a bagel.

Zack regards it as if it were fried octopus. "I can't eat this."

"You're eating something," Roger says. They compromise on Cheerios. After breakfast they pile into the car and set out for Morgan Peak Park. This morning's game against Massapequa is the biggest of the season. Both teams are undefeated, and the winner of today's match will clinch first place in the division. At Emma's invitation, Zack sits up front beside his father. They talk strategy. "Use your wings," Roger says, to the bemusement of Maggie, who pictures Zack soaring high above the field.

It's apparent as they drive through the village that Morgan Peak takes its Halloween dead seriously. Lawns are transformed into miniature graveyards, trees festooned with white cloth ghosts, chimneys topped by witches on broomsticks. The village resembles a theme park.

"Amazing," says Maggie, staring out the window like a tourist on safari. "This is all quite recent, you realize. Do you know what Americans currently spend on Halloween?"

"No," says Emma, "but I'm sure you're going to tell me."

"Two point five *billion*. Do you realize what two point five billion could do for low-income housing in this country?"

"Halloween's not new. We used to go trick-or-treating."

"In the building," Maggie says. "Remember the time Mrs. Feinblatt gave out gefilte fish?"

Emma makes a gagging sound.

"Distribute the ball," Roger says. "Take shots from the outside. Keep the defense honest."

"Tell that to Mr. Ball Hog," Zack says. "Dylan Sanders wouldn't pass the ball if he was triple-teamed *and* had a gun to his head."

When they reach the park, Zack runs off to join his team without a backward glance. Roger, Emma, and Maggie follow after, carrying the folding chairs they never use. The nine o'clock game is still in progress, the sidelines crowded with parents and kids. Beyond the field on the far edge of the park is a small wilderness of oaks and maples in full autumn foliage. Above the canopy of crimson and gold, the sky is so blue you could cut your eyes on it. Emma casts a sideways look at her sister. Does she see? But Maggie's attention is riveted on a nearby flock of soccer moms in matching head warmers and woolen car coats.

Zack's teammates are stretching on the practice field, where Yolanda, ensconced in a director's chair, has set up shop. True to her word she is painting the boys' faces. Roger joins her husband, who is watching the Massapequa team warm up with a one-touch pass-and-shoot drill at the other end of the practice field.

"They're huge," says Gerard.

"Fast, too," Roger observes.

"You believe the hands on that goalie?"

Emma and Maggie watch as Yolanda, with a few stripes and a suggestion of whiskers, transforms Zack into a tiger. She holds up a mirror when she finishes, and Zack yelps with delight. "Now play like one," she says, sending him off with a smack on the butt. Then she turns, and her warm smile takes in Maggie as well as Emma.

"Great work!" Maggie nods at the circle of boys. Marcel is a sleek black panther. Dylan Sanders, with his long blond mane, makes a perfect lion. Each face is different, all are fierce. "But what do you expect from an artist?"

"Today *ich bin ein* soccer mom."

"Talented lady. Emma says you used to teach?"

"Seems like a long time ago," Yolanda says.

"Where?"

"Couple of city schools."

Maggie casts a signifying look at Emma. The wife and mother of the two who died in the accident had worked in a New York City school. That her name was Linda Johnson and the fact that the little girl was her only child were all they know about the woman; they know it only because the news reports mentioned it. Emma never spoke to her, never laid eyes on her. She did defy the orders of the insurance company lawyer to write her a note, expressing her sorrow over the accident and the other woman's loss, but the letter came back several days later torn to shreds. That was the beginning and the end of their correspondence, unless you counted the annual greeting cards, which Emma did. Six so far, and the seventh anniversary looms in November.

Maggie has given up quizzing Yolanda and is staring

with a pointer's intensity at the field. Emma follows her eyes and smiles. "Down, girl."

"Married?" asks Maggie.

"Divorced."

"Who is he?"

"Nick Sanders. Zack's coach."

"And Emma's conquest," Yolanda adds with a Janis Joplin cackle.

Maggie's eyes swivel. "You sly thing!"

"Don't listen to Yolanda. She'll say anything." But Emma feels the blood rush to her face.

Her sister smiles knowingly as she turns back to the practice field. "Not bad. Worth kicking over the traces for."

"Shut up, Mags."

He's coming over. All three women turn to await him. A lesser man might have quailed; not Nick, though, he barges right in. "Yolanda, great faces! I thought the ref would have a fit; turns out there's no rule against it, though."

"I offered to make him a zebra, but he turned me down. How 'bout you, darlin'? Want me to do you?"

"More than anything," he says. "But I'll pass on the face-painting."

"Sure? You'd make a beautiful wolf."

Watching him flirt as naturally as he breathes, Emma catches a glimpse of the misery in store for any woman fool enough to fall for him. It is not, to her surprise, a painless discovery. Now he turns to her and says her name, as if to say that were to say it all.

"Nick," she says, "my sister, Maggie."

Nick grabs his chest and staggers backward. "Be still, my heart. Two of you is almost too much."

"One married," says Maggie, "the other not."

"Think of the permutations." He smacks his head. "No, don't. Think of the game."

"Think of shutting up," Emma says. "Go away, Nick. Tend to your team."

There's a weighted silence after he's gone.

Maggie asks, "Is he always so . . . ?"

"Yes," say Emma and Yolanda in unison.

"Ah." She looks after him. "Still . . ."

A whistle signals the end of the nine o'clock game. Both teams move their gear to the far side of the main field, while the parents stake out positions on the opposite sideline. Not just parents; today's game seems to have attracted the better part of Morgan Peak's soccer community. The Pirates are the only Morgan Peak team currently in first division, and many townspeople have come to see Sanders's boys take on mighty Massapequa.

The captains trot out for the coin toss, Zack and Dylan Sanders for the Pirates. Morgan Peak wins the toss, and the teams take to the field.

The sideline falls quiet as each set of parents sizes up the opposition. The visitors in their maroon uniforms tower over the local boys. "Massapequa has three travel teams in this age group," Emma tells Maggie, who shows unprecedented interest. "This is their A team."

"How many does your town have?"

"Just one. That blond kid, playing striker? That's Nick's son."

"Wasn't that Zack's position?"

"Used to be. Now he plays center half."

On the field, the referee blows the whistle. Dylan Sanders taps the ball back to Zack, and Zack passes to

Marcel on right wing. The offense surges forward.
Massapequa's left fullback makes a play for the ball, but
Marcel puts on a burst of speed and cuts around him.
The defender, seeing he's beat, plants both hands in the
small of Marcel's back and shoves. Marcel goes down
hard just outside the box.

The whistle blows; the ref signals a direct kick.
Marcel gets up slowly. "Did you see that?" Yolanda
says, grabbing Emma's arm. "That was deliberate.
What's that ref thinking?"

"He called the penalty," Emma says.

"Shoulda been a yellow card."

Nick yells for Zack to take the kick. Zack sets the
ball in place and backs off. A wall of maroon shirts
forms between him and the net. Just beyond the far post,
loosely guarded by just one man, Dylan Sanders raises
his hand.

The referee blows the whistle. Zack takes his run, but
instead of shooting at the wall he passes to Dylan.
Dylan leaps over his defender and heads the ball; it hits
the near goalpost and bounces off.

Morgan Peak's sideline lets out a synchronized
moan. Moments later, Massapequa scores on a breakaway.

AT HALFTIME THE SCORE is unchanged, one to zero in
favor of the visitors. Nick calls the team over. They huddle around him, sucking on orange quarters.

"Do you want this game?" Nick asks.

"Yeah!" they chorus.

"No, I mean, do you *want* this game?"

"YEAH!"

"Then act like it! There's a lesson here, guys: You

want something in life bad enough, you gotta reach out and grab it; you gotta do whatever it takes. Go hard out there! I don't give a damn they're bigger than you. Size doesn't matter unless you let it matter. I see anybody playing scared, I'll yank him right off the field. Anybody here intimidated?"

"NO!"

"They're laughing at you now. They think you're beat. Are you beat?"

"NO!"

"They play hard, you play harder. No concessions; we fight for every ball. I want pressure, constant pressure. Keep them off balance; don't give 'em time to think. Do you want this game?"

"YEAH!"

"Then go out and fight for it."

YOLANDA NODS AT the referee, who's standing under a tree smoking. He's a pale, sleepy-eyed man with wispy yellow hair, inordinately tall, with long skinny legs. "Just our luck, drawing that doofus."

"You know him?" Emma asks.

"Hell, yeah. We had his sorry ass lots of times. Kids call him Ichabod Crane. That lazy bastard don't call nothing 'less it's right under his nose, and even then he call it wrong."

They watch him stroll back onto the field and blow his whistle. The Pirates huddle up and pile their hands on top of Nick's. "Go-o-o-o, Pirates!" they yell, and then they spill out onto the field, where Massapequa's already lined up and waiting. It's clear from the first moments that this half is going to be rougher than the first. The Massapequa team's making the most of their size advantage, leaning all over Morgan Peak, but the Pirates give as good as they get; elbows fly, shirts are pulled, with little attempt at subtlety. Both teams have the measure of this ref.

Marcel is being specially marked. Every time he touches the ball he's double-teamed and fouled. Finally he gets the ball on a breakaway, puts a move on the sweeper, and closes in on the goal with nothing but the keeper between him and the net. But as he swings his leg back to shoot, the sweeper tackles him from behind, sliding full force into his legs. Marcel flips in the air and lands on his back with a sickening thud.

He doesn't move.

Dead silence on the sideline. The referee trots over, but the coaches don't wait for his signal; they sprint onto the field. Emma looks for Yolanda, who's disappeared; then she spies her on the field, making a beeline for the referee.

Emma sprints after her. She catches hold of Yolanda's arm; tension runs through it like current through a live wire. "Don't, Yolanda."

"Get off me!"

"Forget him. Look at Marcel."

The boy is sitting up, talking to Nick and the other coaches. Nick stands and reaches down to Marcel. When the boy rises to his feet, a great cheer of relief breaks out on both ends of the sideline.

Shaking off Emma's restraining hand, Yolanda wheels on the referee. "This is all your fault," she says, shaking a finger in his face. "You let this game get totally out of hand."

Ichabod doesn't answer her; he walks away. But

Yolanda's just warming up. Trotting beside him, she offers up a full and frank critique of his professionalism, manhood, and parentage.

The official reverses direction and stomps over to Nick. Without a word, he pulls out a yellow card and snaps it aloft.

On the other side of the field, Maggie turns to Roger. "What's that mean?"

"It means the coach is going to get kicked out if Yolanda doesn't shut up."

Nick takes Yolanda's right arm, Emma her left, and they walk her across the field to the parents' side. Gerard comes out to meet them, and Emma leaves Yolanda to him. She rejoins Maggie and Roger.

"Wow," Maggie says.

"Shut up," says Emma. "She was scared."

"She was furious. I was that ref, I'd watch my ass."

"What's your point? That she loves her kid and gets upset when he's mugged? Well, call out the FBI, this woman's dangerous!"

Maggie raises her hands. "Have it your way. She's okay, you're okay; everything's fine and dandy in Sleepyville, USA."

Play resumes with a penalty kick. Zack takes it and scores, tying the game with under ten minutes to go. Now Massapequa has the ball. Their coach orders everyone up, leaving only the sweeper and goalie back on defense. The players move the ball up. From deep in the corner, the left wing centers the ball into a scrum of players. Leaping, Zack heads the ball out toward Dylan Sanders. Dylan takes off, with only the sweeper to beat. The sweeper comes out cautiously, not attempting to tackle the ball, just channeling Dylan outside while he waits for help to arrive. Zack, sprinting full speed down the center, calls for the ball and gets a perfect leading pass. At once the sweeper veers toward him, but Zack doesn't wait; twelve yards out, in full stride, he shoots on goal. Every eye on the field follows the ball as it sails over the outstretched arms of the keeper and into the top left corner of the net.

The whistle blows. The game is over and the Morgan Peak Pirates, to their own amazement, have won.

23

AFTER THE GAME, after all the back-slapping and arm-pumping and the gathering up of gear and the sloughing of cleats and shin guards, Emma's family splits up. Zack goes home with Marcel, to go trick-or-treating in his neighborhood. (Marcel, Zack tells his parents, has a list, painstakingly compiled and updated annually, of the houses that give the best treats.) Emma and Maggie decide to go into town and gorge themselves on bookstores. They invite Yolanda, who makes a face. "I wish. Gerard invited two of his stuffiest clients and their wives to dinner tomorrow night, and guess who's cooking?"

Roger, too, declines, on the indisputable grounds that if bookstore-crawling is the plan, they will have more fun without him. He offers to drop them off in town and pick them up several hours later.

"Aren't you afraid we'll talk about you?" Maggie teases.

"What can you say that you haven't said to my face?"

"What will you do?" Emma asks.

"Errands," he says. "Home Depot. Manly stuff like that."

He drops them at Starbucks. For Maggie, every good outing begins and ends with coffee. They carry their cups and cakes to a table by the window. Outside, children parade by in costumes: three little girls dressed as M&M's, slews of Freddy Krugers, and a handful of miniature Barneys.

"Well, Emma," Maggie says, licking cream from her fingers like a cat, "you've been holding out on me."

"About what?"

"*About what?* 'Emma!' " Maggie's husky delivery mimics Nick's, with echoes of Marlon Brando crying, "Stella!"

Emma shrugs, stirs her coffee. "You saw how he is."

"Uh-huh. Saw how Roger is, too."

"Meaning what?"

"Meaning after the game, everyone's all huggy and kissy, those two come face to face and Roger looks at him like something crawled out of a cereal box."

"Roger chooses to regard Nick as a threat."

"Is he?"

Emma stares. "Of course not."

"Just checking," says Maggie.

"As if!"

"Now you've got me wondering. One denial is convincing. Two are suspicious."

"You're projecting."

Maggie gazes out the window. A woman dressed as Amelia Earhart strolls by, leading a German shepherd in a raffishly tilted leather aviator's cap, a pair of goggles dangling from its neck. "I ain't saying he's not pretty—"

"Too pretty."

"—but I am not about to take a number."

"You go, girl." Emma raises her cup.

When Maggie has finished every last crumb of her cake, and Emma's, they walk two blocks, up a hill and down a hill, past the Jewish deli and the Italian bakery and the library to the Literary License, the largest of the village's three bookstores and Emma's favorite. Inside the store they drift apart in their accustomed directions: Emma to the crowded shelves of discounted and remaindered fiction, where past forays have yielded many treasures, Maggie to wallow happily in the social-science section. After nearly an hour Emma comes away with three pearls: an early book by Jane Smiley, which she somehow missed; a copy of Russell Banks's *Continental Drift*, which she's read but doesn't own; and a volume of short stories by Amy Bloom. She finds Maggie sitting cross-legged on the floor, surrounded by a dozen books in various stages of perusal.

"Damn you!" says Maggie, flushed, as Emma is herself. For these sisters, shopping for books is the sort of sinful self-indulgence other women seek in Bloomingdale's or Cartier. "Do you have any idea what this binge is going to cost me?"

"You're *not* taking all of these."

"I'm winnowing," Maggie says defensively. "But they've got a hell of a selection for a—"

"A store in the boondocks? Why don't you just admit there's more here than you expected?"

"Don't get cocky, girl. It's not exactly the Gotham."

Maggie ends up buying five books. The owner holds

the door for them. They hit the next bookstore, a small Waldenbooks outpost. No luck here; the remainder tables are full of glossy books on gardening and cooking and the collecting of various objects. The rest of the store doesn't bear looking through: stacks of best-sellers, point-of-marketing displays, flowery jackets and paperbacks with die-cut covers, and a great many books with numbers in their titles: *101 Ways*, *Seven Habits*, *The First 12*, *Seven More Habits*. Maggie finds a volume on depression glass in the psychology section, which gives them a good laugh. By the time they finish, it's two-thirty, time to meet Roger. They stroll back to Starbucks and arrive just as he pulls up.

"Did you get what you wanted?" Emma asks as they pull out from the curb.

"A few shelves and some hardware. Looked at some snowblowers." Roger drives slowly. The streets are full of children walking in groups, attended by watchful parents.

"Do you think any came to the house?" Emma wonders out loud. "I should have left the candy out." But the closer they get to the house, the sparser the clumps of children, till there are none at all. Framed by the Sound, the house looks as stark and lonely as a lighthouse.

Caroline's car is in the shared parking area. Roger parks beside it and takes two Home Depot bags from the trunk. Casey barks at them through the side vents, wagging his tail so violently that the whole dog shakes. Inside the house, Maggie grabs the downstairs bathroom and Emma runs upstairs. As she enters her bedroom, something odd, out of place, catches her eye. She turns and looks at her bed. In the middle of the turquoise quilt lies something naked, pink, and flaccid. A small thing, the size of a woman's hand; half-formed, yet possessed of four discernible limbs, a tiny torso, a large head with sealed, translucent eyelids.

A fetus.

Time takes on a sputtering, discontinuous quality. One minute Emma is in her bedroom. The next she's sitting in the hallway, rigid, back to the wall, legs splayed out. Screams pour out of her throat and down the hallway; she observes this but is powerless to stop. She is drowning in fearful, guilty thoughts. The fetus is hers, she imagines. Her own baby, prematurely expelled in a moment of supreme negligence, delivered without notice and left unattended.

The dog reaches her first. Whimpering, Casey sniffs her all over, licks her face. Emma wants to wrap her arms around him but she's frozen stiff, a Popsicle scream. Then iron fingers clamp her shoulders, and Roger's face fills her eyes.

"What?" he says urgently. "Are you hurt?"

The screaming ends.

Emma tries to speak. She opens her mouth, but no words come. She jerks her arm up, pointing at the bedroom door with a hand that trembles violently.

He turns, faces the door. She must have shut it behind her, she doesn't remember. He twists the knob, shoves the door open, and quickly scans the room. He steps forward, out of Emma's sight.

Now Maggie is here, kneeling beside her. Maggie's face is as pale as Wonder bread. Her hand is on Emma's wrist; her lips are moving but Emma can't hear a word she says. She is straining for the sound of Roger's voice; but from the bedroom comes only silence.

Maggie shakes her. "Talk to me! What happened?"

Roger's silence terrifies. Emma begins to doubt herself. What if there is nothing on the bed, nothing at all? What if the thing she saw was an hallucination? That would prove she was crazy. But she couldn't possibly have seen what she thought she saw.

"Go in there," she croaks, her voice returning. "Tell me what you see."

Maggie rises, hesitates, then plunges through the open doorway and disappears. Emma hears her cry out: a sharp, involuntary yelp, then silence.

Eons pass. Ages. Emma thinks of going in after them, but the tendon connecting thought to action has been severed; she can no more stand and walk into that room than she can levitate.

Roger emerges. She watches him approach. It feels as if her whole life hinges on what he will say next; how strange, then, that she should have no idea what that will be. He kneels, takes her face between his hands, waits till her eyes meet his. Emma's hands are clenched over her belly.

"It's a fetal pig," he says.

"A pig," she echoes.

"Did you think it was human?"

"I thought it was ours."

His face crumbles. He pulls her to him. His arms are like seat belts, strapping her into the world; they are bands of warmth that spread through her body.

"DRINK," MAGGIE says, watching critically as Emma sips her tea. While it is true that a cigar may sometimes be just a cigar, for the Roth sisters tea is never just tea; it is also maternal love and consolation. Hot, sweet, milky tea was Rosie Roth's prescription for every ailment from common colds to broken hearts. Emma's throat aches from screaming, but with every mouthful she feels comforted, restored to herself.

There's a blanket around her shoulders, a fire in the hearth. Maggie hovers nearby. Roger stands apart, talking on the phone. "No," he says. "Not a Halloween prank. Someone broke in."

"Don't know. Haven't checked yet."

"Problem's not what they took, it's what they left."

"A fetus."

There's a long pause.

"We'll be here," Roger says.

He hangs up.

"They're sending a detective," he says. He doesn't look at them. His jaw is clenched so tightly his lean face looks skeletal.

"What will we tell him?" Emma wonders.

"Everything." His eyes, shuttered, inaccessible, touch her face and move on. "Should have done it months ago."

TWO COME, A MAN and a woman. Detective John Thigpen, Detective Maria Wong. After introductions in the front hall, Roger leads them upstairs. Emma follows with Maggie. They stand in the hall outside Emma's bedroom and eavesdrop shamelessly.

"That ain't human," the male detective says. He sounds disappointed.

"No," Roger says. "It's a fetal pig."

"On the phone you said human."

"I didn't actually specify." A weighted silence, then Roger's voice again. "I didn't want a patrol car, okay? I wanted someone we could talk to. This isn't a stunt or someone's idea of a joke. This is another vicious attack on my wife."

"Another?" The woman this time.

"In a series."

To anyone who doesn't know him well, Roger would seem cool, even unmoved. To Emma he sounds like a man walking blindfolded on a razor-thin ledge. Steeling herself, she starts toward the bedroom. Maggie lays a questioning hand on her arm, but Emma shrugs it off. It's only a pig, she tells herself. And she has to do this. She has to see the thing itself, to replace her skewed first impression.

She enters the room. Her eyes are drawn to the bed, but Roger and the cops obstruct her view. She crosses to Roger's side, looks over his shoulder. Now that she sees it clearly, the snout and ears, though immature, are unmistakably porcine.

How strange the mind is.

"What kind of attacks?" says Thigpen. He is forty-ish, five-eight or -nine, with a wrestler's solid build and a square, immobile face. To look at him you'd think he found fetal pigs on people's beds every day of the week.

Roger tells them about the sabotaged computer, the threatening messages, the worms in the sugar bowl. Emma throws in the Raggedy Ann doll for good measure. Neither mentions the condom incident. Thigpen listens without interruption, jotting occasional notes in a small black pad. When Roger finishes, the detective looks at him for a while, his broad, flat face expressionless.

"How long has this been going on?" he asks.

"Since we moved in. Four months."

"Four months," he says. "And all that time, you never thought of giving us a call?"

"No."

Emma winces inwardly. Roger on the defensive is Roger at his haughtiest. His tone is curt, almost contemptuous. He is not an arrogant man, but rather one in whom the possibility of arrogance is never entirely absent.

Then the detective turns his baggy-eyed gaze on Emma. "How about you, you ever think of calling us?"

"My sister suggested it." Emma glances at Maggie, standing by the door. "I didn't think we'd be believed."

This seems to interest him. He doesn't say anything, though, just watches her and thinks it over.

Meanwhile his partner wanders through the bedroom, hands in her pockets, looking at this and that. Tall and willowy with delicate features, Maria Wong looks some ten years younger than Thigpen. There's a kinetic quality about her; she is air to his earth. Emma would have pegged her as a dancer, never a cop.

Wong's eye falls on a magazine lying atop Roger's bureau; she pauses to read the mailing label.

"*Dr.* Koenig," she says. "What kind of doctor?"

"Physicist, not M.D."

The detectives exchange a look. Emma sees that they are like a married couple, like Roger and herself, adept at reading each other's thoughts.

"Someone's sending you folks a message," says Thigpen, who seems to be the team's designated speaker. "This being a fetus, she was thinking maybe it's about abortion."

Roger shakes his head impatiently. "You're missing the point. This was aimed at my wife, not me, and it had precisely the effect intended: It scared her half to death."

"Maybe it was meant to do more," Maggie says from her post at the door.

Roger, all of them, turn to her.

"You should have seen her. White as a ghost, drenched in sweat, pulse racing, hysterical. It's a miracle she didn't lose it." Maggie looks at the uncomprehending faces of the detectives. "Didn't they say? My sister is pregnant."

THE DETECTIVES SEPARATE husband and wife. It's subtly done—Wong asks to see Emma's office, while Thigpen enlists Roger on an inspection tour of doors and windows—but Emma has watched too many episodes of *NYPD Blue* to miss the ploy. Her suspicion is confirmed by the turn in Wong's questioning.

"Do you think you were meant to miscarry?" Wong asks.

In a sudden vivid flash, Emma sees again the tiny half-formed creature that had lain on her bed like something carelessly discarded. She shudders. "I know it sounds crazy, but my first thought when I saw it was, *Oh my God, I lost the baby.*"

Maria Wong winces in sympathy. Later, when they talk it over, Emma and Maggie will agree that it is at this point her attitude changes. It's not that she had been dismissive before; reserved is more like it, cautious. But now Wong resumes her interrogation with a focused edge of concentration that Emma for one finds less troubling than validating. She isn't crazy after all; something very wrong *is* happening here.

Wong glances at Emma's flat belly. "Who knows?"

"No one, just my sister and husband. I just did a home test; haven't seen a doctor yet."

Wong nods. "How's your husband feel about it?"

Emma stares. "He's delighted," she says stiffly. "We both are."

"Anyone else know? Anyone he might have told?"

Emma avoids looking at Maggie. "No, no one."

Wong picks up a glass paperweight from the desk and tosses it from hand to hand. "So who would want to hurt you, Emma?"

"Certainly no one in this household."

"Outside it, then. Anyone with a grudge? A rejected lover?"

"I've been married for twelve years," Emma says frostily.

"Forgive me if I'm telling you something you don't know, but marriage doesn't always equal fidelity."

"It does for me."

"And for him?"

Emma's face is a fortress, cheekbones primed to repel. "For my husband as well."

"How about a spurned would-be lover?" Maggie offers.

THEIR TOUR OF the house, having produced no sign of forcible entry, ends in the kitchen. Roger notices Thigpen eyeing the half-filled coffeepot and offers him a cup. Thigpen says he wouldn't say no. They sit facing each other at the table, and the detective asks about keys.

"My wife and I each have a set. We keep a spare in the dining room. Still there; I checked. No one else. Zack's too young. Our son," Roger adds, in response to a look. "He's ten."

"Where's he at today?"

"At a friend's, thank God."

Thigpen looks at him. It's the first display of emotion Roger has allowed himself. "Anybody else? Neighbor? Real estate agency? You said you just bought this house."

"I changed the front and back door locks when we moved in. Changed the French door lock a month or so later."

"No alarm system?"

Roger's mouth tightens. He shakes his head, a barely perceptible movement.

"Might want to think about it. You folks are pretty isolated out here."

"Got a recommendation?"

The detective shrugs. "Talk to a few. See what they offer. So, if nobody has a key, Dr. Koenig, who's walking in and out of your house?"

Is there a faint satiric emphasis on the title? Roger thinks there is. *You might be a Ph.D.*, he hears, *but you're no brain surgeon.* He grips the edge of the table. "Don't you think I've asked myself that? I don't have a fucking clue."

Thigpen sticks out his lower lip and nods ruminatingly. The bags under his eyes look like catchalls for the world's woes. "Seeing anyone?" he asks, as if he were asking, "Seen any good movies lately?"

A log settles in the fireplace. Casey raises his head and growls.

"What?" says Roger.

"Girlfriend, mistress, whatever. Hey, it happens, and it don't necessarily mean squat, except if that's the case I'd a lot rather you told me than I find out myself."

Roger stares. "Tell me something. Have you looked at my wife?"

Thigpen's smile is humorless. "I've looked at her."

"Any more questions?"

"Don't mean a thing. Look at Prince Charles, dumping a babe like Diana for that old bag Camilla. Look at all them rich Hollywood stars cruisin' around for skank. When it comes to sex, there's no accounting for taste."

"You're barking up the wrong tree, Detective."

"I'd like to think so, Doctor," says Thigpen, and this time there's no mistaking the undertone. "Only you don't seem to want to answer my question."

Roger tries staring him down. It's like staring down a rock. Despite his anger, he feels an unwelcome stirring of respect for the man.

Thigpen waits.

"It's an offensive question," Roger says stiffly, "but one can see why it has to be asked. The answer is no."

MARIA WONG pauses in front of the face-out display of Emma's books. She picks one up, turns it over and inspects the photo. "That's you!"

"What a detective!" Maggie whispers. Emma pinches her hand.

"You wrote all these?"

Emma confirms it.

"Ever get letters from readers?" Wong asks.

"Sure."

"How do they reach you?"

"Through my publisher, usually."

"Never directly to your home address?"

Emma thinks of the packet of flowery "Thinking of you" cards tucked away in Kant's *Critique of Pure*

Reason. Those had come directly to the apartment, delivered every year like clockwork on the anniversary of the accident. As if she'd needed reminding. But that's not what Wong's asking and besides, why open that can of worms?

Can of worms, she thinks. Major cliché. Suddenly, somewhere deep in her brain, a new synapse forms; a connection is made.

"No," she says. "I'd remember that."

"Any that seemed threatening, out of line somehow, maybe overly personal?"

Emma shakes her head. "The odd kook now and then; all writers get 'em. Nothing that ever worried me."

"You keep these letters?"

"I've got a file. You're welcome to see it, but I doubt you'll find anything."

Wong studies her without speaking. She comes toward them, turns the desk chair around and sits with her knees inches away from Emma's. The sudden closeness is invasive, even intimidating.

"I'm hearing a lot about who it isn't," says Wong. "Your family, this guy Sanders your sister mentioned, your loyal fans. I'm hearing nothing about who it might be."

"If we knew, why would we have called you?"

"See," Wong continues as if she hadn't spoken, "my sense is that your husband's right: You are the target here. Someone doesn't like you, Mrs. Koenig, someone who's gone to a lot of trouble, taken risks. So I gotta figure there's a connection between you or your husband and this person. I gotta figure there's a history. You see where I'm going with this?"

"She's right," Maggie says. "This Pollyanna attitude

of yours has gone on long enough. *Someone* is pulling your strings, and chances are it's someone you've already eliminated."

Emma shoots her a look: *Et tu*, Maggie? Easy for her and Roger to say tell all, when it's Emma's secret that has become the luxury they can no longer afford. Still, she knows they're right; but her words, usually so obedient, desert her now.

"A lot of people," Wong says, "what they do, they call us in and then they hold stuff back, which is like going to the doctor and concealing your symptoms. It doesn't do any good."

Emma stares at the floor.

"Oh, for God's sake," Maggie snaps, "tell her! What's the point of all these mysteries? Tell everybody everything; get it all out in the open."

Both of them stare at her, waiting. Emma senses a third pair of eyes, a concentrated gaze coming from behind the desk; but when she raises her head to look, there's no one there.

Her forehead is bathed in sweat. A cold rivulet runs down her side. "There is someone," she says at last. "You might say she has a grudge. Two, in fact."

Wong flips open her pad. "What'd you do to her?"

"She didn't *do* anything," Maggie says resentfully. "She was as much a victim as they were."

Emma silences her with a look. She turns to Wong. "I drove the car that killed her husband and daughter."

"SANDERS," ROGER SAYS. "Lives in town."

Thigpen looks up. "Nick Sanders?"

"Yeah, you know him?"

"Used to coach my kid. Why him?"

"He's obsessed with my wife."

"Obsessed, huh." Thigpen smirks, not a pretty sight. "Not to take nothin' away from your wife, but Nick's got quite a reputation as a ladies' man."

"He's the one who found that CopyCat program on my wife's hard drive."

"So?" says Thigpen. "Sounds like he did you a favor."

"Ever hear of a fireman setting a fire?"

"LINDA JOHNSON," Emma says. "She's a teacher. They both were; the papers said they worked in New York City schools. His name was Lucas. The little girl was Rachel Johnson."

Wong scribbles a note. "I can maybe find out where she's at now. But it was an accident, you say. Why should she blame you?"

No way this woman has kids, thinks Emma. She gets up, goes to her shelf of college texts, and extracts the *Critique of Pure Reason*. The book falls open in her hands, revealing a packet of greeting cards, all but one bound by a rubber band. She hands the packet to Maria Wong.

"Thinking of you, thinking of you," Wong reads, thumbing through. "Are they all the same?"

"Yes. And all delivered to my house on the anniversary of the accident."

Wong pulls out one envelope and examines it front and back. No return address. Name and address printed in block letters. She takes a large plastic Ziploc bag from her jacket pocket and drops the cards inside. "What's that?" she asks, nodding at the one Emma held back.

"This was the first." Emma passes it over. "Look inside."

As Wong opens the card, a photograph slips out and lands facedown on the floor. She picks it up, studies it closely. Maggie goes and stands behind her. Emma watches their expressions change from smiles at the sight of the handsome father and daughter to distress as the realization of who they are sets in. She herself needs no picture; the image of those two faces is seared in her heart.

"This is them?" Wong asks.

Emma nods.

"You never showed me this," Maggie says reproachfully.

"Are you happier now that you've seen it?"

Wong adds the picture to the bag and puts the bag in her pocket. "I don't know," she says doubtfully. "Seven years go by, all she does is send cards. Suddenly she decides to invade your life? Why? What changed?"

"Simple," Maggie says. "Opportunity. They moved here. Tell her about Yolanda."

"Jesus, Mags!" Emma stares. What's come over Maggie, spewing names like rice at a wedding?

"Who's Yolanda?" Wong asks.

"My friend."

"Her new friend," says Maggie. "A young black woman who happens to be both a widow and a former New York City schoolteacher."

"What's Yolanda's last name?"

Emma sticks out her chin. "My son has played at her house; hers has been here. Do you think I'd permit that if I had the slightest doubt about Yolanda?"

"You're probably right," Maria Wong says soothingly. "But wouldn't it be nice to rule her out for sure? What's her last name?"

"It's Dumont now. I don't know what it was before she remarried, and I'm not going to ask."

"THE LITTLE HOUSE by the road," Thigpen says, putting down his empty cup, "that occupied?"

"Yes. We have a tenant." Roger's tone is as stiff as his back. Thigpen has just finished asking, politely but with unmistakable intent, about his own movements that day.

"He home, you know?" says Thigpen.

"She. I believe so. Her car's out there."

"Want to take a walk?"

In the front hall they meet Emma, Maggie, and Detective Wong.

"Detective Thigpen thinks Caroline might have seen something," Roger tells his wife. "We're going to ask."

"You think?" asks Emma. "Could we get that lucky?"

FOOLISH QUESTION, it seems.

"I'm so sorry," says Caroline, pressing her hands together. "I wish I could help."

She has brought them into the living room, the two detectives, Roger and Emma. Like her kitchen, Caroline's living room resembles an Ikea catalog picture. The colors are neutral, the wood is beech; the general effect is pleasing but impersonal, the work of someone, Emma thinks, with money and taste but very little time. She imagines Caroline striding in high heels through the store, salesclerk in tow. *I'll take that, and that, and two of those.*

"Where were you?" Thigpen asks.

"Upstairs, mostly, in my office. The room facing Emma's house."

"So if anyone had approached the house you'd of seen?"

"I'm sure I would have noticed a car."

"How about someone on foot?" he says.

"What kind of burglar comes on foot?"

There's a brief silence. Then Emma answers, "The kind that doesn't take things."

Caroline scans her face. "He left something," she says after a moment. "What?"

"A fetal pig."

"A *pig!* What kind of sick . . . Who found it?"

"I did," Emma says.

Caroline shuts her eyes, then reopens them. She turns to Thigpen. "If this person came on foot, it's possible I might have missed him. Although I did keep an eye out for visitors; thought we might get some trick-or-treaters."

"Did you?" he asks.

"No, not one. Anyone care for some candy?"

"So you saw no one all day," Thigpen says glumly but without surprise. He looks at his partner and starts to rise.

"No," Caroline says regretfully. "Not on the property."

Thigpen sits back down. There's a sudden, dense silence

Caroline looks from face to face. "There was a hiker. But he didn't approach the house. When I saw him from my bedroom, he was already past our drive, walking toward the dead end. I figured he was taking the public access path down to the shore. Lots of people do."

"When was this?" Thigpen asks.

"I was about to have lunch. Twelve-thirty, one, there-abouts."

The detective turns to Roger. "Is there a path from the shore up to your property?"

"Yes, behind the house."

"So someone could go down this public access path, walk fifty yards or so along the shore, and climb back up without being seen by Mrs., ah . . . ?"

"Dr. Marks," Roger supplies. "Yes, easily."

Detective Wong flips open her pad. "Can you describe this person?"

"Not really," Caroline says. "Tall, male, Caucasian. I think he had on a knapsack, that's why I figured him for a hiker."

"Hair color?"

"Couldn't see his hair. He wore a cap, though. A Yankees cap."

"Sanders wears a Yankees cap," Roger remarks.

"There you go," says Emma. "Case closed."

"I'm just saying."

"Anything else?" says Wong. "Clothes? Age?"

"Didn't notice his clothes. Age? Not old, not a kid." Caroline shrugs apologetically. "I wish I'd paid attention."

But Maria Wong rewards her with a luminous smile. "Thanks; you've been very helpful."

Caroline sees them to the door. Emma is the last one out. Their eyes meet. "I'll call you," Emma promises.

24

AFTER THIS LATEST intrusion, Roger is like an arrow shot from an overstrung bow. To Emma it seems as if the only way he can relieve his stress and anxiety is to do things, take action, take charge. That evening, after the detectives leave, he sits down with the Nassau County yellow pages and phones one home security company after another, eliminating those that will not send out a salesman on Sunday. He sets up three appointments for the following day.

At six o'clock that evening, Zack comes home, dropped off by Gerard. Zack's mask, a lovely rotting-corpse concoction that he bought with his own money, rests atop his head. Over his shoulder he carries a pillowcase full of candy. "You are *not* eating all that," Emma says, jolted back to normalcy.

"Casey'll help," says Zack, "won't you, Case?"

Over dinner Roger mentions that they're having an alarm system installed. He says it's a normal precaution for houses such as theirs. He says nothing about an intruder—this based on a decision reached unanimously by Emma and Roger, with Maggie's dissenting vote disallowed on grounds of nonjurisdiction.

"But why not tell him?" she'd protested. "He's not a kid."

"That's precisely what he is," Roger had replied with a terrible coldness.

"You know what I mean; he's not a little kid. He has

eyes and ears and a pretty good brain. Maybe he could help."

"He's my son. It's my job to protect him, not his to protect me. When the day comes that I can't perform that function, I will put him up for adoption."

"You don't protect someone by keeping them in the dark," Maggie had said, knowing she was out-credentialed in this matter but unwilling or unable to give up. "Not when the danger's real you don't."

Though the argument has faded by the time Zack gets home, its echoes permeate the walls. Zack listens to his father's voice, and as he listens he glances around the table. Maggie is eating grimly, spearing her Swedish meatballs with no respect for neutrality. His mother is watching him. When their eyes meet she offers up a meaningless smile and returns to her plate, barely touched, he notices.

"Why?" he asks Roger. "Did something happen?"

"Just a precaution," Roger repeats, fashioning his face into a smile. "Don't want to take chances with all those trophies of yours."

The next day, Sunday, Maggie goes back to the city. The home-security men come in intervals of two hours. By evening Roger has made his choice. On Monday, he stays home while three men install the system. Doors and windows are wired, window latches installed, flood-lights mounted. Because of the dog, motion detectors are of no use, but at Roger's insistence all the door locks are changed again. When the installation is finished, the foreman shows Emma, Roger, and Zack how it works. It's a silent alarm system, he explains. A violation will trigger an immediate phone call from the company headquarters to the house. If the alarm is a false one—if, for example, Emma forgets to disarm the system upon entering the house—she must identify herself to the caller with a code word. If no one answers, or if the person answering fails to give the proper code, the police would be notified.

Zack gets to pick the code word, since it has to be one he'll remember. "Soccer," his first pick, is rejected as too obvious. Next he comes up with "hat trick," and they settle on that.

Roger is as pleased with his new security system as Zack with a new soccer ball. Though she knows she should feel grateful, Emma takes little comfort in the exercise. "What would you have us do," says Roger, "throw open the doors and windows and hang a sign from the balcony: 'Come on in; easy pickings'?"

"Why not go all the way?" she retorts. "Pull a Rapunzel. Brick up the doors, nail shut the windows, and whenever you need to go in or out, I'll let down my hair from the tower."

Roger stares. "Grow it," he says.

ON TUESDAY ROGER stays home from work again. In the morning he goes out, carefully resetting the alarm, and buys a portable phone for Emma and a beeper for himself. "Keep it with you whenever you go out," he tells her. "I want to be able to reach you at all times. And you can reach me by beeper." In the afternoon he buys a car. They've talked about a second car—Roger dislikes depending on public transportation—but Emma, for whom one is bad enough, has been dead set against it. This time he doesn't ask. He goes out by taxi and comes home ninety minutes later in a three-year-old maroon Honda Accord.

"What the hell?" says Emma, coming out onto the porch.

He mounts the steps to stand before her. Takes her right hand, turns it palm upward, drops in a set of keys, and walks past her into the house.

Emma has no idea what all this is costing, and nothing in Roger's demeanor encourages her to ask. He is closed, intent, driven. When they speak, which is not often, he avoids her eyes. To Emma it seems he's angry with her. Perhaps he blames her for bringing the trouble down upon them. Or maybe that's her own guilt speaking. That night, on the phone, Maggie says of course he doesn't blame her, he's just worried sick; she says it as if she knows. Emma remembers the other phone call late at night, while she was in the shower. Do they talk, Roger and Maggie? She starts to ask, then changes her mind, having run up against the boundary of a curiosity she once flattered herself was boundless.

If Zack wonders at his father's rare weekday presence, he gives no sign, asks no questions. To Emma this seems ominous, but then everything seems ominous to her these days. Her nerves are shattered. The least little sound makes her jump; she braces herself before opening doors, scrutinizes rooms before entering. She has trouble sleeping and no appetite at all, though that could be due to her pregnancy.

Deprived of sleep, Emma's mind is like a hive without a queen, buzzing with pointless and circular speculation. Maggie's Pollyanna reproach has struck home. It's true that for too long Emma has buried her head in the sands of denial. Someone is doing these things: coming into her home, planting vile and disgusting things, infiltrating her work and her life. As this person has taken on form and reality in the eyes of others, so has he in her own. Though lacking the essentials of name, face, and gender, her enemy has become a solid presence in her life.

"Chances are it's someone you know," Maggie had also said, "someone you've eliminated." But if it is one of the people Emma has eliminated, then she is dealing not only with hatred but with betrayal.

It is possible. She won't deny it. All along it has seemed that her enemy knows too much about her. But it's so easy for Maggie to draw that conclusion. For her it is all academic, or nearly so. Not for Emma. Because once she admits the possibility of betrayal, no one is immune, no permutation unthinkable. Nothing is secure anymore.

Stress is known to depress the immune system, and Emma knows hers has been compromised. She feels it not in her body but in her mind. Vile thoughts and fancies assail her; memories, long suppressed, burst into bitter bloom. More and more she finds herself thinking of Roger's parents. What comes back to her most clearly is the contempt in Alicia Koenig's ice-blue eyes as she pronounces sentence on Emma's marriage. *Sooner or later, he will realize what his marriage has cost him . . . He will blame you . . . It will end in disaster.*

More than a prediction, it was a curse. The man Alicia described is not the man Emma married; and yet sometimes, lately, Emma has wondered if any mother could be altogether mistaken in her child. She knows Roger loves her; but might he not, in some secret cache in his soul, harbor regret for paths not taken?

The lowest moment comes late at night, with Roger

sleeping at her side. She lies in bed with the quilt drawn up to her chin, the wakeful house murmuring about her, and she watches scenarios unfold before her like coming attractions at the movies, one more lurid than the next. Her own private late show of horrors.

No one is spared. In some of her fantasies, Nick Sanders stars as a mad, *Collector*-type predator plotting to drive a wedge between Emma and Roger. Another features Yolanda as a vengeful widow, a black Melina Mercouri intent on exploiting the opportunity that fate has bestowed. In still another, Emma's in-laws make cameo appearances as a pair of dotty schemers determined to recapture their prodigal son and grandchild. "I warned you!" Alicia Koenig screams in the climactic scene, just before they carry her away kicking and screaming. "I told you it would end in disaster!"

The worst are the scenes in which Roger plays the lead. The model exists and lends form to the fantasy: *Gaslight*, in which Charles Boyer plots to kill his wife after first driving her mad. In Emma's cinema these scenes appear in black and white. The characters all wear evening clothes; Roger in a dinner jacket looks, to Emma's biased eye, like a nineties Cary Grant.

"Divorce was out of the question," he declares in the obligatory confession scene. With his right hand, he extracts a cigarette from a silver case and taps it against the arm of his chair. With his left he points a gun at Detective Thigpen's ample midsection.

"Forget the money," he says. "She might have won custody."

Not even Maggie is spared. Emma's little sister appears in several guises. Once as a latter-day Bette Davis, chasing Emma down endless corridors while slasher music pulses in the background. "I'll show you who Mother loved best!"

That one's laughable. But Maggie appears in another, and that's the one that finally propels Emma out of bed and into her second scalding shower of the night. In that scene—glimpsed for only a moment before patience pulls the plug—Maggie and Roger are lying in bed, tangled in each other's arms.

They aren't making love. They're laughing.

ON WEDNESDAY ROGER returns to work. At nine-thirty he calls to ask if Emma remembered to reset the alarm after Zack left for school. An hour later he calls to ask if Casey's in the house. He reminds her to take the portable phone with her if she goes out and to set the alarm. Does she have his beeper number?

"Roger," she says, "chill."

That morning Emma does something she's been putting off for days: She phones Yolanda to ask about an ob-gyn. Emma doesn't know any doctors out here and can't bring herself to choose blindly. The reason she's delayed inquiring is that she knows how Yolanda will react.

Sure enough, Yolanda lets loose her full-throated laugh. "Girlfriend," she says, "you got a little something to tell Yolanda?"

"If you must know," Emma says, "I have a yeast infection."

"Whatever," Yolanda trills. She gives Emma the phone number of Dr. Nancy Frobisher, who is, she adds slyly, an excellent obstetrician. Emma calls and sets up an appointment for the next week.

One more cup of coffee to carry upstairs. Just as

she's pouring, the telephone rings. Emma starts, and the coffee splashes onto the counter.

"Roger," she says.

But it's a woman's voice. "Didn't want you to think we'd forgotten you," Detective Wong says, which is exactly what Emma has thought. After all, apart from its weirdness, what does their story have to compel the attention of the police? Nothing has been stolen, no one injured or killed.

"Any luck?" she asks Wong.

"Not yet. Haven't been able to ID the hiker. As for that prior accident, since there was no crime committed and seven years have gone by, there's not a whole lot to go on."

"You haven't located the wife of the man I . . . the man who died?"

"We're working on that, but there's a whole bunch of Linda Johnsons who've taught in city schools. And that's assuming she went by her husband's name, which nowadays is a big assumption."

"How about the fetal pig?"

"Standard item in high schools and universities. You can mail-order them from any laboratory supply outfit."

Emma traces her initials into the spilled coffee. *They'll never find out, that's what she's really saying. They're blowing us off.* In the background she hears voices talking, telephones ringing.

"Reason I'm calling," Detective Wong says, "I noticed those envelopes are all dated mid-November."

"The accident happened on November fourteenth. The cards were delivered on that date."

"The fourteenth's coming up. You get another, do me a favor and don't open it. Call us. Okay?"

"Okay," says Emma.

"Anything else happens, you give me a call. Don't hesitate."

Emma thanks her and hangs up. She wipes up the coffee spill and rinses out the sponge. After that the house seems quieter than ever. She trudges upstairs to her office.

Her computer is pushed to the far-right side of her desk. She checks it once a day for E-mail, but for everything else she uses the laptop, which stands in the center of the desk. Beside it is her manuscript, a substantial stack of some 260 pages. Emma's work seems to move in inverse proportion to her personal life; the worse things get, the faster and better she writes. Writing has always been her refuge, but lately it has become something more. Her book is the only aspect of her life Emma can control, the only thing subject to her will.

The notion of including the ghost's point of view has proved pivotal; the whole book has coalesced around those sections, and now she can see her way clear to the end. Another two, three weeks and she'll be there.

She carries the latest chapter to her armchair, settles in, and starts to read. As she turns the first page over, a slash of purple strikes her eye. In the margin of the second page, next to a passage of dialogue, someone has written "Fragment!"

This time, the initial spurt of fear is speedily overtaken by irritation. Ghostwriters are one thing, Emma thinks, ghost editors quite another. This is a first draft, goddamnit. First drafts are sacrosanct.

"They're not meant to be read by outsiders, dead or alive," she says out loud. "Much less edited."

Whom is she addressing? Emma doesn't ask that

question. The point is, it's intolerable to have someone standing over her shoulder, reading every word *and* taking it upon herself to comment.

She moves to the desk, opens the laptop. Her fingers fly over the keyboard. "You want to read my stuff," she mutters, "I'll give you something to read."

```
To: VH
From: ER
Re: my work.

1. First drafts are private.
2. I didn't ask for your comments and I don't
want them.
3. I will use sentence fragments whenever and
wherever I damn well please.
4. No editor in their right mind would correct
the grammar in dialogue.
```

She reads it over. Too harsh? No, simply straightforward. Somehow she and Mrs. Hysop have gotten off on the wrong foot. Emma has allowed herself to be cowed by Mrs. Hysop's teacherly authority, her seniority in the house, and her tricky ontological status. No more. She prints out the page. That afternoon, when she finishes working, she will leave it on top of her manuscript where no prying eye can miss it.

WHEN SHE NEXT enters her office, Emma senses she's not alone. There is nothing to be seen, only dust motes floating in the light-filled room, an air of expectancy, and a faint scent of lavender.

The memo lies atop her manuscript where she left it.

From across the room she sees purple markings on the page. As she comes closer, she sees that the words "editor" and "their" are circled in the sentence, "No editor in their right mind would correct the grammar in dialogue." In the margin, written in the quivery yet determined hand Emma has come to recognize, is the comment, "Tsk, tsk."

"Je-sus," cries Emma, smacking her forehead. "What a diehard!" Then the aptness of the word strikes her, and she starts to laugh with a touch of hysteria. There is no longer a doubt in her mind that Virginia Hysop, or some remnant thereof, lingers in this house, in this very room. How can she doubt it, when she has met the woman herself? Not in person, but on paper. There is a mind behind the purple pencil, a mind with consciousness and even humor—for clearly "tsk, tsk" is a joke, a fitting response to the indignant author whose declaration of grammatical independence contained an elementary error of agreement.

There is a mind, and Emma has met that mind. They have acknowledged one another; they have communicated. This fact ought to scare the pants off Emma. For some reason it does not. Maybe she's too tired for fear; maybe she's used it all up. Or maybe Mrs. Hysop just isn't that scary, once you get to know her.

THE DAYS THAT follow are extraordinary in their ordinariness. Nothing happens, not a single disturbance. Is it the alarm, the new locks, her switch to the laptop? Whatever the cause, the barrier between inside and out seems to have been reconstituted. After a week of nothing but work and laundry and meals and soccer practices and shopping, the most wonderfully boring week of her life, Emma dares to wonder if somehow the storm may have passed by, leaving as inexplicably as it arrived. A mixed blessing to be sure, since it would deny her the understanding necessary for closure, but one for which she would nevertheless be thankful.

She uses the time well. Her book is now very close to completion. At times like this, Emma is like a traveler who, having journeyed long and hard, at last catches sight of her destination. She enters into a kind of trance state. She doesn't want to stop, feels compelled to push on to the end, and resents anything that gets in her way. Zack and Roger, who've been through the drill many times before, hunker down and prepare to wait it out. Zack tiptoes around the house. Roger lays in stores of macaroni and cheese and frozen chicken pot pies.

NANCY FROBISHER turns out to be a tall, energetic blond, a few years older than Emma, with a strong handshake and a friendly, unaffected manner. "From the look of things," she says as she examines Emma, "I'd say you're about eight weeks along. Want to try for a heartbeat?" Without waiting for an answer, she squirts a cold fluid on Emma's belly and presses a disk to her abdomen. At once a rapid beating fills the room, a sound like galloping horse hooves.

"Oh my," Emma cries. It's official now, it's real. There's a whole separate person in there, a second heart beating.

"Perfect," says the doctor. Later a nurse comes in to take blood. It doesn't hurt a bit. Emma thinks about names.

Driving home, she turns on the radio and Gloria Gaynor is singing "I Will Survive." Emma taps out the rhythm on the steering wheel. The Honda's feel is different from the Buick's. The steering is tighter, the car rides lower and clings to the road. If Emma liked driving, she would like this car. Hearing that heartbeat must have done something to her hormones, because suddenly she feels great, flush with optimism. "I will survive," she sings along, "I will survive!"

Caroline's car is parked in the shared lot. Emma parks beside it and gets out. It's a still, sunless morning, nor'easters brewing far off the coast. Instead of going home, she walks down the drive to the carriage house and rings the bell.

Caroline, dressed for work, flinches slightly at the sight of Emma, as if anticipating more bad news.

"Coffee?" Emma asks quickly, to dispel the fear.

Caroline smiles. "Borrow or drink?"

"Drink if you have time."

"I'll make time."

"And I'll make coffee."

They walk up to her house. This time Emma remembers to punch in the security code as soon as she gets inside. Last week she forgot twice; each time the phone rang within two minutes of her entry.

"This is new," says Caroline.

Emma calms Casey down. He hates being left home alone and always greets her as if she's been gone for months. Caroline merits a polite nuzzle and lick, no more.

"Roger had it installed the day after the break-in," she says.

"Better late than never."

Emma bustles around the kitchen, lighting a fire in the fireplace, brewing a fresh pot of coffee. That galloping beat still sounds in her head, animating her movements. She pours two cups and carries them over to sit beside Caroline at the kitchen table. To tell or not to tell? Well, why not, why ever not? Maggie was right: a pox on secrets.

"I just came from the doctor," she says. "Guess what?"

Caroline examines her face, and her eyes grow wide. She sets her cup down on the table, and a little bit sloshes over. "You're not pregnant?"

Emma confirms it with a smile.

Caroline doesn't smile back. She doesn't say a word. She just stares.

"Okay," Emma drawls, looking down. Already she regrets the impulse that led her to knock on Caroline's door.

"Sorry; you just took me by surprise."

"Right."

"It's just that with all that's been going on . . . but of course, if that's what you want, I'm happy for you."

"You think I'm a fool."

"Definitely not," Caroline says quickly. "But you wouldn't be the first woman to see a baby as the cure for marital difficulties."

Emma scowls. "What marital difficulties?"

"Oh, please. Have you forgotten I was there when you found that condom?"

"Roger had nothing to do with that. He was as shocked and upset as I was."

"Uh-huh," says Caroline, and for one appalling moment Emma is shocked into seeing herself through the other woman's eyes. Weak, self-deluded, almost a willing victim: It is an image so at odds with Emma's view of herself that her first instinct is to reject it out-right. Caroline is prejudiced, she distrusts men, she doesn't know what she's talking about.

Equally offensive is the corollary, the implication that Roger is deceiving her. Images of last night's horror show flicker through her mind, but Emma dismisses them. She might torture herself on sleepless nights with visions of betrayal, but it is one thing for her to doubt her husband, quite another for Caroline to do so. Who is this stranger to cast aspersions on her husband? Roger is not, it's true, the easiest of men; he is brilliant but shadowed with areas of darkness, icy patches that correspond, in Emma's view, to the conditional quality of his parents' love. One thing, though, she knows with all the certainty of twelve years together: At his core, Roger is a good and decent man.

"I believe him," she says, her voice quiet but force-ful. "I have no reason to doubt him. Neither do you."

"None," says Caroline, "save common sense."

"How dare you!" But no sooner does it emerge than Emma's anger is undermined by the sight of Caroline's miserable face, **pale and** haggard beneath her perfectly applied makeup. This woman never asked to get involved in her problems. It's Emma who dragged her in, imposed on her. Her intentions are good; she simply doesn't see the whole picture.

"You have to look at things in perspective," she explains. "The condom didn't happen in a vacuum. It was one of a series of sick pranks."

"Pranks?" says Caroline, a strange look on her face. "You call them pranks?"

"For want of a better word."

"You're a writer. You should find a better word."

Emma stares.

"Emma," Caroline says sharply, "it's time you took a good, hard look at Roger's role in all this."

"So, finally you come right out and say it. You've been hinting at it long enough."

"And you've been avoiding it—none too success-fully, I'd say from those circles under your eyes. Try to look at it objectively. Roger is the one person with constant, easy access to the house and your computer. He's the one who initiated the move out here, effectively cutting you off from your entire support network. He's had every opportunity in the world to carry out these attacks."

"Funny," says Emma, "that's what he says about you."

"Naturally. He would resent any outside relationship you form."

"Anyway, why go to all that trouble? If he hates me so much, why not just put a gun to my head and shoot me?"

"Maybe he's hoping you'll do it yourself."

Emma looks at Caroline as if for the first time. "Roger always said you hate men."

"Not true; I hate abusive men."

"Roger's not abusive."

"You mean he doesn't hit you."

"I mean he's not abusive. And now, if you'll excuse me, I have to get to work." Emma stands with as much dignity as she can muster. Caroline allows herself to be escorted to the door but there pauses, as if hoping to be called back. Emma says nothing.

Caroline takes her hand. "You're too smart to blame the messenger."

"Good-bye, Caroline."

"I know you're angry. I only hope that when you've had a chance to reflect, you'll consider the fact that I have nothing to gain by saying what I did, and a great deal to lose."

Emma's face is wooden. "Thanks for coming. It's been real."

"Would you promise me one thing, Emma? Will you think about what I've said?"

"I will not," she replies. To her rage and disgust she feels tears gathering in her eyes. "I won't give it another thought."

"THAT BITCH!"

Emma hushes him, looking toward the open door of the bedroom. "You'll wake Zack."

"How dare she?"

She gets out of bed and shuts the door. Now the only illumination comes from the muted television. Emma feels her way back into bed. "She's worried about me. She doesn't *know* you. To her you're just the husband."

"And you listen to her," Roger says bitterly. "You entertain her crackpot theories."

"Hey, you know, the cops asked questions, too."

Poor choice of words; she knows it as soon as they leave her mouth. Emma studies her husband by the flickering light of the eleven o'clock news. Maybe it was wrong to tell him; certainly it was a betrayal of Caroline's good, though mistaken, intentions. But Emma is sick to death of secrets, sick of parceling out information like portions on a soup line: so much per customer, selection may vary. Caroline forced a choice and Emma made it. Confiding in Roger was meant as a declaration of faith, but in this she reckoned without the refraction of his own complicating passions. From her point of view she is taking sides, not against Caroline, but against her version of events. From his, she is using Caroline to post her own doubts.

She takes his hand, presses it to her belly. By now Emma is feeling pregnant. Her breasts are swollen and tender, her womb is heavy inside her. "I heard his heartbeat today. That's our baby in there. That's our son down the hall. Don't you dare question my allegiance."

Roger draws her to him, kisses the top of her head, then cradles it in the hollow of his shoulder. But there is distance and distraction in his absentminded stroking of her hair.

"Who the hell is she?" he mutters. "Mrs. Nobody from Nowhere; where does she get off? She's got her own baggage, don't tell me she hasn't."

"She's trying to help me," Emma says. "Give her credit for that, at least."

"Bitch," he says between his teeth. "Presumptuous, interfering bitch."

25

IMMURED IN HER tower, Emma is deep in the final chapter of her book. When the phone rings she is tempted to ignore it, let the machine downstairs pick up; but given the state of Roger's nerves these days, that's not really an option. She reaches for the phone without taking her eyes off the computer screen. If it's him she'll be short. If it's a telemarketer, she won't even waste time being rude; she'll just hang up. "Yes?"

"I'm disturbing you."

What a psychic, Maggie would say. Under any other circumstances, Emma would have been glad to hear the familiar nasal tones of Ida Green. Now, though, she has to wrest eyes and thoughts away from her book. "Hello, Ida."

"You've been on my mind lately," the psychic says. "I'm thinking should I call, should I not call? I don't want to bother you, but I'm a little worried."

She now has Emma's full attention. There's an indecipherable blur of voices and laughter in the background: a radio, perhaps, or a TV talk show.

"I keep seeing a date," Ida says. Another wave of tinned laughter ends with an abrupt click. "Does November fourteen mean anything to you?"

Depends; does a knife to the heart mean anything? Emma slumps in her chair, blindsided, and not just metaphorically. Dark spots spin before her eyes like pieces in a melancholic kaleidoscope.

"Yes," she says. "It means plenty." Ida waits, but Emma doesn't elaborate. "Is something going to happen on November fourteenth?"

"Possibly. I know it's a dangerous time for you."

Emma hugs herself. "Could you be more precise?"

"If I could, I would," Ida answers tartly. "It's not a wire service."

"Sorry."

"No, no. That's my own frustration talking. I wish I did know more, but better something than nothing. Especially in your condition, you need to be very careful."

Emma says, "In my condition?"

"You are pregnant, aren't you?"

She touches her stomach, still flat as an ironing board. "How did you know?"

"Doesn't take a psychic, dear," Ida says with a laugh. "At my age, a person should know a pregnant woman when she sees one. But tell me, on that other front, how are things going?"

"My houseguest, you mean?" She glances around the room, lowering her voice slightly. "Actually, there've been some developments. We've made contact." She tells Ida about her memo and Mrs. Hysop's apt response. Emma is talking to the one person of her acquaintance who would believe this story without question; yet in the process she herself feels a stirring of doubt where none was before. As a tale, Mrs. Hysop's ghost is utterly convincing; yet the same story, presented as fact, evaporates in the open air like water sprinkled on a red-hot skillet.

If Ida is not amazed, neither is she amused. "You don't want to encourage them," she scolds Emma. "It's like feeding stray cats. They're meant to move on."

"Then why doesn't she?"

"Who knows? It's not so unusual, I'll tell you that. People get confused, they get lost, they want to say good-bye. My husband, God bless him, wanted a salami sandwich."

Emma says, "Excuse me?"

"He passed suddenly in St. Louis, on a business trip to some clients. Heart attack in his hotel room, late at night. I was home. Middle of the night something wakes me up. Can't get back to sleep, so I figure I'll make a nice cup of tea. Murray's in the kitchen, peering into the fridge. 'Murray,' I say, 'what are you doing here?'

" 'I was hungry,' he says.

" 'But you're in St. Louis,' I say.

" 'So what could a little salami hurt?' he says. Then he shuffles down the hall to the bathroom, and that's the last I ever saw of him."

Maggie would ask if he flushed. Even Emma succumbs to a twinge of doubt. Much as she likes Ida, it's almost too good a story. But who is she to say? Lately she herself has been feeling like a character in a paperback original, jerked around for the sake of someone else's lurid plot—hardly the author of her own destiny, hardly the omniscient narrator she envisioned when she first spied this lofty glass tower. After Ida's call, Emma wraps herself in an afghan and huddles cross-legged in her armchair. The book will have to wait. If Emma's learned anything these past few months, it's the necessity of rolling with the punches. No good pretending they don't hurt; just roll with 'em, get up, and come back.

Ida's message is a blow. *It's not over.* Well, she never really thought it was, did she? The final chapter is missing; the question is, who's going to write it?

This notion of her antagonist as the author of a plot both elates and empowers Emma. After all, when it comes to writing stories, they are on her turf; she has home-field advantage. What she needs to do is step back. To look at the story from the outside, see where it's going and where it comes from. For that, too, should be possible; by analyzing a text she ought to be able, in a limited field, to derive the author.

She may not be as brilliant as Roger or as sharp as Maggie, but Emma knows her own strengths. If stories were cars, she'd be an expert mechanic. Give her a set of symbols and she'll deconstruct them in a flash, a flat character and she'll infuse him with incident. Faulty plot engines? Fuhgetaboutit; specialty of the house.

Suddenly energized, she tosses off the afghan, fetches her journal from the bottom desk drawer and carries it back to the armchair. She opens to the first page and begins to read.

To every writer's brain there are two sides, the creative, where plots, characters, and symbols are born, and the critical, where they are edited. It's the critical side of Emma's brain that is engaged now. As she reads, she scribbles notes on a sheet of looseleaf.

Access?

Worms. Can of worms = buried secrets.

Fetal pig—why? (Human hard to come by.)

Fetus > pregnancy.

Which?

She underlines the last word, then lays down her pen and stares straight ahead. Which indeed? Maggie had jumped to the conclusion that the fetal pig incident was both a reference to and an assault on Emma's pregnancy, and they all jumped with her. But now Emma sees there is another way to read that particular text. Seven years ago, the accident that killed the Johnsons, father and daughter, had taken another life as well. Emma's unborn child, a six-month-old fetus, died when the impact of the air bag and seat belt caused the placenta to separate. In the hospital, unable to detect a fetal heartbeat, doctors had performed an emergency C-section; but they could not revive the baby, a tiny, perfectly formed girl.

Everyone close to Emma at that time knew of this tragedy, far more than know about her pregnancy now. Countless strangers must have perused the brief newspaper articles. To the extent that this public event is now a secret, it is one of the slow-forming variety, created by Emma's subsequent refusal to allude to it and by the fitful nature of memory itself. It is an event encrusted by tact and forgetfulness, like a buoy so coated with barnacles that its original shape is lost.

The fetal pig may have been intended as a taunting reminder of that earlier loss. Had she not been pregnant at the time, that would surely have been Emma's first association. That her enemy knows about the accident she has no doubt; the Raggedy Ann doll beneath her car wheels proved that. Ida's message about November fourteenth seems to confirm the connection, if a psychic's warning can be taken as evidence.

Turning to a fresh page, Emma lists everything she knows and surmises about her enemy.

1. Clever
2. Computer literate
3. Access to house
4. Knowledge of past—accident, illness
5. Knowledge of family movements
6. Organized
7. Patient
8. Driven
9. Vindictive

She reads the list over and over. Does she know this person? Up through number seven, the list could describe most of the people she's close to. (Though not all; hard to cram Maggie and patience into the same sentence.) Emma can't even eliminate those who didn't know her at the time of the accident, for that was public knowledge; any reasonably adept researcher could find it out in an hour.

Add items eight and nine to the mix, though, and she doesn't recognize a soul.

But of course, this person doesn't want to be recognized. "10. Deceptive," she appends.

Emma still doesn't know who's behind it, but she feels a step closer to knowing. Feels better, too, for having in some small way taken arms against her sea of troubles. She is not, after all, a character in someone else's twisted tale. She is her own potent and capable self; she is Emma Roth.

A PERVERSE BUOYANCY carries her through the rest of the day. That evening, Zack's team is having a pizza party to celebrate their victorious season as first-division champs. Parents and siblings are invited. Before driving Zack to the Morgan Peak Pizzeria, Emma takes the trouble of changing out of her working sweats into jeans and a turtleneck, brushing out her braided hair, and putting on makeup. She does this for no one's sake but her own, she tells herself; it's part of getting a grip. Just because one's ordered world is rapidly devolving into chaos is no excuse for walking around like poor mad Ophelia. The widening of Nick Sanders's eyes as she walks into the restaurant, while gratifying, was certainly not her aim.

The pizzeria is narrow in front, just wide enough for a long counter in front of the ovens and a passageway to a back room that houses a dozen tables and booths.

Three tables have been placed end to end in the middle of the room for the team to sit at, while parents congregate along the edges and in the booths. Emma and Zack are among the last to arrive. As they enter, Nick Sanders leaves a group of men standing near the back room entrance and comes out front to meet them. "Yo, Zack," he says, holding out his hand. Zack slaps him five and races back to join the other boys.

When Emma starts to follow him, Nick slides in front of her. "Where's Roger?" he asks.

"Couldn't make it, unfortunately. He gets home around seven."

"Too bad. How's that laptop working out for you?"

"Great, thank you." She wants to go in and join the others, not stand here talking privately with Nick; but as she starts past him, he takes hold of her wrist. "I need to talk to you, Emma."

"You need to take your hand off me."

He lets go at once. "What, Emma Roth scared of a little small-town gossip?"

"You bet," Emma says, with Mrs. Hysop in mind. "Stuff's lethal."

"Then meet me somewhere else. Have lunch with me."

"I don't eat lunch."

"We need to talk."

"About what? The laptop's great. Problem solved, case closed."

"Case closed my ass. It's not just the hacking." Nick braces himself. "I read the rest of that journal, you know, that day in your office."

Her hand twitches, itching to slap him, but Emma overrules it. They're being watched—obliquely by the men, overtly by the moms. She keeps her voice down. "The fuck you did, you bastard."

"What'd you expect, doling out those little bits and pieces? Ever since then I've been thinking."

"Dangerous pursuit; better stick to coaching." She brushes past him, walks back into the restaurant. Yolanda is standing at the foot of the boys' table, pouring Pepsi into paper cups and passing them out. "S'up with Nick?" she asks as Emma draws near.

"What's always up with him?" Emma answers. They lock eyes and laugh. Once again Emma is embraced and comforted by Yolanda's deep, rolling laugh, like distant thunder on a summer afternoon.

"Got something to tell you," says Yolanda, but before she can confide, the pizzas arrive and they are swamped by a tide of ravenous boys. After the initial feeding frenzy subsides, Nick taps a spoon against a glass and the room quiets. At first it's the usual coach speech; Emma's heard it a dozen times before. Thanks to the assistants, thanks to the parents for their support, yada yada yada. Then Nick turns to the team.

"I shouldn't say this," he says. "I don't want you walking out of here with swollen heads. But I gotta tell you the truth. This is the best damn team I ever coached."

Cheers from the boys. Nick raises a hand and they quiet down.

"I'm proud of you guys," he says. "Not just for winning, though I gotta admit the winning felt great." More cheers, mixed with laughter. "More than that, though, I was proud of the way you conducted yourselves, the character you showed. The times you came back from being down, the times you played hurt, the times you stepped up your play to beat a better team. I want to thank you guys for the best soccer season of my life."

A moment of silence. Then one of the boys cries out, "Let's hear it for the coach!," and they all join in, yelling and banging on tables and stamping their feet in a racket that continues until the parents intervene to stop it.

Yolanda, drifting to Emma's side, does a Sally Field imitation. "They like him, they really, really like him."

"He's a fine coach, I'll say that for him."

"That's not all he's good at, what I hear," Yolanda teases. "Or am I preaching to the choir?"

"In his dreams! Is that what you think of me?"

"Easy, girl. I don't, but you can't blame a person for wondering, way he looks at you. Shit, look at the fool now, staring over here."

Emma doesn't look. She keeps her back to Nick.

"Anyway," says Yolanda, "what I wanted to tell you before? One of Gerard's clients is a set designer for *Lion King*. The guy was so blown away by the job Gerard did on his country house, he comped him tickets to the show."

"Lucky you! I tried getting tickets; they're sold out a year in advance."

"He gave us four. If it's okay with you, Marcel would like to invite Zack."

A faint twinge of unease raises its head, only to be swamped by a wave of gratitude. What a treat for Zack, and how kind of Yolanda! Emma accepts immediately, with thanks.

"Means being out late on a school night," Yolanda warns. "Probably won't get home before midnight, one o'clock."

Emma shrugs. "So he'll be tired in school the next day. When is it?"

"Next week. November fourteenth." Then, observing Emma's face, Yolanda says, "Is that a problem?"

"No," says Emma. "No problem."

Suddenly the room closes in on her. Too many people, too much noise. The men are smoking cigars, and the smell makes her sick. She looks around. Zack's engrossed in a video game. "Be right back," she tells Yolanda, then grabs her jacket and heads outside.

Her car is parked in the back of the restaurant's side lot. Emma walks over and leans back against the hood, imbibing the cold, salty air, her mind spinning with thoughts about Yolanda, the fourteenth of November, the nature and limits of coincidence. What should she have said? On that date of all others, is it better to keep Zack close or have him at a safe distance? The doubt she would not heed earlier asserts itself now, speaking in Maggie's voice. *Coincidences happen in real life. Someone you know. Someone you've eliminated.*

But have you heard her laugh? Emma answers the voice. Have you sat with her, talked with her? There has to be a bottom, she thinks. There has to be some faith in one's ability to judge, the courage of one's instincts. Hers are wholly with Yolanda . . . but what price error?

She shivers and starts back. Just then a man emerges from the restaurant and walks toward her, moving purposefully. With the streetlight behind him, she cannot make out his features, but she recognizes him by his gait, that easy, athletic stride. "Son of a bitch," she mutters to herself.

"You can run but you can't hide," Nick says as their paths intersect. He's in shirtsleeves but shows no sign of feeling the cold.

"I don't appreciate you following me."

"Then why'd you go outside?" he asks with a cocky grin.

"For peace and quiet and fresh air, out of which I got the air. Jesus, Sanders, you are the most obnoxious, ego-tistical—"

"Skirt-chasing asshole," he finishes. "I know what you think of me, and it's my own damn fault you think it. But that's the old Nick Sanders. Since you came along, there's a new one."

"Oh, really?" she says. "How many of you are there?"

"Go ahead, mock me. Tear my heart to shreds."

"Flirting again. You disappoint me, Nick. I thought we were past this."

"You're mistaken, Emma; how could we get past what we've never gone through? But interesting as that subject may be, I'm afraid this is not the time to be thinking about us."

"What *us?*" she sputters. "There is no *us,*" but he goes on as if she hadn't spoken.

"It's clear to me that someone is setting you up, and you don't have a clue who it is. Am I right so far?"

"What if you are?"

"Then maybe what you need is a fresh pair of eyes, an outside point of view. I'm a pretty smart guy, Emma, when I'm not making a total ass of myself. You ought to let me help."

His open, steady gaze vouches for him, and the dis-tance he keeps, and the hands jammed into his pockets. He is one of those men in whom the boy shines through, making him seem better than he is: less cunning, more impetuous. His motives and desires appear transparent, in stark contrast to Roger's brooding opacity; he's a babbling brook to Roger's still waters. As to her own motives, Emma suspects a certain passive complicity. Half a second's thought would have told her that if she left the restaurant, he would follow; his type always does. They make it seem so easy. No need to decide, no need to choose; just stop resisting for half a minute and see what happens.

Not likely. Roger called this move, he said Nick would try to muscle or worm his way into their lives; and Emma had promised to keep him out.

"Thanks," she says, "but Roger and I will handle this."

"Roger, right. Like he's handled it so far?"

Emma scowls. "Crossing a line here, Coach."

"What is it with that husband of yours?" She turns and heads for the restaurant, but his voice follows her. "If you were my wife, I'd have got to the bottom of this thing long ago; I'd have put a stop to it. What's he done, besides bust my chops for trying—"

She slams the restaurant door behind her.

26

MONDAY, NOVEMBER 11. There's a storm coming, a huge nor'easter slowly working its way up the coast. Right now it's pounding the southern tip of Florida. In three days it may hit Long Island. On the other hand, it could take an eastward turn out to sea and miss the Island altogether. Three days is forever when it comes to weather prediction; just ask Roger.

Still, it gives Emma one more thing to worry about. If the storm does hit, it will arrive on November 14, the anniversary of her accident and the day Yolanda is taking Zack and Marcel to see *The Lion King*. Emma hasn't forgotten Ida Green's call. If anything happens to Zack, it will be the end of her. She wants to keep him home. Roger won't hear of it.

"It's one thing for us to indulge our fears," he'd told her last night. By *us*, she understands, he means *you*. "It's another to impose them on Zack."

"But why tempt fate?" she'd asked. "It's not as if we haven't been warned."

Roger's face had curdled with disgust. "Have we been reduced to ordering our lives by psychic prediction?"

Of course they haven't . . . not quite. Nevertheless, Emma can't help fearing the thing she's always feared: poetic justice. What goes around, comes around. Magical thinking or true perception? Perhaps they are not as different as she once thought. If God exists, surely his middle name is Irony.

Too nervous to work, Emma wanders about her office window-gazing. The bay is singularly still today, its waters glassy smooth. Wispy cirrus clouds hover, stationary against a sky the fervent blue of robins' eggs. Viewed from up here, the bay appears so much more a painted seascape than a living scene that the appearance of a small fishing dory strikes a note of incongruity.

The room shimmers with a fine azure light, charged with apprehension. Emma is suddenly aware of Mrs. Hysop's presence; and she feels certain that Mrs. Hysop is equally aware of her. It's as if they are floating up here, cut off from the rest of the house, enclosed in a bubble. There is a bond between them, Mrs. Hysop and herself, that goes beyond coincidence, beyond their asynchronous sharing of this room. All that she has heard and learned of Virginia Hysop has coalesced over time into the image of a flesh-and-blood woman to whom Emma, had she known her in life, would surely have been drawn. There is a familiar tartness to her temperament, a caustic humor that has survived even death. And how many people in this world possess a passion for punctuation? Not many, but Emma is one, Mrs. Hysop another.

Pity for the poor remnant of a woman is compounded by Emma's sense that there but for the grace of God. . . . The same disease had laid claim to them both, only Mrs. Hysop, having no family to intervene and force help upon her, had succumbed to hers. Even her clinging to this house, symptomatic of a greater refusal to move on, arouses the deepest empathy. Hadn't Roger, by his insistence on their moving, implicitly accused her of that same failure of nerve?

For all her sympathy, however, Emma has no desire to further her acquaintance with Mrs. Hysop. No doubt her fictional protagonists, in a similar situation, would have reached out through seances. Not so their author; in this respect alone, Emma is anti-integration. Even allowing for some sort of survival after death, which she has most reluctantly done, one can still hold out for separation. The living and the dead belong to separate spheres. Ida Green was right: Mrs. Hysop ought to move on. Emma's room, her home, will never fully be hers until that happens.

Though she has no desire to speak to Mrs. Hysop, and shudders at the very thought of seeing her, there is

one mode of communication common and comfortable
to them both, through which Mrs. Hysop might be
gently shooed along. ("Where to?" is a question Emma
does not ask; she imagines only that some provision
must exist, otherwise the world would be teeming with
spirits, and we would think no more of meeting one than
of encountering a neighbor on the street.)

She sits at her desk, boots up the laptop. "Graduation
Day," she types, then continues without pause; indeed
the words come so quickly that her fingers can barely
keep up. Never before has Emma written so quickly, so
fluently. In essence it is their story she is telling, or
rather the intersection of their stories; but the prevailing
point of view belongs to the teacher, whom Emma calls
Lavinia Bishop.

> Lavinia Bishop woke from a long, stuporous
> sleep to discover that her house had been sold
> right out from under her. She was not pleased.
> To add insult to injury, the new owner, who
> styled herself a writer, turned out to be an
> ill-educated person seemingly incapable of com-
> posing a single paragraph without a sentence
> fragment. Although her writing had a certain
> energy and was not utterly devoid of talent, its
> "creative" use of punctuation betrayed a de-
> plorable spirit of laissez-faire.
>
> It was only by the greatest good fortune that
> the writer had chanced upon the home of a re-
> tired English teacher. Old plow horse that she
> was, Lavinia did not hesitate to apply herself
> once more to the yoke: She took upon herself the
> editing of Miss Thing's opus.

In the exercise of this thankless task, however, Lavinia experienced unprecedented difficulties. She found that she was very weary. Her hand quivered when she wrote, and it was only with enormous effort that she could manage to underline an error or scribble a word in the margin. When she read, the words shimmered on the page like amoebae under a poorly focused microscope. Her eyes were failing, and no wonder; after forty-five years of poring over thousands of student essays, the wonder was that she could see at all.

Lavinia not only lives and breathes but also walks and speaks in Emma. After months of steady incubation, she emerges fully formed, like Athena bursting from the brow of Zeus. Emma types steadily for an hour, barely pausing to think. When she takes her hands from the keys, the story is finished. Rough, to be sure, but a story in all its parts, with a beginning, a middle, and an end.

The beginning and the middle are based on reality—Emma's version, not Roger's. The end, in which Lavinia, realizing that her work is done, graciously departs the house forever, is pure invention; but it's invention that fits what comes before. Emma's strategy is simple. No one can resist a story about one's own self. Mrs. Hysop will read it, she will be drawn in, and perhaps—such is the writer's abiding faith in the power of artful language—she will be persuaded.

Emma prints out the story and reads the hard copy, editing as she goes. No point leaving a sloppy draft for Mrs. Hysop; she'd just use it to justify sticking around.

* * *

EMMA IS MAKING dinner and Zack doing his homework at the kitchen table when Roger walks in at a quarter to five. She is uneasy, Casey ecstatic, and Zack opportunistic. "Dad," he says, throwing an arm around Roger's shoulders, "old buddy, old pal, as long as you're home early, how about a little practice?"

"Maybe later, sport. Right now I want to talk to your mother."

Zack looks from one to the other, and silently leaves the room.

Roger looks toward Emma but does not meet her eyes. "Let's take a walk."

He's leaving me, she thinks as she takes her jacket from the closet. He's had enough; there's someone else; he's leaving.

ONE AFTER THE OTHER, Roger leading, they clamber down the cliff to the beach. Beside the path are the wintered-down remains of summer's salt-spray roses: bare vines and imploded blossoms the color of dried blood. There is not the faintest breeze off the bay, all wind having been sucked out of the atmosphere by the impending storm. Though not unfamiliar with the conceit of pathetic fallacy, Emma can't avoid the notion of Mother Nature holding her breath. As they reach the bottom, she turns to Roger, struggling for composure against the panic that assailed her the moment he appeared in the doorway.

"Tell me," she says.

Roger pushes the hair out of her face. Deep trenches bracket his mouth. There is trepidation in his eyes, but something else as well, a muted excitement. "This is going to come as a shock," he says.

"Just tell me."

"Your friend has been lying to you."

Emma sits down hard on the shingled beach. Roger, mistaking relief for anxiety, hunkers down beside her.

"What friend?" Emma asks.

"Caroline," he says, with a curl of his lip. "Dr. Caroline Marks."

"What about her?"

"Doesn't exist. No such person."

"Bullshit," says Emma. "This is so obviously you getting back at her for what she said about you."

"Emma, I looked into her background. She doesn't have any."

"You invaded her privacy?"

Suddenly he shouts. "What about our fucking privacy, ever think about that? What about our right to live in peace?"

He is a volcano on the verge of eruption. Emma stares straight ahead, hardly breathing. Roger drops his head onto his arms with a deep groan.

Presently she says, "Why are you so angry?"

He raises his head and looks at her. "Why aren't you angrier?"

Their eyes meet in a moment of extreme clarity. A very good marriage might have three or four such moments, in which each sees so clearly into the other that the boundaries between them disappear. Roger's question resounds in her head. The times they found the doll in the road and the pig on their bed, Emma was struck dumb with horror; but Roger was galvanized with rage. Looking back, she sees his as the rational, human response. What's wrong with her? she wonders with disgust. Might as well change her name from Emma Roth to Emma Soft if she can't rise to her own defense, stand up and shout wholeheartedly, "Enough, we don't deserve this, no one has the right to do this to us!"

But she's not a coward; Emma knows this. She was nineteen when her parents died, leaving her with a fifteen-year-old sister to raise. As frightening as these past few months have been, they don't come close to the practical and existential terror of finding herself and her sister alone in the world. Emma had met that challenge, had succeeded for both Maggie and herself. Pride in that accomplishment is the crystalline core of her self-confidence.

What has become of that confidence now? What has become of her open-hearted anger? She knows the answer. They bled out on a rainy street, one dark night in November. Since then, convinced there's a big black mark against her name on the karma chart, Emma has lived a life of tragedy-in-waiting, as haunted as her fictional creations, as trapped as Mrs. Hysop.

Now Roger, seeing her lost in thought and liable to remain so, stands and offers her a hand. They proceed along the shore, pausing atop a stone jetty to gaze out at the bay. The dory Emma saw earlier is now putting back to port, trailed by a flock of raucous gulls. Sandpipers perch at the far end of the jetty, pecking at shellfish between the rocks. The air smells of far-off places.

Roger reaches out, tucks a strand of hair behind her ear. "Are you ready to talk about Caroline?"

She blanks her face. "I'm listening."

"There's no certified psychologist by that name in this state or Pennsylvania, where she claims to come from. She's not registered with any professional association in the country; she has no employment record prior to her current job; she has no financial or credit history predating that job, which started shortly before she showed up at our door."

Two images assail Emma in quick succession: Caroline's face as she hands over her rental application, filled with blanks; then her living room, the brand-new furnishings, the lack of mementos, photos, magazines, books, or any other accouterments of private or previous life. Out of the blue she had come to them, like Mary Poppins; but even Mary Poppins had her carpetbag.

Still, Caroline had explained all that, hadn't she? Divorce, the desire for a fresh start—resuming her maiden name was part and parcel with the rest.

"Simple," she tells Roger. "She changed her name when she divorced. Women do it all the time."

"She didn't change it legally. There's no court record of it in New York or Pennsylvania."

"So she did it somewhere else, or she did it de facto. Does a woman really have to go to court to take back her maiden name? Besides, that women's center hired her; they must have been satisfied with her credentials."

"We don't know what kind of cock-and-bull story she sold them."

"We?" she says.

He looks out to sea. "This guy I hired."

"A detective?" Emma is amazed at how utterly, in time of crisis, he has reverted to his roots. "You had no right—"

"*No right?*" he howls. "Do you have any idea what I'd like to do to that bitch?"

"For changing her name? Are you nuts?" Emma

turns and scrambles off the jetty, heading toward home. Roger catches up. He tries to take her arm, but she shakes him off and walks faster.

"Changing her name is just the tip of the iceberg," he says. "Calm down a sec and think it through."

Five strides later Emma comes to an abrupt halt. "You've got to be kidding."

"It all adds up. Plenty of opportunity, a bird's-eye view of our comings and goings—"

"And no motive."

"No known motive," he amends. "Maybe she's nuts. Maybe someone put her up to it. I don't know. Tell you this: I intend to find out."

"How, by shaking it out of her?"

He stares at the ground. In the waning light, Emma sees as if for the first time how gaunt he has grown, how deeply etched his face.

"I'd like to," he says. "But I'll let the police handle her."

"The cops? No way!"

"Actually, dearest, I'm not asking permission."

"No, Roger. You don't do that where I come from. You don't go to the cops."

"Oh, really? Where I come from, we're encouraged to report daily on one another."

Emma laughs. Can't help it; he sounds so much like his old self. They used to enjoy fighting back in the time she thinks of as Before; they used to indulge in long, luxuriant four-course arguments. A taste of politics and religion for starters, then on to the relative merits of science versus art, fiction versus nonfiction, and then the really contentious stuff, like the proper way to eat a bagel and the names and sexes of their four children-to-be. And finally, dessert: the pleasure of bridging their differences with their bodies.

She shakes off the nostalgia; this is one argument that won't be settled in bed. Roger takes her arm again, and this time she doesn't pull away. They walk homeward, carefully picking their way over the rocks as evening settles in around them. Presently Emma, in a calmer voice, says, "She may have reasons of her own, reasons that have nothing to do with us."

"Right," he says.

"The point is, you don't just go to the cops without giving her a chance to explain."

"Fine. If that's how you feel, I'll talk to her myself."

"Absolutely not. You'll fight with her, I know it; you'll drive her away."

Roger stops and stares at her in wonderment. "Emma, darling, open your eyes. The woman shows up out of nowhere. Every word out of her mouth is a lie. What does that tell you?"

"That paranoia's catching?"

He doesn't laugh. Emma licks her lips, which have gone dry. Her head aches desperately. The phrase "splitting headache" comes to mind, and for the first time she fully comprehends it. When the mind splits in two, naturally it's painful. Roger's revelations were the wedge; now half of Emma cleaves to the friend whose support has carried her through these past few months, while the other half stands aloof, questioning and reexamining every encounter, every word. She feels like one of those cartoon characters with a devil whispering in one ear, an angel in the other.

Roger's accusation has shaken loose a flock of doubts, insignificant in themselves but alarming in the aggregate. She cannot deny that Caroline's constant, Socratic questioning of Emma's most basic assumptions lends itself equally to two opposing interpretations. It could be—Emma has supposed it to be—a therapeutic delving, a form of tough love. Looked at from another angle, though, the angle that Roger has foisted upon her, challenge becomes insinuation, and sympathy a subtle undermining of Emma's deepest ties.

Like a juror who may not believe the defendant but finds for him on the basis of reasonable doubt, Emma believes in Caroline's innocence, but acknowledges that Roger has raised reasonable suspicion. Though his method shames her, she cannot ignore the results. Questions must be asked, but not by him. Feeling as she does about Roger, Caroline would never tell him anything.

"I'll see her myself," she says.

"Not without me you won't."

They agree to go together.

27

"It's none of your business," Caroline says, sitting erect on the edge of her Scandinavian chair. "You had no right." Bright red patches burn in her cheeks. The air around her crackles. From the moment she opened her door to them, her gaze has been locked on to Roger's face. Only once, when he admitted to having had her investigated, did she turn to look at

Emma; but what a look that was. Emma's face still tingles with it.

"Your signature on the rental application gave me the legal right," Roger says. "And if I didn't have that, I'd have done it anyway."

"I don't have to tell you a goddamn thing."

"No, you don't. You can tell the cops instead. That was always my preference; it was Emma who insisted we give you a chance to explain."

Caroline narrows her eyes. "Don't think for a moment that I don't know what you're up to."

"What *I'm* up to?"

"It's obvious. You're trying to deflect attention away from yourself by targeting the outsider, the stranger."

"Lucky me, finding one with so much to hide."

"Perhaps you'd care to explain *why* I would do those terrible things to Emma?"

He is silent.

"Just for the hell of it?" she prompts. "Maybe I'm crazy; is that the theory? But even crazy people have motives. What's mine?"

"You tell me."

"Can't. You may not have noticed, but I've grown quite fond of your wife." Caroline turns to Emma. "Please tell me you don't believe this."

Roger's eyes bear down like heat-seeking missiles. Seated on the couch between their chairs, Emma feels like the rope in a no-holds-barred game of tug-of-war. She has not said a word so far, her silence arising not from embarrassment—like a woman in labor, she has passed beyond that state—but rather from concentration. Hawklike she has watched, from a far, still place. Nothing has escaped her eye, she is alert to every flutter of expression on Caroline's face, every movement of her body. So far she sees a woman outraged and hurt; she sees no trepidation in those indignant eyes.

Emma says, "I don't understand why you lied to us. I told you everything. You told me nothing."

"Can't you just accept that it has nothing to do with you?"

"I wish we could."

Reacting to that marital *we,* Caroline gets up and glides to the empty fireplace. She takes a cigarette from the box on the mantel, a lighter from her cardigan pocket, and lights up, inhaling deeply. Resting her forearm on the mantel, she stares pensively into the empty grate. Emma is struck by her composure, her indefinable air of consequence. Caroline resembles those willowy, self-possessed heroines of forties' movies, whose demeanor proclaimed, "I may be a character in your drama, darling, but I'm the star of my own."

Now she turns with an air of decision to Emma. "I'm going to tell you my story. Not because you have a right to know—you don't. And not because of your husband's bullying and threats—I don't give a damn about them or him. The reason I'm telling you is because if I don't, I'd be playing into his hand. He's already cut you off from your city friends. Now he's trying to sever our bond as well."

From ten feet away Emma is singed by her husband's rage. But he grits his teeth and keeps quiet. Caroline carries the ashtray back to her chair. She sits, crosses one stockinged leg over the other. She smokes her cigarette down to the filter before speaking. "It's not easy to talk about this. They drum it into you, over and over:

Tell no one. Put the past behind you. Don't confide, don't hint, don't even remember."

"They?" Emma prompts.

"The people who helped me. I call them the new underground railroad. But that's the end of the story. The beginning goes back to when I met my husband. We were married for eighteen years; still are, for all I know. Six months into the marriage, a week after we moved into our first house, my husband beat me for the first time. After that the beatings occurred periodically, every five or six months, more often toward the end.

"I can't—I won't—go into all the gory details. There was always a pretext but the pretexts weren't the point; his enjoyment was. The beatings always ended with sex. If I tried to resist, he'd . . . well, let's just say I gave up resisting."

She lights another cigarette, draws hard on it. Her eyes are fastened on something Emma can't see; except for a slight tremor about the lips, her face could be carved of stone. Emma tries to imagine this proud woman cowering before a man and fails dismally; yet the flat, almost clinical tone of her recital rings true. Caroline is hardly an open, confiding sort of person. Forced to reveal a humiliating secret, she would naturally, it seems to Emma, do her best to distance herself from it. Had she wept or waxed hysterical, Emma would not have believed her; but this tamped-down rendition is compelling.

Roger, on the other hand, doesn't buy a word of it. "You expect us to believe that an educated woman, a psychologist, puts up with this kind of crap for eighteen years?"

Caroline turns on him. The hectic color has faded from her cheeks, leaving her wan; her long neck is corded and tense. "Do you really think only poor, uneducated women are beaten by their husbands?"

"One who specializes in spousal abuse, no less!"

"The specialty came after," she snaps. "And why do you think I chose it?"

Roger, momentarily silenced, scowls at the floor.

"Oh, yes," Caroline says to Emma, "we know his opinion, don't we? Women who stay in abusive relationships have only themselves to blame."

"I'm not blaming you," Emma says gently. "But I don't understand."

"It was fear. He told me many times that if I ever left him, he would find me and kill me and get away with it. I believed him."

"That's it?" Roger scoffs. "One threat and you're his prisoner for life?"

Caroline looks at him. "My husband is a very successful criminal defense lawyer, a former homicide prosecutor. His entire career has been spent in the criminal justice system; I, on the other hand, had no job, no money, no access to his, no family, no resources. I didn't doubt for a minute that he would come after me. I still don't."

"And no one knew, that's your contention? In eighteen years, no one ever picked up on this ongoing abuse?" He sounds like a lawyer cross-examining a witness.

"Why would they? My husband was a powerful man; I was nobody. They took pains not to know."

"And you never told?"

She shakes her head vehemently. "We always kept up appearances—I needed that as much as he did. Life would have been totally unbearable if people had known what I endured from him. Most of the time we presented as the perfect couple."

"But there would have been signs," Roger says. "Marks, bruises."

"He was careful. He never lost control, never broke any bones or put me in the hospital. When there were visible bruises, he made me stay home, sometimes for weeks. His colleagues were told, in confidence, that I had psychological problems. He got a lot of mileage out of my infirmity, a lot of sympathy fucks. And of course it explained his watchful solicitude whenever we did go out together."

"Didn't you have anyone to help you?" Emma asks.

"Who could I turn to? Our friends were his friends; he'd made sure I had none of my own. My parents were dead. Controlling men," Caroline says, with a signifying look at Emma, "like women without family ties. I did try once, though. I told his mother."

"What did she do?"

Caroline laughs dryly. "Sat me down for a woman-to-woman talk. 'Now dear,' she said, 'a woman's got to take the good with the bad. I didn't hear you complaining when he bought you that nice big house, and I didn't hear you complaining when he bought you that fancy car and your beautiful clothes. So how come I hear you complaining now?' "

"Bitch."

"Actually, she was sympathetic. She put ice on my bruises, she made me tea, and she never told my husband what I'd done. She just didn't think an occasional battering was worth ending a marriage over. Wasn't till later I found out she'd been taking them herself for years. Like father, like son."

"A family with traditions," drawls Roger. "Isn't that special?"

"Roger," Emma warns. She turns to Caroline. "What changed?"

"The beatings became more frequent, more severe. I was afraid he would go too far, and I knew that if he did, he'd sooner kill me than send for help. Once I realized that, I had nothing to lose by running."

"How?" Roger demands.

"I found help." Her tone says, Don't go there. Naturally he dives right in.

"From who?"

"From some very good people, and fuck you if you think I'm naming names." Roger and Caroline stare at each other. It's like flint striking flint.

"What's your real name?" he says.

"Caroline Marks."

"What was it before?"

"I'm not telling you that," she says calmly.

"Why not? If you changed your name, there must be a record somewhere. You could clear this up in a second."

"I told you who my husband is. Do you really think I'm fool enough to register a name change?"

"So basically you're operating under an alias."

"Common-law name changes are perfectly legal, as long as there's no intent to defraud."

"How about intent to destroy, would that qualify?" He doesn't pause for an answer. "It takes money to start a new life, Caroline. Where did you get yours?"

"I took it from him," she says with a brief smile. "It's not a fraction of what any divorce court in the land would have given me; but then, I'd never have made it to divorce court."

"Yet you claim he kept you penniless." Roger cuts his eyes at Emma. "You said you had no access to his money."

"I got access," Caroline says. She waves her hand, leaving a trail of smoke. "I told you I had help. That's all I'm going to say."

Though she holds herself as straight as ever, her back seems to long for the chair's embrace. Emma sees that she is yearning for them to leave; she is spent, held erect by spite and pride.

"You realize," Roger remarks to Emma, "that for all the talking she's been doing, she hasn't given us one bit of verifiable information."

"Good," Caroline says defiantly. "I wouldn't trust you with my secrets and I'm sure as hell not confiding anyone else's. Some people went to a great deal of trouble to help a total stranger, and I'm damned if I'll repay them by siccing you on them."

Though Caroline is careful not to glance in her direction, Emma knows these words are meant for her, a not-so-subtle reproach. Like Caroline, Emma had turned to a stranger for help; unlike her, she had betrayed her befriender.

A short time ago, a few hours ago, even, Emma would have succumbed to a full-fledged guilt attack, as her overactive glands sprang into full production. It doesn't happen now. Her talk with Roger on the beach has in some mysterious way inoculated her. Though Emma feels sorry for her tenant and sorrier still for their friendship, which now seems unlikely to survive, she is free of guilt. True, they have invaded Caroline's privacy, forcing confidences she had no wish to give; but their need is great, their situation dire. Caroline ought to see that. Perhaps she will, when tempers subside. If not, thinks Emma, to hell with her.

ZACK IS PRETENDING to be asleep. Emma sees his eyes flutter as she enters his room. She doesn't say anything, just pulls the covers up to his chin and kisses the top of his head.

Roger is in the kitchen, making coffee, both of them parched. Caroline had offered nothing and taken nothing herself, though by the end she'd seemed in dire need of sustenance. It was, Emma suspects, a matter of principle not to offer hospitality to the enemy.

Caffeine's the last thing she needs, though sleep's a long shot anyway. But she gratefully accepts the cup Roger hands her. The kitchen is cold. He lights a fire in the hearth and they sit close together, drawing comfort from the heat and light.

"So," says Emma, "back to square one."

"You think?"

She looks at him. "You don't?"

"We've heard a story," he says. "It's a good story. I'm just not sure if it's fiction or nonfiction."

Emma is shaking her head before he's halfway through. "She couldn't have made that up. Too detailed, for one thing. For another, it makes sense. It explains everything, including her hostility toward you. She's projecting her experience on to mine; naturally you get cast as the villain."

In the fire's glow Roger looks fretful. He may not be convinced of Caroline's innocence, Emma thinks, but he's no longer sure of her guilt. "Can you really see that woman sitting still for years of abuse?"

"That's hard," she admits. "But who she is now isn't

who she was then. I can imagine her life now as a reaction to what it was before. It makes sense that she would work with other battered women. It makes sense she'd live alone; solitude would have to look good to a woman whose life has never been her own. Even the fact that she refused to name the people who helped her—to me that's very plausible, it's the kind of person she is."

They watch the fire. A log settles and sparks fly up the flue. Emma suddenly thinks of Mrs. Hysop. Has she read the story yet?

Roger's hand is on her neck. Emma starts at first, then relaxes as his thumb makes deep circles in the hollow at the base of her skull. She leans back and shuts her eyes.

28

THE NOR'EASTER, a solid phalanx of wind and rain, has made its way up the coast. Now battering the Jersey shore, by mid-afternoon it will hit Long Island. Outside, the slate-gray sky lets down a steady drizzle; the treetops sway rhythmically. In the kitchen Emma keeps the radio tuned to the all-news station. Coastal flood warnings, travel advisory, a reminder from Lilco to prepare for possible power outages. More than ever she misses the city. Safely ensconced in her cozy apartment, surrounded by concrete walls and double-glazed windows, she would have enjoyed watching this storm batter itself senseless against the stolid buildings. Here atop this cliff, she feels as exposed as Lear on the heath.

It's not just the storm that's stripped her nerves raw. Today is the day Zack goes to the city with Yolanda and Marcel. Their plan is to meet Gerard and have dinner at Jekyll and Hyde, one of the new crop of theme restaurants popping up all over the city, before going on to *The Lion King*. Zack's talked of nothing else for days; last night he didn't fall asleep till well past midnight. Emma knows because she, too, was awake, obsessing over scenarios that began with her waving good-bye and ended with a phone call, a stranger's voice. "Is this Mrs. Koenig? Ma'am, are you the mother of Zachary Koenig?"

Emma doesn't need Roger to tell her her fears are irrational. Dreading something doesn't make it any more likely to happen. So never mind about what day this is, never mind what anniversary: What about her rational fears—are they, too, outlawed? Does it make any sense to risk Zack's life, let him drive thirty miles through pouring rain and gale-force winds for the sake of a Broadway show? Even if that's what he wants, surely it's her duty to ensure his safety—or, if that is impossible, at least protect him from unnecessary risk.

Roger will be angry if she keeps Zack home, but that would not deter her. What gives her pause, trivial as it seems, is the risk of losing Yolanda's friendship. Yolanda wouldn't understand, and her hurt would be magnified by Marcel's disappointment. Emma has forfeited one friend already this week; she can hardly afford to lose another.

For there is little doubt that her friendship with Caroline is mortally wounded. They spoke yesterday— Emma made the call—but the conversation was brief and went nowhere. Caroline's tone was distant—not unfriendly, but distracted. Emma couldn't get a purchase. She said she was sorry for causing pain; Caroline replied that she understood. Emma assured her the matter would go no farther; Caroline thanked her. They'd reverted to an earlier stage of communication, all surface politeness and deep reserve.

That Caroline must resent her Emma fully understands. The woman had fled from a cancerous marriage, reinvented herself, embarked on a new life, or perhaps laid claim to the life that she would have led had she not been derailed; then suddenly along comes Roger, threatening to expose her to the very danger she thought she'd escaped. Caroline must rue the day she spotted their little carriage house.

But Emma's regret over their estrangement, though real, is not quite as great as she might have expected. There simply isn't time for it now. She has been pushed and pushed and pushed some more; and now she's in a corner, fighting for her life. Nothing like desperation to concentrate the mind. There's a core of ruthlessness in the best of us; Emma, at last, has tapped into hers.

The wind picks up, whistling through the trees, rattling the windows. The house, creaking in every joint, hunkers down to await the storm. Emma's coffee has gone cold. She decides to call Yolanda. Just as she reaches for the phone, it rings.

"Hey," Yolanda says.

"Hey yourself. I was just about to call. Have you looked out the window?"

"Hell, yeah, just got back from dropping Marcel. What's up with that shit?"

"It's supposed to hit this afternoon. I'm a little nervous," Emma says carefully, "you driving in."

"Way ahead of you, girlfriend. If it's bad we take the train."

With that, Yolanda knocks out the only rational objection Emma had. She is less relieved than she ought to be. "Is the train safe, do you think?"

"Safe as houses. You do sound edgy. What's up, Emma?"

"I went driving once in a storm. Lived to regret it."

Silence comes over the line: Yolanda waiting for more or weighing her response.

"Don't worry," she says at last. "He's in good hands. I promise you, I'll take the same care of your child as you would mine."

EMMA GOES UPSTAIRS to work, accompanied halfway by Casey. The first thing she does is check the story she left for Mrs. Hysop. Feels silly doing it—it reminds her of Passover seders in her parents' apartment, when they would set a glass of wine outside the door for the prophet Elijah, and every half hour or so the children would check to see if it was gone. Emma's not sure what she hopes to find; "Sayonara" would be nice, "Thanks for the memories." But if Mrs. Hysop has read the story, she has not been moved to comment on it. The pages remain as Emma left them, virgin copy, unmarred by penciled annotations.

She stands by the window overlooking the bay. By now the wind has gathered so much sand, pebbles, leaves, and other debris that it is visible; she can actually see the currents swirling around the house. Beneath a blanket of gray cumuli, the bay surges and swells upward like a woman arching toward a lover's body. The shoreline is obliterated, the lines between water, land,

and sky are blurred: an Impressionist's rendition of a bay, more Monet than Turner, with a van Gogh sky.

Roger should see this. She remembers the first time she viewed the house, Roger standing behind her at the bedroom window, whispering in her ear. *Imagine this in a storm.* For him, a storm is chaos made visible, a reminder of all man cannot control. For Emma, it is a window into that which is intractable in nature; and like the art of tragedy, it is best appreciated from a safe vantage point. Well, here is the storm; and where is her husband? Safe in the city, where she longs to be.

He did offer to stay home. Not because of the weather, but because he knows what this day means to her. Emma, though tempted, turned him down. She has something to prove, as much to herself as to him; and the way to prove it is to act as if this were any other day.

She sits in her armchair and picks up the final chapter of her book. Now that the novel is nearly finished, she finds herself lingering, deliberately slowing her pace, as if taking a final stroll through a neighborhood she knows she won't be visiting again. When she finishes this novel, she'll do that kids' book with Yolanda to cleanse her palette, like sherbet between courses. After that, who knows? Not another ghost story, that's for sure; she lacks the requisite disbelief. Maybe a book more like the books she reads, a braver book than any she's written before.

For a couple of hours Emma works steadily, editing yesterday's pages, then writing the next scene. She forgets her problems, forgets what day it is; the story carries her like a river, and she steers the course. When she comes to the end of the scene, she gets up and stretches, surprised to find that the room has grown darker. Rain, heavier now, slants against the windows; the world outside is reduced to streaks of watery color.

She sits at her desk with the laptop in front of her, and once again the world recedes. She fixes the old pages, types in the new. Waiting for the pages to print out, Emma decides to check her E-mail. She turns on the desktop computer and logs on to Compuserve. There's a message from Gloria, her agent. One word: "Nu?," which, decompressed, means, "You're two months late and I'm tired of fending off Arthur. What's happening with the book?"

Emma hits Reply and types an equally terse reply: "Imminent." She sends it and hits Exit. A box comes up on the screen. "You have messages in the outbox. Do you want to exit?"

What messages in the outbox? Emma opens it up and finds a note addressed to Roger. She pulls it up on the screen.

Roger,

    You win. I've had enough.

    I know this is where I'm supposed to say I'm sorry, it wasn't your fault, you did your best, try to forgive me, blah, blah, blah. But to hell with that: If there ever was a time for honesty, this is it. The truth is, I don't want your forgiveness and I sure as hell don't offer mine. I'm sorry for Zack, but for you, nothing. You drove me to this. Think of me while you're lying with your floozy bitch, and remember that the prayers of the dying have a special potency.

    See you in hell, you bastard.

    Emma

There's a tingling throughout her body. Someone walking on my grave, she thinks dully. Or digging it. When she tries to read the words again, they lose coherence, dancing and gyrating on the screen. Emma thinks it's the computer until she looks up and finds the room itself in motion. Her throat fills up with bile; she tries to rise, but her legs have no strength, and she leans over and vomits into the wastebasket.

She wipes her mouth on her sleeve. The room is still spinning, and her body is bathed in clammy sweat. She feels a gentle pressure on the back of her head, like a hand pushing downward. Bending forward, she puts her head between her knees and breathes deeply. In a few minutes her dizziness passes.

When she sits up, the words are still on the screen. Emma reads them again, this time through Roger's eyes. He wouldn't believe she wrote this. He knows her too well. Even if he had someone, this is not a letter she could write.

He'll figure it out, she thinks, but not instantly. There'll be a moment when he reads this as coming from me, and he'll be devastated, destroyed. Emma thinks about the sickness of the mind that could devise such a torment. What an enemy she has drawn, what a twisted soul.

But why wasn't it sent? If its purpose is to frighten Roger, why leave the message in Emma's outbox?

Maybe the person was interrupted, she thinks. But how long does it take to press Send?

Maybe it wasn't meant to be sent; maybe Emma was meant to find it. This makes sense; she's been the target all along. In that case, this note is just another in a series of cruel hoaxes.

But there's another possibility. Emma forces herself to look it square in the face, and it stares back unblinkingly. I'm meant to die, she thinks. Here's my suicide note, all typed and ready to go when I go. I'm meant to die, and it will look like suicide.

In a moment of explosive clarity Emma sees that everything has been building to this end. Like the point in a novel where all the plot lines converge, there is a sense of inevitability, a sense that everything, all along, has been leading her here. If she were to die today, and her death were construed as suicide, she would be thought unbalanced; and everything that came before would be looked at in that light. It would be a chicken and egg conundrum: Did the persecution give rise to the madness or the madness to the persecution? Did someone's cruelty—and the letter, written in her name, clearly accuses Roger—drive her to the point of suicide, or did mental illness lead her, first to invent, then to succumb to those torments?

She ought to be terrified. She has been floored by lesser shocks; this one ought to have her cowering in a corner, wetting her pants. Maybe it just hasn't sunk in yet, but Emma finds herself thinking more lucidly than she has in a long time. It's pouring outside, but inside a summer sun is beating down, burning off the fog. There is a place, deep inside, that radiates calm.

Emma reaches for the phone and with a steady hand punches in Roger's number. India answers. For once Emma skips the small talk. "Is he there?"

"No, sorry. He's in with the dean; they're working up next year's budget. Want me to transfer you?" India makes the offer with obvious reluctance, on orders from Roger, no doubt. God knows what he's told her, what she imagines. Wifey on the verge of collapse, probably. Emma feels that way for a moment, so acute is her disappointment.

"Have him call when he gets back," she tells India.

"Is something wrong, Emma?"

India's syrupy voice, oozing concern, wakens deep instincts of self-preservation. Emma calibrates her pitch at casual. "Nothing's wrong, I just need to talk to him."

She hangs up and turns back to the computer. The message is still on the screen, but it occurs to her that this could change in an instant. She opens a file called "Perp" and files a copy there.

Just a precaution. A few years back, a local teacher was car-jacked on her way home from a lecture. Though in fear for her life, the woman had the presence of mind to switch on a small recorder in her purse. The car-jacker, a clean-cut young man with no criminal history, drove to a wooded area where, despite her pleas for mercy, he murdered the woman. Guided by information revealed on the tape, the cops caught him within hours.

The story comes back to her now. Of course, Emma is not going to die. Locked in her house, with Casey downstairs, she's not even in imminent danger. But if somehow things go very wrong, if in some unforeseen manner her enemy is to succeed, Emma is damned if she'll let it look like suicide. Someone has to be told, and told now.

With sharp regret, she thinks of Caroline, whom she's lost the right to call. Even if she could, though, she knows what Caroline would say. Some way or another she'd blame this on Roger.

Emma reaches for the phone again and dials Maggie's office number. Not much chance of catching her in, and sure enough Emma gets her voice mail. "It's me," she says, in a calm, big-sister voice. "Something else has happened. I'm okay, but check your E-mail and call me back."

She turns back to the computer, chooses "create E-mail" from the options list, titles her message "Urgent," and addresses it to Maggie and Roger.

"Dear R & M," she types, "I found the following in my E-mail outbox, addressed to Roger. DON'T WORRY. I'm fine. The doors are locked, the alarm's on, and Casey's in the house. Call me when you get this." She appends the original message and hits Send. When the confirmation appears on the screen, she breathes a deep sigh of relief. This adder, at least, has been defanged.

One more call to make. Where did she put that card? She finds it buried under a pile of papers on her desk and punches in the number. It rings five times before a deep voice answers, "Detective squad."

She identifies herself and asks for Wong or Thigpen.

"They're off today," the deep voice says. "This is Detective Randall. Can I help?"

Emma laughs under her breath. Figures. Not her day; never was.

"Never mind," she tells Randall. "I'll call back."

"Something wrong, Miss, uh, what'd you say your name was?"

She leaves a message, hangs up. What now? She rises and restlessly passes from window to window. Sheets of cascading water enclose her; she feels as if she's been swept out to sea, no land in sight. The liquid air is filled with rumbling and cracking sounds, as if something large were breaking apart.

There's a sour taste in her mouth, a foul smell rising from the wastebasket. Emma carries it downstairs, holding the banister with her free hand. Casey jumps her just outside the spiral-stair corridor. Tail wagging frantically, he presses up against her leg. Emma can feel him trembling. "What's the matter, pup, scared of a little weather?" Casey sniffs the wastebasket, then looks up at her face. "Stinks, huh? Mama's not feeling too good today."

The dog follows her into the bathroom. Emma rinses out the wastebasket and brushes her teeth. She's drying her hands when the phone rings. Let it be Roger, she prays as she rushes into her bedroom. Please let it be Roger.

But it's Detective Wong.

"They said you were off," Emma says.

"I got your message," Wong says. "Been meaning to call anyway. What's up?"

Emma tells her about the E-mail addressed to Roger, reciting the text by heart. When she finishes there's a silence broken only by static.

"Detective?" says Emma.

"That's a suicide note," Wong says slowly.

"Only if I wrote it, which I didn't."

"Where's your husband, Ms. Roth?"

"Work."

"You're home alone?"

"I've got the dog. The house is locked. We put in an alarm system."

"I'd stay put, I were you. Not much of a day for going out, anyway."

"I'm not going anywhere," Emma says fervently.

"Tomorrow I'll have a word with our expert on com-

puter crime—hacking, stalking, stuff like that. I've got a
bad feeling about your situation, Emma. You did right to
call."

Sounds like a sign-off. Emma clutches the receiver
like a lifeline. "You said you were meaning to phone.
Did you have any news?"

"Oh yeah," Wong says. The line's so bad Emma has
to strain to hear. "That accident you told us about—we
got a line on the wife."

Emma pats the bed, and Casey jumps up beside her.
She leans into him. "Where is she?"

"I don't know. So far we just traced her back to
where she used to work. I talked to the principal. He
remembers her well, says she had some kind of breakdown after the accident, took medical leave, and never
came back to the job."

"You don't know where she lives now?"

"We checked her old address. She moved the year
after the accident, no forwarding. DMV had nothing
more recent."

"Isn't there any way to track her down? Social security, bank records?"

Wong's sigh percolates through the static. "Need a
warrant for that, and that's not going to happen based on
what we've got."

Emma carries the phone to the window. The trees
along the cliff edge bow and sway like syncopated
dancers against a charcoal sky. There's a beauty to the
storm that beguiles even as it threatens.

"Is there anything else you can tell me?" she asks.
"Do you know what she taught?"

"She didn't. That's what took so long, us looking for
a teacher."

"But I remember—"

"She worked for the board of ed, but . . ." Wong's final words are lost in a burst of static.

"What?" Emma yells, covering her free ear. "Talk louder!"

Another burst of static, then the detective's voice comes through loud and clear. "She was a school psychologist."

EMMA'S BACK in her office with her journal open on her lap. She just read through the whole thing, looking for proof that Caroline isn't Linda Johnson.

She's found none.

Is she paranoid for even making the connection? So they're both psychologists; so what? The country's lousy with them. The coincidence is suggestive only because Emma and Roger have no idea who Caroline really is, they know nothing of her history beyond what she told them three nights ago. They don't even know her real name; all they know is that it's not Caroline Marks.

Emma thinks about Caroline's story of abuse and escape. It answers many questions; moreover, it was not thrust upon them but extracted under duress. But is it true? As a novelist Emma might be expected to know fiction from truth at a glance; but in fact, for her, good fiction *is* truth. She'd believed Caroline's story because it was plausible and enlightening. Now another story has presented itself, equally plausible, equally enlightening. It's possible that Caroline Marks is Linda Johnson; there's simply no proof either way.

Emma turns to a fresh page in the journal and starts a list. At the top she writes: "C.M. = L.J.?" She draws

a line down the center of the page, heads the left col-
umn "No" and the right "Yes." Under No she writes,
"The child was black." Under Yes, "The *father* was
black. Child was lighter. Mother could have been anything."

Under No: "Caroline married to a black man?"

Under Yes: "Why not?"

Under No: "She wouldn't hurt me."

Under Yes: "Vengeful." Her pen falters. The room,
the books, the storm itself fade from view, and she is in
Caroline's stone-white kitchen, and the book on her lap
not a journal but a volume of plays that has fallen open,
as if by habit, to the first scene of *Medea*. *Shakespeare's
women don't hold a candle to the Greeks,* Caroline is
saying. *Cross those women, you'll wish you'd never
been born.* Then the kitchen morphs into the interior of
Starbucks, a table overlooking the street, Caroline leaning toward her. *I never thought living well is the best
revenge. Living well and sticking it to the other guy,
that's more like it.*

It occurs to Emma then that the time for making lists
is past. There is one simple way to find out what she
needs to know. She shuts the journal and crosses to the
window behind her desk. Caroline's car is gone.

Emma bends over the desktop computer and taps out
a note, summarizing what she learned from Detective
Wong and detailing what she plans to do. She addresses
it to Roger and Maggie and hits Send. "Dialing
Compuserve" comes up on the screen, followed a
moment later by an error message: "Dialing incomplete.
No carrier." She tries the phone; sure enough, the line is
dead. The cellular phone is downstairs in her purse, but
she has no idea how to send E-mail over a cordless

phone. No point phoning again, either. If Roger were back he'd have called by now.

She switches the printer jack from the laptop to the desk computer and prints out the message she'd tried to send. Folding it twice, she slips it inside her journal and heads downstairs to her bedroom. She feels foolish, hiding the journal inside Roger's pillowcase; she accuses herself of melodrama. But if things go well, she'll be the one to retrieve it and no one will ever know; and if they don't, Roger will find it.

She promised him she'd take no chances; she promised Wong she'd stay home. Emma is about to break both promises. It's not a question of foolhardiness, she tells herself. She just cannot abide sitting at home, making lists and waiting for whatever is slated to happen, knowing that ten minutes alone in Caroline's house will yield a definitive answer.

She leaves her purse on the bed, taking only her keys and the cellular phone.

Downstairs, Roger's bulky anorak is hanging in the front-hall closet. Emma puts it on, pockets the keys and the phone, and fetches the carriage house key from the dining room sideboard. At the last minute she adds a flashlight.

Casey barks pleadingly as she opens the front door. She considers taking him; she'd like someone watching her back, even if it's only a dog. But the ground is too muddy; he'd track up the whole house and Caroline would know that they'd been inside. Emma is still operating on the premise that Caroline's feelings matter.

"Take care of the house," she tells the dog. She resets the alarm before locking the door behind her.

The moment she steps outside, the wind grabs the

screen door from her hand. She puts her shoulder to it and slams it shut, then descends the porch steps, holding on to the railing. With head lowered and eyes narrowed against the gritty wind, she tacks across the open ground to Caroline's house. She rings the bell and bangs on the door before letting herself in.

The kitchen's as tidy as ever. Beside the sink, a cup, a bowl, and a spoon have been set out on a dishtowel to dry. "Caroline?" she calls, moving out into the hallway. Her voice echoes hollowly.

She goes upstairs. She hasn't been up here since Caroline moved in. Three doors open off a short corridor, one on each end and one in the middle, opposite the stairs. Emma starts with that one. It's a bathroom: white-tiled walls and floor, an old-fashioned claw-footed tub, a rack with two neatly folded blue towels and a small rug of the same color. The counter is bare, not so much as a toothbrush in sight. The cabinet above the sink is empty. Emma touches the stainless-steel towel rack, the doorknob, the mirrored cabinet door, and the tiled walls. Invisible to Caroline, her fingerprints will be clear evidence to the police that she'd been here, if it should come to that.

Someone, after all, wants her dead. Someone thinks she's halfway there, too scared and worn down to function. Emma knows she's stronger than her enemy believes; but she also knows, better than most, that anything can happen.

Leaving the bathroom, she enters the room to her right. This is the room that faces Emma's office; it was at this window they'd stood when Caroline had turned to her and said, "I'll take it, if you'll have me." Now the room is an office. Like the living room and kitchen, this room is strictly functional. There's a bookshelf, a desk, and a chair, the sort of generic office furniture sold in Staples and Office Max. The desk, a concoction of oak-laminated particle board with two drawers on each side, faces the window; the chair faces the view. All Emma, peering through the window, can see of her house is the light shining in her office. Her office is on the third floor and Caroline's on the second, but the two rooms are very nearly on a level; the carriage house is built on a small knoll and the first-story ceiling is uncommonly high. If the day were clear, Emma would be looking directly into her office. Her own desk is similarly placed behind that window, but her chair, unlike Caroline's, stands between the desk and the window, facing into the room.

Emma sits at the desk. Caroline's chair is on casters, the seat and back upholstered in a black, nubby fabric. The computer is an IBM, top of the line, fully compatible with her own. She turns it on, then starts looking through the drawers. One thing Emma knows with certainty: If Caroline had a child and lost it, somewhere in this house there are pictures of that child.

The two top drawers contain a neatly ordered assortment of bills, receipts, and checkbooks, all in the name of Caroline Marks. Emma rifles through quickly; they're not what she's looking for. The bottom-right drawer holds office supplies, stationery, stamps, and envelopes.

The bottom-left drawer is locked.

She searches for the key. She tries the other drawers, the shelves, the bottom of the desk and chair: nothing. Kneeling, she shines her flashlight into the keyhole. Emma knows a thing or two about locks the way she knows a thing or two about all sorts of odd subjects: She'd needed it once for a book. A local locksmith had

obliged by teaching her the basics of lock-picking. She's
pretty sure she can pick this one.

She runs down to the kitchen, selects a steak knife
with a sharp point, and returns upstairs. She sits on her
heels in front of the drawer, flashlight in one hand, knife
in the other. Her hand is a bit unsteady. The knife slips,
then catches. She turns it gently. There is no hearing
anything in this storm. Between the wind whipping
through the trees and the water pounding the shore,
Emma is deafened. She feels rather than hears the tum-
bler click open.

She puts the knife up on the desk and slides the
drawer open. A leather case lies at the bottom. She lifts
it out, opens it, and takes out a pair of high-powered
binoculars.

Breathing rapidly, Emma sits at Caroline's desk
and trains the glasses on her office window. The rain,
like a gray scrim, wipes out color, but the black-and-
white image that appears is a perfectly focused view
of the back of Emma's chair and her desk, as close as
if she were standing in the room between the window
and the chair.

The binoculars drop onto the desk. Blood rushes to
her head. God, she thinks, what a fool I've been. Roger
was right all along; I've been played like a goddamn
fish. She covers her face with her hands.

"Hello, Emma," says a voice behind her.

She wheels around. Caroline is standing in the doorway. She wears a belted, rain-streaked mackintosh,
leather gloves, and a wide-brimmed rain hat that casts
the upper half of her face in shadow. A black gym bag is
slung over her left shoulder. Her right hand is in her
pocket.

"My phone is down," Emma says. "I needed to send an urgent E-mail."

The locked drawer gapes open. The binoculars lie in plain sight on the desk. Only the knife is hidden, behind Emma's back. Caroline smiles dismissively and remains where she is, blocking the door.

"Mine, too," she says. "I had to go out to call in sick."

"Are you ill?" asks Emma.

"No," says Caroline. "I needed some personal time. This is a special day for both of us, isn't it, Emma?"

"Linda Johnson," Emma breathes.

Caroline bows mockingly.

Emma's phone beeps. At once both of them reach into their pockets; Emma's hand emerges with a phone, Caroline's with a snub-nosed gun. "I wouldn't answer that," Caroline says. "I'm not much of a shot, but I don't think I could miss from here."

Emma's body feels too large for her; she hunkers inside it like a house. She feels the cold air passing through her nose, pushing past her sinuses, inflating her lungs. She feels adrenaline pumping through her veins. She feels the slumbering fetus stir uneasily. Her eyes are like slits in a fortress wall. She watches and waits.

"Put the phone on the floor. Slide it over here."

Emma obeys. She sits back up, placing her hands on the desk behind her. In her mind she sees the knife, flush against the keyboard.

Caroline picks up the phone. It continues to ring for a long time in her hand. When it finally stops, she glances down. In the moment it takes her to turn off the power switch, Emma has grabbed the steak knife and slipped it under her sweater into the back of her jeans. She's put on a few pounds already; she prays the waistband is snug enough to keep it from slipping.

Caroline pockets the phone but keeps the gun leveled at Emma's chest. "That's better," she says. "We don't want to be interrupted."

29

"THERE'S NO answer," Roger says, appearing in the doorway of India's office.

She doesn't look up from her monitor. "Maybe she's gone out."

"On a day like this?"

India shrugs. The vagaries of Roger's wife, the shrug says, are no concern of hers.

In two seconds Roger reaches her and shuts off the monitor. She feigns astonishment. He brings his face close to hers. "What, exactly, did she say?"

"I offered to transfer her, like you said. She said don't bother. I asked if there was a problem; she said no, just tell him to call."

"Why did you ask if there's a problem?"

India hesitates, then says reluctantly, "She sounded upset."

Roger backs away. "You should have paged me."

"She said not to," India calls after him, but he's already gone.

Half a dozen people are loitering outside his office, waiting to talk to him. Roger passes through them as if they were air. He enters his office, shuts the door. The

E-mail icon is blinking on his computer. He clicks on it. Five messages appear, including one from Emma marked "Urgent."

He opens the letter and reads it. Blood drains from his face; he curses himself for a fool. How could he leave her alone today? Pacing the office with the cordless phone, he dials the operator.

"The line is down," she reports a moment later. "I can connect you to repair, but there's a lot of damage from the storm. You'll have a long wait getting through."

He hangs up. Someone's knocking on the door. He ignores the sound and eventually it goes away. Don't panic, he tells himself. She's probably working in her office, oblivious to the world, unaware that the phone is out.

He tries the cell number again. This time it doesn't ring through; instead he is shunted immediately to Emma's voice mail.

Which means that in the interval between his two calls, someone has switched off the phone.

His coat is in his hand and he's halfway to the door before he stops to think. He's thirty miles from home: nothing as the crow flies, but in this weather he could be stuck in the car for hours. The train, then. He returns to his desk, grabs the schedule from his top drawer. The next train leaves in ten minutes, no chance of making it. The one after leaves an hour later. Two hours at best, then, to make it home, and if the train is delayed or gets stuck somewhere en route, he's fucked, totally helpless.

He *is* helpless, and he brought it on himself. *She* never wanted to move; he'd pressured her into it, convinced in his hubris that he knew what was best for them. If they'd stayed in the city, he'd be home by now; if they'd stayed, none of this would have happened.

Cursing, he slams his fists down on the desk. The constant murmur outside his door ceases, then resumes. *Pull yourself together,* Roger orders himself. *This isn't helping.* If he can't make it, someone else will have to. Thigpen springs to mind. The detective's card is on him somewhere. He empties his pockets, pounces on Thigpen's card, and punches in the number.

"We're sorry. Due to weather-related difficulties, your call cannot go through at this time. Please try again later."

He calls the operator again. She tries the number for him and gets the same message. "But it's the police!" he protests.

"Their lines go down, too," the operator chirps. "We're sorry for the inconvenience. Have a nice day, and thanks for choosing Bell Atlantic."

"NEVER EVEN OCCURRED to you, did it?" Caroline taunts. "I knew it wouldn't. You phony liberals are all the same: You claim to be color-blind, but you're blinded by color." She has pushed her hat back. Her eyes shine with triumph; her face is flushed with the joy of finally speaking her mind. "You looked at me and thought you had me pegged, you and that big-shot sister of yours."

Emma's laboring to make the adjustment. "And that story you told us about the abusive husband and your escape—that was all made up?"

"Borrowed, from a client. And you bought it, hook, line, and sinker."

"And all your accusations against Roger, all that distrust and animosity . . . ?"

Caroline permits herself a tight-lipped smile. "Had you wondering, didn't I? Had you spinning like a top."

"I trusted you."

"Which makes you stupider than spit," says Caroline, "but has no effect on me."

Emma searches her face for a trace of compassion, some tiny port of entry, but Caroline's face is nailed down tight. The woman Emma thought she knew, the woman who'd befriended, comforted, and counseled her, is gone. Did she ever really exist?

"Caroline," she says softly, "I know how much you've lost."

"You have no idea what I lost." Without removing her eyes from Emma, Caroline fishes in her bag, pulls out a small leather case, and tosses it to Emma.

Emma opens the snap, and the case unfolds into an accordion-pleated cascade of photos. Emma can see that the pictures, some dozen in all, have been handled nearly to death. There are pictures of Rachel as a baby, naked on a fluffy pink towel, Rachel at the beach, riding atop her father's shoulders, Rachel perched on a stone tortoise at the Central Park Zoo, Rachel hand in hand with her mother in a field of wildflowers. Though the child is an incipient beauty, all eyes and cheekbones, it's the mother's laughing face that rivets Emma's attention: for here is still another Caroline, one as far from the vengeful virago now pointing a gun at Emma's heart as from the austere, professional mannequin of the past months. Age alone does not account for the hardening of those features, the loss of humor, joy, and spontaneity.

Tears come to Emma's eyes. "Caroline," she murmurs, "I'm so sorry."

"I'm sorry," Caroline mimics savagely. "Sorry is for stepping on someone's toes, dialing a wrong number. You wipe out a person's family, sorry doesn't cut it."

"What do you want?"

"I want justice. I want to set the world right, put time back in joint. Did you think I would stand by and let you build your world on the rubble of mine, as if my family were so much landfill? Did you really believe there'd be no price to pay?"

"You're not the only one who suffered," Emma cries. "You know what we lost."

"Oh," Caroline says with a sneer, "your little miscarriage. Boo hoo. I had four before Rachel, *four.*"

"Caroline, if I could give you back your daughter and husband, you know I would."

"Empty words. You should have died with them and saved us both a lot of trouble."

"You're not a murderer." Emma gazes into her implacable eyes. It's like staring into a black hole: no return at all, not even an echo. "When it comes right down to it, you won't pull that trigger."

"You know what, Emma? Hold that thought." Caroline backs into the hall, aiming the gun at Emma's heart. "Let's take a walk."

ROGER IS SHOUTING into the phone. A small crowd has gathered around his door; through the glass he sees them milling and turns his back. The moron from the security company is telling him for the third time that there's nothing they can do. They're not the police; their job is merely to notify the emergency services in case of fire or break-in, neither of which has occurred in the Koenig residence.

Roger is not accustomed to being denied. He works his way up the company hierarchy to the manager. This oily bastard never raises his voice or shows impatience; he just parrots his refrain over and over, interspersed with phrases from the customer relations' handbook. "With all due respect, Dr. Koenig, allow me to suggest that you're overreacting. It's not surprising you can't reach your wife. Lines are out all over the Island, sir. Our own lines went out for an hour this morning, and what with alarms shorting out all over the place you can imagine what kind of chaos we're dealing with."

"I don't give a damn about your problems," Roger says furiously. "I care about my wife. In the time you've wasted arguing, you could have been to the house and back." He slams the phone down and leans on the desk, arms rigid. He forces himself to breathe deeply. Outside the wind and rain are unrelenting. There'll be trees down, roads flooded. He is hours away from home.

CASEY GROWLS AT Caroline. Emma is amazed. He's never done that before. How does he know?

"Put it out," Caroline says.

"In this weather? That's inhuman."

Caroline drops the gym bag on the floor and points the gun at Casey, who growls again, this time showing his teeth. "Put it out or I'll shoot it."

Emma looks at her flat eyes and decides the dog will be safer in the storm. Muttering an apology, she grasps his collar and pushes him out onto the porch. He's too surprised to protest.

Caroline slams the door and locks it. "Now enter the security code."

"What for? It doesn't work when the phone's down."

"Don't fuck with me, Emma. That alarm goes off, it'll be the last sound you ever hear."

Emma punches in the code. She turns toward the kitchen.

"Where do you think you're going?"

"Making us some coffee."

"Isn't that cozy." Caroline sneers. "We're going upstairs."

"Lighten up, Caroline. You've waited years, what's another few minutes? Besides, even a condemned prisoner's entitled to a last meal. I just want coffee."

"Upstairs, right now, or I'll shoot you where you stand."

Emma answers with more certainty than she feels. "If you were going to shoot me, you'd have done it by now."

"Shooting you isn't the plan, but it's a perfectly acceptable backup. I'll give you to the count of five. One . . . two . . ."

On three Emma moves to the stairs.

HIS PRIVATE LINE rings. It could be anyone, but Roger is so convinced it will be her voice on the line that he moves from relief to anger in the second it takes to answer. "Emma?" he barks.

"No, Maggie. Did you get her E-mail?"

Her voice breaks his heart, so like the one he'd expected to hear. "Yes," he says. "I can't reach her. Have you—"

"No. I've been trying both lines. What do you think we should do?"

Roger fills her in on his calls to the detectives and the

security company. "I've got to go home. But I'm afraid of getting stuck in the car for hours."

"We don't know she's in trouble," Maggie says.

"Someone turned off the cell phone. It rang the first time I tried. Five minutes later it was switched off. Why would Emma do that?"

"Did you try nine-one-one?"

He had, he says, and wasted ten precious minutes trying to explain the situation to the moron who answered before slamming down the phone.

"Oh God," Maggie wails. He can see her on the other end, tugging at her hair. "Isn't there anyone else in that godforsaken—what about Caroline, have you tried her?"

"Forget her," he says curtly. "I don't want her near Emma."

"Yolanda, then."

"I tried. She's out."

He'd wrestled for fully five minutes over that call. It was different from calling a man. With Gerard, it would have been enough to say "Emma may be in trouble; could you get over there right away?" and Gerard would have been on his way. A woman would ask questions. To enlist Yolanda, Roger would have to tell her things Emma had chosen not to tell her; he would have to betray his wife's privacy. Which he could live with; but there is a streak of old-fashioned chivalry/ chauvinism in Roger that made him loathe to send a woman to fight his battle. Besides, if Em is in trouble, what can Yolanda do?

In the end, though, fear for Emma had won out and he'd placed the call, which rang through, but no one had answered.

"I can't wait any longer," he tells Maggie. "I'm leaving now. You keep trying the police. Ask for Thigpen or Wong."

"Have you got a car phone?"

"No, but—hold on." He steps out of his office. Half a dozen faces turn his way.

India glides forward. "Roger, what's going on?"

"Anyone got a cell phone?"

"I do," she says.

"Good girl. Lend it to me, would you." He gives Maggie the number and hangs up. India follows him into his office. Roger is gathering up and replacing the contents of his jacket pockets. He slips the phone into his briefcase and shrugs on his coat. "I'm off. If Emma calls, tell her I'm on my way home and give her the cell-phone number." He walks past her and turns left in the corridor, hurrying toward the back door and parking lot.

India trots alongside. "You're supposed to see that guy from the Santa Fe Institute at three o'clock."

"You see him."

"The dean's office rang while you were on the phone; they want you to call back immediately. Also—"

"Not now," he says impatiently, in a voice so distant and unmindful of her that for India it's like walking into a wall. She stops short; he strides on, heedless. She watches him go away from her, knowing he won't turn back.

EMMA BIDES HER time. Caroline doesn't know she found the E-mail. As long as she hopes to pass this off as suicide, she can't shoot Emma in the back or even bruise her. Despite the gun, Emma's having a hard time adjusting to the idea that Caroline is her enemy. How could Caroline have fooled her so thoroughly? She didn't fool Roger; he distrusted her almost from the start. Did Emma's own fear and isolation blind her to the truth? Perhaps, yet she wonders how Caroline could have borne it, hating her as she does. That stalwart friendship and concern, was it really all pretense, all show? Was she gloating all the time, reveling in Emma's pain, or was there some part of Caroline's tormented soul that truly sympathized with the torment she herself inflicted? Emma desperately wants to believe that on some level, Caroline must be conflicted.

"Caroline," she says, in a voice pitched low for persuasiveness, "you don't want to do this."

"Don't I?" The other woman cracks a smile. "That's funny, I was sure I did. Move."

They are passing Emma's bedroom, heading toward the stairs to her office. Emma walks as slowly as she dares. "What's the plan here, Caroline?"

"The plan is you do what you should have done seven years ago."

"What happened then was an accident. You said so yourself."

"I said what you wanted to hear. You and I know the truth."

"What truth?" Emma cries. "Do you think I deliberately skidded into your husband's car?"

"You killed them and you failed to accept responsibility. People are responsible for their actions, not just their intentions. The Greeks knew that; Oedipus certainly knew it. You know it, too. That's why you conjured up that ghost of yours—out of guilt. Up now, slowly."

They have reached the spiral staircase. Emma climbs up first, followed at a prudent distance by Caroline.

Well, Mrs. Hysop, Emma thinks, if you're here, this would be the time to show yourself. The house is full of ghostlike moans and knockings, but they come from the storm; no sign of Mrs. H.

"Up against that wall," Caroline says. "Assume the position."

"Assume the *what?*" Emma risks a smile. "You've been watching too many cop shows, Caroline."

The gun rises. "We can always go back to plan B."

She braces her palms against the wall. The steak knife slips an inch, biting into her butt.

"Bring your legs farther back. Lean forward all the way. Put your face to the wall."

Emma obeys, and suddenly the logic of the position comes clear to her. Off balance, she cannot strike, would have to right herself before attacking. What Caroline has failed to notice is that the darkness outside has turned the windows into mirrors. By turning her head to the side, Emma can see the other woman's watery reflection. Caroline is kneeling before the gym bag, unzipping it with her left hand; the gun is still in her right. Then the bag pops open, and Emma glimpses a thick coil of rope.

Panic presses in on the edges of her consciousness, like the onset of pain as Novocain wears off. She can't allow herself to be tied up. The gun is bad enough; she couldn't stand the utter helplessness of being bound. This is the critical moment. Caroline can't tie her up without putting down the gun, but without the gun she's got nothing. Emma remembers her saying that everyone at the women's center, staff as well as clientele, has to study martial arts. Doesn't matter. With the gun out of the equation, Emma's a cinch to prevail.

She has so much more to lose.

"Caroline," she says urgently, "think for a moment. You'd never get away with it. The police are already involved; don't you think they'll find out who you are? You'd be throwing away your own life."

"What life? Now, turn your face to that wall or I'll have to shoot you." She speaks with matter-of-fact briskness, as if Emma were a child refusing to take her medicine. The lack of affect in her tone is more chilling than any bombast could be.

Emma faces the wall, straining her ears, but the howling of the wind leaves her no hope of hearing Caroline approach. Legs tensed to leap, she awaits the touch of her enemy's hand.

But the first touch she feels is a stunning kick to the outside of her right thigh. Already off balance, Emma falls hard, landing on her shoulder and hip, then flops onto her stomach. At once Caroline drops onto her back, landing with both knees between Emma's shoulders. Before she knows what has happened, her right hand has been grasped and wrenched back, and a silky noose tightened around her wrist.

Emma can't breathe, she's close to fainting from the pain of her swollen breasts crushed against the floor, but she flings herself to one side in an effort to dislodge Caroline. For a woman her age, Caroline is amazingly lithe and strong. She captures Emma's left hand, forces it back, and slips a loop around it. When she's finished tying her hands together, she swings around to attend to Emma's legs. Emma kicks backward and connects squarely with Caroline's face. "Fucking bitch!" Caroline cries. A short, brutish struggle follows, but Emma has no hands, no leverage, no

chance. Within moments her legs are pinned and her
ankles tied together.

Bloodied, sweating, Caroline gets to her feet.
Flustered for the first time, she walks away, comes back
and delivers a swift, hard kick to Emma's side.

"Goddamn you," Emma cries, "I'm pregnant!"

"I wouldn't worry about birth defects," Caroline
says, panting.

THE FDR DRIVE is flooded. Traffic crawls along for a
mile, then stops altogether. Roger is caught between exits,
hemmed in on all sides. He peers through the windshield,
trying to spot an exit sign; but even with the wipers on
High he can't see more than a car length away.

He takes out India's phone and dials Emma's cell
number. Voice mail again. If she's okay he'll kill her
himself for doing this to him. Roger feels an unbearable
helplessness. The nightmarish quality of this ride—moving as fast as he can, yet making no progress—brings
back a dream he had years ago, when Emma was in the
hospital. In the dream, he was in the Antarctic as part of
a scientific expedition, and Emma was there to write a
book. She went out alone and got lost, he set out in
search of her, and somehow they ended up stranded on
different icebergs, floating apart from each other toward
open water.

Events are occurring now over which he has no control. Volition has slipped a gear, lost its connection to the
world. There may come a day when he will look back
on this day to retrace every mistake, error of judgment,
failure of trust, second lost, wrong turn taken, everything that led to—to whatever he will find when he gets
home.

The car in front of him sloshes forward eight yards, then shudders to a halt. The rain falls aslant, and gusts of wind rock the car. At this rate he'll reach Morgan Peak by June.

This is stupid. He needs help. There must be someone he can reach out to. Once again, Roger feels the sting of dislocation. In the city there were a dozen men he could call on who'd respond in a minute; out there the only friend he's made is Gerard Dumont, and he works in Manhattan.

Suddenly an image springs to mind: He sees Nick Sanders holding out his card to Emma, sees himself snatching the card away. *I'm never far,* Sanders had said. *You work in the city. Think about that.* Roger had taken it as a taunt, a warning to watch his back; in retrospect those words are as welcome as a beacon to a sailor lost at sea.

He switches on the interior lights and for the second time that day empties his pockets. The car in front lurches forward another ten yards, then stops. Roger closes the gap. There are half a dozen business cards among the papers on the seat beside him, none of them Sanders's. Then his eye falls on a crumpled ball of paper. Carefully he opens it up. The card is torn and stained but still legible. "Nick Sanders, President and CEO, Acorn Technologies," followed by an address and a litany of numbers. A car honks behind him; Roger looks up and creeps forward another dozen yards before once again coming to a halt. Those few seconds suffice for him to ask if he really wants to do this. Sanders must be the last man on earth, save Roger's father, to whom he cares to be indebted. It's not that he suspects Sanders of anything besides trying to get into Emma's pants.

Obnoxious as he is, the coach doesn't fit the part of their tormentor. He might welcome the chance to make Roger look bad, but he wouldn't plow through Emma to do it.

Sanders would help, no question about that; probably thank Roger for the perfect opportunity to play white knight. But so what? The coach, big, strong, and athletic, makes a hell of a better emissary than Yolanda would have.

He flips the phone open, dials Sanders's office number.

We're sorry. Due to weather-related difficulties—

"Fuck!" he shouts and hangs up. Drives forward another eight yards. No exit in sight. There's a cellphone number on the card. Hopeless now, but determined to try every avenue, Roger punches it in. The phone rings twice. Someone picks up; a man's voice says, "Hello?"

He gasps, amazed to have gotten through. "Sanders?"

"Yeah, who's this?"

"Roger Koenig. I need your help."

"WHY ARE YOU fighting this?" Caroline, sitting in Emma's desk chair, seems genuinely puzzled. Head canted back, bloodied handkerchief pressed to her nose, she regards Emma with the wary pride of a fisherman who's just landed the biggest catch of his life. "Don't you see it's necessary? Don't you feel how inevitable this is?"

Emma lies on her back, not flat, because her hands are bunched behind her, but leaning on her elbows. Her wrists and ankles are tied with silk handkerchiefs. Why not rope? To avoid leaving marks; Caroline still hopes for the appearance of suicide. But then, what's the rope for?

Panic threatens to overwhelm her, but she forces it down. In its place comes a rare lucidity, a state of diamond-sharp perception and watchful serenity. Fear is not gone but rather sealed off. The knife, miraculously, is still lodged in her pants, its sharp teeth pressed up against her ass.

"Nothing's inevitable," she says. "Nothing's happened yet that can't be undone."

"Can you undo my husband's death? Can you bring my daughter back to life?"

"Would killing me do that?" Emma hikes herself a little higher and twists her hands together in a praying position. She forces her index fingers down the waistband of her pants, feels the knife handle, but can't quite grasp it.

Where is Roger? She reaches out to him. *Help me, come home; I need you now.*

At once, very close beside her, a voice answers, not Roger's, but a woman's voice, crotchety, ancient, lavender-scented. *Pull yourself together, child. God helps those who help themselves.*

Caroline is lecturing earnestly. "You can't act as though their lives were nothing. You can't go on with your own life like nothing happened, writing books, having babies, giving speeches and interviews—as if you had anything to say to the world. In your heart you know it's wrong. That's why you wanted this to happen."

Emma's hands are down her pants, feeling for the knife. Her waist is so constricted she can hardly breathe, but she keeps her voice even. "How can you think I wanted this?"

"You invited me in. You made it so easy. If I hadn't existed, you would have invented me."

"Wrong. I didn't want this and I don't deserve it. Accidents happen in life. Cars skid, drivers lose control . . . things happen and there's no way to stop them."

"Think of me," says Caroline, "as one of those things."

"What if your husband had survived, and I hadn't— would he deserve to die for killing me?"

Caroline grimaces. For a moment Emma thinks she's reached her, penetrated her turtle shell; then she sees that Caroline's frown is just the impatience of a director with an actor who keeps fluffing his lines. Caroline must have imagined this conversation countless times, just as Emma has: two parallel but totally different conversations, one about forgiveness, the other vengeance.

Now the knife is in her grasp.

Caroline lowers the handkerchief and feels her nose gingerly. The bleeding has stopped. She wads up the handkerchief, drops it in the open gym bag, and takes out the rope. It's a thick nylon rope, eight feet in length, one end of which has been fashioned into a noose.

Now, as the full horror of Caroline's plan bursts upon her, Emma gasps. "Oh Jesus. You evil bitch."

"We're beyond good and evil here, Emma. We're in the land of necessity, the realm of inevitable response."

"Caroline, please—whatever you feel about me, you can't do this to Zack. He'll be home soon; he'd be the one . . . you wouldn't hurt him like that."

If Caroline is moved at all by this appeal, it doesn't show in her face, as smooth and adamant as a Greek goddess. "Should have thought of that sooner. Never would have come to this, you'd done the right thing."

"What, killed myself?"

Caroline's smile is pure insinuation. Emma wonders how she ever found it comforting. "I know you thought about it. That day on the beach, wondering if you were crazy—you were thinking about it then. Should've done it, Emma; should've drowned your evil ass." She drops the gun into her pocket, carries the rope to the staircase and ties it to the balustrade. Her gloved hands move with practiced dexterity; when she's done she tests it with a hard yank. "Would you believe I was a Girl Scout? Earned a badge on knots. Never know what's going to come in useful." She drops the noose end of the rope down the center of the spiral stairs and watches it fall.

Emma hacks downward with the knife. The point rips through the fabric and embeds itself in her palm. She barely registers the pain, just pulls it out and tries again.

Caroline hauls the noose back up and turns purposefully to Emma. Suddenly she stops and sniffs, frowning in puzzlement. "What's that smell?"

It's lavender. The scent permeates the room, as strong as if a whole bottle of perfume had spilled out onto the floor.

"It's her." Emma cuts through the scarf, freeing her hands. She clutches the knife behind her back.

"Whose?"

"Mrs. Hysop, my imaginary ghost."

"Bullshit. It's a trick. How'd you do that?"

But Emma isn't looking at her, she's staring wide-eyed at a spot just behind Caroline. "Oh my God," she murmurs.

There's nothing there, nothing visible, at least; but Caroline wouldn't be human if she didn't look. As she turns, Emma jackknifes forward and slashes the scarf around her ankles. She jumps up, staggering as her ankles give way.

Caroline wheels around. Draws the gun from her pocket, levels it with both hands.

Emma wields the steak knife. Eight feet separate her from Caroline—too far to lunge without getting shot. She dives to the ground and rolls so hard into a book-case that books rain down around her.

Caroline turns with her, tracking her with the out-stretched gun. She shoots, and the recoil sends her staggering. A bullet whines past Emma's head. She grabs a book from the floor and chucks it at Caroline. It hits her in the chest, and her next shot goes wide. A tiny hole appears in the window nearest Emma. As she watches, a spiderweb radiates outward from the hole until the entire window is rimed with delicate cracks. Then the wind puts its shoulder to the glass and sends it crashing to the floor. As the pages of Emma's manuscript rise from her desk and dance through the room like spirits from a graveyard on All Hallow's Eve, she is rocked by a powerful attack of déjà vu. It's her dream come to life, the dream she had just after they moved in. But there's no time to think about that now. Caroline, batting pages away from her head, is taking aim again.

Emma hurls another book, and another. Thank God for hardcovers, she thinks. "Knock it off!" Caroline yells furiously as *Pride and Prejudice* clips the left side of her head. She protects her face with her left arm while aiming with her right. Another shot, another miss; *Huckleberry Finn* takes it in the heart. Emma grabs the largest book she sees, *The Name of the Rose,* and heaves it with all her strength. It strikes Caroline's right arm; the gun flies out of her hand and skitters across the floor to Emma.

Emma grabs it and points it at Caroline. She rises carefully, keeping her back to the bookcase. The gun feels good in her hand, heavier than she had expected, a solid chunk of power. Without it, Caroline looks diminished.

The other doesn't move, but watches Emma with an odd, unreadable expression. "Go on," she says. "Shoot. You've taken everything else from me."

"I never meant to hurt you," Emma tells her. "All the malice was on your side."

"Do it. Finish the job."

"No." She lowers her arm. "You're a sick woman, Caroline. You need help."

"Been there, done that." Caroline takes a step forward.

The gun rises smoothly. "Don't you move."

Another step. Caroline's eyes fasten on Emma's, taunting, daring. "Do it, Emma. Or else shoot yourself, 'cause there's not room in the world for both of us."

The storm has moved inside. Both women are soaked, windblown. Suddenly, beneath the roar of the wind, comes the distinctive clatter of breaking glass elsewhere in the house, followed at once by the sound of Casey barking.

A deep voice bellows from downstairs: "Emma!"

"Up here!" Emma screams, but her voice is swept away by the wind. Then Caroline throws back her head and lets out a cry so hopelessly despairing that a portion of Emma's heart shrivels on the spot. In pity she lowers her gaze; and Caroline is on her at once, punching, flailing, grabbing for the gun.

Emma spins away and pushes her off with her left arm; she holds the gun out of reach, unwilling even now to shoot. Then there's a clattering on the stairs, and Casey leaps into the room.

Emma hardly recognizes the dog. His thick coat is plastered to his body, his ears are laid back flat along his skull, and his upper lip is drawn back to reveal long white incisors. He crouches, leaps, and sinks his teeth in Caroline's calf.

Screaming, Caroline backs away, dragging the dog with her. She beats his head with her fists, but Casey holds on. There's blood on her pants and on the floor.

Emma tosses the gun out the broken window. Then she gets behind Casey, grabs his collar, and wrestles him away from Caroline. He continues to snarl and lunge; it takes all her strength to hold him. "Go," she gasps.

"Emma!" The cry is closer now, on the second floor.

Caroline looks at her. Then she limps to the head of the spiral stairs and starts down, leaning on the banister. Emma, still clutching Casey's collar, follows cautiously. Just as Caroline reaches the door at the end of the hall, it bursts open and a man barrels in behind it. He sees her, takes in her age and gender, and for one crucial moment hesitates.

She doesn't. Without breaking stride, Caroline slams her knee into his groin, then continues past him out the door.

Emma skitters down the spiral steps, followed by Casey. She bends over the fallen man and sees to her amazement that it's Nick Sanders.

He's ash gray in color, breathing in short, wheezing

gasps. His knees are drawn up, his arms crossed over his chest. On his face is a look of perfect self-absorption.

Concussion is her first, irrepressible thought; but she attends to the stricken man with dispatch and sympathy. Gradually his breathing calms; he sits up and once again takes note of his surroundings. He gapes at Emma, bloody, bedraggled, and wet, with tattered remnants of colored silk about her wrists and ankles, like a Maypole after the dance.

"Hello, Emma," he croaks. "You're looking lovely today."

Despite everything, she laughs. "Now I know you're concussed."

"Tell me, who was that Fury?"

" 'Fury' is the word, all right," she says. "What are you doing here, anyway?"

"Your husband called, said you maybe needed help. Glad to see he was wrong."

30

SHE LIES IN the hospital bed, black hair streaming across a snowy pillow. Eyes closed, skin so pale he can see the fine blue tracings of capillaries in her eyelids. Her left hand rests atop the thin white blanket and it, too, is white, wrapped in a bandage.

She hears him come in and opens her eyes. Roger watches her reach for a reassuring smile, and the gallant effort pierces his soul; he feels he has never loved her as much as he loves her in this moment. He goes to her and gathers her into his arms, holding so tight that her bruised body lets out a groan; but when he tries to release her, she hugs him tighter still. So waiflike and vulnerable in that skimpy hospital gown, and yet so indisputably, solidly alive: Roger's heart expands and contracts at once, threatening to break. "Emma," he breathes.

"I know," she says. "I'm okay."

"And the baby?" he asks fearfully, for this time is so like the last.

She smiles. "Fine. I heard the heartbeat."

He puts his forehead to hers, breathes in her scent, and offers up a silent prayer of thanks.

"Well," says a languid voice from across the room, "I can see I'm not needed anymore."

Roger turns. In a chair against the far wall sits Nick Sanders.

Roger goes over and shakes his hand. "Sanders, I owe you."

"You have no idea," Nick says feelingly. "I'll take your firstborn."

A smile flickers across Roger's drawn face. "Emma always said if it came to choosing between her and Zack, you'd pick the soccer player."

"Don't kid yourself; I just know when I'm beat. Classy move, calling me. Was I your first choice?"

"Last. You were the only one I could reach."

Nick laughs. "Anyway, much as I hate to admit it, I didn't exactly rescue your wife. Thing ended with her picking me up off the floor."

Emma says, "I never thought I'd say this, Nick, but you're too modest. If you hadn't shown up, there might have been a whole different ending."

Nick walks to the door, moving stiffly. "Tell you one

thing, you owe that dog a steak dinner. Second I broke the window, he was through it like a heat-seeking missile."

Roger glances at Emma in surprise. "Casey went up to your office?" She nods. "I'll be damned."

EMMA HAD GIVEN the paramedics a hard time, refusing to go to the hospital until arrangements were made for Yolanda to take Zack. Reached by cell phone, Yolanda had asked no questions, just listened to Emma's rambling, incoherent account and said of course she'd take Zack, what a question; in fact she'd keep him for the night, if that would help.

Now Zack stands in the door of Emma's hospital room, looking from her to Roger. Yolanda is behind him. "He needed to see you're okay," she says over his head to Emma, who nods.

"Come on in," Emma says. Zack approaches slowly, pulling his cap down over his eyes. She sits up, puts her arms around him. He's shaking. "Hey," she says gently. "I'm still here."

"What happened to you?"

"Well, I was in a fight."

"You?" Zack gives her a considering look. "Who won?"

"Me," she says, messing his hair. "Definitely me."

"Hey, champ," says Roger. Zack just looks at him. And says, in a voice he's never used before, "I want to know what happened."

"All right," Roger says. "Tomorrow."

"I mean it. No more secrets. The whole story."

Roger raises his right hand. "The truth, the whole truth, and nothing but the truth."

Yolanda steps forward. "Zack, honey, your mama's tired. Tomorrow's time enough." She steps up to the bed and Emma holds out her arms. They hug. "Sorry about the show," Emma murmurs, but Yolanda just rolls out her red-carpet laugh and says, "Never mind about that, girlfriend; the Lion King will roar another day."

BY THE TIME Emma is released at eight-thirty that night, the storm has passed. A shimmering caul of newness lies over the hills of Morgan Peak, and the air tastes of the sea. Escorted by a patrol car, Roger and Emma drive past old Victorians that glisten in the moonlight like iced gingerbread castles, past bungalows aglow with yellow light, teeming cafés, village streets full of people. When they turn onto Crag Road Emma is amazed to see it lined with cars and television news trucks. A crowd has congregated at the foot of their drive, held back by a uniformed cop. As they drive past, faces peer in at Emma and flashbulbs explode in her face; a man with a camcorder on his shoulder trots alongside the car. At first Emma buries her face in Roger's shoulder; then, thinking of Arthur and her book, she raises her head and gives the cameras what they want.

"ABOUT THE GUN," says Detective Thigpen.

"What about it?" Emma sits on the living room couch, flanked by Roger and Maggie, who was waiting in the house when they got home. The sisters had clutched each other silently, Emma too exhausted to talk, Maggie for once without words.

"We recovered it," he says. "Four rounds spent, like you said. Mind telling us how you took it away from her?"

"I hit her with a book." Emma offers up the ghost of a smile. "I guess the pen really is mightier than the sword."

Maggie stares. "You threw books at a woman with a gun? She could have killed you."

"No, duh! She put a hole in poor *Huck Finn.*"

"For which she'll no doubt burn in hell."

"As well she should."

Maria Wong interrupts the sisters' duet. "Once you had the gun in your possession, why throw it out the window?"

"I was afraid she'd take it back and use it."

They look at her in silence, the same question on each face.

"She told me to shoot her," Emma says. "She said, 'Go on. Shoot. You've taken everything else from me.' "

Roger groans. "I wish to God I'd had the chance."

"Should have done it," Maggie says.

"I couldn't," Emma says.

"She had every intention of killing you."

"Maybe."

Maggie, Roger, all of them look at her.

Emma shrugs. "She missed four times. It's a small room."

"You dreamer, you," Maggie breathes.

"I'm not saying she wouldn't have. I'm saying we don't know."

"What I'm wondering," Thigpen says after a moment, "is how she got access in the first place. You never gave her a key, did you?"

"No, but she knew where we kept the spare set." Emma had time to think in the ER. She tells them about the time shortly after Caroline moved in when she locked herself out of the carriage house and asked to borrow Emma's key. She'd followed Emma into the dining room, watched her search through the keys in the sideboard drawer, then waited downstairs when Emma went up to fetch her purse. Caroline could have taken the house key then, duplicated it, and returned the original before they even knew it was gone.

"Haven't you found her yet?" Roger asks. "What's taking so long?"

The detectives fill them in. Caroline Marks didn't flee in a panic; she planned her escape. Between the time she limped out of Emma's house and the first patrol car arrived in response to Nick's 911 call, no more than ten minutes elapsed; yet the police found the carriage house stripped of personal belongings. Every stitch of clothing gone, along with her computer. Some papers had been left behind, but nothing useful. The move was organized; Caroline was packed and ready to go before she encountered Emma snooping in her house.

Emma hears them out with an air of puzzlement. "But the computer was on her desk; I saw it."

"She went back to her house before leaving," Thigpen says. "Must have taken it then."

"But if she was going to run anyway, why go to the trouble of staging a suicide?"

"I'll tell you why," Roger says furiously. "Because murder wasn't enough for her. That twisted bitch wanted to destroy us all. She wanted Zack to walk in and find his mother hanging. She wanted me to believe you died blaming me."

Wong says, "You've got to realize that, as far as she was concerned, everything was on track. She didn't

know you'd found out who she was. She probably figured we'd buy the suicide."

"Then why run?" Emma says.

"Too dangerous to stay. She knows we'd look at her,
and no way she stands the scrutiny."

Thigpen glances at his partner and says, "We talked
to the director of the women's shelter. When she applied
for the job, Caroline Marks represented herself as a battered wife who'd escaped her abuser by changing her
identity—same story she told you. Yesterday she goes in
and tells her boss someone has found out who she is,
and they're threatening to tell the husband. Says she
might have to move on. This is her setting up a motive
for disappearing unrelated to Emma's death."

Roger cocks an eyebrow. "And all this time I'm
what, sitting on my thumbs?"

Thigpen shrugs. "Wouldn't have worked anyway. No
way we'd have bought the suicide. Forensics aside,
there's a history of menace. But amateurs always make
the same mistake; they think they're smarter than the
professionals."

"Meanwhile," Roger says impatiently, "she's out
there and we're holed up in here."

"We'll find her. There's an APB out on her and her
car. We're checking the hospitals and clinics for dog
bites; judging by the trail of blood, she's gonna need
some treatment. It's just a matter of time," says Thigpen.

BUT THEY DON'T find her. They find her car, parked in
the long-term lot at Kennedy, but not a trace of its
owner. Days, weeks, months pass; no sign of Caroline.
Gradually life returns to normal. By spring Emma's
belly is huge, and her book, rushed into print by

Arthur, is flying out of the stores. Zack has decided that the baby is a boy; ever since Roger told him that unborn babies can hear, he's been holding long conversations with her belly about life, liberty, and the pursuit of soccer.

Yolanda, too, is pregnant, for the very first time—a reminder to Emma that not all surprises are bad. Their due dates are barely a month apart. This fortunate coincidence serves to solidify their friendship; they move from bonding over baby furniture and layettes to a seamless professional collaboration. Emma has no intention of switching permanently to kiddie lit; indeed, her mind is already churning with ideas for her next novel. But the book she and Yolanda are creating is something special, a love offering to their sons.

Roger is delighted by their friendship, the more so because he is busier than ever with his assistant gone. India left before his return; she left without saying good-bye. On the day of the nor'easter, Roger had been scheduled to meet with a colleague from the Santa Fe Institute of Chaos Studies. India parlayed the meeting into a dinner invitation, and dazzled her way to a job offer that she accepted on the spot.

What a shame, Emma had said.

Good riddance, you mean, Roger replied. *You never liked her.*

I like her fine, now that she's gone.

ONE NIGHT EARLY in May, the baby wakes her with three booming kicks to the ribs, one after another. Emma sits up and massages her belly. Zack's right about one thing; she's incubating another soccer player. The baby responds to her soothing touch with another barrage of kicks. The clock on her bedside table shows 5:30. She's wide awake; no point trying to get back to sleep.

Roger doesn't stir as she slips out of bed and crosses to the window. In the east the sky is lightening, and the desire comes upon her to see the sun rise from her tower.

The house murmurs in its sleep, undisturbed by her passage, for it knows her now. After the storm, after Caroline's attack, Roger had offered to sell it and move back to the city. Emma flatly refused. To the victor go the spoils, she told him; this house is theirs.

A point even Mrs. Hysop seems to have conceded. As Emma emerges into the tower, she has no sense of the other's presence, nor does she expect to any longer. Mrs. Hysop is gone; the old schoolteacher's retired at last. There's not a cough or sigh to be heard, not a whiff of lavender; the emptiness in the tower has lost its density, the corridor its chill. Emma is free to write fragments and run-ons to her heart's content.

Emma is pleased, not only for herself, but also for Mrs. Hysop. Whatever state she's in now must be better than her captivity here; with all her heart, Emma wishes her peace.

Roger professes himself relieved as well that the ghost is gone, but she knows better; he's relieved that she thinks it is. He never believed in the ghost; like Caroline, he'd written it off as a by-product of Emma's guilt. Thus, to his mind, its disappearance speaks more of Emma's peace of mind than of Mrs. Hysop's.

It's a theory. It's logical. But Emma knows she didn't imagine that final overwhelming scent of lavender. Caroline smelled it, too; it rattled her. Mrs. Hysop may very well have saved Emma's life, and Emma's one regret is her inability to thank her.

There's a fine blue mist rising from the bay, and the cliffs glow pink and gold. Emma recalls the fantasy that first drew her to this aerie: the idea that somehow working in this high, sheltered place with its panoramic view would foster a sort of real-life omniscience. As if, through foresight, accidents can be banished, chaos subdued.

Foolish hope. Chance is woven into the very fabric of life; it cannot be avoided. Somewhere in the wide world, Caroline is thinking of her. She may come back, she may not; there is no way to know for sure. Roger chafes at the lack of closure, but Emma is secretly content. If there's anything worse than the thought of Caroline at large, it's Caroline incarcerated. And somehow Emma seems to have emerged from her ordeal with a heightened threshold for uncertainty. There are unforeseen advantages to living with the consciousness of impermanence. Nothing is taken for granted. The taste of ripe strawberries, the smell of her son's hair, shared laughter at the dinner table, the baby kicking inside her belly: all graces are sweeter for the knowledge that nothing is guaranteed, and nothing lasts forever.

Also available from

BARBARA
ROGAN

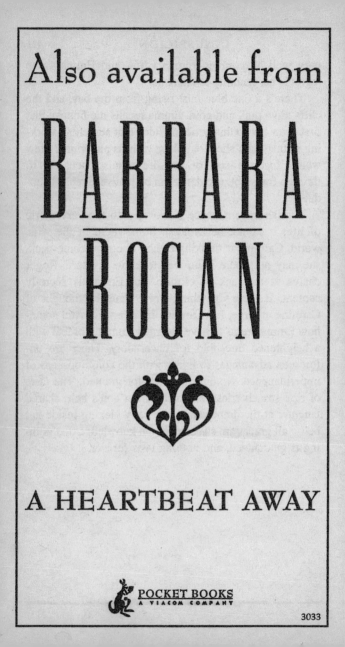

A HEARTBEAT AWAY